raise for Elizabeth Gill

'A w…lerful book, full of passion, pain, sweetness,
…ists and turns. I couldn't put it down'
Sheila Newberry, author of *The Gingerbread Girl*

'Original and evocative – a born storyteller'
Trisha Ashley

'An enthralling and satisfying novel that will leave
you wanting more'
Catherine King

'Drama and intrigue worthy of *Call the Midwife*'
Big Issue

'An enchanting read for all true romantics'
Lancashire Evening Post

'Elizabeth Gill writes with a masterful grasp of
conflicts and passions hidden among men and women
of the wild North Country'
Leah Fleming

Elizabeth Gill was born in Newcastle upon Tyne and as a child lived in Tow Law, a small mining town on the Durham fells. She has been a published author for more than thirty years and has written more than forty books. She lives in Durham city, likes the awful weather in the northeast and writes best when rain is lashing the windows.

Also by Elizabeth Gill

Available in paperback and ebook

Miss Appleby's Academy
The Fall and Rise of Lucy Charlton
Far From My Father's House
Doctor of the High Fells
Nobody's Child
Snow Angels

Available in ebook only

Shelter from the Storm
The Singing Winds
Under a Cloud-Soft Sky
Paradise Lane
The Foxglove Tree
Snow Hall
The Preacher's Son

. . . and many more!

Elizabeth Gill

The Guardian Angel

Quercus

First published in Great Britain in 2017 by Quercus Editions Ltd
This paperback edition published in 2017 by

Quercus Editions Ltd
Carmelite House
50 Victoria Embankment
London EC4Y 0DZ

An Hachette UK company

PB ISBN 978 1 78648 263 1
EBOOK ISBN 978 1 78648 262 4

10 9 8 7 6 5 4 3 2 1

Cover design by Debbie Clement

Typeset by CC Book Production

Printed and bound in Great Britain by Clays Ltd, St Ives plc

For my cousin, Christine, who introduced me
to the beauty of the lakes

One

Stanhope, Weardale, County Durham, 1855

Alice didn't know what prompted her to begin writing to the murderer. The new Methodist minister, Mr Martin, had suggested it, but then he was young and knew no better. As far as she knew, Zebediah Bailey's name had not been spoken of in Stanhope for the past eight years. The minister must have realised as soon as he mentioned the man that he should not have done so but he ploughed on.

'From what I understand, this young man has had no visitors, in all this time.'

Nobody in the parlour spoke. Into the long silence that followed old Willie Harding offered, 'He killed Alec White. They should have hanged him. I don't know why they didn't.'

'Mr Martin, we are Christians.'

'I know what the Bible says: "An eye for an eye and a tooth for a tooth".'

'That's in the Old Testament,' the minister said. 'Jesus taught us to forgive—'

'Well, I don't hold with it,' Mr Harding said and he and his wife walked out into the nasty east wind. From the draughty window, where she sat in a very tatty armchair, Alice could see them. Mrs Harding was hanging on to her Sunday best bonnet, trimmed with grey ribbon, as the couple made their way down the long narrow lane which led out on to the cobbled street and beyond.

She envied Mr Martin his front garden. It was big and he could do useful things with it. Mr Martin, however, seemed to have decided that it was either beneath him or else he didn't have the time or money, because although the garden wound its way around the house like a scarf, the grass was long, the trees were neglected and the whole place was overrun with weeds.

It offended Alice's sense of tidiness and practicality: so many things to eat and use could have been grown there, and it was wasted. It was well known that the minister had neither gardener nor anyone in his house other than a kitchenmaid to help his wife. It was said that he was so badly paid that he could afford nothing more.

Mr Martin, however, wasn't having any of Mr Harding's ideas.

'I went to the prison but Mr Bailey wouldn't see me.' He looked sadly around him. 'Hasn't anybody ever contacted him?'

Alice wondered what had prompted this. It was well known in the village that Zebediah Bailey had been the only child of the Methodist minister who was the incumbent at the time and for several years afterwards.

'He has no family left here,' Mr Willis, the grocer, said. 'You no doubt already know that, what with his father having been minister. It broke his poor mother's heart.'

'Eight years is a long time when you are nineteen,' Mr Martin said.

'Alec had a wife and a bairn,' Mr Fairbairn contributed. 'We have long memories around here and you won't endear yourself by going around saying such things, Mr Martin.'

Several people nodded at this and Mr Fairbairn, who owned the hardware store, looked about him with some satisfaction.

'I understand the wife married again and has had three children more,' Mr Martin said. 'All I ask is that one of you looks into his heart and writes a few lines to him. Is he never to be forgiven?'

Nobody spoke.

It made Sunday interesting at least, Alice thought, as she made her way back down Church Hill and into the main street. Stanhope was a small dales town in Weardale, County Durham, and it had only one long main street that followed the river Wear down to Frosterley, Wolsingham, and up out of the dale into the rest of the county. It was mostly pit villages towards Durham City.

If she turned right in the main street, beyond the castle and the parish church, the road meandered down a slight hill and then into the top end of the dale with its neat fields. Two small stone villages, Eastgate and Westgate, used to be entrances to the Bishop of Durham's deer park. Further up, amidst quarries and lead mines, it was harsh land, the farms tiny and the dale itself steeper and narrower until it burst up on to the tops where it led to Cumberland.

Alice turned left. Her shop was only a few yards from here. She opened the gate that led down into a narrow tunnel and the backyard.

She wanted to dismiss Zeb Bailey from her mind, but she – along with everyone in the area – could remember the incident. Before it even occurred, people had been saying for years that he would come to a bad end. As a child he had been wilful and his father, the minister, had been mortified by his behaviour. His mother had taken to weeping a good deal, so her friends had said. Alice hadn't liked either of them but was not involved with them. And she knew the boy as well as any person could when she is ten years older than he is.

He wouldn't go to school. And while it was well known that he was ungovernable, people were ready to let it go if he attended his classes and settled down and got past his childish behaviour. Then he failed to pass the school certificate. His friends began work in the big, limestone quarry that overshadowed the village, but his parents refused to let him go. They tried to keep him at home with his books and to stop him from seeing such lads but it did no good.

He ran away, lived in a hostel with other workmen and never saw his parents after that day. He drank and fought in the streets.

It had been a Saturday night when he killed Alec. Alice had been working late making sweets so she wouldn't have to work on the Sabbath. It was her only day off, so she liked to make the most of it. And because she lived just along the road from the pub on the corner, the big, square Bonny Moor Hen, she heard the men fighting.

She thought nothing of it; it was common on Saturdays. They had worked hard in the quarry all week, and back-breaking work it was. The Methodist lads would be at home with their families, reading their Bibles and sitting quietly over the fire, Alice thought, wincing as the noise grew. She hoped the merrymakers would not come any nearer. She didn't want her windows smashed in. Two years ago she suffered a cracked pane when some lad fell into it during a fight.

The commotion was getting worse, more yelling and roaring, so that eventually she could not stop herself from going outside. There she saw the young men fighting on the pavement and in the street, Alec White and Zeb Bailey were nearest to her and there was a little circle of space around them as though the others could see that this was more than a drunken skirmish. Bailey got hold of his opponent and knocked him so hard against the wall that the other lad fell and there was a silence then or just afterwards – she could never remember exactly – and Alec White paused. Then he slid down the wall and then they were all standing, looking.

Alec didn't move. She waited and waited for him to try to get up but he didn't and the lads began to melt away and the shopkeepers came out of their houses and Bailey stood as though transfixed, as though he could not believe what had just happened.

Mr Fairbairn, who kept the hardware store, got down beside Alec and somebody else shouted that he would go for Doctor McKenna.

Mr Willis, the grocer, said to Bailey, 'What the hell were you doing? What were you doing, lad?' in a hoarse disbelieving voice as Alec lay still on the wet dark pavement.

'I think he's dead,' Mr Fairbairn announced, and his voice too seemed broken as though something so terrible could not happen here on the street of the little dales town. It was like some personal insult to the town's inhabitants.

Alice truly believed that it had been an accident – What drunken lad would mean to murder another in cold blood like that? – but nobody listened when she tried to tell them that she thought it had been a mistake. Looking back, she was the only woman on the street that night. Zeb Bailey was taken away and she had not seen him since.

Two

Alice had been adopted when she was very small. Her parents had been fairly old even then, or was that just the way that she saw them? She had been told that at the time they were fifty. They had despaired of having a child for over twenty years but when an unmarried mother died after childbirth, they were offered the baby. There was no one else to take her. And so she had found a home; she was lucky.

Nothing had ever been said about her biological mother and she did not like to ask, not wanting to hurt her adoptive parents when they had been so kind to her. There had been no father in evidence and from what little gossip she heard as she got older, her mother had put herself in the river after giving birth, leaving Alice on the bankside where she had been found by some local boys as they were fishing.

Her father was a good shoemaker but when she was about ten he became ill and could not work any more. Her mother had always helped him, kept house and looked after Alice, but she had no special skills. For a while they managed on their savings, but they had to be careful. Since her father was confined to bed and they could no longer afford anything but plain food, it was difficult.

There was an old lady in the village, Miss Frost, whom people went to if they couldn't afford a doctor. Her father had been a travelling medicine man and although she claimed nothing, she grew lots of herbs and helped people with sore throats and bad coughs.

Alice thought that a lot of people went there for sympathy more than anything, and her home, up in High Street along from the chapel and overlooking the village, was a haven for many. It was a big house, almost as big as the vicarage, which was the largest estate in the village. It stood alone, surrounded by huge gardens back and front.

Miss Frost took in poor folk, those who weren't well – who were just tired perhaps because they had led such hard lives. She also harboured animals – abandoned cats and dogs, chickens and foxes, which some farmers didn't agree with but wouldn't have dared to say so to her – as well as injured crows and hurt rabbits.

She tramped miles over the moors with her two collies that had been no use as sheepdogs but that she claimed were good companions. Because of this, she was always having her boots repaired and she and Alice had become good friends.

Her house had such a welcoming atmosphere that the minute Alice went into the garden, taking some boots back to Miss Frost after mending, her body seemed to fall into a sweet sigh, as though nothing in her life could go wrong.

Miss Frost had interesting friends who would come and stay: musicians, poets and actors, people she had met on the road with her father as a small child. There was always room at her house for such folk, the locals said, some with disapproval. But she was so good to people that they forgave her these oddities.

'You ought to sell sweets,' Miss Frost said one day when Alice was helping her mend her shoes – not very well since father was too ill to cobble now. Alice found the work difficult and boring and therefore wasn't good at it. 'Your heart clearly isn't in this. I used to make sweets but I've rather given up in recent years,' Miss Frost told her. 'The villagers still ask for them, though; the demand is there.'

Alice, musing over her family's future, began to consider this. One day she went to Miss Frost's house and shyly suggested she teach her to make sweets. True to character, Miss Frost threw up her hands in enthusiasm.

'Of course, Alice, how truly brilliant of you!' she exclaimed, as though it had been Alice's idea right from the beginning.

Alice spoke to her parents about her idea to turn their cobbler's into a sweet shop, and with their relieved permission, she began the transformation. Over the next few months Miss Frost showed her how to make a dozen different kinds of sweet. They bought bottles and jars cheaply, from markets and junk shops, and Alice got Ted Ward, the local handyman, to refit the shop with the right shelves. It didn't take much doing – the counter was in good shape and the existing shelving merely needed adjustment. She bought small paper bags from the post office and ordered more. Miss Frost unearthed the scales that she had used in her own sweet-making days, and Alice got Ted to paint the outside white and hang a sign across the top of the door that read, 'Alice Lee, Confectioner'.

After her parents died, all Alice had was the shop. She didn't understand how the chance of other lives had passed her by. The night when Zebediah Bailey had fought with and killed Alec White outside the Bonny Moor Hen, she had been twenty-nine.

It had never occurred to her that she might marry. She stayed at home, though through school she knew most of the village lads. She was not beautiful – but then, other girls no prettier than she had gradually found partners. Looking back, Alice had always been alone. At school she had no friends and in a sense had not expected it. She was born to a loose mother and an absentee father, so other children avoided her.

It didn't matter so very much, her adopted parents were kind. She would sit over the fire and read to them in the evenings. They told her how happy they had been to take her in, how blessed they were that they had found her. She had completed their lives and she loved them in turn.

Her problems at school had been made worse because she had a good head for facts. Her classmates grumbled every time the teacher called on her. Her parents did not boast of her being a good scholar but she couldn't remember a time when she wasn't able to read and her arithmetic was always well ahead of everybody else.

Some people didn't send their daughters to school – they had younger children that needed looking after. The boys went to school when they were small, but as they grew older, they were needed on the small farms, in the lead mines and at the quarries. And anyway, a lot of them did not care whether they learned or not.

Most of the boys she grew up with were restless. They liked to be outside, kicking a ball around the schoolyard, racing one another. She kind of understood what had happened to Zeb Bailey due to the company he kept, except not quite. After all, he had been given more advantages than almost every lad in the area. Yet he had tossed them aside and ruined himself. He blighted his parents' lives and those of the wife and child of the man he had killed. Nobody here had ever thought he should be forgiven until this minister suggested it, and most thought Mr Martin should be taken aside and told to forget it. Zeb Bailey – if ever he chose to come back, and why would he? – would never be accepted.

Alice lay awake that night. Usually she slept well; she had a full and comfortable life. She had buried her parents with dignity, she ran a successful business, and she went to chapel every week. But tonight she was restless and glad of the half moon that spread light over her bedroom through the open curtains. She always left them open, whatever the season: she felt hemmed in unless she could see outside, and she loved the view where the hillside went up to the top of the valley, beyond the quarry where the sounds of hammering went on all day as the stone was broken up and frequent explosions ripped it from the hillside.

Up on the tops the grouse flew, the partridges flourished and in September, her favourite time of year, she would walk on Sunday afternoons to where the heather cast a purple cloak on the land. She liked to look back down at the tiny square fields and little white dots of sheep.

She had been so lucky, she thought, but tonight it made no matter: she couldn't sleep. She didn't understand it. This murderer was nothing to her. But she could not forget how the minister said that Zeb Bailey had no one.

The following evening, when the shop was shut, she went up the back road to the chapel to see the minister. She was half-glad and half-sorry to find him there. If he had been out she could tell herself that she had done her best and leave it be. But when she opened the door to the sanctuary, there he was in the front pew. He turned and smiled.

'Miss Lee,' he said, 'how are you?'

'I've been thinking,' she began, and he cocked his head on one side as though genuinely interested. 'About Zebediah Bailey.'

His shoulders slumped. 'I wish I had said nothing, yet how

could I keep silent?' He spoke more frankly than perhaps he should have done, though perhaps he knew that she would not judge him.

She nodded. 'I thought it was kind,' she replied. 'Do you think – would you consider that a single woman of middle age should not write a letter to such a man?'

He looked at her. 'How good you are to consider it.'

'Being alone is – is so very hard and I would think horrible in such circumstances.'

'Yes. I have wished there was more I could do, though it is difficult since he has refused to see me or indeed I think any charitable person who has tried to help. I would deem it a great favour if you would attempt some form of correspondence. He may not even reply, he may throw away your letters, but I am convinced that it is worthwhile.'

It was only then that Alice understood she had been hoping the minister would tell her what a bad idea it was. She was already repenting the impulse. What on earth was she thinking? Was she nothing more than a frustrated old maid who wanted to take what little pleasure she could from interaction with a man – someone who had *killed* another man?

Her life was oddly free of men. Only women and children came to the sweet shop. If buying a present for their wives, her male customers would send their children or mothers. She had so little male conversation outside of church, she barely remembered what it was like. She had forgotten the frail voice of the only father she had known.

Dismayed and slightly fearful now, she made her way back down the steep hill, through the little passage, into her yard and inside.

*

The September days were bright and warm, but the mornings were white and silver on the fields beyond her house. It was a lovely month to have a birthday – or rather, the day they had guessed it to be when she was found – even though she had no one to share it with.

Her birthday was just like any other day at the shop. Nobody knew any different. Alice served her customers, pondering how her birth mother must have looked on her as nothing but a burden and given up on her before her life had really started.

When the shop was finally closed – it felt as though the day had lasted a week – she ate her evening meal then sat down over her little table by the fire. She found a big piece of cream notepaper – she didn't know where it had come from – and began to write.

The Sweet Shop
Stanhope
September 4th, 1855

Dear Mr Bailey,

'Dear' sounds ridiculous since I barely know you. I was twenty-nine when they took you away and only remember a little bit about it. I try not to judge any man or woman, so I thought that there was nothing wrong in writing to you. Even if you get this and throw it away, it will have been pleasant for me to write it.

It was my birthday today. Nobody knew it. I'm thirty-seven now. Birthdays mean a lot to some people, I dare-say, but since I live alone and work most of the time, it just got by. I'm trying to pretend that it didn't matter, but I wish someone saw me as more than an orphan from disreputable parents, on this of all days.

I run a sweet shop, as you can see. I don't suppose you get sweets? If you ever come back here, I could make your favourites. Can you recall what they were? Perhaps not since you have been in prison for so very long . . . or does that make you remember things even better? I cannot imagine what it must be like, not being able to go outside when you want to.

The minister says you don't like visitors. I should think not. What could they understand of the life you lead? Do you mind me writing to you? I suppose if you threw the letters away, I wouldn't know. It might give me just a little pleasure to write to you. If you want to, you could read what I say, and if you don't, what does it matter?

Shall I tell you what the dale is like now? This morning we had a white frost and when it lifted the grass sparkled. The sun beat down and the afternoon was warm. I'm always grateful on days like this that I was adopted and raised in such a beautiful place.

There is a quarter moon tonight, I can see it from my window. I hope you can see something comforting from yours. Though it has just occurred to me that perhaps you have no outside window. How very hard that would be, not to be able to see the way that light and darkness fall on the land and the seasons changing and all the other distractions that make life bearable.

I shall stop now and let you throw this away if you choose, but I shall write to you again.

God bless and keep you,
Alice Lee, Miss

September 10th

Dear Mr Bailey,

Perhaps you would like me to send you some of my sweets? I don't know why I didn't think of it before. You may not like letters but I never met anybody who didn't like some kind of sweet. Do you like boiled sweets? I make a lot of them because the children like them, especially when they become sticky against the paper bag. They are not very exciting though they are quite difficult to make. You have to time the mixture exactly or it burns and you lose it. Then you have to turn it out and work with it quickly or you lose it again. It took me such a long time to get it right but I'm good at it now.

Or I could send you chocolate. Everybody likes chocolate. Even people who say that they never eat sweets enjoy it. If you let me know whether you have preferences that would help. In the meantime I will send you different types of sweets and put them in a plain parcel so that no one should suspect anything and steal them.

Alice Lee

September 25th

Dear Mr Bailey,

This morning the quarry owner's wife, Mrs Almond, came into the shop. They say she was nothing but a poor lead miner's daughter who lived near Killhope when she had the good luck to meet Mr Almond. He was just starting up the quarry then.

They are very well off now and have a big place called Ash House halfway up Crawleyside Bank, but for a long time they lived in a tiny house in the village. That's where they had their child. They must have had a hard time of it to begin with because folk say they were so poor that Mrs Almond went out cleaning other people's houses.

People say she gives herself airs and graces but I think it must be hard to become rich and still live among the people who knew you when you weren't. She doesn't say much and rarely comes into Stanhope, but when she does, she buys chocolate for herself and her daughter. I think she probably finds it easier to have everything sent to the house but I don't do deliveries. She's quiet and polite and I'm the same with her.

This afternoon I found two small children stealing. Their parents would have whipped them. I simply put them outside, locked the door and told them they could not come back inside until they had learned better manners.

I do Lucky Dips. Have you heard of these? A big bran tub full of mysterious, coloured parcels. These have inside them a motto, a small toy and sweets. Can there be anything more exciting than the anticipation of not knowing what is inside? Is it a small sugar mouse in pink or blue or white? Lemon drops that make you screw up your face from the acid? Fudge that sticks to the roof of your mouth, or toffee with hazelnuts? I shall send you these in small quantities to try. Do let me know what you think of them if you have leisure or privacy for such things. Perhaps you don't write because you are never alone, or work so hard that when you are done all you care for is to sleep. Or maybe you simply have neither pen nor paper.

Can you even receive parcels? I had not thought of that. I shall send them anyway and hope for the best. If I don't hear from you over the next few weeks I shall assume that either there is corruption in the gaol (which I am sure of) or that you do not like my dainties (which could not possibly be true).

Yours, as ever,
Alice

Three

September turned into October and Alice heard nothing back. She sent two parcels of sweets but presumed that they had not reached him.

The days and nights were sharp with frost and she was working toward Christmas. It was the best time of the year for making money though she made sweets for every occasion. She was in some debt to the Christian calendar, for Easter was also a boon. But Christmas was the best and busiest because even people who did not usually eat sweets would splash out for the holidays. Alice bought in lovely white boxes and tied them up with green and red ribbons, evoking summer grass, robins, and cheer.

She had sent away for moulds so that she could fashion various shapes of chocolate. Hearts were popular for Valentine's Day but she did a good trade all year round in spades, diamonds and clubs. The Methodist community liked bows and squares, oblongs and triangles.

Alice knew there was a lovely tradition that once the chocolates were eaten, the pretty white box with the coloured ribbon would be used for keeping love letters. She had never had one herself, but she liked the sentiment.

She sent more sweets to Mr Bailey in November and again in December. Christmas for her was hard. She didn't take the same delight in chocolate as other people did and she had no family to spend the day with. She got through as best she could and went to chapel on Christmas Day. She was grateful that she had enough money to get through the cold winter months, and went home to sit over her back-room fire, reading the books she had borrowed from the subscription library, her one luxury.

New Year's Eve, though not officially a holiday, was taken as such by a lot of the quarrymen. Many of them were Scots and would never have gone to work the day after Hogmanay, and the Irish ones would drink upon any given occasion.

Alice went early to bed and extinguished every light to prevent someone from calling on her at midnight. It was traditional for a first-foot to visit – a tall, dark man that would step over her threshold in the New Year to bring good luck. He was meant to carry coal for warmth and bread for food, the goods acting as a blessing so that you would not be cold or hungry through the year.

Many people here were superstitious and thought it bad luck for a woman to be the first over the threshold, but Alice thought it a good deal safer than letting some man into her house late at night and having to give him whisky. She hoped that some drunk would not think it sport to call on her. Even though she had long since made it a rule to lock her doors and not answer them after dark, she always slept badly on New Year's Eve.

She could hear the drunken sounds in the street. It reminded her of Zeb Bailey. When would he be free and what would he do then?

Four

Dear Mr Bailey,

I hate January. The celebrations are over and all we have
to look forward to in the dale is snow and ice and a bitter
wind that screams down from the tops to the river, cutting
through man, beast and buildings in its way. The farmers
have to pull sheep out of snow and it is very bad this year,
worse than I have ever seen it. Some of the farmers have
lost several of their flock. Having to pull a suffocated lamb
out of a snowdrift must be one of the most dispiriting
experiences imaginable.

After Christmas nobody can afford sweets. The children
press their faces against the windowpanes while I attempt
to ignore them. They are for the most part well-fed and
well-kept and I will not make a better living for over-
indulging them.

Luckily next month is Valentine's Day. You may think
that these people with plain hard lives would not care for
frivolity – and indeed the men, embarrassed at any show of
affection or anything which might raid their pockets, would

like it not to be remembered – but this is my living and I cannot allow any holiday to go uncelebrated. I make up tiny gifts, worth not more than a few pennies, but sufficiently meaningful to make it an occasion for people. Any festival is worth celebrating when you lead as hard a life as they do here in the dale.

It is the only time that many a bashful lad will conquer his fear and hover just outside the door so that he can point to the sweetmeat that he thinks the chosen lass might like. It brightens up the coldest, darkest month of the year. After that we get Lent, which I detest because people give up sweets. But everything improves in the spring with the arrival of Easter and its Sunday celebrations and new bonnets and pace eggs and chocolate.

Yours, as ever,
Alice

Five

'Nice, Bailey,' the lag said, tossing a crumpled box onto his bed.

Zeb said nothing. He never did say anything. There was no point. It was not conversation, it was nothing but a joke, an invitation for you to endure words and blows. He gazed at the paper but didn't touch it until the lag had gone, laughter echoing behind him. Then he leaned forward and picked it up and even then he worried someone was watching so he just slipped it into his pocket. It was probably some kind of mistake, he thought, but when it was candles-out that night he opened it. A sweet smell transported him to his childhood and the little shop around the corner down from the chapel.

Whatever it had been, there was nothing now but a single crumb. He could feel it in his fingers and when he put it into his mouth it tasted of childhood heaven.

He looked more closely at the paper when daylight came but there was no clue as to where it had come from. He wanted to throw it away but he couldn't help clinging to the hope that it really was meant for him. Why else would the lag throw it at him? But for some of them, this could be just another way of trying to evoke a response so that they could taunt him further.

If he said nothing and didn't lift his gaze, they would forget about him. The key to surviving here was to be boring and invisible. Then he wouldn't be singled out for whatever form of torture they had thought up on that particular day.

It did not occur to Zeb Bailey that he might receive another package, but this one had sparked a notion that always existed deep down inside of him – even after eight years of near-starvation, verbal and bodily abuse – that there might be something else, something more beyond this. It was a hope he tried to deny to himself, especially when feeling down – that there could be anything other than the prison – but then a sunbeam or a raindrop would lift his mood and it resurfaced. He told himself that such a dream was ridiculous, but he couldn't help it.

He hated the winter but at least it killed off the lice and the fleas. In winter the meals were always half-frozen. In the beginning his stomach could not endure it but now he could eat anything. He didn't notice the colour or the texture or the taste.

For weather, he liked the rain best. It was variety. He liked to see it change the shape of the ground, the shininess it gave dull surfaces. Rain altered the day to darkness. He had not known that there were so many shades of grey until he came here.

The prison walls kept out the sun and muted the wind, but could not keep out the rain. He didn't mind this; sometimes he even wished for the reassuring signs of weather so that he would know he was still alive. It was never warm except in high summer.

From the very beginning it seemed to him that he had died and gone to hell. He had been a toy, first for the warders and then for the prisoners. He had been a victim and there was no escape. Day and night you were nothing and anybody could have you who could overpower you and when you were fine-looking and nineteen you had no friends.

There seemed to be so much blood from the beatings and

abuse, thick red blood which nobody noticed or cared about, the soreness and the pain and the aching. You got used to anything after a while. You ceased to exist. Night and rain were the only difference.

He forgot that he had a voice. In the night he dreamt about what his parents had done for him, his comfortable home, their reasonable demands. How could he not have wanted to please them? He wanted it now, when his body was just a vessel for other men. He wanted to go back to being a child and to have his mother's lips, her sweet breath, upon his face and his father's kind voice forever in the background.

He had ruined everything.

Dying is not that easy. The body goes on. It wants food and drink. It wants a place to get rid of its waste. It craves warmth. Much as he wished to give up he could not do so. Every morning he awoke. During the day he slept when he could, from exhaustion, from spending nights when there was no rest, the blows and words hurting, his body bruised and aching, seeping blood.

He did not protest. He did not cry out. He did not weep. That is no game for cruel men so gradually he spent his nights alone and was grateful for any kind of peace. He also learned how to defend himself. He discovered that when he fought a man, he must win the fight – no matter what – before it even began.

They didn't know that. They would come at him with little skill, perhaps nothing more than weight and a clenched fist. He became adept at stepping aside, catching them in the places that hurt most, and winding them before he became tired. In a place like this with very little food, no care and hard work every day, he was always on the verge of exhaustion, so he learned to resolve conflicts quickly.

H took on whatever he had to. The warders didn't care what

happened, didn't intervene. If an inmate died, they buried him in any convenient soil within the precincts of the prison. Those who had been hanged were buried in the same place. For years he had thought he would end up there.

He could not call on God. He had denied God so many times to his father's hurt face; he could not go back.

He didn't need a Bible, he remembered it. He could still recall the stories he was told when he was a small boy. The Christmas story of course, the Easter story uneasily, but he particularly enjoyed the story of the boy David, who had slain Goliath the Philistine and become a king.

He also liked Joseph and the coat of many colours, but his favourite was the one about the good shepherd, who went out and found the one lost lamb and took him home.

The weather was vile. It was February, the hardest month of all. He had long since given up on spring or even a softening of the air upon his skin. But one day, Mr Perkins – the one decent warder, the main man – came to him, looking at him as though he still couldn't quite believe Zeb was there.

'This came for you.'

It was a package. Zeb stared.

'Take it, man,' Mr Perkins said, so he did. It had his name written on it. 'And these. Don't know how long they've been in a drawer or why. I nearly threw them out, clearing up as I do.' Mr Perkins gave him the letters and went off, whistling as though it was nothing special.

Zeb gazed at his package and the letters. Why would anybody write to him or send him a parcel? He knew nobody any more. He had deliberately isolated himself, hating himself for having killed. He had been in prison for so long in his silence. His first instinct was to hide the bundle but he didn't think anybody would bother him, and Perkins would tell nobody. Now that he was an efficient fighter, nobody dared touch him or the little that belonged to him. And his silence frightened them. So he secreted the package and secured the letters inside his shirt. For the first time in memory, his mood began to lift in a way that had nothing to do with snowflakes or sunshine or the distant sound of bells on Sunday afternoon, which made him think he could hear the cathedral.

His happiness made him anxious. He could not afford to look cheerful. The warders would see it, and they were the only ones left who would lay a hand on him. One upward glance and they would beat him so that he couldn't move for weeks without pain. And yet he would have to: work was required every day but the Sabbath. They usually had him doing something pointless; for a long time he had been digging holes and filling them in again. He didn't care; all he had left anyway were his memories and the Bible stories and his dreams.

He went outside with his package and the letters. He went as far away from anybody else as he could and in that cold, wet yard he took the package from inside his clothes and turned it over and over in his thin, trembling fingers.

It did have his name upon it. His hands shook. Did this have anything to do with the time that the minister had come to see him? Did the man not understand that he could bear no one's company?

And then sense asserted itself. A minister would send in no package, except maybe a Bible, and this was too small and too light for that. Yet it was heavy enough to be something interesting. He thought back to the smell of the box the lag had thrown at him.

He put it against his nose. He was quite alone but even so he turned to face the wall. The smell was possibly the most wonderful of his whole life.

He didn't unwrap it. He put it back inside his shirt. The prisoners were not searched unless it was a visiting day. These were rare and he had never had a visitor, so the warders would think it unlikely that he had anything to hide, especially after all this time. Eight years in, with nothing for anyone to complain about; he was free from scrutiny.

For several days he kept the package and letters warm against his body until, given a little more time on the following Sunday, he had enough space and solitude to unwrap it.

He had a cell by himself. He still didn't know how this had happened. He thought at the time some cruel bastard wanted to keep him in solitary confinement but now he wasn't sure. It was tiny but it was his. After work every day, coming back to this place was almost a comfort.

He took his time opening the parcel. He curbed his impatience and slowly and carefully removed the string and brown paper. Nestled within was a pure white box with a delicate blue ribbon wrapped into a bow around it. He was astonished.

He carefully untied the bow. His tastebuds and sense of smell were going mad by then. And when he – more deftly than he would ever have thought – managed to open the box without tearing anything, there inside was a blue sugar mouse.

He stared at it. Who on earth – and for what reason! – would send him such a thing? He fought a smile.

His mouth filled with saliva. Determined not to eat the entire mouse at once, he nibbled at one of its ears, closing his eyes. He gingerly put it back into its box and opened the first of the letters.

Six

Alice had no reply from the prison but in a way that made it easier. Not knowing what he was like, she could write into the air and say anything she chose. No one was judging her; no one else was involved. She didn't even care whether he was receiving them. The simple act of writing became a secret pleasure; the letters turned into a journal of sorts. She wasn't sure she should be indulging herself, but she enjoyed putting pen to paper so much. Since she had nobody close to whom she could tell such things, the diary made her gleeful, like a child with a treat.

The minister would ask her from time to time whether she had heard anything back but even when she told him that she had not, he was still encouraging. He thought it was a fine thing she did. That made her feel guilty: the letters themselves had become her greatest pleasure; she was no longer writing them just to raise the spirits of a prisoner.

Was it a sin to write to a man she didn't know? Was she wrong to enjoy it? She liked to imagine that her words might cause him to smile, that the blue sugar mouse could have reached him and showed him that somebody cared, even just a little bit.

*

Easter was a bonanza for Alice. Just when the snow and ice and cold winds seemed as if they would never go away, and all she was selling were cough sweets and honey and lemon drops, spring arrived and with it all the fuss which surrounded the church and the chapel. She liked the way that the whole dale seemed to pick itself up. The weather gentled and the lambs dried off and danced in the fields. Rabbits ran around the hills, so many of them that she even spotted the odd black one.

Alice provided a variety of chocolate shapes, big and small so that everybody could afford one and this year added a new creation: a big chocolate heart on a ribbon to go around the neck, which the young girls seemed to covet. She used her new dying techniques on the chocolates and her little shop was full of colour as the softer wind blew down the dale.

She liked Carling Sunday, where the pubs gave everybody who went in some peas with a little vinegar. Palm Sunday always felt like a day of peace to her. Her favourite, though, was Easter Sunday. People would come into the shop that week and order their sweets and Alice would distribute tiny chocolate squares to the chapel and the minister's house to add to the celebratory atmosphere.

She made up a little box with half a dozen chocolate shapes and sent it off to the prison.

After Easter, summer promptly arrived. Sometimes it happened like that in the dale: hot weather came when it should have been spring and then rain might follow for weeks on end. So one had to make the best of it. Children frolicked outside in the main street and everywhere trees and flowers came into bloom. Alice loved to see the children playing.

The farmers were happy because the ewes who were lambing late got the best of the warmth. Every year Alice thought that the warmth had never been so welcome and that she could not remember what the sun felt like on her face. It was a season that never stopped feeling new. It made her drowsy in the evenings and made her wish for a bigger garden. Beyond the backyard, her garden sloped gradually before it began to climb steeply as it made its way towards the tops.

What it really needed was terracing with a set of steps in the middle but in lieu of that, she filled her beds with her favourite flowers: daffodils in the spring, roses and peonies in the summer. In the immediate backyard she had paving with a few shrubs, all in containers of one kind or another. Two of them were large stone troughs such as the farmers used in their fields for feeding animals. These had been there for as long as she could remember. She had a tiny shed for anything she wished to overwinter.

She grew mint to make chocolate peppermint leaves which were a big hit with the older women, thyme and rosemary to go in oils for other sweets, and sage which she liked having in her stuffing when she had a pork chop dinner. She grew parsley to have with fish for when Mr Ward caught trout in the river and offered her one, and bay leaves because they went with everything.

She had also begun to experiment with wines. As a good Methodist, Alice drank nothing stronger than ginger wine at Christmas, but Miss Frost taught her that country wines were good for certain conditions. Since Miss Frost's father had been a travelling medicine man, Alice trusted the advice. When it was in season she made elderflower wine, which left to itself fermented for a second time and produced champagne. She also made elderberry wine, thick and dark red, and buttercup wine which tasted so awful it had to be good for clearing coughs. Her aloe vera plants she applied to cuts and bruises and used to soften her hands when she had been busy with sugar all day.

When her evenings were free she took a sandwich and a bottle of cold sweet tea down to the river. She enjoyed splashing her bare feet in the cool water.

It was hard not to neglect her work in warm weather. It also took longer and chocolate could not be made. She would work with the back door open because the kitchen was her workshop but often there was little breeze. She sweated so much that the drops ran into her eyes and down her neck and under her arms, making her feel so sticky that she longed to throw off her clothes and drench her body in cool water.

Any kind of weather which went on beyond its usual time was a disadvantage, not only for the farmers but for the farmers' wives making butter and cheese, and for the school children stuck inside on lovely days. Alice thought they would have been better running about the dale and plodging in the river where it ran through Stanhope, shallow over big wide stones.

By May the good weather had gone. The days were dark and dreary and there was no breeze to help anything along. It didn't rain and the farmers started to worry about their crops. Alice knew that a bad year for farmers meant less money for everything else, and sweets came at the bottom of the shopping list and slid off the end.

When the weather broke, it was in the middle of the night and thunder crashed so loudly above her house that Alice awoke. Lightning split the sky and she got up and went to the window. It was forked lightning and every few feet it struck, followed by the sheet lightning, so close that it blanketed the sky and shook the buildings.

And then it rained. It battered the streets for weeks. It reduced flowers to slime in gardens. It caused the Wear to flood so that nobody could go near the ford for fear they would fall in and be swept away. Her roof leaked in so many places that she hadn't sufficient vessels to contain it. The road and pavements had been dry and dirty. Now mud splashed up people's boots and on to stockings and trouser legs and skirts. Every time Alice went out she got soaked and was reduced to drying her clothes over doors and chairs.

It was the first week in June when she got a letter. It was written on cheap paper so that she could almost see the writing through the back. Her name and address were in letters so badly formed that she doubted this man had had much education, but when she opened it and read, the sentences denied this. It was written in pencil and so small that she could barely decipher it.

Seven

'Mr Perkins?'

The head warder turned in surprise. Bailey never spoke. Mr Perkins could not even remember the man's voice. But there it was, halting and scratchy. Mr Perkins had to remind himself that this bent over skeletal-like figure was still comparatively young. But after more than eight years of prison – which would have broken most men – there was nothing young left. He waited for the second utterance.

'You wouldn't write a note for me?'

Mr Perkins was astonished. Nobody asked such things. But then, a lot of the men couldn't read or write.

'Can't you write?' he said.

'Yes, sir.'

'Then I will furnish you with pencil and paper.'

Bailey looked astonished in his turn and why wouldn't he? Mr Perkins had already done him favours by giving him the letters and parcels, and now he'd supply him materials for letter writing? He didn't need to; he could easily say no. Zeb realised that the new governor must be changing things. He had heard rumours, but hadn't seen any evidence of it himself. Though since Zeb had asked for nothing in years, Mr Perkins wasn't likely to deny this request, harmless as it was.

And Mr Perkins knew something Bailey didn't: the new governor was considering releasing him in the coming months. If this happened, Mr Perkins needed to make sure there was no hint of wrongdoing. Bailey had been ill-treated for years. Now he had a cell of his own, tiny but private. He had grown into the kind of man that the other prisoners avoided and they never did such a thing without good cause.

As far as Perkins knew, Bailey had not killed another man since being in gaol but he had certainly damaged more than one. Perkins didn't mind that; he understood the necessities of survival. He was more worried about Bailey's despondency. The governor did not like suicides, and prisoners with no hope left often tried to kill themselves just to get out of this place. Perkins had seen this before and it scared him. He was more than happy to give Bailey his package and the letters. In the depths of that almost black gaze there was a hint of light. Perkins did not want to extinguish it.

Perkins also had a son, almost eighteen, and he was causing him no end of trouble. He was beginning to understand what young men were given to doing and he was so afraid that his son would make the same mistakes that Bailey had. And how would he feel if his son was treated like this? So Bailey had a good right to look surprised. Nobody owed him anything. He should have been a dead man long since.

'You would?' Bailey said.

'You can pay me?' Perkins needed to justify it somehow.

The inmates were given a very little amount of money for their labour and this could cost it all, but Bailey nodded.

It was such a difficult thing to do: not just getting the letter out of the gaol, but the actual writing of it. He hadn't used a pencil in years and kept making mistakes. Also he had only the one shot at it, a single piece of paper. But whatever would he say? It took him three days to work it out. He had lain in the darkness and composed it over and over again and it never sounded right to him. What did you say to somebody you have never met who for no reason had sent you sweets?

She must be very religious, was his final conclusion. It made his heart sink. He had always disliked the whole idea of religion. He understood that people led hard lives and found comfort and strength in the concept of an afterlife – and from time to time, he too had wanted to call on God – but he couldn't do it. If there was a God, it wasn't fair to ask Him for help, and if there wasn't, it was all just a waste of time.

His opinion of Alice was modified by the presents she sent him. There was something decadent about sweets, something almost lover-like about chocolate. And she had bothered to make these, wrap them carefully and send them off to a man who had no redeeming features left. He found it very odd.

He liked the sound of her letters: she was practical and yet warm, and he liked hearing about the little place where he had been born, even though he had always thought he hated it.

He struggled over his letter. He spent a great deal of time on Sunday when he had the afternoon free. He finally finished it but when it was done he was unhappy with it and almost ripped it up. But he knew this may be his only chance so he didn't.

He told himself there was no point in it; he didn't want to think there was anything beyond these walls. He couldn't bear that other people might lead decent, perhaps even happy, lives. All he could bear was this, the routine, the way that it was quiet and secluded. In a sense it was almost monastic. He made himself laugh thinking of it like that, since it was the least religious place anybody could imagine. Life in the gaol was all about lack of hope, failure, pain and hate. He didn't want hope but he couldn't throw the letter away, so, trying not to think about it, he put it into the envelope and gave it to Mr Perkins. He trusted that he was kind enough to post it since he had been paid to do so and it had cost tuppence, a great deal of money to him.

Durham Prison

May

Dear Miss Lee,

I am writing to thank you not only for your letters but also for your gifts. I don't know why you have sent them to me but they are by far the best thing that has happened to me in eight years. I don't know how to thank you for your kindness. I don't like to ask for more sweets but they tasted so wonderful. If you can spare the time I would very much like to hear from you again.

Best wishes,
Z Bailey

Alice carried the letter around with her. She was so pleased that her efforts had borne fruit and she kept reading it again and again and was more pleased with herself than she had been in years. She had finally done something for somebody else which had brought a little joy. She never got letters so the minute it was in her hands, she was happy. She was so glad that he had received at least some of the sweets, though he didn't say which.

Now she knew that she had an actual correspondent she was intrigued, enthusiastic and somehow cowed. This was turning into something real. What if there might be some responsibility that she had not thought of? She didn't know why she felt like taking a step back, but the idea of not writing was like staring into a huge empty space that stretched into the future with no end in sight.

Should she be more careful about what she wrote? Would he think that she owed him something when he came out? What if he charged up to Weardale and forced himself – at least his presence – on her? She panicked and didn't know what to do.

She thought she might ask the minister but he was naïve and would only encourage her without thinking it through. She then thought of Miss Frost, but she knew what her answer would be: she should go on doing the right thing and brave the future. She felt sick with anxiety for several days. It was only when she realised she missed the act of writing itself that she decided to continue. She could stop any time she liked.

Stanhope
June 7th

Dear Mr Bailey,

I was so glad to receive your letter. I had begun to think you had not got the parcels and the letters so it was a great relief to know that these had reached you.

I have been making ice cream and lollipops. My good friend Miss Frost has a big house that is very old and has an ice house at the back of its garden. It looks like the kind of thing you catch swarms of bees in and has a lovely brick dome. Things keep cold there so I make my dainties and take them up there to set and then bring back as many as I can sell before they melt. Alas, I can send you none or you would get nothing but a soggy parcel!

The lollipops are easy but ice cream has to be turned and turned so it's a time-consuming task. But nothing draws people to a sweet shop in hot weather than knowing they can have something sweet to cool themselves down with. I also make cold drinks with ice cream and I fill them up with different colours that are basically cream of tartar, sugar and water.

Does it get too hot where you are or are the prison walls so high that you do not catch much of the sunlight?

Chocolate would melt so I am sending you some boiled sweets. At least they last longer than others because you have to suck them. I hope you like them.

Your friend in correspondence,
Alice Lee

Eight

Zeb was aware that his father had used his influence to prevent Zeb from hanging. People had suffered like that for much lesser crimes than his. He hated his father more for this, that he had helped him even when he had killed another man. He would rather have died. He acquitted his father of hoping he suffered more in living: his father was too religious, too worthy for such thoughts. But after the first days in the gaol, Zeb wished himself dead.

There was no future. He knew that he would be there the full ten years and it felt endless. He might not live to be twenty-nine here: most prisoners didn't last. But then most of them were not as young as he was.

From the beginning, he could not believe that he would have to endure ten years of this hell. When he first arrived, the chaplain at the time had come to talk to him after the obligatory Sunday service. Zeb had no interest in speaking to the chaplain and knew that if he was shown favour, it would be the worse for him from the other prisoners. He stayed silent during the chaplain's speech and then again during subsequent services. He hated every second of them; it was his childhood all over again.

The prisoners knew what he was doing here. If he wasn't a murderer, then he was a debtor and debtors were much better treated.

It was not until he received the sugar mouse and the letters from Miss Lee that he wanted to alter the way that things were. He fought against his newfound hope. Nobody cared. Most of the prisoners who had been there when he was first brought in had died or been released. Some were back repeatedly and could not read or write and had no interest in such things.

Cigarettes, whisky and any kind of drug were valuable here. On the rare days when they were allowed visitors, all these would be smuggled in and then the trading began. He took no part in any of it. He had nothing to sell and wanted to buy nothing.

The second letter for some reason was harder to write. This woman had become a part of his reality and that was very strange. He hadn't seen a woman in eight years and he had never been close to one. All he remembered was his mother's sweet words, and now Miss Lee was sending sweet words and sweet-meats to him.

It was not easy to think of what to say. Nothing changed here; there was no news or activity to report. That was part of its trap and its ease: it was quiet and orderly and things went on and on. He had to do only what he was told. Even making the decision to write again was very hard.

Day after day he thought but did nothing about it. The frustration turned into resentment against himself, that voice which he thought had gone forever. It came back, saying that he was too afraid to try and jeering at his loneliness, his fear. It called him coward that he could not even write a note to some dried-up old spinster who no doubt from a fit of religious conscience had sent him presents. He swore at her under his breath at night for bringing him back into some kind of outside world where there might be hope. He hated it.

His mind, however, having something to think about for the

first time in eight years, was ready to go forward. It tortured him in the darkness and there wasn't much of that, it being summer now. The gaol was not that far from the river. It was the same river where, as a boy, he had run over the stepping stones beside the ford in Stanhope and played with his friends.

How odd to think of all that now, when he had sworn to put the dale and his youth and all the wrongs he had done out of his mind forever. The sweetness of his childhood came rushing back to him. He had thought he would allow none of it to get to him and here it was, glaring at him in the brief summer darkness.

He remembered hating school lessons, always wanting to be out of the door and up on the tops. He kept running away and they kept bringing him back. Now he had to work but he liked the fresh air, even when the weather was bad and after it he found himself in a cold cell. If he was to die of pneumonia surely it must be a comparatively easy way to go compared to living like this.

After all these years he could not help thinking about the dale and the little town that had been his home and where this woman lived, making her sweets, going to chapel and bothering to send him a sugar mouse. He had broken his silence with his first letter and could not resist doing it again.

He told her about Mr Perkins and described him in such a way that it made him smile as he wrote it. He was convinced that Mr Perkins could not read or write much and so it was doubly good, he told her, that Mr Perkins had made sure he got her packages and letters. Mr Perkins looked at a letter as some people looked at the Bible: with reverence, care and a slight amount of fear.

Zeb wrote, 'I remember you and your wonderful little shop. I went there as a small child with my mother. She would buy humbugs, which she liked, and sherbet in rainbow colours for me. You used to put it into a cone-shaped bag open at the top and I would lick a finger and insert it in the bag to suck out the sharp taste of the sweet. I liked how as I went on it would change colour.'

Alice sent him more boiled sweets. These were her own favourite. They looked like the marbles boys played with on the pavement in front of her shop. She made big batches of them with different colours and flavours and was proud of her ability to do so. They were very difficult to get right. Timing and temperature were important but Miss Frost had been a good teacher and had equipped her with a sugar thermometer, copper pans and a healthy fear of what boiling sugar could do to her hands and face if it spattered up.

People called sweet-making a craft but she thought of it more as a trade, such as a welder might on ship-making or a man pouring white-hot metal to make steel castings.

She was rightly proud of what she did but best of all she liked how people came back again and again for their favourite sweets. One old lady came in especially for black bullets, which she fed to the local horses in the fields down by the river. A lot of children loved acid drops and she had shapes and flavours to produce orange and lemon segments.

Turkish delight she had come to late but so many people enjoyed it that she became an expert. She made Turkish delight in rose and vanilla from different essences. People bought these for birthdays and anniversaries, dusted with icing sugar and pretty in white boxes with coloured ribbons to match.

Mint humbugs were another favourite with older ladies and lots of people bought her classic mints, in both soft and hard, for their digestive systems. She advised them to drink mint tea, though she knew they wouldn't. Here everybody drank tea almost black, sweetened with condensed milk even though there were cows at every farm. She could not see them infusing mint in their teapots, even though it flourished in their gardens.

The boiled sweets she sent to Zeb reminded him of being a child in the schoolyard and playing marbles. They were perfectly round and raspberry-coloured with clear and white swirls in places. They stuck to the packet as they had always done and they lasted longer than any other sweet. That was the best thing of all: he sucked them until they were mere slivers on his tongue. When they finally melted, he was left sitting there with a sense of blissful satisfaction. It was almost happiness.

The night after receiving these, even though it had turned cold and the rats came in from outside and polished their whiskers in the corners, he slept and dreamed of playing conkers. He remembered the horse chestnut trees at the edge of a big field, how the trees would sway in the wind and he and his friends would stand beneath them and wait for the spiky green balls to fall down.

If they were ripe, they would split open as they hit the ground. The boys pierced the shiny brown insides and put a string through, and used these against the conkers of other boys.

He was happy. He felt as if he wandered by the river and he could see the stepping stones. Conkers were all around and the wind swept across the river so that it rippled, reflecting the autumn sun and the leaves turning orange and lemon and lime. Horse chestnuts were so big, wide and bold, and gave up their fruit for others' pleasure.

They were, he thought drowsily, like Alice Lee, making people happy with her bright sweets and her kind letters.

'The raspberry-tasting boiled sweets were a triumph and they were 'so right in shape and texture,' he wrote to her. 'I don't know how you do it. It's very clever. Thank you so much for taking an interest in me. Why would you when I have so little or nothing to offer in return?

You do know who I am and what I did. I cannot ever undo that. I took another man's life. For all this time, I have wished that I was dead but now I'm beginning to doubt myself. I know it's stupid but I can't help the hope that has sprung up in me. I almost wish you hadn't got in touch. I could have gone on living like an icy stream forever; where spring never arrives and hope does not flourish.

This awakening hurts and is just as hard as learning not to care. I am remembering all the things that were so nice in my life, and how little I regarded them. My parents gave me everything and yet I cast them off. I was their only child but I didn't care. I see now that I had so much and I threw it all away and for what?

I can hardly bear to think of who I turned out to be and how awful I was after they had given me everything.

My mother died. I can't say that I killed her, that would be dramatic and credit me unduly, but she died from sadness and disappointment and she didn't have other children to bring her comfort. Single children have a huge burden to bear and it isn't right to have to carry all your parents' expectations upon your back. Why couldn't she have had others? Maybe a clever bookish son who would have gone on to study for the ministry, as my father had hoped I would, or a daughter to bring them comfort and perhaps grandchildren?

They must have been heartbroken that they had no other child to make up for my shortcomings. If they had another, notably one kind or talented, they could have borne it better when I turned out to be such a bad son. Other sons, before and after, would have diluted their hopes. I know it would have meant so much for my mother to have daughters, because she had one sister who died before they were grown. My father was one of six and burdened by that, too. In a family of hugely intelligent boys, he was average. His five brothers went to Oxford, helped there by rich relatives who cared very much for such things. Two of them took double firsts.

He went to Durham, did theology and his PhD and stayed, thereafter becoming a Methodist minister. How that played out at a time when all was confusion in the church, I don't know. My mother was the daughter of a dean. What he and his wife thought of Methodism, I don't know that either, but I don't think anybody would have been very pleased.'

Alice had always been alone in so many ways but this correspondence made her feel quite different. She had never had letters from a man. Her confidante was Miss Frost who was very old and becoming frailer by the week. It was strange to have an audience. It was only one person but still somebody to talk to. He didn't have to read her letters; he didn't have to reply. She had been abruptly and inordinately pleased that this murderer liked her sweets, was sufficiently interested in her letters. In mitigation who else was he to talk to? Who would send him sugar mice, be they pink, blue or white?

Alice was nervous about how much she enjoyed their writing. She half-wanted to stop and she wished she had never told Mr Martin that she was doing it. Every Sunday the minister asked her about the state of her correspondence with the man he deigned to call 'Mr Bailey'.

He was no longer so discreet about it and on the second occasion that he asked, the sharp ears of Mrs Harding overheard. She put down her cup and saucer and even the partially-eaten raisin bun that Miss Hope, the schoolteacher, made, which were so dry that they stuck to the roof of the mouth. Alice didn't blame her not wanting to finish it.

Alice did not look at her, pretending she didn't know that Mrs Harding had overheard, but that woman was never one to keep anything to herself. She gazed at Alice questioningly.

'Am I hearing properly, Miss Lee, that you are actually writing letters to this murderer?'

Alice wanted to tell her that listening to other people's conversations was rude and that butting in was the height of bad manners, but she couldn't bring herself to do it. Consequently, Mrs Harding conveyed to the whole of the congregation who huddled in the manse – which was no small crowd, especially on days like this when it was wet and the whole valley was grey with mist – that Alice was corresponding with a prisoner.

Everybody stared, even Mrs Martin, who looked very hard at her husband, though she would never have contradicted him in public. Perhaps she did it in private, Alice did not know. The minister, God save him, intervened.

'I asked all of you if you would take it upon yourselves to write just a line to this wretched young man. Miss Lee was the only one to do my bidding and I am most grateful to her.'

'Well, I think it's scandalous,' Mrs Harding said, 'that a maiden lady like Miss Lee should have anything to do with a man in gaol.'

The silence that followed would have burst open the chapel doors. Then Mrs Goulding, a woman who had gone to school with Alice and now had five children, asked in a curious tone, 'Does he write back to you?'

'Yes, he does.'

'I'm surprised a man of that calibre could write,' Mrs Harding said.

'He went to school here, his father was the minister,' Mr Martin put in coldly, 'and both his parents came from very learned families. Even Methodist ministers have sons who lose their way.'

Mrs Martin had three daughters and looked satisfied at that point.

Alice dearly wanted to leave. Everybody was staring at her. She wished Mr Martin had held his tongue but then why should he? He saw nothing wrong with her writing to Zeb. As she stood there, she felt her cheeks flush, her neck burn, and even her ears, thankfully covered with the ribbons of her Sunday bonnet, tingle in shame.

She said nothing more and soon she left for home. But after that she no longer attended chapel on Sundays, or on any other day. She was saddened that her writing to such a man was depriving her of something she had always taken comfort in and even enjoyed. And church was one of her few social outings. She still met people in the shop, of course, but although sociable it was still business. She met other women when she went shopping but now she was very aware that they were talking about her so her peace of mind was gone. In the shops nobody spoke and the shopkeepers looked askance at her over their countertops.

In the streets people whispered, and even though she told

herself that they were not necessarily talking about her, she could not help the feeling that they were. Not much scandal happened here; they would have to make the best of it.

In her saner moments, Alice knew that she had done nothing wrong and resented how harshly they judged her. But at night, or when she was tired and couldn't sleep, she judged herself. She had not written to this young man for generous reasons; she wanted somebody of her own. She could not manage by herself.

Three weeks later, in the early summer, the chapel held a fund-raiser. Alice always contributed sweets for these sales and decided this one would be no different. She made special candies, put them into transparent bags and tied them up with white ribbon. But when she went to the Sunday school, where the trestle tables were laid out and women were busy covering them with white cotton and embroidered tray cloths and knitted tea cosies, nobody told her which table she was on or even looked at her. They bustled around laying out Victoria sponges and small rock cakes and the tiered cake stands that shone under the light, and nobody spoke a word.

Alice, having lived in shame for three weeks now, was growing tired of it. She knew there was a chance that this would happen but she would not stop taking part in something she had always done. She took the bags of sweets from her big basket and put them out on the table beside the cakes. Mrs Harding stopped and pointed.

'Those don't belong on this table.'

'On what table do they belong?'

'I have no idea.'

Alice looked around but nobody was looking at her. They

were remarkably interested in smoothing out the final touches of the table arrangements. Usually they drank tea together at this point but she could tell nobody was going to offer her any. So she went across to the big teapot, put down her basket and poured the tea herself.

At that point Miss Frost walked in. Alice couldn't have been better pleased if Jesus himself had turned up. Miss Frost was often absent on these days; she was now in her eighties, frail, and walked with a stick. Alice was amazed that she had managed to get this far. Miss Frost came straight across to her.

'Why, Alice,' she said, 'how lovely to see you. Pour me some tea, dear. Now where do I put these?'

She picked up her lavender bags and kettle holders and headed for an empty table. She added the contents of Alice's basket with hers and laid them all out together. Miss Frost, though no Methodist, tried to take part in every worthwhile cause, and her cause in this case was Alice.

'The sweets don't go there,' Miss Hope said.

'Oh, I think they look very nice,' Miss Frost said innocently. 'What a treat your rock cakes are, Miss Hope, they always go down so well with a pot of tea.' She beamed at the woman and arranged Alice's bags of sweets at the very front of the stall. 'And Alice is always so kind to do this when she already works so hard. I'm sure all of you must appreciate her efforts here.'

The women went silent and Alice and Miss Frost left together shortly afterwards. Halfway down the lane Alice burst into tears and turned away.

'Oh, my dear, don't worry so much,' Miss Frost said.

'What have I done?'

'Your Christian duty, which is more than could be said of any of them. I've got nothing against Methodists, my dear, since you are one, but I have to say they can be awfully smug. And if I ever have to eat another one of Miss Hope's rock cakes I shall need new dentures.'

Alice laughed just a little at that.

'Come along,' Miss Frost said, and she took Alice to her house where her companion and housekeeper, Susan Wilson, was just finishing the Sunday roast. She smiled at them in greeting. Alice could smell gravy and Yorkshire puddings. Miss Frost insisted on her having a rather large glass of sherry.

'Medicinal in your case, my dear, indulgent in mine,' said Miss Frost, gulping back hers and filling her glass again. They sat down at the table and Susan brought the tureens of vegetables and a joint of beef to the table.

Alice knew that her friend loved her independence so she was worried at how frail Miss Frost had become. When Alice later ventured into the kitchen she found Susan of the same mind.

'She shouldn't be living on her own with me in this big house,' Susan declared, throwing cutlery into the sink so that the soapy water splashed up at her face.

Alice knew that this was not altogether altruistic. Susan Wilson was, like herself, an orphan. She had come to Miss Frost as a two-year-old child and been here ever since. She had no security: when something happened to Miss Frost, she would be homeless. It was well known in the area that Miss Frost had family, though Alice could not remember when they had last been to see her.

Alice had always liked Susan so she ventured to say now, 'Miss Frost is very old but you won't be alone when she dies. I'll be here and I'll take care of you. Don't be frightened.'

Susan smiled at her through the tears.

'That's so kind of you, Miss Lee.'

'Not at all. You make the best dinners in the history of the world,' Alice said and that made Susan smile.

The trouble was that Alice no longer saw her correspondence with Mr Bailey as her Christian duty. She took far too much pleasure in it. She looked forward to the evenings when the hour was late and she could sit down at her desk and tell him what she had been doing, as though he were a diary.

She felt free on paper as she never had before. She even took the train to Crook to go to the stationer's and there she bought pens and ink and thick cream paper, glorying in her purchases as though they were hidden delights.

She spoke to no one of what she was doing. She swore to herself that she would go back to the chapel on Sunday; there was no point in hiding away.

That week business was slow at the shop and she saw several children pause outside and their mothers hurry them past. Alice was astonished. It was as though she had committed some sort of crime.

She went to bed and worried about what it would be like when nobody came to her shop for sweets, when she had no money. Whatever would she do? But then she reprimanded herself: 'Pull yourself together, Alice, they have to come to you if they want sweets. They have nowhere else to go. Their boycott won't last, no matter what they think of you.'

'Did you really think it wise to encourage Alice Lee to write to a man who was in prison?' Mrs Martin said that night when she and Mr Martin were getting into bed.

'I didn't encourage her specifically at first, I only asked generally that people might. It is part of our duty surely.'

'It just seems hard that she was the only one to do it; unmarried women are such an easy target.'

'She's a very good woman. People should appreciate that. I think it was brave of her. You could do one thing, you know, Ella.'

'What's that?' his wife asked, snuggling down in the comfort of their bed.

'Call in and buy the children some sweets and make sure there are lots of people about when you do it.'

'James,' was all his wife said, but she kissed him.

Nine

Dear Mr Bailey,

The lambs are very big now in the fields at either side of the village. The pheasants are walking proudly around the edges. The rabbits appear on the horizon with ears aloft and the partridges are half-grown, almost hidden in the long grass.

You must be restless at this time of year, constricted as you are. It's bad enough being stuck in a shop. As the summer heats, so the desire for work cools, because making sweets is a very warm occupation. You don't say what your work is but I am sure it is much harder than mine and you must think me faint-hearted having so many advantages.

I keep the doors open while I labour in the evenings, wiping the sweat from my brow and eyes. My nose sweats the most. How awful is that? I have to be careful, I don't want any salty sweat dropping into my sweets. I spend half my time wiping my face with a damp cloth.

I wish I could go away somewhere from here. I have never been to the sea. Have you been there? As a child of the dale, probably not. Not many of us have. I have heard of what it is like to put your feet into the North Sea. They say your toes freeze and that the dark sucking sand comes up around your feet. I would like to run along a beach, to feel the warm sand up above the waterline, as soft as people say it is. I would like to see a sand dune fifty feet high so that I could climb up to the top and throw myself down it and roll all the way to the bottom like a pace egg at Easter. '

The following Sunday after the morning service at the prison Zeb lingered. Nobody noticed. Nobody cared. He had been there for so long that he was invisible. He walked up to the chaplain, Mr Samuels, who was standing at the front near the altar. Zeb wasn't used to talking so it took courage. It also took time because he didn't want to do this, yet he couldn't help it. The chaplain noticed him and looked surprised, as well he might.

'I wondered, sir, if I might have a Bible?' Zeb said.

He had recalled many Bible stories but for the first time in eight years, possibly in his whole life in fact, he hungered to read, to see the words on the page.

'You don't have a Bible?'

'No, sir.'

'I thought everyone had one. Did somebody steal it?'

Zeb could have smiled. It was a long time since he had found humour in anything but his lips attempted it. How sincere this man was. Didn't he know that most of the inmates couldn't read or write and that to them there was no worth in a Bible? They would never steal it; to them it was a useless object.

'No, sir.'

The chaplain looked sympathetically at him. Zeb was astonished.

'Is it true that you are a minister's son?' the chaplain said.

'I was, sir.'

'You don't have to call me "sir".'

'In here everybody is "sir".'

'I'm Nathan Samuels. Do you have other books?' the chaplain asked.

This was astounding. Even in many homes in the dale the Bible was all people owned. It was the only book that denoted respectability. Zeb shook his head. He was wearied with 'no sirring' the man and already exhausted by the encounter; it had taken every ounce of courage he possessed.

'I shall talk to the governor,' Mr Samuels said.

'No!' Zeb said quickly. When the chaplain stared he added, 'I mustn't stand out, you see, or ask for anything or it would go badly with me.'

The chaplain faltered and then nodded. He went to the front of the chapel and came back with a Bible, a book of psalms and a prayerbook.

'No one could object to these, I think,' he said grimly, 'but I shall say nothing. If there is a problem, refer the warders to me. If they have any sense then they fear God and I am his representative. Who knows? If they cross me, I could rain down fire and brimstone upon them.'

He smiled again and touched Zeb on the shoulder. Nobody had touched him in friendship in a very long time. It was just a brush of fingers but it seemed to Zeb that the minister's hand was indelibly printed upon him.

He went back to his cell, openly carrying the books but nobody said anything. They probably didn't even notice. He went into his cell with them and sat down on his bed and turned them over and over in wonder. To anybody who knew anything about books, they were lovely, not just your usual worn copies. He looked in the front of the Bible and saw Mr Samuel's name written inside and sweated slightly. If a warder thought he had stolen these they would kill him without even asking. He could only hope he was shielded by the length of time he had been there.

Unknown to Zeb, the warders had been instructed by the new governor not to hurt any prisoner. Nobody except Mr Perkins came to his cell, anyway: Zeb had not caused any bother in years. He was too old to be a toy and too tough to bait. He had little money, no friends, and if some old dear wrote him the odd letter and sent him mint humbugs it was nothing to him. Zeb received all of his mail after the governor's proclamation, and it was little that the warders cared for.

If they noticed the religious volumes, they were too scared of God to say anything. They also were aware that he was a minister's son and they equated God with Father Christmas and the devil and all kinds of other mysterious beings. So he read his books with nobody but the rats for company.

It was five weeks later when Mr Samuels nodded at him toward the end of the service so that Zeb lingered reluctantly.

'Do you need the books back, sir?' Zeb asked. He felt the loss already.

'No, no, my dear boy.'

Zeb blinked. He had never been anybody's dear boy before.

'I brought you some other reading material.' The chaplain offered him three more books.

'Are they sermons, sir?'

'No, indeed.' The minister beamed. 'They are stories and fairy-tales. I'm sure you are much too old for such things but they have lovely illustrations and I just thought they might bring you comfort. And this – ' he magicked another book from the pocket of his coat and said in a low voice, as though it was sinful – 'is a novel.' He spoke very softly. 'It is a wonderful tale. I thought you might enjoy it.'

'That's – that's so kind of you.'

The book was big and called *The Warden* by a man named Anthony Trollope.

'Not at all,' the minister said. 'My children have loved these fairytales and my wife thought the novel was wonderful. Perhaps you will think so too. If you like it I can bring you more; it's the first of a series. It's about the Church of England.' He gave a quick smile. 'My wife is an insatiable reader and once she has read a book she doesn't want to keep it so if you like it you may have the others. I have told Mr Perkins that I am giving you these books and he didn't seem to mind – or even be interested – but I thought after the last time I saw you that I had better make everything straight. I don't need to have them returned.'

Zeb didn't know what to say except to thank Mr Samuels several times. He was surprised and pleased and excited, three things he could not remember feeling during his time in here. The chaplain went off to see the sick in the prison hospital and then home for his Sunday dinner. Zeb remembered Sunday dinners and put them out of his mind immediately. It was too hard to think of. Meals here were bread, water, and soup with strange things floating in it. Anything sweet had to be sucked hard because it was so dry.

That afternoon, the only afternoon when he did not work, he became engrossed in the novel. It was so well-written and he loved the characters in it; the writer was amusing and clever. So when he heard a sound he dreaded and almost didn't comprehend, he had to drag his attention back. Mr Perkins came in.

'Reading, eh?' he said. He looked impressed but in a way that showed he didn't think much of such things. He eyed the book as though it was a large insect.

'Mr Samuels loaned me the books,' Zeb said slowly, getting to his feet in respect.

'Aye, he said,' Mr Perkins responded hastily. 'He told me. Just watch yourself, lad. Don't think all this reading and writing will earn you any favours.'

'No, sir.'

Mr Perkins came over.

'The Bible, eh?' he said, picking up the book of psalms. 'You like the Bible?'

'Yes, sir.'

'What for?'

'It has lots of stories in it.'

Mr Perkins frowned.

'Like what?' he said.

'Like David and Goliath.'

'Oh,' Mr Perkins said, obviously at sea.

Hesitating, Zeb went on to tell the story. Mr Perkins didn't speak until it was finished.

'Well, by damn,' he said, 'and here's me thinking it was all about going to hell. Who learned you all that?'

'My – my father.'

Mr Perkins looked enviously at him and then shook his head.

'And you still ended up in here. I never had no father nor school teaching. It takes all my time to read, write and add up. I don't know what that says,' Mr Perkins wondered out loud, and then he went off back to his duties.

*

A young lad was brought in the following week. It was always awful when new blood arrived. Zeb had seen and heard it many times. There was nothing you could do, just listen to his cries as the warders had him. When they were finished, he was passed to the other men.

'Haven't you got a dick then?' one snarled to Zeb.

'Shut the fuck up,' he responded as he had learned to, in a deep growl that none of the other men dared to get past.

His reputation protected him. He had fought his way to here and they left him alone but that was all he got. He could not protect another prisoner or they would kill him. Thank God there were no women here. There had been a time not long before he got there when men and women were imprisoned together and the women would give themselves to anybody who wanted them, hoping that they would be able to plead their bellies if they were to hang. It could get them transportation instead.

Times were good now by comparison. As long as he didn't cry or complain or ask for anything, as long as he worked and was silent, he could just disappear almost into the very walls of the gaol.

From the beginning his reputation had helped. Rumours had gone around that he had strangled a lad with his bare hands, that he had butchered more than one man. He was still treated like a plaything because he was only one lad and they were many, but he said nothing. He was starved and put on a plank bed and beaten and still he said nothing. So it eventually came to an end. Then, after half a dozen encounters in the prison yard, things had changed. Zeb had learned to fight. Years in the quarry had strengthened his hands and no man could compete with his punch.

The warders tried to teach him not to fight, using their fists and their boots, but in the end they too remembered his silence and the look in his dark eyes, and gave him space. As Zeb grew stronger and older, he could take on any task they gave him with apparent ease. It didn't matter how hard or repetitive it was, he bore work that finished many men. Those few years in the quarry had been useful.

Friendless, alone, half-starved and cast out, he dealt with anything they gave him. Between that and his fists, it became no pleasure to them to taunt him. There was nothing to be gained from trying to break the mind or spirit of a man who did not respond. They grew bored and moved on to easier prey.

They didn't know that his disinterest stemmed from having no reason to stay alive. When one was past caring, everything became easy. That was the problem. It was like being a little kid in winter when you got chilblains on your hands and feet because you were so cold: you didn't notice it until you were back inside the house and everything got warmer. Then the chilblains turned from white to blood red and they itched. God, how they itched.

Now it was as if he was wrong again. His fucking frozen heart had decided to thaw. He wanted to tear up her bloody letters, to chuck away the sodding sugar mouse which he still kept. He wanted to give the books back to the chaplain and return to the place he had been before, where nothing mattered.

He couldn't stand that he should thaw. It had taken him so long to get hard. Why should he give it up? It would do no good. At night his brain came alive and showed him visions of chocolate and raspberry bonbons.

He remembered how kind the chaplain had been, how Mr Perkins had stood there enamoured at the thought of David beating Goliath, how he killed the Philistine with a stone and a sling.

'Well, by damn,' Mr Perkins had said, very pleased.

Zeb even cared about Goliath, who no doubt had had a pitiful childhood. Oh God, his whole world was collapsing. He had been content in his numbness. He had thought that his numbness would never go away and now it was like an ebbing tide and he was standing naked and freezing on the bitterly cold shoreline.

That night he cried. He hated himself so much that he wished he had a means of doing himself in. But prison prevented such possibilities. It wasn't that they cared, it was just that it would have looked bad to the governor. He did not approve of suicide; he preferred people to die a slow death of despair and loneliness and the sheer bloody stink of prison life.

Punishment had moved on in lots of ways from hanging and deportation as the only options. The first was too quick and the second gave you hope, and hope was not allowed here. To lose hope was your punishment. To despair was your lot. And after you stopped despairing, you moved into the place where Zeb had been for all these years. But now he was losing sight of that loneliness.

He may be too cold or too dirty or too hungry, but he was not bored because Mr Samuels gave him books every week and he devoured them. He had never thought that he would count books his friend. They changed his life, that and the friendships – such as they were – of the prison warder and the chaplain and Alice.

When a package arrived and was brought in by Mr Perkins with an almost-smile, Zeb wanted to throw it out of the window or back at the warder, but he knew he couldn't do it. This man had bothered to be kind. Zeb sighed.

'Why don't you have these for your bairns?'

'Me?' Mr Perkins looked suspiciously at him.

'Aye, it's usually sweets.'

'You don't like sweets?' The warder sounded incredulous.

'Open it,' Zeb said, handing him the package. The warder, as though it was Christmas come far too soon, unwrapped the paper. Inside were sugared almonds, pink and white. Zeb thought they smelled like the sweetness of home.

'But lad – ' Mr Perkins protested.

'Please take them. You've been kind to me for no reason.'

Mr Perkins gazed at him.

'It's my Missus's birthday this week.'

'She might like them.'

'That she would,' Mr Perkins said and then he looked back and at the package and he held out a letter to Zeb before he went off. He held the sugared almonds tightly in his hands, like they were gems, and Zeb was so pleased that he was embarrassed of himself.

Dear Mr Bailey,

Sugared almonds are very difficult to make, I would have you know. All confectionery is a terrible mess and it puts you off sweets for life. Why I have a backside like a carthorse I have no idea, I haven't eaten a confection in twenty-five years.

Oh dear, how personal was that, referring to such things. I beg your pardon. I always wanted to be pretty and dainty. Alas and alack, as they say in books, I never shall be. I hoped I was going to be the sort of girl who could get away with wearing pink but it looked extremely foolish in my case. I also hoped that I would be admired by somebody, anybody, but I am so ordinary and my mother was what they call 'a fallen woman'. What a stupid expression. What did she fall from, a state of grace? Nobody is in that state. And was there no man of equal guilt? Obviously there was since I am here, but he was not about when she had me.

People never seem to blame men. It is as though babies came from nowhere but the woman and she is the only one to blame. Presumably she had to take all the responsibility and should have stopped him. But maybe she couldn't. Or maybe she cared about him. How awful for her then that he left her and then she had to leave me.

I was adopted by an older couple and brought up with no reputation to lose since I never had one in the first place. When my father became ill, I started making sweets instead of shoes. I realise I have had so much in so many ways but now at almost forty, I do wish I could have been married. Though I will confess I look around at so many people's marriages and children and I don't envy them; I have my shop and my freedom and my own life now.

Perhaps God plans these things. Some people He seems to look after. The rest of us are thrown to whatever grey winds there really are. That's you and me, I think.

I do remember the night they took you away. I live just feet away from the pub and what transpired was nothing unusual. I did try to tell them but who would listen to me? You were just one of a crowd of drunken lads who didn't know what they were doing. I saw it happen. I came outside because the noise was so bad and I know that Alec White banged his head off the wall and died. I know you were partly to blame, I know you hit him, but I didn't for a second believe they would accuse you of killing him. Nothing was deliberate as far as I could tell, and to be honest I never liked him. It was common knowledge that he beat his wife and she was expecting when he married her.

It wasn't fair, but things never are. Some people get the blame and the hatred and the casting out from wherever they were. I don't know which bit is worse.

I suppose they are glad it isn't them. And they stand back and see you marched away and blame you in their turn, like whited sepulchres. I shouldn't use that term – Mr Martin, the minister who asked me to write to you in the first place, would definitely object. But how smug some people manage to be.

The days are fine; we are having an Indian summer. I'm still making ice cream and iced lollies and storing them at Miss Frost's.

She is a very old lady now and I dread losing her. She is my only real friend. The women at the chapel are mostly married and have children and some have grandchildren. I have nothing in common with them. There are other single women but most of these are widows. The rare exception is the one spinster and oh dear, although I am one myself, I do have to say that the scones she makes for chapel are as hard as she is. She's a schoolmistress. Pity the poor children.

Old maids tend to get together and talk about luckier women. I stay away. I miss my father's company and the voices of men. I know it's hardly respectable to say so, especially to someone I have never met, but my father always made me laugh. I miss both my parents; I feel that I shall never get used to the loss of them.

When you come out – and I believe it is next summer – if

you come back to the dale I will make for you the best ice cream in the history of the world. I promise.'

Unhappy at the intimacy of this letter somehow, he tried to throw it away. The honesty of it worried and comforted him, all at the same time. He swore to himself for days that he would not reply. He ignored the chaplain on that Sunday and the one after it while the unkind weather declared it summer over again and the prison stank of body sweat and water-logged cabbage.

He tried not to think of the ice cream that Alice Lee might make for him. It would be so cold and so sweet and as he licked it, it would melt beneath the warmth of his tongue. If it was a particularly hot day, it would begin to slide like tears.

He lay there during the airless nights, sweating beneath a single sheet. He talked to his favourite rat, who had become so friendly that not only did he not run away or scuttle across Zeb while he slept, but he would sit there, looking almost sympathetic as Zeb recounted his problems. He called him Eli. Sometimes even Eli grew bored and drowsy and was only held to attention by the respect that gave him a small amount of room in Zeb's place of rest.

Finally they would sleep and Zeb found comfort in Eli's twinkling brown eyes as he curled at the foot of the bed.

Ten

Dear Miss Lee,

It was nice for you to say that I was not responsible for Alec White's death but I was. I wanted to kill him and I did, so there's no use in putting it any other way. He crashed into the jagged part of a stone lintel, which aided it, but mine was the fist that put him there and I had done it on purpose. I hated him.

He had that lass by force; their parents made them get married and he was never there with the bairn he had given her. I had wanted to wed her. She wouldn't have me and she wouldn't have him. I accepted it but he wouldn't. Why should she settle for a quarryman when she was the bonniest thing in the dale? But when he couldn't have her by decent means he dragged her up an alley and had her anyway.

I'm sorry to be this blunt to a decent woman like you and I know it's no excuse for what I did. I think of how he would knock her about. Alec and I called one another all kinds of names that night and he was scornful, told me what he had done.

He bragged in the pub week after week about how he

had forced her and got her in the family way. He boasted that now she was his wife and had his bairn, he could do what he liked with her. As far as her family was concerned she had disgraced herself and they wanted nothing more to do with her.

I had wanted to kill him a dozen times but once was all it took and now I'm paying for it. That's fair enough.'

Zeb began to notice other things around him: how one of the old men who went with him to Elvet pit where they sorted the stones from the coal was ill and struggling with the labour. Zeb had worked with the old man for a long time; he had known him as long as he had been inside.

Zeb had heard the rumours. The old man, Josiah Wearmouth, came from the dale, just as he did. He had done his wife in. That was the only thing Zeb knew about him. They did not talk, even about their background in common. The old man, as far as Zeb could remember, had never spoken of his home or his family but it was nothing unusual.

They were encouraged to be silent in gaol, and after a while nobody noticed that they barely spoke. It was just part of prison life and in some ways Zeb was grateful for the quietness; it was one of the few good things about prison. You didn't have to endure anybody wailing over you, or expecting sympathy. Nobody thought that anything would improve and it was just as well. At least it had been up 'til now.

Zeb didn't see why the old man was still alive amid such treatment and hard work but there came a day shortly after Zeb had begun corresponding with Miss Lee when the old man began to falter. It wasn't quick and the old man tried to hide it but after the first few weeks he was so obviously in pain that Zeb wanted to help him. The warders didn't care but Zeb had found compassion, for God's bloody sake, and did additional work so that they wouldn't notice the old man couldn't keep up.

Jos Wearmouth didn't acknowledge this for the first couple of weeks. Maybe he thought he was going to get better. Since he had never been ill before it was a fair hope, unless one took his age into account. But Zeb could see how much he was failing and as they worked together, he would do both his own work and the old man's. They were separating coal from stone at the pithead at the Elvet pit where they were taken to daily. Zeb was glad to be off digging duty.

It was hard work even when one was fit, but the old man couldn't keep up and nobody cared. He could die there and they would just drag him away. So Zeb helped and nobody noticed. The lags were not that keen. It was easy for Zeb to do both their work and he made the old man lean on him so that it should not be too obvious that he was so poorly.

'You're a kind lad,' Josiah said.

'Nay, I'm nowt of the sort,' Zeb said and his new friend smiled at the effort he was making to ease his day.

After the week was over, Zeb was called into the office. He sweated with anxiety. To be called into the office meant that he was going to get a beating, even if he didn't know what it was for. He was cold with sweat and fear. He knocked on the door and was told to come in. There was nobody in the room but Mr Perkins.

Mr Perkins made him wait. When that happened, you really were in for it. Zeb could not help considering what it would be like to be kicked to the ground and hanged in the prison yard, even though you were mostly dead by the time they got that far.

'So, Bailey, you think you can do two men's work?'

'No, sir.' That was obligatory.

'You obviously do as you have done Wearmouth's work all this week. Perhaps even before that, since nobody appeared to notice.'

Zeb said nothing.

'You could try lying to me,' Mr Perkins suggested.

'He's dying.'

'He killed his wife. You know that, don't you, since you come from the same part of the world. You killed for a woman, so they say, and he killed a woman, which would give you a great deal in common. Tell me, Bailey, what is it about the Durham dales that men go killing so very often?'

Zeb was angry and he found it hard not to let the feeling show on his face. He must not because if he did that, he was a dead man. He said nothing. Mr Perkins waited.

'Well?' he said.

'I wondered if he could share my cell and I could do his work just for a day.'

'Do you know, Bailey, you astonish me. Few men in here do such things. They are stupid and they are vile and they are not worth my time but you – you are a new thing altogether. Did you know this man when you lived nearby?'

'No, sir.'

'Then why do you care how he dies? You haven't gone all religious on me since Mr Samuels gave you those books, have you? Because if you have I will make you sorry.'

'No, sir.'

'No sir, what?'

'No sir, I haven't gone religious.'

'Soft then?'

And that was when Zeb looked him in the eyes. You should never do that. They punished impertinence, and not lightly. But Zeb looked him in the eyes.

'No, sir,' he said.

Mr Perkins relaxed and shuddered at the same time.

'Sometimes, Bailey, you frighten me,' he said. 'You are a very dangerous man. It's your unpredictability that worries me, and also that you can be moved to compassion for no reason at all. But all right then: you can have him and you can do his work.'

The old man was therefore allowed into his cell. In a way Zeb resented it. He had liked having his privacy; he had liked how he and Eli could talk in the evenings. Eli now huddled in the corner with his friends. Zeb was sure they were talking about him and how he had moved on and got another man in here, as though there was room for any more.

Jos Wearmouth mumbled his thanks and fell on to Zeb's bed. There was not room for two men and a rat on the narrowness. Zeb would have to take the floor. The old man was so tired that he fell asleep immediately but it was not for long.

The old man pissed, warm and sour, and there was nothing Zeb could do. Jos didn't even wake up; he merely stirred as the urine ran down his legs and onto the bed and then down to Zeb on the floor. Half an hour later his bowels gave up and the stink was so bad that Zeb could almost see the rats moving back against the odour.

Zeb had nowhere to move. The old man did not awaken but as soon as it was light, Zeb took water and mop and swilled the whole place down, cleaning off Jos, as well. Josiah awoke at the cold and shivered and Zeb was sorry, but he had to. They could not go on in filth like that.

Zeb took off his coat and placed it over the old man before

he had to go to work. That day the warders were on him all the time. He was not working hard enough; he was not shifting enough. Did he really think he could do two men's work? Every time they went by they cuffed him so by the end of the shift both eyes were almost closed, his nose was bleeding, his mouth was bleeding and the blood was running down his neck.

When he got back to his cell the old man needed water and he had pissed himself again. Zeb cleared up once more. He went out for dinner and saved most of it and brought it back but the old man couldn't eat it. What he did eat he spat up and the saliva slobbered down his chin.

'Don't bother with me, son. You've done too much already.'

'I'm fine,' Zeb said, 'and you will be, too.'

'I would like to write to my son before I die.'

Zeb was astonished. Getting paper and pencil in here was almost impossible; he knew from experience. He still had his personal supplies, though, so when the dawn came he sat the old man down and let him write. Later that day he appealed to Mr Perkins to send it, offering almost all the money he had, so that Jos Wearmouth could send a letter to his son before he died.

Mr Perkins took the letter and the money though Zeb was never sure that the letter went to where it was addressed. He only hoped so. That night the old man did not piss himself and his bowels did not empty so Zeb shared the narrow cot with him. It couldn't have been that bad because Eli came back to him and slept, cuddled between the two men for warmth. The bedding still stank and was sopping from the night before.

In the morning when Zeb awoke, the old man was very still beside him. Josiah Wearmouth no longer breathed.

Eleven

Zeb cried over the old man and then hated himself for doing so. He had gone soft with this woman writing to him and sending him sweets. He dreamed of his childhood and his parents, he dreamed of being cast out of the dale forever. He dreamed that his parents never wanted him back and he was there, holding out his arms as he had not done before.

He woke up in a sweat and wished things otherwise. And yet he had been a rowdy child, then a naughty young boy and finally a rebellious young man; they should have put him on a ship or sent him away to fight for some cause. He saw what fighting was all about: although war was a bloody pestilence for some men, the activity was needed, if not the killing. And yet he had killed at home, among his friends and his parents' friends. He felt like the dog that had shit on the rug in the living room.

He would never be free of what he had done; he had ruined his parents' lives. His mother had died because of him. His father had been disappointed and ashamed. He felt as if he would never be done with the scorching that he felt when he considered his childhood. He had sinned as badly as any man could and it would be better if he were dead.

*

At the beginning of November when the warm weather had finally given way to the constant rain that Zeb loved because it was a change and made noise and cleaned everything, the governor called him into the office. Mr Perkins was there.

'Sit down, Bailey,' the governor said.

Zeb was dumbfounded. He had never been asked to sit down.

'It has been decided that you should be let out,' the governor said.

Zeb stared at him.

'You have served nine years and it seems to us that for a crime such as yours you have done enough.'

Zeb went on staring at him.

'We thought we would let you go at the end of the month.' The governor smiled as though he should be congratulated. 'On the thirtieth.'

Zeb was then dismissed and Mr Perkins went outside with him and actually grinned.

'Aren't you the lucky one?' he said. 'Home for Christmas.'

Zeb had never thought about leaving. He had been here for a third of his life. He couldn't sleep. He managed everything. He did the work they wanted him to do; he didn't care about how bad the food was. He didn't mind the solitary cell.

'Oh hell, Eli,' he said to the rat who sat on his chest washing his own whiskers with great diligence as he always did, 'what am I going to do? And worse still, what will you do without me? The next bloke in here won't want you, or share his awful food with you.' Zeb looked at the rat, drew the half slice of bread he had secreted from his pocket and offered it to him. Eli looked carefully at it and then at Zeb. 'That bad, is it?' Zeb said. 'I hope you have a wife and children, I really do.'

The rat almost smiled.

'I don't think you have anybody or what the hell would you be doing here? Yes, I am in your debt. I've given you nothing and I hope you have a home to go to because you can't come with me. I've got no place to go. Do you want to end in the river? Can you swim?'

Zeb laughed and then lay there terrified. They put you out with the few shillings that you had earned over the years. It was a very small sum because they deducted for every time you broke a rule, for every infringement. His cell began to look like sanctuary. The prison became home and Mr Perkins was like having a dad. Oh God, whatever would he do? Winter, Christmas. Holy hell.

He could not tell Alice Lee that he was coming out. It wouldn't be fair. She had been so very kind to him and there was no reason why she should face the reality of him. He would write politely and give her no indication that he was getting out early.

Twelve

The first week in November was bliss in the dale. It was mild. Everybody said how good it was for this time of year and that October had been so cold.

Alice loved the run up to Christmas, not in a Christian way but because she made so much money. Christmas, her cynical self told her, had been invented for business people. If she didn't make more money at Christmas than at any other time then she was finished. She also paid off scores. All those people who had been upset about her writing to Mr Bailey in prison were stuck now because she was the only confectioner in the area.

If they did not come to her shop, they could not go anywhere, so she worked very hard to make up all the specialities that she knew people liked. She also charged huge amounts for them so that those who had been unkind to her paid up before Christmas.

When she went to chapel, Mr Martin asked her if she could stay for a few minutes after the tea and scones were given to everybody before they went home for their Sunday dinner.

She was uneasy. She didn't know what he wanted; she hadn't talked to him for weeks about Zeb Bailey. But now as the sitting room in the manse emptied, and from the kitchen came the smell of Yorkshire pudding and carrots, she smiled and waited for what he had to tell her.

The minister looked down for a few moments as though unsure what to say.

'Yes?' she prompted him. When he looked up, she could read very little in his face.

'Zebediah Bailey is coming out of prison at the end of the month.'

'Oh,' Alice said.

'According to the prison chaplain he has nowhere to go.'

'Oh,' Alice said.

'We have no room here.'

'Has it been suggested to him that he might come back to Weardale?'

'I don't think so.'

'Then what is he to do?'

'I was rather hoping that you might have some idea.'

'I can hardly take him in.'

'I know that.'

'Surely somebody will help.'

'I have asked everybody I know.'

'I don't understand why you are telling me this; it is most unfair of you.'

'I didn't mean it to be like that. I though that perhaps your friend Miss Frost might help.'

'That's very kind of you. Since she appears to be the only Christian in the area, I'm sure she would.'

'Miss Lee—'

'No, no. Don't say anything more that you would be ashamed of,' Alice said and she walked out.

*

That afternoon Alice went to see Miss Frost, who was working in the garden. She was cutting rosemary and bay leaves and putting them into a wicker basket where a few cream roses in bud resided. She was by now very frail indeed but Alice wouldn't have dared say so.

'Don't you think roses at this time of year are at their best somehow, when so many other flowers have stopped growing?' Miss Frost said.

'So brave.'

'People think that only people are brave but animals and roses are in there somewhere. You look worried, Alice. Come inside and have some beetroot wine.'

Miss Frost always maintained that beetroot wine was not alcoholic but somehow Alice always came away from Miss Frost's house after drinking it with a happy glow about her. It was, so Miss Frost insisted, the colour of claret. She didn't say that it had the same effect. They sat down with two large glasses, lovely ones shaped like tulips and dark red. Susan was busy with dinner and wouldn't sit down with them but Miss Frost poured her a glass too.

Alice told Miss Frost about Zeb Bailey coming out of prison before Christmas.

'I can't take him,' she said.

'Of course you can't,' Miss Frost said, wrinkling her brow. 'I would take him but I must ask Susan first because I think she might be afraid of a man like that. And we are two women, neither of us large.'

'I couldn't ask you to take him. I thought that perhaps you might know of someone who could help.'

Miss Frost wrinkled her brow and thought for a few moments and then she looked at Alice.

'I don't,' she said decisively.

'Then I will have to let him manage alone.'

'Oh Alice, you can't. He won't last five minutes alone out of that place. He'll put himself in the river.'

Over dinner they talked about it some more and Susan said that even though she was nervous, she couldn't think to let anyone come out of prison after all that time with no prospects at all.

'Besides,' Susan said, 'he was a decent lad once, that's what everybody says.'

'Nine years is a long time,' Miss Frost said.

It was agreed that Alice would go to the prison on the morning of his release and bring him back. It sounded so simple but they all knew it wouldn't be.

Thirteen

One early evening when she was making sweets for the Christmas onslaught she heard a banging on the back door. It was unusual for anybody to come in the front way unless they needed to buy something. But she couldn't imagine who it could be: though she did get visitors from time to time, people knew that she worked through the evenings so they weren't likely to come calling. She also had few friends, especially now that it was well known that she had written letters to a murderer.

Luckily she was not at a crucial stage or she would have ignored the door. But since she was tired and didn't want to do any more work anyway, she stopped and wiped her hands and her brow and made sure nothing would burn or catch fire and went to open the door.

It was dark out there so she hesitated for a moment but a little voice called out.

'It's me, Susan, Miss Lee.'

'Susan?' Alice's heart gave and she pulled the door open. The girl came in out of the cold night and burst into tears. 'It's Miss Frost,' she said. 'She's died and he put me out. He wouldn't even let me have my things.'

'What happened?' Alice said, gently taking her in toward the fire.

'Miss Frost just passed; I'm sorry I wasn't able to come sooner to give you the news. The doctor said it was her heart and the next thing I knew this man named Mr Turnbull appeared and said he was her nephew. He said that I had no right to be there and he put me out. Somebody must have told him that she died but it all happened so fast, I don't know who it was and I don't know him. He's never been there before and now that Miss Frost is dead—'

Susan cried and cried. Alice soothed her as they sat by the fire. She gave her chamomile tea and told her that she was not to worry about anything even as her own heart was aching. She could not imagine that Miss Frost had died; they had been friends for so long. But Miss Frost had been so very old. She had needed a stick to walk, her hands were veined and gnarled, and her face was far too thin. But they had never discussed it. Miss Frost had probably known that she would die soon, but she wouldn't mind. She was like that.

It was hard on Susan and Alice tried to reassure her.

'Don't worry, you can stay here and we'll sort it out.'

'But Miss, she's dead. She's all the family I ever had and now look.'

Susan cried herself to sleep in Alice's front bedroom with a good fire and a big warm nightdress. Alice sat over her own bedroom fire until very late, grieving and also worried. What would she do about Zeb Bailey?

That week it became obvious that young Susan had options. As soon as folk discovered she was alone and available, they came to the sweet shop and asked to see her.

Farmer Beeston visited and brought with him an overwhelming

odour of thick manure, sour urine and sweaty, long-unwashed clothes. He was well known for bedding his maids and turning them out afterwards, usually when they were having a child.

'I'd like to see Miss Susan,' he said.

'What for?' Alice said coldly.

'That is my business.'

Alice went into the back where Susan was busy preparing dinner.

'Farmer Beeston wants to talk to you.'

A panicked look entered her eyes.

'You are not going near him. Susan, you don't have to go anywhere. You can stay here with me as long as you choose to.'

'But I can't put on you.'

'You can. Now go through and get rid of him,' Alice said, with a wicked smile.

Then there was Mrs Kirkstone, who had nine children. Alice considered that just about as bad. When she came in Alice said that she had no idea where Susan was but she was sure that she was busy.

Miss Frost's nephew had taken over the house as he was en-titled to do, according to the solicitor when Alice went to see him. But Alice could not believe that Miss Frost would not have made provision for Susan.

Alice too had lost her best friend. The other women in the dale were not like Miss Frost, and though it was awful to think of it like that, Miss Frost was so clever. She knew about politics and she gave books to Alice to read and they would sit over the fire and talk endlessly about them.

The morning after Miss Frost's death, Alice left Susan in charge of the shop. Susan was worried about it but Alice knew she could perfectly well manage. She trudged up the icy bank toward Miss Frost's house and banged on the front door.

It was hauled open and a tall man, vaguely resembling Miss Frost, stood there looking down at her.

'Yes?' he asked irritably, as though she was an intruder.

'I am Alice Lee, the confectioner,' Alice said. 'Miss Wilson came to me and I have come for her clothes and her wages.'

'I know nothing about it.'

'She is due six months' wages.'

'You'll have to apply to the solicitor,' he said.

'I would like to come in and collect her belongings, if I may.'

'She's got nothing.'

'Mr Turnbull,' she said, 'Susan needs her things. She has clothes and books here and various other items and you have no right to deny them to her. If you cause problems I will—'

'Very well then, you have five minutes.'

To Alice it was awful, coming into that house where her dearest friend had lived. The house still smelled of cinnamon and beetroot wine and chocolate, all so familiar. She remembered how many winters they had sat over the fire and how many summers Miss Frost had given her the ice house for her confections and how often they had sat in the garden. Susan, a wonderful baker, would make Victoria sponge, Alice's favourite.

The house was cold now as it had never been. Draughts were already screaming through the hall because the wind had got up and Miss Frost's voice had ceased forever.

Alice made her way upstairs, knowing that Susan had the room opposite to Miss Frost's. She went inside and took down two big bags from on top of the wardrobe and then she started to decant Susan's belongings into them.

Susan had lots of lovely dresses, warm clothes, half a dozen pairs of boots and several pairs of shoes. There were books, scarves, ribbons and a silver brush, comb and mirror set. Alice wasn't sure she could carry it all but she would not leave any of it here. She had no doubt that he would take everything.

When there was nothing left in the bedroom she hauled her load downstairs. Mr Turnbull was, predictably, in the study, rifling through drawers at the desk.

'I would like Miss Wilson's wages before I go.'

'That's nothing to do with me. Like I said, the solicitor will sort it.'

Alice didn't see how she could do more.

'I do so appreciate your help,' she said. 'Will you be staying here?'

He frowned at her impudence.

'My wife and five children are due any day now.'

'I wish you well,' Alice said and she smiled thinly at him, picked up her burdens and staggered on along the road and down Church Lane. She had to stop several times because they were so heavy but when she got to her front door, Susan came out of the shop door in a scurry and relieved her.

'Thank you, Miss Lee. I am so grateful to you.'

Miss Frost's funeral, which was five days later at the parish church, was not well attended. A lot of people had gone to her without telling their families or friends; others thought her strange. Single old ladies were only one up from witches. A lot of people at the chapel had looked askance at Alice's friendship with Miss Frost and now it was showing.

Her great nephew and his family were there at the front and she and Susan were in the row behind. After that there was nobody much. Alice was ashamed: so many of the community had gone to Miss Frost for help of various kinds and she had been amiable to all.

There was no gathering afterwards. She and Susan went home and sat over the fire, the shop being closed for that day. Alice had put a notice in the window saying why so they had nothing more to do.

The following day Alice went into the solicitor's office. She had made an appointment and just after ten she was ushered upstairs. He was an amenable man of forty with a wife and two children, prosperous and rather stout. Too many potatoes with butter, Alice thought, since he and his family rarely came to the sweet shop.

She explained that Susan had had no wages and he shook his head and said it would take time before the will was sorted out.

'I understand that Miss Frost's great nephew and his family are living in her house. It didn't take long to sort that.'

Mr Preston looked levelly at her.

'He was living there before she died.'

'Indeed? Her companion didn't mention it. Miss Wilson came crying to me that he had forced his way in there just after his aunt died. If Mr Turnbull can move in there directly, then surely the law will allow Miss Wilson her wages, which she has put in six months' work for.'

'Not quite,' he said.

'Miss Wilson has little. She has nowhere to go – '

'She could find work on one of the farms. I understand Mr Beeston has offered her a place.'

'Really? And you would expect any decent woman to go living up there with an old man? Are you blind?'

'Miss Lee—'

'Mr Preston. I'm sure you can sort this out to Miss Wilson's satisfaction. I would think – though you have said nothing – that Miss Frost even left something to Miss Wilson.'

'I was going to write to her.'

'You can write to her at my address as soon as is convenient to you. In the meanwhile she is still owed six months' wages and since she has worked more than five months of those she will not mind you deducting three weeks and sending her the balance as soon as you can manage it.'

Alice swept out of his office, wanting to spit all over his turkey rug. She knew that legally nothing could be done about Susan's wages until the will had been sorted out, but morally the whole thing was a disgrace.

Fourteen

Alice tried not to think about Zebediah Bailey. She told herself a hundred and more times that he was not her responsibility and she called the careless side of herself stupid for having become involved. How many sides does one's nature have? Alice's various sides were all over the place now. One said she was a dried up old maid and accused her of taking solace from a murderer. Another voice said that she must help him because what would he do? And then a third voice hovered above stupidly, unable to decide. Alice was angry with all these different sides of herself and besides, it was exhausting.

She also had Susan here now, bereft because of Miss Frost. How could she bring a murderer back here? And yet how could she see him leave the prison with nowhere to go while she had pretended to be his friend? She had not pretended, she argued with herself, but what was the point in being kind to someone if when things got really bad you withdrew your friendship?

Two days after her visit with the solicitor, Alice sat down with Susan by the fire and said that she thought she must offer Zebediah Bailey a place in her house. Susan stared at her.

'Didn't Miss Frost say the same?' Alice queried.

'We talked about it but to be honest, Miss Lee, I don't want to be in the same house with a murderer.'

'Neither do I, but he has spent almost nine years in gaol for what he did, which was a drunken quarrel between very young men. I feel as if I cannot condemn him to what could be a very short life and the river.'

Susan was silent.

'He has no money. He has no friends. He carries that stigma with him,' Alice said. 'He is hardly going to murder us in our beds.'

'But we are two women.'

'I cannot turn him away.'

'What will you do?' Susan said, eyes as big as saucers.

'I have to try and give him a home even if it's just for a few days.'

'Then where will he go?'

'I don't know, Susan, I don't know anything, but as a decent Christian I cannot let him come out of that awful place and not try to help him. Don't you think I'm right?'

'You may be right,' Susan said, 'but it doesn't make me any more comfortable.'

'I don't suppose it makes him comfortable either, leaving just before Christmas with nowhere to go and the whole winter to get through.'

'Does that mean you want me to go?' Susan said.

'No. I thought you could share my room.'

'Your room?'

'Well, I thought you wouldn't want to share his.'

The slight humour in this was lost on Susan.

'He's a murderer,' she said.

'Do try for a little perspective. He got into a fight and the man banged his head and died.'

'So why did they keep him there all this time?'

'Because the law, like a good many other things, is at least a hundred years behind anything else. You may of course leave if you wish.'

'I have nowhere to go.'

'Well then, you must try to be civil.' We must both try to be civil, she said to herself as she processed the idea that she would bring him back, that he would come back. Or maybe that he would refuse or be too weak.

She tried to talk herself into not going on the morning that he came out of gaol and couldn't do it. She couldn't leave him there alone. How long would he last without food, money or friendship? Or what if he had become so used to what must be a truly terrible existence that he could no longer cope with the outside world? And could she and Susan learn to handle what he was like now, however awful it may be?

She moved Susan and her things into her room and showed her where she could put her boots and hang or fold her clothes. Susan gave great sighs while this was going on so that in the end Alice put her foot down.

'If you don't like it, you know where the door is. I have done you a favour. You are in no position to behave like a child. You are not my child and while I know how much Miss Frost cared about you, that time is over.'

She left Susan upstairs and heard her start to cry but tried to take no notice. A short time later when the shop was empty Susan came in, stood in the doorway and wrung her hands.

'I'm sorry, Miss Lee.'

'You don't have to call me "miss". Call me Alice. I will pay you fairly for the work you do. Hopefully this man won't need help for long and you will have the other room back to yourself soon enough. '

'I didn't mean to sound like that. I know there are lots of places in the dale where ten share a room. And you've done so much for me.'

'Just try to be kind. He is as alone as you are,' Alice said, embracing her.

Susan choked and held back the tears and said that she would go this minute and put the kettle on and make a decent loaf and stew for when the prisoner came home.

Fifteen

What it would be like the minute he stepped beyond the gates of Durham gaol for the first time in nine years, Zeb Bailey could not imagine. It was as grey as a morning could be, as all those days had been while he was inside. He had imagined he would feel free, but instead his first inclination was to hammer like hell on the doors and shriek to be let back in. It was all he knew of home, all he could remember.

He was so scared that his hands were shaking and he wasn't sure his body would hold him up. His stomach felt heavy and was going round inside him like a spinning top. He felt sick, as though he would lose his bowels and throw up at the same time. It made him panic. He could not do that here, it was not the gaol where people shit their pants and threw up every time they were ill-used and it didn't matter. This was the rest of the world and you were meant to control your body.

The street was empty. He didn't know which direction to go. All he had on him were the clothes he had worn when he came in here. They were huge on him now; if he didn't hold his arms tight against his sides they slipped to his waist and to his feet.

He had no idea what to do. The day started to brighten and he hated it. Yesterday he had known where he was and what he was doing. Now he was like a small boat on a huge sea with no sail, adrift. The shadows became varied and even that seemed strange, and in among them he thought he saw a person's form, a tall, thin person, dressed so plainly that he had to accustom his eyes to the gloom. Then he saw the hat and the hands that were clasped across the front of her. It was a her. It was a woman. Women stood so differently from men, at least he remembered that.

She moved only so far and then she stopped. It became obvious to him that she was waiting for something or somebody and as time crept forward and she did not move away, he saw that she waited for him. And then he realised who she was. He wobbled very slowly toward her – he had not crossed a street alone in so long that he didn't see how he could do it – and when he was just a couple of feet away he stopped.

'Mr Bailey?'

'Yes.'

'I am Alice Lee.'

This was the woman he had been writing to. She was plain and years older than he was. Although he had known that, it had not been as obvious when he couldn't see her. She wore the most hideous clothing he thought he had ever seen and a dark hat over her hair, which was grey at the sides. Her eyes were also grey and sharp.

She was pale to wan and she wore a coat that was so old that it drooped at either side of her. It was pale black, as if it had been worn for many years and not retained any colour. He wanted to run back inside the gaol and even looked back. The huge gates were secured against him so that the only life he had known for nine years was gone forever.

*

She was appalled at the sight of him, small and bowed and old because of the life he had led. He had long, black, stringy hair, made worse by his having no hat. His face dropped inward so that his cheekbones looked like mountain peaks. He had a long black beard and his eyes were so dark that she could see nothing in them. His gaze went downcast as though it was all he knew. She had never seen anybody so thin.

'Will you come back to Stanhope with me?' she asked.

His wrists protruded from his frayed shirt cuffs and the suit that he wore was almost falling off him. He stopped and took off the tie that was around his neck and fastened it at his waist to hold up his trousers.

They began to walk slowly away from the prison and Alice thought it would take a very long time for them to get anywhere at his pace. He kept faltering and looking around as though he were being chased. And the further away they got the more his steps faltered. After five minutes he stopped. 'You go,' he said, his voice scratchy like gravel, as though he rarely spoke. 'I can't.'

'You're coming with me.'

He shook his head.

'Do you have someplace else to go?' Alice asked.

He shook his head again but wearily.

'No. But I'm nothing to do with you. You don't owe me a thing. You've been kind but I'm so very tired now. Please go.'

The road that passed the prison was beginning to fill up with people as the day advanced. He stood like someone frozen and watched like a beaten dog. Alice didn't know what to do. She could see now that he was so unused to people and to voluntary movement that he was mesmerised and terrified and couldn't move.

She saw a cab putting down some people at the end of the street. She called and it came across.

'All you have to do is get in,' she said.

'Just go and leave me here,' he said and he sounded so tired that she despaired.

'I will not do that. Get in.'

Seemingly, getting into things was easier than getting out of them because he managed.

Even as they set off, she was panicking. She had thought to find a seemingly young man, not this hunched bundle of broken humanity. He stank from body odour and mould from his clothes and sour breath from the prison diet. She couldn't see his face because he still didn't look up but she could also smell the fear on him. It had not occurred to her that he would be afraid. She thought that after so long one would be glad to step to freedom, but he sat there in the corner like an encaged bird let go, breathing hard.

It was luckily not far to Elvet Station but it seemed hours before they trotted down the cobbles of Old Elvet, and up the steep bank which led out of the town towards Sunderland.

She paid the cabbie but still Bailey didn't move.

'Come along,' Alice said briskly, as she would have done to an errant child, 'this is where we get out.'

Still he didn't move. She was afraid. She didn't like to say anything but the cabbie obviously needed to move on to his next fare. But if this man wouldn't get out there was no way in which she could make him. She got back in and then she spoke very softly.

'You have to get out now.'

His breathing quickened but then very slowly he pushed his body from the corner and like someone a hundred years old, as though every bone and muscle ached, he followed her out of the cab and on to the pavement.

She had not known that mornings in Durham were so busy. People were hurrying backwards and forwards along the pavements and here in the station they moved even more quickly. She began walking at a very slow pace and gradually he began to follow her, looking around him at the movement and the noise, shrinking with every step.

By the time they reached the platform there was a train but once again he stood back. She thought of the noise of the engine, of the steam and the smoke and the general grime, and how the train looked like an enormous black beast. She could understand how somebody who hadn't seen a train in nine years would shrink in front of it. His eyes searched the whole place for escape.

'We have to get on it,' Alice pointed out. 'It will take us to Bishop Auckland and then we will board another train which will take us to Weardale.'

He shook his head.

'It will soon be leaving,' she said, 'this is your chance.'

'Chance?'

'Yes, this is your chance to get away from Durham. It's all you have.'

He didn't speak. Alice was more than half-inclined to get on the train, leaving him there and never seeing him again. She was regretting having ever had anything to do with this man. What was he to her? He was beyond help. He wasn't a person anymore; he was just a thing, like a dying animal.

Around her nobody noticed, nobody saw. Nobody stopped and stared. Why would they? Didn't they see crippled people every day? Those who couldn't cope, those whom fate had condemned, those who were diseased and corrupt and those who had murdered? He certainly looked very odd with that long, black hair and huge, black beard and pale, sunken face.

The train would set off soon. People had stopped getting on it and the guard was coming to close the doors. He glanced at her.

'Are you getting on, Miss?' the guard asked her.

She could do nothing but look at him.

The guard looked at Bailey. And then slowly he smiled.

'Aye, seems like it might eat you, doesn't it, sir, but it won't. Howay then,' and he took Bailey by the arm like he was an old man. He certainly looked it. Alice held her breath; she thought if Bailey was touched he might lash out or cry or scream. The guard helped him approach the train, talking all the time in a low, level voice.

Perhaps Zeb knew so little of gentleness that he could not distinguish it from any other behaviour. To Alice's surprise, very soon the guard had guided him towards the door and then he helped both Alice and Zeb up. He closed the door. She wanted to thank him but the words wouldn't come. The train was beginning its movement, its puff puff that she loved, the wheels grinding as it went on its majestic way.

Bailey sank to the floor as the noise started and covered his ears, his knees hard up against his chest. Alice stood in front of him. She wanted to get him up but she didn't know how to. Neither did she feel that she could go into a carriage without him. It was a very long way to Bishop Auckland but nobody said anything, nobody stared.

The train kept stopping. People had to walk over him to get out but they didn't twice look at him. Alice stood and pretended she was not there, she was back at home, she had not started on such a ridiculous charade with this shred of humanity.

When they finally got into Bishop Auckland station she got off and waited and everybody else got off and then he twisted on to his knees and stood up and then he followed her on to the station. His slouch had slightly improved and she could almost see the back of his head.

The morning was by now well advanced and the café at the station was open. Alice told Zeb to sit down on the nearest bench. She wasn't going to spend time getting him there. Without looking back, she went inside and bought tea. She put sugar and milk into his and just milk into hers and then she bought scones with butter and put them on a tray and went back outside.

He was motionless on the bench. She put down the tray and handed him his tea without looking at him. She gave him a plate with a scone then she ate hers and sipped her tea.

She thought the scone was going to choke her, her throat felt so tight. But unlike Miss Hope's scones, this one was as light as air. She watched the passersby and from the corner of her eye she saw Zeb lift his tea and then he took half of the scone and began to eat it. He bit into it and then stopped and then very slowly began to chew it. She had never seen anybody eat half a scone at that pace. He didn't eat the second half but put it into his pocket for later, as though somebody might try to take it from him. He drank his tea just as slowly.

They got on the train from Bishop Auckland. He did better this time. They didn't speak but she was already fearing what would happen when they got off. The station was a three-mile walk from her house and she wasn't sure this man would manage the distance. It was not physical tiredness, she saw. She knew that prisoners did hard work day after day. It was fear of what might happen that stopped him.

Worse still, snow was starting to fall. It was not unusual here at this time of the year but she knew that it would make the walking worse. She kept on telling herself that once they reached her house, things would get better but how she would manage with this strange, old-looking creature, she had no idea.

Once again they got off the train and she could have cried with gratitude that she had got so far. She set off to walk without speaking to him and he followed at some distance behind as though he had not walked for years but, she thought, it was that he had not seen this place in nine years. Had it changed?

His view of it, his perspective, must be so different. He faltered again and again as though he wanted to run away but had nowhere to run to. He kept stopping. Perhaps he recognised buildings. Or was it just that all he saw was the prison he had come from? Maybe he even wished he was back there because it was the only thing that he could remember.

She kept stopping and waiting for him. It was getting colder and colder and she was having to martial her patience. She tried to understand how the narrow valley and small fields must look to him, and the snow falling into the pale grey river and on the streets. When they reached further into the little town, the trees, the market place, the church and the castle were covered in white from the big square flakes as if clean. Finally they reached her house. She had never been so glad to get there. She could have wept.

She took him around to the back, through the gunnel and into the little yard. There she put her key into the door and opened it. It smelled warm and welcoming.

Susan came to the door and stared and took in her breath and put up her hands to her face at the sight of him. He drew back and Alice, worried that he might run, but trying hard to get him out of the bad weather, drew past him and told him encouragingly that there was food inside and a warm fire.

Alice only noticed then that he had no overcoat and was shivering. She poked at the kitchen fire until it burned freely and pulled up a chair and bade him sit down. He looked longingly at the fire but hung back and she realised then that he had not seen a fire in nine years, never mind sat near one. And this was her most comfortable chair so no wonder he was eyeing it like it had teeth.

'Come on,' she gestured. 'Sit down.'

He didn't. Alice gave up and let him stand there. She put the kettle over the fire to boil and she put the pan on where it was not so hot so she wouldn't burn Susan's stew. She set the table carefully and lit candles as she always did at this time of day. She loved their light, their softness and the way that they made her table look so warm and attractive.

She had even brought rosemary and thyme inside so that the whole place smelled good. She didn't know why now; he didn't speak and he didn't move. He looked as though he would run away. He watched the kettle boil and then the stew bubble. She felt so lucky to have Susan there.

She could never have had him in the house when she was by herself, however brave she felt. Miss Frost was dead and Alice hated that, but she was glad that she wasn't having to deal with this as old as she was. He could rest here with these two women in their joint respectability and hopefully nobody would think otherwise.

She made tea and gave him a big mug thick with sugar and milk. He cradled his thin fingers around it as he stood and stared into the fire.

She wished she could have bidden him to wash his hands, which were almost black with grime, but she couldn't do that, he wouldn't understand. He gazed in front of him, then around the room, and his hands started to shake. She thought that he hadn't seen a table and chairs or decent food like this in a very long time.

'Sorry,' he muttered.

'Don't be sorry. You're all right now. Nobody means you harm. This is Miss Wilson – Susan – and she knows your name and she is a lovely lass. We work in the shop together. Susan, this is Mr Bailey, who has come to stay with us.'

Susan nodded and tried to smile at him but Alice could see that she was astonished at how ill and skinny he was. Alice had noticed since she had come into the light that his eyes held a dark fire, not quite extinguished, something she had not seen before and it did not make her easy. This man had endured where most men did not. His past life was there in his look. He was beyond ordinary feelings, she thought and that frightened her. What had she done by bringing him here?

He said nothing to Susan but merely inclined his head.

Alice took the stew to the table in its big pot. Susan put out plates and cut big chunks off the loaf of bread and then Alice invited him to come to the table. When he had sat down, she ladled the stew on to his plate and offered him the bread. He took a first bite, chewed very slowly and then sat back just a little. Then he began to eat, much more slowly than they did. It took him a long time to finish even though it was a very small portion. She offered him more but he only shook his head and sat back.

For the first time in her life, Alice couldn't think of a single thing to say. Susan was the first to move. She began clearing up and when it was done she sat by the fire. She had started knitting in the evenings. She was just learning so it was nothing but a scarf, but it gave her fingers an occupation and it meant that Alice could pick up a book. She asked Zeb if he would also like to read. He looked at her small bookcase like it was going to leap out at him. She picked up her book and started to read while he went on gazing at the books.

She persuaded him to sit down by the fire with them. It was the longest evening that Alice could remember, though she had been awake at night for the last week and more, worrying about what she had promised herself she would do and regretting that she had become involved.

She had spent hours debating whether she should go to Durham when he was being let out. Nobody expected it of her, and now that Miss Frost was dead and she had Susan there, it was not fair to expect a young girl to sleep in the same house with an ex-convict, a man who was just coming out of prison, who was totally unknown and unpredictable. Alice had slept only when she had talked herself out of it. Then every morning she went back over her thoughts and returned full circle: she could not let him come out of that awful place to nobody and nothing.

The argument went round and round in her head and she was so weary with it all and silently cursed Mr Martin and cursed how she had got herself into this mess and now she didn't know what to do.

They sat there until Alice considered it a respectable time to go to bed. He hadn't moved from his chair. Alice closed her book. Susan stopped knitting and wound up the wool and put the needles through it. And then Alice didn't quite know what to say.

The jugs in which they put hot water for washing were there by the fire and the kettle was boiling now so she filled three jugs. Susan took two of the jugs and her candle and went up the stairs. While she was gone, Alice braved the issue.

'I can give you a candle if you need to go down the yard but there is also a chamberpot under your bed. If you are happy to go upstairs, I will show you the way.'

He nodded and she took the third jug and urged him up. On the landing she opened the door on the right. She had always preferred her own room because it was on the back and she could open her window to fields and sheep in the early mornings. When she slept at night with the window open, she could hear the lambs crying in the fields and the sheep calling to one another and the cock pheasants with their throaty noise and the flapping of their wings as they took off. The little birds sang in the dawn.

She went into what had been her parents' room. She had asked Susan to keep on the fires up there and so the room was warm.

'You can sleep in here.'

She turned to her guest who was surveying the room as though it housed wasps. She put down the jug in the ewer on the marble-topped dresser. There was also soap and a towel. The bed was big and had a feather mattress. She had found a nightshirt of her father's and clean clothes that would be much too big but would have to do. The boots she thought might fit.

He then actually raised his eyes in astonishment for a few seconds.

'Who else sleeps in here?'

'Nobody.'

'It's for me?'

'That's right.' Alice would have turned and walked out of the room but he spoke again.

'But why?' His face was full of wonder.

'So that you would have somewhere to go. Goodnight, Mr Bailey.'

When she reached her own room, a few feet across the landing, her heart was pounding so much that she thought she might pass out. She was so grateful for Susan, sitting up in the double bed and whispering.

'Is he all right?'

'He seems to be.'

When her door was closed she turned the large key that secured it. She tried to undress normally for bed but she peeled off her clothes in haste and dragged on her nightdress, pulling it around her as though in protection. She climbed under the blanket and she and Susan whispered furiously.

'What have I done?'

'Your duty as a good Christian woman.'

'I'm starting to wish I hadn't been one.'

Neither of them slept at first. They were frightened. He was unpredictable and he was strange, and although she put it all down to prison life she couldn't help thinking that they were two women in a house with a man who had killed and had been in gaol for nearly nine years.

Zeb walked around his room. Alice had such good hearing that she heard every step. She always heard the people next door. They were old and Mr Crosby was always walking up and down at night as though he couldn't sleep and Mrs Crosby snored so loudly that sometimes Alice couldn't get to sleep for the noise. But Zeb went on walking around and around like a bird who had just found himself in a cage, rather than the other way about.

She turned over and over. The church clock struck the quarter, the half-hour, the three-quarter and then a single note at one. She was so tired and so pleased when she felt herself falling into sleep. She could not think any further. She was so grateful for the way that Susan's regular breathing went on that she fell asleep herself.

The bedroom where she left him made Zeb blink. It had a little black fire surround and the fire had been kept going and was beautiful in its various flames and blackness. There was a big bucket of coal and also sticks and paper and matches but he was already far too warm. There were big thick curtains to shut out the front street and he was glad of that, he had such horrible memories of it. He was now only feet away from where he had killed another man.

The walls were white. His parents' house had been all dark brown and green, nothing like this. Here, she had used what light she could and it was pretty. The bed was very big, covered in a pink and green quilt on a white background and the pillows were white and edged with lace. There was a desk with a little chair by the window and on it paper and pens and ink. There was even a small bookcase that he liked better than anything else in the room, though he didn't look at the various books and their titles. The idea of having something to work toward was new.

He ventured across to the washstand and here the water was hot. He had not known such luxury. He took off everything he wore and soaped and washed his body, even running the wash-cloth into his hair. It was such bliss, letting the water run down his beard and neck and body. When he was clean he sat over the fire and let his hair dry, running his fingers through it so that it would not tangle badly. He sat there for a long time, watching the fire die, something else he had never grown used to.

The bed looked too soft. He had not slept on a proper bed for so many years that he didn't think he could do it. He would have to get down and sleep on the floorboards, such as they were, sanded and oiled and covered with a big, rag rug. But when he got into bed he sank into the feathers and pulled over him the lavender-smelling sheet and burrowed his face in the pillows and the eiderdown wrapped itself around him. It was pink and shiny and had various feathers protruding from it here and there. As he blew out the candle he thought that he would never sleep.

He was more scared now than he had ever been. He tried to remember what prison had been like when he had first arrived there but it was so awful that he couldn't get his mind round it. Here everything was strange. Each noise made him jump. Each sound was alien. He was sweating now.

He got out of bed as softly as he could and tried not to walk around and around but there was nowhere to go. He couldn't get out and then he knew he could, all he had to do was walk down the stairs and unlock the back door and be gone. But where to?

All these years he had imagined getting out but it had not occurred to him that it would be as hard as being inside. He lay down on the floor but the room was so hot that he got up and unlatched the window. But then he could hear the sounds of the men in and outside of the pub and it brought back so many memories that he immediately shut it again. It was as though it was that night again. It was in fact not the worst night of his life but it was the beginning of the worst nights of his life.

He was so scared that he shivered. If he shut out the sounds of the pub and the street, how would he endure the strange noises that he was so unused to? There were people next door. He could hear snuffling and even talking.

He pulled the quilt off the bed and the pillow. He had forgotten that things smelled good. Nothing had smelled good for so long but he was clean and fed and he had the most beautiful bedroom in the whole world that had been given to him by an old maid with the kindest manner that he had ever met.

Why would she take him in? She didn't want a man. If she did, she would have looked everywhere else for one, never in a prison. And she was middle-aged, past that stage. She didn't need an encumbrance, surely, she had already taken in that tiny little lass with the frightened eyes.

She was self-assured, she knew who she was, and yet she had turned up at the prison and was waiting outside for him. She had got him here even though he had done so much to prevent it. He knew how dearly it would cost her to have him in her house. She should not have done it; he was not worth it.

The floor smelled of lavender polish. He thought he might learn to love the smell if he was there long enough but maybe he wouldn't be. She would grow tired of how he could not cope with anything. But if she had not wit to turn him out, it would not be so bad dying here where he had been born. And if the weather was bad all you had to do was lie down in it and go to sleep, or so he had been told. It could not be that simple, his experience told him, nothing was.

There was always something to leave. Even that morning he had looked for Eli as the rat had been there when he went to sleep. It was so late that it was almost early and he was so afraid of going beyond the gates. But Eli had gone. The rat knew that he was leaving; he didn't have to say anything more.

Sixteen

When Zeb awoke the following morning he knew that something was very wrong; nothing felt familiar. But when he opened his eyes he could see the room that he was in and it could not have been more different from his prison cell than anywhere in the world. He sat up. His body, unused to the floorboards, was aching and sore and stiff but he was cleaner than he had known and the sun was up behind his curtains. He drew on some clean clothes that were hanging on the wardrobe door and boots that were almost the right size. He put on an extra pair of socks and they were fine. Then he went over to the window and pulled open the curtains and saw the streets outside which he had known as a small child.

He tried to keep out the memories that swept through his mind – he had held them at bay for nine years and was not going to allow them back now – but the trouble was that Durham City was miles and worlds away and he was here, a place he had sworn never to come back to. He was here only because he had had no option. He had no money and no place to go and she was waiting for him.

She was downstairs now, he could hear her moving about and the girl talking. He was so afraid to go down there. He would have stayed in his room forever but he could not, she had done so much for him. So he made himself walk down the stairs and into the back room that was her personal space behind the shop.

He had noticed little the night before other than the fire, the meal and being in a strange place. He made his way softly down the stairs and into the room. It was as he had thought: the only room down there that she could call hers. It was a pleasant room. Somebody had cared enough to put in glass doors which led out to the yard, letting in all the light, and in the yard before the garden which led up to the hills were pots of different plants. He knew nothing about plants, just that it was full of sunshine on snow. He wasn't used to the brightness; it made him blink.

There were easy chairs at the back of the room but it was mostly a kitchen. There were three armchairs and three seats around the table. It was as though she had bought an extra armchair and an extra dining room chair. For him?

Miss Lee turned as she heard him and the girl stood up straight from where she was bent over the fire.

'Mr Bailey. How are you feeling this morning?'

Zeb said that he was very well, thank you. He thought he would always be in her debt, be apologising for as long as he stayed here. He had seen himself in the mirror that morning and was horrified. He looked like some kind of barbarian. He couldn't understand why she had taken him in. His eyes were black and narrowed, his mouth was thin and his face was almost caved in with malnourishment and bad treatment and with the guilt which he had never come to terms with and knew now that he never would. His teeth were all right – and that was about it – from never having anything sweet and from all those mouldy carrots and hard turnips which made up most of his meals.

His body would barely hold him up. He was surprised at this because in nine years of ill treatment it always had. He was so tired he could scarcely stay awake. Worst of all, his hair was thick and halfway down his back and his beard was so long that it got in the way.

After breakfast Miss Lee said to him that he could spend the day by the fire. Nobody had said such a thing to him since he had been a small child with some slight illness, and back then he had hated books. Now he could not resist the idea of sitting over the fire with a book. There were bookshelves in the back room and in his bedroom. He had seen such things only at home when he was a small child and then they were religious books. Miss Lee's books were a mixture of books about how to make chocolate and sweets, about herbs, how to grow them and use them in all kinds of ways. She also had a great many cookery books. But a lot of her books were stories he had never read. He didn't settle immediately. It seemed such a strange and idle way to spend a morning but there was nothing else to do.

As she was about to go off to the shop, he asked her for a pair of scissors. She went pale.

'What for?' she said.

'Because I want to cut my hair and beard.'

'Oh, I see.' Miss Lee hesitated. This was a new problem. She couldn't direct him to the barber along the street: she didn't want him to have to try to go out and she didn't think the barber would have been willing to help.

'If you trust me,' she said finally, 'I used to cut my father's hair. I could also take off most of the beard and then you could take hot water upstairs where I have left you a razor with your soap. It would be much easier than you doing it yourself, if you could stand the idea of somebody that close and touching you. It'll only take a few minutes.'

How did she know such things, he wondered.

'You wouldn't mind?' he ventured.

'Of course not. Susan can manage the shop.' So she did. She was very deft and he thought that came from her profession and when she had finished and let him look in the mirror he looked much better.

'Twenty years younger,' she said with a smile.

He thanked her and went off upstairs, armed with hot water to shave. The razor hadn't been used in a long time but it was all right. He liked the shaving brush which must have been her father's. He put the soap on thickly so that the razor wouldn't cut him. He thought he looked better again after that, though it showed his hollow cheeks and scraggy body the more.

She and Miss Wilson had gone off and shut the door that led presumably to the front where the shop lay. Everything was clean and tidy, including himself, and the fire was burning high and bright.

He tried to settle but in the end he found that he lay on the rug before the fire and went to sleep, like a cat.

He awoke only when they came back inside and then he apologised for sleeping.

'That was what you were meant to be doing,' she said. 'We thought you might manage soup.'

He did. The only soup he had ever had outside of prison was of his mother's making and it was a broth with lots of vegetables. But this was carrots, very orange, and not much else and they had been cut so small that they were falling to pieces. It was one of the most delicious things that he had ever eaten and he told her so.

'I put onions, thyme, and rice in it. Miss Frost is responsible for most of my recipes, and Susan's, too,' and then she explained to him about her friend and how she had died. She and Miss Wilson looked at one another, rather wet-eyed. 'We do miss her.'

'What can I do to help you?' he asked, when the meal ended.

'Get better,' she said, 'go back to sleep.'

That afternoon, not intending to do so, he did, only this time he really indulged himself by going to bed. He had never done such a thing during the day and the bliss of giving himself up to the daylight – when he should have been breaking up stones and loading them or separating coal – was overwhelming. He lay down and closed his eyes and knew nothing more and by the time he awoke the light had gone. He went downstairs shame-faced and found that Miss Lee or Miss Wilson must have come back at some time because the fire was still burning bravely.

That evening after supper, the two women made sweets. The smells were so good and he was fascinated by the way that Miss Lee deftly stirred the mixture to the right temperature and then got it to the table and pulled and twisted it. The colours were so bright, orange and green, that it almost made his eyes hurt.

As soon as she thought his attention was taken she stopped being aware of him, he thought. He enjoyed watching her work; it was so soothing that he fell asleep again and to his shame only woke up when she touched him gently on the shoulder to tell him that it was bedtime.

The two women went up and left a candle for him so that he could go down the yard. It was so different from the night before. He went down the yard, came back, locked the door and was so tired that he could barely manage the stairs. He pulled off his clothes, extinguished the candle and fell into bed and this time he could believe that he was in Miss Lee's house behind her sweet shop and that he was safe. He was not in gaol, he did not have to go and break stones, he did not have to put up with lice and fleas. He did not even have Eli to keep him company and that was his main loss.

He did not have to worry, as he had when he had had first reached the prison, that men would come in the night and knock him to the ground just for being there. Nobody touched him, nobody hurt him, nobody asked anything of him. He listened to the quietness. He had thought it would be like his childhood when he came back here and that he would hate it but it wasn't.

He felt safe for the first time in nine years and his body, aware of it, dropped off into sleep as sweet as sugar mice.

The following evening, when it was cold and dark, and they were sitting around the fire and he was just thinking that he might get used to such a thing and even feel a little bit happy, there was a tremendous crash from the shop. When they ran in with a lamp, somebody had put a huge piece of stone through the window. There was glass everywhere.

'All my sweets for Christmas,' Alice said. 'Somebody will steal them. There's nothing to stop them now.'

'Yes, there is. I'll sleep here,' he said.

'No, you can't. What if you get into trouble again, chasing somebody away?'

He gazed at her in the lamplight.

'This is because of me. I will stay here tonight and guard the shop and in the morning I will go. You can't have this.'

'You will not go because of this; I won't have it. I won't have people treat you or me or Miss Wilson like we have done something wrong. You have paid for what you did and just because other people don't like it that doesn't make the difference.'

'If you have some cardboard and nails and a hammer I could repair the window until the glazier can come.'

Alice said she did. Susan took the lamp and went into the back and came with the necessary materials and held up the lamp as Alice and Zeb repaired the window as best they could.

After that he said he would stay there and Alice said she would not let him do it alone in case there was any problem. He argued back that it wasn't respectable. In the end they brought the armchairs in from the back, built up the fire in the shop and sat around it. Susan fell asleep.

'I'm sorry to bring all this trouble on you, Miss Lee,' he said.

'You didn't.'

'If I wasn't here, it wouldn't happen.'

'And if nobody helped anybody nothing would happen. Why don't we have some chocolate?'

He couldn't think of a good reason not to so she rummaged in the cupboards and came back with something that smelled amazing.

'It has coffee in it,' Alice explained.

It was the best thing that he had ever eaten. He told her and sensed that she was pleased.

As the night grew late, he urged her to waken Miss Wilson and for them to go to bed but she wouldn't. She sat there with him and though nobody said anything much after that he was content to sit there.

There was no more disturbance that night. In the morning he repeated his willingness to go.

'I should never have come here.'

'Is nobody ever to be forgiven?' Alice said. 'All those awful years that you spent in there, was that not enough? Have not men done such things when drunk on Saturday nights before?'

'But you belong here and the people won't tolerate it.'

'Then they will have to learn to. I am going to see the glazier and you are not going anywhere because other people are so intolerant. It was one window and I will stand the cost and you will not think about it any more. We will not let them win because they have not the intelligence or the will to be kind.'

The following night when he did sleep he had terrible dreams that he was being flung back into gaol and was being beaten and when he awoke he knew that somebody was screaming, but he didn't know who it was or why until he sat up and saw a thin, white figure attempting to wake him up. It was no ghost, it was Miss Lee, standing by the bed with a candle.

'Mr Bailey? Mr Bailey?'

It seemed to Zeb as though he was being called from his dreams. He was half-sure that she was there and yet he could not make his way free of them. He was like a fly in a spider's web and everything was sticky and he could not get beyond it. The more he tried to free himself the more entangled he became and the spider with its huge legs and its big head was coming towards him and he cried out.

'Mr Bailey?'

He came to and saw Miss Lee properly now. She was really there. She looked different in a nightgown. It was plain and white and high-necked and as virginal as anything he had ever seen in religious books, like an angel. Her hair was plaited and her face was full of concern and it was a good face, not just kind but beautiful in a certain way. The planes of her face were so equal, so neat and her eyes were like a winter dawn.

'Are you all right?' she said.

'It was just a bad dream.' He was shaking but he tried not to let her know it.

'You don't have to worry,' she said and she smiled at him.

'Miss Lee. How kind you have been to me.'

'Go back to sleep. You're safe now,' she said.

Zeb thought it was the most wonderful thing that anybody had ever said to him and his mind repeated it over and over again.

Seventeen

Susan's money came in time for Christmas. It was not just wages: Miss Frost had left her a hundred pounds.

Mr Turnbull and his wife and children were not Methodists but Alice heard that they went to the parish church. Since it was just along from her shop, she thought they must have decided to honour the will in order to ingratiate themselves in the little town they had moved to. It would not do for them to owe Miss Frost's companion, lest she talk disparagingly about them.

Susan had said nothing to anyone; she was too close for that. And Alice did not gossip, she had her business to think of. She just wished that Susan was known as more than Miss Frost's kitchenmaid because she had been so much more than that. But she was glad of the money.

Alice told Susan that she could do what she wanted, though what Susan would do Alice had no idea. She had nobody to go to and nowhere to go and Alice had the feeling that when Susan had free time she thought very much of Miss Frost. She grieved in private that the old lady who had loved her so much was gone for good.

That was the trouble with grief, Alice thought, you imagined that you would be soon beyond it but you never got there. Miss

Frost would not fade from Susan's mind. She awoke one night not long before Christmas, crying.

Alice lit the candle as Susan cried into her pillows.

'I dreamed that Miss Frost was still here and when I woke up she wasn't. I dreamt I could go home to her and I can't even go to the house or step foot in the garden. Whatever will you do for ice cream in the summer months, Miss Lee?'

It made Alice feel warm, that Susan's second thought was for her and the business.

Alice was worried about Zeb and Christmas. She was worried about herself and Christmas and about Susan and Christmas. Susan was not a Methodist and she didn't imagine Mr Bailey would want to go to chapel. She didn't think he could manage anywhere with people staring, so whatever he did other than staying at home wouldn't work.

He hadn't been beyond the yard yet and showed no signs of caring to. Alice didn't want to go to chapel herself; she hadn't been since Zeb's arrival. She knew it was cowardly and eventually she would have to show her face. If she didn't, the mean people in the chapel would have won.

She knew they were talking about her and was glad for the respectability of having Susan live with her. The Sunday before Christmas she made herself go to chapel. She went in just before the service started but even so everybody stared. She took no notice. Let them talk.

After the service she went to the manse with everybody else and there she had the pleasure of Mrs Martin approaching her.

'Miss Lee, I think you are close to sainthood!' she exclaimed for all to hear. 'Not only have you taken in Miss Frost's dear companion when she had nowhere to go, but also Zebediah Bailey. You are to be admired by all for the important work you are doing for the sake of the people in this village, besides which you have the loveliest shop for miles around.'

Alice was astonished. She had not known that the minister's wife would do such a thing. She smiled back at the sunbeam that had taken over Mrs Martin's face.

'Why, thank you,' she said.

Mr Martin also came to her and congratulated her on her generosity and benevolence. After this nobody dared say anything. Alice swore to herself that the minister and his wife and children should have enough chocolate that Christmas to make them sick, even if they had no more than a farthing for each child's sweets.

She went home in triumph but said nothing to her little family. Susan had Sunday dinner ready for the table, and made as good a Sunday dinner as Alice's, possibly better. Alice was happy to let Susan make it and she didn't think it was a bad idea to leave Susan and Zeb alone. They had barely spoken to one another yet.

Everything was organised. They sat down to the perfect Sunday dinner, stuffing themselves with pork and crackling and apple sauce and parsnips and carrots and potatoes and lots of Yorkshire puddings filled with gravy.

It was snowing outside but the fire was burning bright. After dinner they sat down by the fire and Zeb dozed. Then Alice saw that Susan was looking into the fire.

'Have you plans?'

Susan, startled, looked quickly at her as though she had been caught doing something wrong. 'Me, Miss Lee, no.'

'You can call me Alice,' said Alice for perhaps the hundredth time.

'It wouldn't sound right.'

No, Alice thought, she was as old as Miss Frost to this half-child.

'We have a very narrow life here and you have some money now. And because of your help here, I owe you money.'

Susan butted in and said that no, she didn't. Miss Lee had been so kind after Miss Frost died.

'Isn't there anything you want to do?'

Susan laughed at that.

'Of course,' she said, 'I want to marry a lovely rich man who can look after me. I want to have his children and be adored by him, live in a fine house in the city, and have a country place and own a carriage and for him to deck me in jewels and velvets. Isn't that what every girl wants?'

'I suppose so.'

'Isn't it what you wanted, Miss Lee?'

So far in the past tense, Alice thought with a smile. She had always known that such things didn't happen. Nobody married the prince; there was no fairytale. Most women had a bad time in marriage with children. They were poor because they could count on a child each year and husband who was never going to earn enough. She was better off as she was but she mustn't disillusion Susan, that would be unfair. Susan had her own life to lead and must make her own decisions.

'If there is anything else you want, Susan, I would be glad to help you. I have money put by.'

She could see the panic in Susan's face.

'But Miss Lee, all I want is to stay here with you forever and ever.'

'That's fine, then,' Alice said.

She wondered if somebody had offered her such when she was seventeen what she would have answered. She would have loved to have got away from here, to places she didn't understand, where ideas were different and language was strange and she might learn.

'I'm like you,' Susan said. 'I don't know where I came from, I don't know who my parents were. I have nobody. All I had was Miss Frost. I was so frightened when she took ill and she was so old. I didn't know what I would do without her and there you were, like a shining angel.'

'A shining angel?' Alice pulled a face and Susan laughed.

'You know what I mean. If you want me to go I will – '

'I don't want you to but I wanted to give the opportunity if it was something for you.'

Susan looked shyly at her.

'I like when I sleep that you're there. I know this sounds daft but I think mothers are like that and I know you're too young to be my mother but the comfort of you is like that, I imagine. I have no memory of anybody loving me before Miss Frost. I know there are hundreds and thousands of children who feel the same and are never helped and die but I have been helped and you have done so much for me.'

At that point they decided to think about tea and wash up the dishes. They put the kettle on to boil and it occurred to Alice that she was quite old enough to be Susan's mother.

'Do you think he's all right, Miss Alice?' Susan said, nodding at the ex-prisoner who was still sleeping.

'He does seem to be getting better.'

'I think he has bad dreams. Sometimes I wake up and hear him crying out.'

Alice didn't mention that she too knew of his nightmares.

'You aren't afraid of him?' she said.

Susan looked astonished.

'I never thought about it since the first night you brought him here. I was a bit worried before then but when I saw him I saw he was just like everybody else that had never been looked after, so skinny and dirty and lost. Miss Frost said it wasn't justice to put a lad away like that for banging another lad's head off a wall. I think he was probably a really nice lad once. Being shut up like that must do horrible things to you but he seems nice to me.'

'It will get easier for him,' Alice said.

Privately she thought that nine years in prison left the kind of mark that he would struggle to get beyond and that given the right circumstances he could be dangerous. But not here and not with her and not with Susan. She had confidence in him and tried not to doubt herself.

At first – once it sunk in that he was no longer in gaol – Zeb was glad that he was free. He had a bed and room to himself and lots of good food and peace. But after that, he was afraid. He couldn't face going outside. He kept remembering the long difficult journey from Durham to here and every time he thought about it he didn't want go any further.

Nobody said anything to him. Nobody made him aware that he should leave the house. He went on eating and sleeping and he began to feel ashamed that he could not venture further out. He went down the yard to the outside lavatory and then he would rush back and cocoon himself in his bed or the chair by the fire.

He was aware all that time that he was living off a woman – two women. It was a very bad situation and he was taking advantage of them. He slept and slept. Some days he could scarcely speak before he fell asleep again and daily the guilt crimsoned his face. He stopped saying much or eating much and he began to excuse himself from meals. He didn't think Miss Lee had noticed and she didn't say anything anyway because she was too good to do that.

One such day when he was sitting dazed in front of the fire and Miss Wilson was serving in the shop, Alice Lee came to him.

'I want to say something to you,' she said.

'I know. I'm sorry I'm not pulling my weight, I will go out and find work and repay everything I owe you – '

'No, no, no.'

Alice had a quiet decisive voice that stopped him.

'I want you to take your time,' she said. 'You're not doing that. You think you should be out there being useful. You are worn out. You have withstood a thing that would kill most men. Now you need time and space to recover. Why don't we give you until the spring – and it is always a late spring here, April or May – to see if you feel better? In the meanwhile you should eat and rest and not take upon yourself the guilt of not being able to go outside.'

He bowed his head.

'You noticed?'

'Other than the backyard you need go no further. You are safe here. Why don't you go to bed and sleep? There will be lots of time when you are well and then you may work. Now I must go and see if Susan has sold out the shop while I was away,' and she went off with a little smile and left him sitting in wonder.

Zeb staggered up the stairs; he had become so tired that he could not stay awake any longer. He pulled the covers around him and the winter sunlight made its soft way inside. It wouldn't last long but it was enough to lull him to sleep.

Eighteen

Zeb was ashamed that the tiredness went on, despite Alice telling him it was okay. Rather than doing more as he hoped, he did less and less. Although he tried to fight the fatigue, Alice let him do nothing and kept sending him back to bed as though he was a sick child. And in some ways, he thought, perhaps he was. Maybe you were always a sick child until somebody rescued you and the tragedy for most people was that nobody ever rescued them. He was lucky.

He struggled and tried not to sleep, but the trouble was that the more he tried, the more tired he became, until he was looking at life through a perpetual mist.

Alice made him huge meals and after each one he went back to bed. If he tried to stay downstairs she banished him and there was no arguing with her so he gave up his conscience.

It was a cold, dark winter and many were the days when he lay in bed and watched the sleet run down the windows in the semi-light. He could hear Alice's slightly off-key voice singing Charles Wesley hymns in the kitchen. Never had Methodism sounded as sweet to him.

There was always bacon and eggs and good bread for break-fast, soup in the middle of the day, and often if things had been busy in the shop, there was cake at six when it shut followed by supper at eight.

Strangely, just when he had thought he would spend the rest of his life in bed, about the end of February, he woke up one morning and was bored and wanted to get up.

He began to sleep less and then he noticed things around him more. He was used to silence and Miss Lee and Miss Wilson did not lead a quiet life. He was less used to women than men and he had no idea what very young women like Susan were like so it was not easy. She blushed when they met on the stairs and seemed startled. She hastened out of the way as much as she could and he couldn't think of anything helpful to say to her. She rarely spoke to him and it was a barrier between them.

Miss Lee he got used to because he would have done anything for her. He tried to interpret her moods. If she had told him to jump off the roof he would have done it. Miss Lee talked and didn't care whether anyone responded; she just got on with things, no doubt as she had always done. She would give brief instructions or ask politely that things should be done.

At the beginning he had had meals in bed and always a fire and the two women had become so used to him that they talked around him in his room and over him and occasionally even to him. On that February morning, he got washed and dressed and went downstairs just in time for breakfast.

That day, while the women were in the shop, he read by the fire but also he brought in the coal. During the early afternoon it snowed and he wanted to go out. He was half-afraid. He hadn't been out in so long. In some ways Alice's little house had become his refuge, though unlike the prison he could put on his coat and boots and leave. He was scared of the freedom.

He ventured into the backyard and lifted up his face to feel the snow as it fell and then happiness came to him, so great that he wanted to thank God for his luck. He was ashamed to call on God now, having loathed the very idea of him all those years, so instead he offered up an apology and stood in the yard while the snow fell silently around him.

A short while later Alice came outside and she saw him and smiled.

'The shop's quiet. Would you like to go out for a little while?'

He was so afraid that he felt embarrassed.

'Just a little way,' she said softly, so he agreed. He saw how she was manipulating him for his own good. She put on coat and hat and boots, and red woollen mittens that Susan had knitted for her, and they went through the passage and out on to the front street.

Zeb stopped immediately. He couldn't breathe. The street was so very wide and the sky was endless. The houses had stepped back for the bare trees that grimaced black at him. Then nothing.

When he came to he was cold and rather damp and as he opened his eyes he could see Alice's concerned face hovering over him.

'Mr Bailey? Are you hurt?'

He reassured her that he was fine and tried to get up and was dizzy.

'Slowly,' she said.

He saw a face and then another and somebody in the background spoke.

'It's only him. It's the murderer.'

He managed to get to his feet.

'He should never have been allowed to come back here,' another said.

He could see Alice's face and she was smiling at him, ignoring everyone.

'Come on,' she said, putting an arm around him. For God's sake, nobody had ever done such a thing. She guided him back through the passage. When they were inside the house his breathing returned to normal and that was wonderful. He had not known how frightening it was when you couldn't breathe.

'I don't know what happened,' he said.

'Perhaps it was just too soon,' Alice said.

The following day he was even more scared. He could not afford to faint in the street like that; men didn't do such things, even murderers weren't allowed. He pretended to himself that it was all right not to go out and then he began to breathe more easily and hovered over the fire.

He noticed that evening that Susan didn't like staying in a room with him by herself. She would make any excuse when Miss Lee went upstairs or into the shop to follow her. That evening Miss Lee went off into the shop to do something and before Susan could follow he spoke.

'I can remember when you were very little, Miss Wilson.'

Susan's look was all surprise.

'You remember me coming here as a tiny child?'

'Yes. I was about thirteen.'

'They found me by the side of the church?'

'The chapel,' he corrected. 'My father discovered you when he went out first thing on a beautiful summer morning. There you were, wrapped up very tightly so that you shouldn't come to any harm.'

'Do you know anything about my mother?'

'I don't, just that she must have cared for you because she left you in a safe place where you would be sure to be found very soon.'

Susan nodded.

'Miss Frost told me the story but I still like to hear it. She thought that my mother must have been very young and scared.'

'I'm sure. I think it's awful that young women are treated so.'

'That's why I feel that I have so much in common with Miss Lee: we were both left and taken in by kind people. But I didn't know that your father had been the person to find me. Did he carry me inside, into the house?'

'I remember him doing it.'

'Do you?' Her eyes were shining now.

Zeb nodded.

'You were so small and my mother wanted to keep you because she had no daughter. My parents always wanted a big family. It was the biggest disappointment of their lives to have only one child. I don't think they ever got over it.'

'Then why didn't they keep me? Was it because I was left like that?'

'No, no, my parents were good people; that would not have stopped them. I think that because Miss Frost had nobody and was so obviously a good woman and had a great big house and money that they were persuaded. She wanted to take you just as much as my parents did; she loved you straight away. Because they thought that she was lonely, they made all the right arrangements.'

'Nobody ever thought of me as her child. They called me her maid.'

It was shortly after this that Zeb, scouring the bookshelves for something new to read, found a compendium of games. There was an exclamation of delight from him as he brought out the box and showed it to the two women.

'We've had that since I was a little girl,' Alice said.

'Would you like to play some of the games?' he said.

'If you don't mind, I'd rather read.'

'Miss Wilson?'

Susan looked doubtfully at him.

'I'm not sure I know how to play.'

'I could show you,' he offered and they played draughts, tiddley winks and snakes and ladders. Susan beamed across the table at him as she beat him after two games of snakes and ladders.

'And you must use my first name,' she said.

The following day, even though he was more afraid than ever, Zeb put on his outdoor clothes and tried again.

This time he reached the front street and, breathing carefully, he set off along the pavement. He saw people staring at him but he ignored them. He wanted to cross the street but he thought it might be too difficult. If he passed out in the middle of the road and people gathered and called him names, that would be too heavy to bear.

He didn't look at anybody, even when a woman guided her two children away as she saw him. He just kept putting one foot in front of the other.

Five minutes later he turned around and walked back and was very pleased when he got to the sweet shop again. Susan saw him and smiled and waved.

The following day he managed to walk across the road. That Sunday after it had snowed and the sun had come out, he and Alice walked all the way to the ford, almost ten minutes.

He thought he had never seen anything as beautiful as the dazzle of sunshine on stone and the river sparkling and the stepping stones that he must have crossed a hundred times as a boy.

Later that evening they had a visitor. It was Mr Martin, the minister.

'I hope you don't mind me coming like this,' he said to Alice, 'but I would like to pay my respects to Mr Bailey.'

Alice was so grateful that she could have kissed him. He came forward and as Zeb got up, Mr Martin reached out and grasped his hand.

'I hope I have timed this well. I'm the local Methodist minister. I'm not here to get in the way, I just wanted to say hello.'

'Thank you, sir, I'm very grateful to you,' Zeb said. 'Mr Samuels spoke well of you and he was very kind to me on your behalf. If it hadn't been for you and Miss Lee I don't know what would have happened to me.'

'He is a very good fellow and I'm most grateful to him.'

Alice gave them tea and cake and Susan sat with them by the fire and they talked of ordinary things, of Mr Martin's wife and children, and of his plans for Easter. All he said to Zeb before leaving was, 'You are most welcome at the chapel any time, if you feel you can come. If not, I understand and am so glad you are back here.'

Zeb didn't realise how much Mr Martin's visit would stir things up inside him. Coming here had been a good thing in many ways but it also brought back childhood memories that he would much rather have left dormant.

His father had been like Mr Martin: a good man, a good Methodist, manoeuvring people for what he thought would aid them. Yet if it hadn't been for Mr Martin, talking to Mr Samuels and introducing the idea of corresponding with him to Alice he thought he might have been dead by now. He had endured so much and had felt as though there was nothing left and that giving up was all he had. And then his father, and he managed to think positively about his father now that he wished his father was still there so that they could be reconciled. His father had prevented his hanging in the first place. It was this contradiction that upset him because if Mr Martin and his father were right, then he was wrong. He couldn't sleep.

He took on the job of the fires so that every room was warm. He was proud of it: such a small accomplishment, yet it mattered to all three of them. Alice and Susan had both said how grateful they were. It was nothing to him to carry buckets of coal upstairs but so heavy for them.

He preferred wood, he liked the smell of it, but coal lasted a lot longer and gave out more heat so he could justify keeping his fire on and his candle lit when he had long since turned down the lamp and extinguished it. Alice insisted on having oil lamps upstairs which gave off a lot more light if he wanted to read.

That Sunday Alice and Susan went arm-in-arm up the cobbled street toward the chapel. Susan had confided to him that Miss Frost almost never went since she was Church of England but that Miss Lee had been so good to her that she felt she should go.

Zeb was half-inclined to ask if he could go with them. He was astonished at this and not very pleased with himself. How could he be won over so easily? Yet it was not easy: it had taken all these years to humble him, and he did want to go and be with other people and perhaps remember his parents. In truth his father was a lot less kind than Mr Martin, at least that was how Zeb remembered him. He had never been a good child that he could remember at all. He tortured himself imagining that he would get to the chapel and Mr Martin would turn into his father, and his mother would be there in the front pew as she always was and they would both tell him he was a failure to them.

He suffered the whole time that Alice and Susan were out and when they came back he couldn't eat the splendid dinner that Alice put in front of him.

She didn't say anything. They went for a walk before it got dark and Alice said that the days were lengthening and soon it would be spring. Susan kept darting ahead because she wanted to see whether various flowers were out. Zeb had become accustomed to people staring at him but now he thought that they were not staring at him as much as they used to.

Alice slipped her hand through his arm. He thought it was the nicest thing that anybody had ever done, as though they were related, family, as though none of this was anything out of the ordinary. How trusting of her.

'What are you worrying about?' she asked softly.

He hesitated, not knowing whether to tell her or not and then he said quickly, 'I half-wanted to go to chapel.'

'Oh, Zeb,' was all she said.

'How could I without picturing my parents there and at the manse where I grew up – I just couldn't do it.'

'I'm not surprised,' she said.

'Do you remember my mother?'

'Yes, of course.'

'My father wrote and told me that her heart had broken over me and she died. I can't bear what I did to her.'

'I think your parents' marriage would have been quite different if they had more children. Being an only child is an awful responsibility; there's nobody to take the weight or the blame or to share your childhood memories with – though it seems to me that most siblings fight and squabble all their lives and learn to hate one another, so it could be a crooked view. I was an only child in a sense and when my father became ill, it was awful. But then older children might have moved away and younger children would need to be fed and clothed and cared for, so there would have been even less money.'

'Your mother drowned, right? I remember knowing something about it.'

'I blamed myself for that.'

'But you were a baby.'

'I know but we do, don't we? We're there so it must have been our fault. If she hadn't been having a child there wouldn't have been the shame, so in a way I killed her. I think you can turn anything around if you choose. Also, you have to understand that your mother had had a lot of miscarriages.'

This was news to him. He stared at her.

'I didn't know that.'

'She died in childbirth, it must be two years ago. They were ready to rejoice because they thought the child was going to be full term but it died. I think she was too old to have another child by then. And besides, they were the adults. How could you bear to bring up a child and then blame it for making a mess of its life?'

This was new information to him; he had thought his mother died of heartbreak.

'To be fair, I never liked your parents,' Alice said. 'I just wished they would have moved on and taken their stupid ideas with them. I'm sorry if that sounds awful – '

'No, I feel better,' he said, laughing.

Alice was glad that she had made him laugh but she also reminded him that because they had been his parents they must have had some love for him. He should forgive them even if it appeared that they had not forgiven him. His mother was dead and she had surely loved him as a child.

Zeb tried to keep in mind what Alice had said. He wanted now to see his mother's grave and possibly to find out where his father was. He didn't ask Alice any more but one fine afternoon he went to the graveyard and found her stone easily. All it said was 'Beloved Wife of John'. There was no mention of him, as though they had erased him completely from their lives because of what he had done.

He could understand that. If they didn't blame themselves, then why should they remember him? And if they did blame themselves, then why not pretend your son had not committed murder and didn't exist? But it seemed harsh all the same. It was one thing for him to abandon his parents when he was fourteen, it was quite another for them to abandon him for what he had done as a young man. Yet he knew that when he had committed murder it changed everything.

The thing that really upset him was that she had not been dead that long. Somewhere in his mind he thought she had died because of him – that she had laid down her life in grief just after he entered prison – but it wasn't true.

All those years neither of his parents went to see him, neither of them wrote; he received the odd stiff letter from his father to begin with but that had stopped after the third one. He had kept his father's letters all those years though they had brought him little comfort but had thrown them away before he left prison.

He couldn't write back; the place was unbearable for so long after he got there and no one would have let him write a letter at the time. It took months before he stopped reading his father's letters and even then he cried over them.

His parents held the grudge and his mother had been alive for seven years after he was put in prison. If she had broken her heart over him, it had been a long time in coming. And even though his father had not written to him in so very long, it had apparently still been his fault.

They must have thought that if she could bear another child they could start anew and cast him off since he was not the person they had expected him to be.

His father then had not left Stanhope so very long ago. Zeb made himself walk up the rough, cobbled street toward the chapel and was glad to find Mr Martin outside. He didn't want to go to the manse or even inside the chapel but he would have steeled himself and done it if he had to. But Mr Martin was just coming out so he was spared.

Zeb explained that he did not know the whereabouts of his father.

'He must be on the circuit somewhere. Perhaps other ministers may have news of him?' Zeb asked.

'I haven't heard anything,' Mr Martin said, 'but maybe he went further afield. I don't necessarily have news beyond Durham.'

Zeb went back and told Alice and Susan.

'But do you want to find your father?' Alice said.

'It's such a shock to know that my parents were here until relatively recently and that he went off like that after she died. He never liked me so what would I gain from getting in touch with him? I just want to stay here and see if I can get a job at the quarry. I'm fit now, you know, so I thought I would.'

They agreed with him and he thought he was all right about it but from then on he felt sick and didn't want to eat and he couldn't sleep. He had to eat because Alice would have noticed, but he saw now how difficult working there would be. A lot of the men he had worked with would still be there and some of them had been Alec's friends. They were the sort who didn't care what he did to his wife or child; hard men they thought themselves.

Zeb was so worried about it that he tried to persuade himself he wasn't well enough to go, that he should have another week at home. He could have. No, he couldn't. Alice would have seen through him and would have thought that he was a coward. He was beyond all the problems that had stopped him from working. He didn't realise when he announced he would go up to the quarry to seek work that he had been hoping she would question his motivation until she didn't.

He went on feeling sick but he couldn't put it off. He itched to be doing more but he was afraid of what he would meet.

'Don't worry,' she said, smiling just a little, 'Susan and I will look after our quarryman.'

He wanted to panic, to say, 'What if they won't take me on? What if nobody will take me on? To some of them I can never have paid for what I did. Will they try to kill me too?'

He didn't sleep well. When he got up, earlier than he had to, he was surprised to find that the women were up before him and Alice had already made him a huge breakfast. He struggled to get it down and then she gave him a large bottle of cold black tea and a big tin of food to get him through the day.

The sickness started to pass the moment he stepped out of the house. There was a fine mist over the little valley, the trees were half-hidden and he was fourteen again and full of enthusiasm, feeling like a man for the first time and free because he had walked out of his father's house after having an almighty row. His mother had scolded and then cried and his father told him that if he insisted on throwing his life away and going to work at the quarry he should get out and not come back. So that was what he did.

The guilt was always there. He had tried to argue that he had been very young and they had been unforgiving but that was how some families were. The expectation and the reality did not come close and could not be reconciled.

He remembered how proud he had been of himself when he moved into the boarding house where the other men lived. He smiled to himself now as he walked, thinking of how awful it was in there and how that place and the quarry prepared him so well for prison with its hard labour and little comfort, awful meals and the loneliness that settled on him. If he had not fitted in at home, he certainly didn't at the quarry.

He was always the minister's son, just as at home his parents were ashamed because he wanted to be a quarryman. He fitted nowhere, not even in prison; he was always apart and alone.

His worry now was in one place: he did not expect the men to accept him. He didn't really care except that quarrymen worked in twos. But he was not afraid, he had become a hard man. He hadn't shown it but he didn't need to in Alice's house. He always called her Miss Lee, very respectfully, but to him she was his guardian angel. She had been kinder to him than anyone in his life and she was the only person he would have died for.

She even seemed to like him. He laughed at himself for needing her approval, as though she was his parent. She had been more like a good parent to him than anyone ever had but he thought that she did what she did because it was her duty.

She was so good, religious but not pious. She wasn't made like that. And she was not sentimental, she was just decent, in a different way than anybody else he had ever met and he admired it. He would work for her now and give her back every penny he had cost her and help her as much as he could. Maybe at some time she might regard him as something more than a broken soul.

He had set off early so that he would not meet the other men at this stage. It would have been too much. He had learned what he could handle and what he could not. It altered as he made progress but he had to protect himself.

He walked on, past the chapel and up the path which led beyond the fields and houses. He had forgotten that it was quite steep initially and then levelled. He got as far as the quarry and he had forgotten how mighty it was. He had loved the awe of its size. It was so long at either side that you could barely see where it began or ended and so deep that it scared him. It had grown a lot in the past years when he had been away and he was glad of it.

There in front of him to the left stood what had once been a little shack and was now a brick building, quite large. There was no point in hesitating. He opened the door and went inside and, to his astonishment, there stood a man he had liked and worked with. And even more than that, he was the son of the old man, Jos Wearmouth, who had died in gaol.

'I heard you were out,' said Daniel Wearmouth. He was no longer a quarryman. He was wearing a suit. He was not smiling but neither was he telling Zeb that he would rather rot in hell than give him a job. He was not the clerk either because Zeb could see a man seated at the far desk, writing. He remembered him too, Angus Paterson. Mr Paterson didn't acknowledge him but as far as Zeb could remember he had always been like that so maybe it was nothing personal. He already felt relief that Daniel Wearmouth had even spoken to him.

The owner, Mr Almond, was also there. He too got up and came forward.

'Bailey,' he said.

'Yes, sir. I wondered if you might give me a job.'

'Why would I do that?'

Zeb was used to being badly treated and was at home with humiliation but he fought to keep his voice steady.

'I'm fit and ready and I'll do anything.'

'And who is to partner you?'

'I'll partner him,' Dan Wearmouth said. Mr Almond looked amazed and he wasn't the only one, Zeb stared.

'You're in the office most of the time,' Mr Almond said.

'We need an explosives man and I can show him how. It doesn't take two if the one man knows exactly what he's doing.'

'What happened to the last one?' Zeb said and Daniel Wearmouth grinned.

'He moved away.'

Zeb didn't quite believe him but then he had heard nothing to the contrary, and if there had been an accident everybody would have known. It was the most dangerous job in the quarry.

Mr Almond was still looking at him.

'Are you afraid of anything, Bailey?'

'No, sir.'

'Then you should be. An explosives man should always be afraid.'

'I would be afraid for the other men.'

'Ah, now that's quite a different thing. All right then, if Mr Wearmouth thinks you're worth it, we'll give you a trial. But be careful.'

'I'm always careful,' Zeb said and when they looked at one another, Mr Almond was the first to break the gaze. That was when Zeb realised that the men here were afraid of him. Why would they not be? He had killed a man and survived nine years in gaol.

Then Daniel Wearmouth took him outside and showed him what to do.

Nineteen

When Daniel Wearmouth had heard from the gaol, in a brief note, telling him that his father had died and would be buried within the prison grounds, he could not believe it. Ten years to other people was different than it was to him; ten years in which he had learned to hate his father. He had gone to the prison five times after his father was convicted but his father would not see him. Daniel thought that his father knew how guilty he was and could not face his son. So he gave up going to the prison but he kept on writing and had nothing back.

People shunned Dan. He hated how they talked, how nobody called on him or offered him a meal. His friends turned their backs when he walked the streets of Stanhope. He hated his father for having killed his mother and his mother for having been so ill.

When he had received a letter just a few months ago from his father it terrified him. After all this time his father had got in touch. Why would he do it now? There were only two possibilities: either he was coming out or he was dying. Both were terrible and Dan's heart thumped so hard and his hands shook so much that it took time to open the letter. When he finally had the single paper and saw his father's handwriting, the tears began to speed down his face.

Mr Dear Son,

I am writing to you now because I don't think I have much longer to live. I'm sorry I didn't see you when you came to visit. I didn't want you to see what this life was like. I have hoped that you found a life of some worth. I know that you could not have forgotten me nor perhaps ever forgiven me for what I did, though in my mind it was for the best. I have paid for it dearly.

I have thought about you every day while I have been in here. I wish that I had cared more about you and less about your mother, because I see now that although letting her go seemed the right thing to do, it deprived me of you and of my liberty and of all the time that we could have spent together. But I could not help it; she suffered so.

Your mother was in such awful pain and had been for so long. Neither of us could stand it any longer. I did what she asked of me even though it was difficult, but over time I have realised it was the wrong thing to do. My duty to you as your father should have been my first concern.

I loved your mother more than I loved you. Some people would say that was right but now I am sure that I got it all wrong. But it's too late; I made my choice, though I did not perhaps realise it at the time. All I could think of was her pain. You will have to forgive me if you can for all the stupid things I have done. I do love you. If there is a heaven then your mother is waiting there for me so don't grieve. Don't give me another thought.

Just one more thing: a lad in here, you probably remember him, Zeb Bailey, he has been so good to me. We have much in common: he killed for the woman he cared about and so did I. These past weeks I couldn't have got by without him. He has been my final comfort.

Your father,
Josiah Wearmouth

The first thing Dan felt was envy that another lad, a man of his own age, who had been shunned by the community for what he had done, was closer to his father than he was and could help him when he was ill and dying. Yet Dan was grateful that anybody had been there to help. He thought back over all those years when he had wanted to be there for his father and had wanted his father to be there for him and there had been no help and no comfort and no society of any kind. Hundreds of times he had thought that he would die of loneliness.

Dan went on with his work all this time. It was the only thing he could do. He moved to a men's hostel because could not find sufficient rent for the house where he had lived with his parents and so had had to give it up along with the furniture, the few books and his parents' clothes. His mother at least would never need them again and his father might not come out of gaol alive. Dan had been convinced that he never would.

The hostel was worse than his own home, but not by much since his home had been tainted by the time he left. His mother had died and his father had been wanted by the authorities for what he did. Dan could not bear to think of it. It was bad enough lying there at night down by the river where they had lived since he was born; the batts, as it was called.

That silence was the hardest way that he had ever lived. He

had not known that silence had its own sound. But here at the hostel, despite the dirty beds and awful food, he was at least with other men and could drink, smoke and find companionship of a sort in the evenings. They didn't care who he was or what his father had done. They had all had dreadful lives and so he could go to bed drunk and get up and do a day's work and not think beyond it. He could lie there and remember his childhood and better days.

He had wanted to leave school as soon as he could, even though he knew how to read and write and was good at figures. His father and mother thought he might want to go to the grammar school; they had put money by for it and saved hard. But he had wanted to join his father in the quarry and at the mine and to be a man as he was.

He was proud to work with his father, who taught him all about lead mining and limestone quarrying. He dressed as his father did and walked as tall as his father would but in his parents' marriage he was not important. They were the sort of people who would have been happy without a child. They never said so but he always felt as though he was in the way, an encumbrance.

He didn't perceive that he had wanted to work with his father so that his parents would be proud of him. But somehow they never seemed to be. It didn't matter how hard he worked, his father and mother never praised him. He was too young to understand that they thought he would go on after them and do well and didn't need the praise. They didn't want to spoil him by telling him how good he was at what he did.

He was eighteen when he came home with his father one lovely sunny June day and found his mother pale and in pain. From that day onwards she cried and complained constantly. She found everyday tasks too much and in the end his father insisted on taking her to the doctor. The doctor prescribed powders to make her better. These worked for a few days and then she was ill again and his parents went once more to the doctor.

This time she went into hospital in Wolsingham while the doctors consulted one another and decided that she had a growth in her stomach and she might not get better.

His parents told him these things when they came home. He couldn't decide which of them was the paler. When they all went to bed somebody cried next door to him and he didn't know which of them it was until he heard his mother's tender voice, soothing, as she took his father into her arms. Dan wept silently into his pillow.

How could things have gone so wrong? Had he done something? He tried to think back over his childhood at what might have been terrible misdemeanours but there was nothing he could bring to mind other than not getting his lessons right sometimes.

He had been a good son, at least he thought he had, and the next day when he and his father went for a walk down by the river and his mother went to bed he questioned his father. His father had looked down and shaken his head. He was more tender to him than he had ever been before.

'Oh Dan,' he said, 'how could any of this be your fault?'

'Mustn't it be somebody's fault?'

'It just happens.'

'But it shouldn't, if we do everything right. Isn't that what the Bible says?'

'People wish it did, they take comfort in thinking some things are within their control. For most folk life is hard and they need the comfort of God and the lovely idea that they will have an afterlife. Why would you not want to believe in such a wonderful thing?' his father said with a sad smile. Dan looked at his father and longed to take the hurt away.

'Do you believe in that?'

'I have to,' his father said softly. 'I love her so very much.'

'Will she die?'

His father hesitated.

'The doctors will do what they can and we must try to stay cheerful.'

'How can we do that?'

'We must, for her sake.'

And they did. They pretended that things went on forever. They went to work and although Dan's mother now had help from Elsie – the girl from next door, who was kind and hard-working and came and did so much – they worried all day about her. Work did not take up your whole mind, Dan saw as his father faltered.

The work was hard. He wished his father didn't have to do it but it was what they did. Then there came a time within weeks when his mother began to get worse, unable to go downstairs or be useful. She spent her time in bed, pale, thin and gaunt with pain and his father didn't want to leave her.

Dan was proud to tell his father that he must stay at home now, that he was needed, and Dan would bring in the money. It made him feel as though he was contributing something important. It also got him away from the house he loved that was now so difficult to stay in.

He didn't sleep very well in those weeks and he could hear his parents talking in the next room and the anguish in his father's voice. His mother tried to soothe her husband but he would choke and cry, and although Dan knew that men were not supposed to cry, he understood that his father loved his mother. That was when he wept.

So his father stayed at home and Dan was glad of it. He found that he preferred being at the quarry without his father because he could pretend that everything was all right and he was important. Mr Almond, the manager and owner, would praise Dan's efforts such as his father had never done. Dan liked to hear how good he was and how if he went on working hard he could train and go on to be a manager.

Always now he came in to find Elsie in the kitchen. Her cooking was bad and although he ate it, he did not enjoy it. His mother did not get better. Somehow he had thought that because he wished it, it would happen but within weeks the doctor was there more often. His father's face grew pale and thin and it was not Elsie's cooking.

Dan made himself go to work. They needed the money but he no longer thought that his mother would get better. Then her pain began to get worse. He thought that she should be in hospital but for some reason she would not go, or his father would not let her, or the doctors thought it could do no good. Dan didn't understand. Only that his mother was dying.

She began to cry out in the night and beg his father for something to help ease the pain. Sometimes Dan would run for the doctor who lived at the far end of the little town and he would come and silence her pain with drugs and all would go quiet.

Dan had never felt so alone. There was nobody to comfort him. It was to both his parents as though he did not exist and he lay there night after night, desolate.

But within another few weeks when he went for the doctor the doctor could not help and his mother was crying out with pain every night. For a while it got better in the mornings and then his father would sleep a little. Daniel, having been awake most of the night, would drag himself to work.

It was summer in the quarry and the days were fine, the work was hard and the sweat dripped off him. He began to wish that he had a wife and a house of his own and did not have to go home to his mother's pain and his father's grief. It was cowardly of him, he knew.

August was hell. The sun beat down as though it had nothing better to do than to turn the animals' thirst to rage and men to insanity. Washing was stiff in backyards. Earth became dust in gardens and flowers and vegetables shrivelled and died.

Daniel's mother discovered another level of pain and was never easy. Their little house seemed suffocating, even with the doors and windows open it was as though the heat bounced off the fields and the street and the shiny rooftops until Dan thought he had forgotten what rain sounded like and he longed for the coolness of it.

His father would pray on his knees that his wife should not suffer so much but even though the doctors came, two of them, they seemed to be able to do nothing. He heard his father through the wall, shouting.

'She needs relief. How could she become addicted to this and does it even matter?'

The doctors' replies were so quiet that he could not hear them. He wished to be away. He wished beyond anything to be out of there so that he could not hear his mother's screams and his father's agitated voice.

This went on night after night so that he would have given anything not to come home. In the daytime it must have been the same but thankfully he was not there to hear it. Elsie fled so there was no food but he didn't care. All he cared about was that his mother should stop screaming. On the night that she did, he finally slept easily. He told himself that she was better, that she would be well.

When he got up, it seemed that September was almost upon them and things would improve. The hot weather had gone and soon it would be harvest time. It was silent in the house. He washed and dressed and went downstairs. Then he heard a banging on the door and when he opened it one of the doctors stood there.

Daniel let him in and up the stairs and things were apparently far from well. In the silence Daniel followed him and saw his father sitting on the end of the bed where his parents had always slept. His father was bowed so that Dan could see the top of his head and the doctor glanced at his father and looked at his mother.

'You smothered her.'

His father looked up, meeting the doctor's gaze clearly.

'I released her, as you should have done.'

'You had not the right to do such a thing and neither had we.'

'She couldn't bear the pain any more.'

'You cannot take her life; it is against God.'

'I cared more for her than for His wrath or yours or the law's.'

Dan always remembered that and was proud of what his father had said and done. If God wanted people to suffer that much then he was wrong. If some people got to drop dead and suffer nothing and others had to go through what his mother had gone through, then his father was right, God was unfair and unjust. His mother had been a good woman and deserved none of that and neither did his father.

*

That afternoon the constable came and the undertaker. The first took away his father and the second his mother. Dan was left with the house, silence and despair. Despair was new to him. He had not known that it was as crippling as he found it. It got him round the middle and in his head, in his legs, in his arms, and in his chest. Everywhere was just a blanket of misery and pain and he couldn't move other than to stagger to bed.

His father did not come back and the vicar came to him and asked him about the service for his mother but he couldn't make a decision without his father. When his father returned, he told Daniel that he was accused of having killed his wife.

Dan thought he had died and gone to hell. He wanted to run back through some wall or garden so that he could get to where he had been before all of this had happened.

His father looked old. His face had deep grooves, not just lines, and Dan had not noticed how thin his father had become. None of them had eaten well in so very long. His father's clothes were slack on him and his eyes had lost hope.

Dan wanted to shout, 'What about me?' but he couldn't.

His father was taken to prison and though there was a trial it did not take long.

During the days before the judgement, Dan lay in bed and imagined what it would be like when they hanged his father and he would be completely alone. He was such a coward; he cried in his bed and was terrified. He couldn't sleep, he shook and then he would watch into the darkness of the ceiling hour after hour and night after night. It was torture.

Once his father was dead he would have nothing left. Prior to this, Daniel had been interested in the local lasses, seeking solace, comfort, and somebody of his own, but once his father was accused of murdering his mother, everything else melted away.

People on the street looked askance at him and he wanted to stop them and ask how they would feel if their husband or daughter was dying in unimaginable pain. He wanted to point out that if they haven't been through it, they can't know how it is. Instead he just stopped speaking to people and he gave up the house which he could no longer afford to keep. His mother was dead and his father was in Durham gaol and all was lost.

His father was not hanged. He was glad of this for the first few days and then he realised that his father would die in gaol. They had given him fifteen years for what he had done. No middle-aged man could survive such a thing. His father would have a living death.

At the quarry nobody said anything and his status had changed. Mr Almond no longer spoke to him in a friendly way or told him he would go on to management. He was called into the office and asked if he would take on the explosives. He hated that he was being asked but he could hardly refuse. What else had he? So he said that yes, of course he would do it, and if he should be blown to hell what difference did it make.

He began writing to his father and telling him anything good that happened but since then nothing, his letters were short and his grief was huge. When he did not have a single reply after eight months, he gave up until even his tears dried at night and he had nothing to give.

All he did was get up in the mornings and go to work. He never took chances with his work: he was employed to get the men through the day. He was better paid than they were but not at first. Mr Almond had not offered him better but after the first few weeks Dan approached him.

'You think I'm going to do this for the same money?'

'You can go elsewhere.'

'I can, but can you?'

Mr Almond thought about it and his flint grey eyes sliced across Dan's gaze.

'How much do you want to stay?' he said and Dan gave him a huge, almost indecent figure. He knew that Mr Almond would pay it because explosives men sometimes died and nobody wanted to take it on.

Dan didn't even smile when he was granted his request; he just got himself out of the office and did what he was meant to do.

He tried not to think about his parents but it was hard. He had to drink an awful lot of beer at night not to envisage his father in gaol and his mother dead. He did start writing to his father again but he had no reply and in time he learned not to go to the gaol or watch for letters.

Twenty

'If you let me down here, you are finished,' Dan Wearmouth said to Zeb as they left the office.

'I will do my best.'

The explosives man was the most dangerous job in the quarry but Zeb didn't care. Why should he worry about things like that after what he had been through? Though to his astonishment he didn't really want to die any more. He had not felt like that in so long that he held the feeling and examined it. It was because of what he had now. Miss Lee and Susan had already become so very important to him that he wanted to be there, he wanted to go back to the sweet shop in the evenings.

He thought of how proud they would be that he had found a job. A man was not a man without a job and he had not been a man for all those years. He wanted to run back to the sweet shop and tell them of his triumph but he kept his face closed and his expression empty. It didn't take much doing, he had perfected it over the years.

Zeb and Dan didn't talk. Zeb didn't want to talk, it was bad enough with all the men staring at him. He could hear whispers and he half-wished that somewhere amidst the beatings he had endured that his ears had been damaged so that he could not hear this.

He was, he thought with sudden hope, in reasonably good shape for what he had been through. Or was that just exhilaration because he was back in the quarry where he had always wanted to be, and at the end of the day he would go home to Alice Lee's sweet shop and her wonderful dinner and a soft bed and all the comfort that any man could wish for? Now he had a whole bookshelf full of books that he wanted to read. He could walk down by the river and watch the fish rising. He could stay in if he wished and talk by the fire and drink tea with the two women.

The whispers reached him.

'What's he doing back here after what he's done?'

'Mr Almond should never have taken him on. Did he think the men would stand it?'

'I've said it before, he should have hanged.'

Zeb ignored it. Being in prison was good for making you resilient. He didn't care what anybody said. He had a job. He hadn't thought he could get one. And it was the kind of job that he had liked and it couldn't be any harder than what he had been doing while he was in gaol.

Things were so good that he couldn't believe it. But he didn't think that the Lord was trying to balance his life. God never did such things. You could go down and down and down and he would never notice until you died or killed yourself. It was nothing more than luck and your own perseverance. Though maybe that was God.

Dan was silent for the first two days other than giving instructions. Zeb listened carefully because he knew nothing about it. Dan told him what to do in short, flat tones. All Zeb did was nod and obey and Dan seemed content with that. Zeb worked hard and was used to not speaking.

It was strange: all those years he hadn't seen or spoken to a woman, and now they were all he conversed with. And their voices were as sweet as the chocolate they sold. The tones of the quarrymen, when they talked among themselves, sounded harsh. Zeb didn't listen to anyone except Dan.

After a week he began to think about the way that Dan had rescued him. Why on earth would he have done such a thing unless he knew that Zeb had helped his father in gaol? Zeb would have done the same for any helpless old man but to Dan it was important. He remembered that the old man had written to his son but Zeb had been brought up far too well to read a dying man's last letter to his child.

His luck lasted into the second week and then just before the end of the shift he found himself confronted by half a dozen men. He hadn't even noticed them gathering and that showed how soft he had got. He would never have let that happen in prison. But then nobody there would have dared do it.

In fact he was somewhat amused that they should think he could be taken that easily. They didn't understand how these things worked and he only had to sort two before the rest would take fright and shift. There was nobody behind him, at least his instincts had kept him that safe. He was so used to these things that with a wall behind him and them in front, life was much easier.

He didn't show humour; he just turned around and glanced at the half circle. He saw that a lot of men were standing back. They wouldn't mind him getting a hiding but they didn't want to be involved. That was how it worked. If he could take the first two down quickly and make it look bloody the trouble would stop. His advantage was that they hadn't been through nine years of hell so they didn't understand what they were dealing with. He was no longer nineteen and a stupid lad.

He had learned the hard way, but it could make life different now. The only weapons they had were mallets and hammers which were too big to swing, too slow to hurt. He always carried a knife on him. He didn't know how to move without it. He could feel it there, small and just heavy enough in his pocket. It could do an awful lot of damage in a very short time and he had become very good with it. He had kept it hidden for years in spite of the lags. That and Eli had been all his comfort. He had thought about getting rid of it. Now he was pleased he hadn't. Now he never would.

'Something up?' he said.

'Aye, you are,' said one whose name he couldn't remember.

'Me? Why?'

'You have no right to come back here and think you can pick things up as if you hadn't murdered Alec White. He bled to death in the main street.'

'I was there,' Zeb pointed out.

'You think you're funny, don't you?' They were all thin, the work made them that way, but a nine-year-old could have made a meal of this short-arsed bugger.

He waited for them to come a bit closer but just as they started to, a good-humoured voice came from Zeb's left.

'Nice one, lads.' Pat McFadden, the most popular bloke in the quarry, came and stood beside Zeb.

'This is nowt to do with thee, Pat,' another said.

'Zeb's done nothing to you. He paid for what he did.'

Zeb was surprised. He and Pat barely spoke and he was surprised to hear his name on Pat's lips.

'They should've hanged him,' somebody else said.

'Who made you the law?' Pat said, holding the man's gaze so that the man looked away. It was something he had perfected, Zeb thought admiringly.

Zeb was about to tell Pat that he could manage just fine but for once he didn't see why he should. Pat was about forty but he was in very good nick. The two of them could sort this lot out in minutes if it came to it.

Pat, of course, was Irish and had known bad times. He had been put out of a lot of places before he got here, Zeb dared guess. The Irish got a bad time from almost everybody. The only blokes that Zeb had seen worse treated were some poor black bastard in the gaol and another feller who came from Persia or some place; he had a brown skin and black eyes and other ideas. Being different just wasn't good around here. And he was now different and a target.

Pat stood and waited like somebody who had all week and in the end the men melted off, like snow by the river on a warming day.

'I could have done it on my own,' Zeb said, in thanks.

'Oh, go and piss yourself,' Pat said.

Every day Alice packed up food for Zeb and it was much better than the stuff Dan got. Living in a boarding house his food was not just dull, it was awful. The sandwiches had curled edges, rancid butter and cheese with mould on it. They smelled vile.

Zeb would have been grateful for such fare only a few months ago but Alice's cooking had alerted his nose and tastebuds. He could not help be aware of Dan watching when he unpacked chocolate cake and cheese scones freshly made and thick with butter.

During the first few days Dan kept going back and forth between the office and where Zeb worked in the quarry. He seemed to have a double role, at least until Zeb could do his job without blowing his feet off. As a result, they were spending a lot of time together.

Zeb offered to share his food. Dan shook his head.

'Miss Lee always makes too much,' Zeb said. 'Go on, she's trying to fatten me up. I need it after nine years in prison. Try this chocolate cake, honestly, it's the best I've ever tasted.'

Dan's appetite and the smell of the chocolate cake bettered him and he took it. It was a beautiful day there up in the quarry and there weren't many of these this early in the year. He thanked Zeb and they sat in amiable silence for a moment.

'I want to thank you for offering to work with me like this,' Zeb ventured to say quietly. 'I didn't expect to be taken on.'

'I owe you,' Dan said shortly.

'I understand why you think you do, but all I did was offer a little help to an old man.'

Dan didn't say anything for such a long time that Zeb wished he hadn't said anything. But he let the quiet grow. He was no longer afraid of silence.

Finally Dan said, looking down the side of the valley towards Frosterley, 'You helped him when nobody else would have.'

'It's hard to look after anybody inside, even yourself, so I didn't do much,' Zeb said.

'He wrote and told me how good you'd been. It might not mean much to you but it means a whole lot to me.'

'What are you still living at the hostel for?' Zeb asked.

'I'm saving money. I thought I might leave the quarry but lately Mr Almond decided that he likes having me help in the office and he's paying me more.'

'Where would you go?'

'I don't know. I've got nothing here but things are changing.

And since you came back here, you've taken over the job I didn't like.'

Dan got up and went back to work at that point, so Zeb followed him. After he told Alice about it that evening, she began to pack twice as much food. Even if Dan was busy, Zeb would put the extra bottle of cold tea and the tin just inside the office door without speaking. They never discussed it but Zeb could see by Dan's face how grateful he was.

The first time Zeb was paid, it was more money than he had ever seen. He went back to the sweet shop and put the coins into Alice's hands.

She stared.

'But – but Mr Bailey, it's yours. You earned it.'

'It's for you and Susan, to help pay for everything you have done for me, the housekeeping and the food and for everything. You have been so – so wonderful.'

Alice blushed. Zeb was astonished but he saw that it was just that she was embarrassed.

'That's beyond kind. You must have some of it back.'

'I don't need money.'

'What if you want to go for a drink?'

Alice looked so lovely that day, he thought; her cheeks were red from the cold and her eyes were bright in the firelight.

'And you a good Methodist, Miss Lee.'

'Yes, but you don't have to stick to my ideas.'

He hesitated.

'I haven't had a drink in nine years and you know where it got me last time.'

'I don't think that was just the drink,' Alice said generously and she gave him back half of the money. 'Don't be so hard on yourself.'

He didn't like to argue with her but he insisted that she take another handful. He thought of what he might buy that would help them. Or maybe he would just save it for when something went wrong, because sooner or later it always did.

Twenty-One

Zeb had been at the quarry for more than two months when Alice said to him, 'Why don't you invite Mr Wearmouth to Sunday dinner?'

Zeb stared at her.

'We aren't friends. We just work together.'

'But he had such an awful time.' What she meant was that they had certain things in common. Zeb didn't think they had but Alice was insistent and he knew how she liked to help people.

'And he must get tired of the boarding house and its food.'

Dan seemed surprised at the invitation but he didn't say no. Zeb had been convinced that Dan, who was almost part of the management, would refuse. Now that Zeb knew what he was doing as the explosives man, he rarely saw Dan. He spent his whole time in the office. Everybody was aware that he was doing good work there and Mr Almond, who had no son, thought dearly of him.

Zeb was pleased that things were working out so well for him and he liked being able to do the explosives himself. He found that the men were kinder and it was because if he didn't get his job right it could cost them time, money and even worse, injuries and possibly even their lives.

So to invite Dan for a meal was a huge thing but Alice didn't seem to understand. Zeb could hardly say anything to her about this, it would have sounded stupid.

'Don't you think we should?' Alice prompted him. 'He has been through a good deal and has no friends.'

That was so like her: she understood things that few people understood. Yet her generosity was puzzling.

'It's very kind of you to ask him,' he said.

'I want to help people,' she said and he thought, yes, Dan was just like he had been, and she would gather him in as she had himself and Susan. It was, he thought, like a chocolate orphanage for adults.

Alice went off to chapel, as though everything was normal on the day that Dan had agreed to come for Sunday dinner. She had been to the butcher for a lovely piece of beef and since the butcher and his wife and two children loved sweets and were favoured by Alice, Zeb did not doubt that the cut of meat would be perfect. She had left strict instructions that they were not to leave it cooking too long or it would be brown and tough. It had to be what she called 'sealed, put in the oven and slightly underdone,' so they kept to her wishes.

Alice returned just before their guest arrived so she was there to greet him and tell him how pleased she was to see him. Susan smiled and held out her hand and Zeb could tell that Dan liked being there and why wouldn't he? The table was set with white linen and napkins, and tulip-shaped glasses glinted in the sunlight. Alice had offered her elderberry wine, which was gloriously red and fruity and claimed to be alcohol-free but obviously wasn't.

The Yorkshire puddings rose golden and high, the gravy was

dense and rich, the parsnips were almost caramelised and Alice had made her raw onion with pepper and vinegar that was the perfect accompaniment. There was horseradish that Alice had bottled when it grew in the garden and it was thick with cream, vinegar, salt and white pepper.

They had poached pears to follow and local Cotherstone cheese with biscuits and from somewhere Alice had procured port to go with it for the two men. It was as though a celebration, Zeb thought. And then he thought, yes, when you had been through a lot as they all had, each day was a celebration.

'What a lovely woman Miss Lee is,' Dan said as Zeb saw him out of the back door and up the vennel to the front street. 'She would have made a good mother. And Miss Wilson is very pretty. Is she eighteen?'

Zeb didn't like this but he wasn't sure why.

'Younger, I think.'

'She's a slip of a thing.'

Zeb didn't like his womenfolk – when had they become that? – spoken of like this. He was sure that Dan meant no disrespect but they had done so much for their guest. He thought Dan might have just said how kind they had been.

'She is a lovely girl,' Dan said.

'Yes.'

They said goodnight and Zeb went back inside, but he imagined Dan treating Susan as men were wont to treat young women they fancied but had no intention of marrying and he was not very happy about it. Did Dan think that Susan was attainable simply because she had no parents, no background?

He hated to think it. When he got back to the house, he was just in time to hear Susan say to Miss Lee that she thought Mr Wearmouth a fine young man.

Zeb, coming in the back way in the darkness, stood with the door open and then announced that he was back and the conversation ceased.

On the Wednesday of that week, Dan said to Zeb when Zeb went into the office, 'I thought I might come round and ask Miss Wilson if she would go for a walk with me.'

Zeb stared at him.

'You can't.' He hadn't meant to say that but somehow it slipped out. He was horrified: he thought of Susan as a child.

Dan looked at him, face white and eyes hard.

'What do you mean, I can't?'

'She's a lot younger than you imagine her to be and she doesn't know anything about men.'

'Maybe you should let her decide. You aren't her father.'

'You're a lot older than she is.'

Zeb decided to say no more when Dan turned a red, angry face to him and they went about their work. Zeb didn't know what to think or do. He had the feeling that if he said anything, it would be misconstrued. After all, what Susan did was up to her. He kept telling himself that he was overreacting because that was what he had done when Alec White had so mistreated the girl they had both been in love with.

He wanted to talk to Alice about it but he couldn't get her by herself. Dan was right, he had no say here, it was nothing to do with him. Alice would doubtless have something to say but on the Sunday afternoon when Dan turned up, all neat in his best and asked Susan if she would go for a walk with him, she blushed and collected a light coat.

After they had gone Alice turned a grim face to Zeb.

'I'm sorry,' Zeb said, 'but I didn't know what to say. It's not my business.'

'He must be as old as you,' Alice said, as though Zeb was in his dotage.

'Presumably he means well.'

'Huh,' Alice said, 'he must be the first then.'

'What could you have said that might have changed her mind?' Alice sighed.

'I'm like you: I'm not her parent, I'm just a friend. But I didn't think he'd do this.'

Zeb couldn't relax. They were gone two hours. By the time Dan brought Susan home her cheeks were glowing and her eyes were sparkling. Alice gave him tea and shortbread. Zeb wished him away and Susan kept turning to him in the way that women have turned to men for centuries, eyes pleading with him to like her. It made Zeb want to shout and swear at her for being so vulnerable and obvious.

After Dan had gone, she had followed him to the door and outside and was there some minutes and then danced inside. Nobody knew what to say.

'Where did you go?' Alice said.

'Along the riverbank. Oh, Miss Lee, it's almost summer there. The wild flowers are pushing their way through the grass. Danny knows all the names of the trees and he showed me fish in the water when we got to the bridge and we ran over the stepping stones and it was lovely.'

'Danny?' Miss Lee reproved.

'He told me I could call him by his first name.'

When it was time to go to bed Susan took herself off with a joyful step. Alice and Zeb lingered.

'I wish I hadn't asked him here,' Alice said.

'You can't help such things.'

'I didn't know that she would react like that.'

'Neither did I,' Zeb said.

Alice was more concerned about Dan than she let on. She didn't want Zeb to get involved, she didn't think it would help, and she couldn't say anything to Susan. After all, what could she add? Girls younger than Susan were given to men twice their age every day. Servant girls like her slept in old men's beds because they had nowhere else to go.

Dan was young and clean and a hard worker, but there were so many potential pitfalls. When Alice went to bed she was aware of the girl lying beside her awake and she knew that Susan thought she loved this man already. She was so keen to give herself away. Alice's heart twisted for her and yet she was also envious. Nobody had ever asked her to go for a walk.

She lay awake while Susan dropped off into the kind of sleep where Alice thought that even in darkness, the girl was smiling. She heard Zeb move about and she knew how hard this was for him because although he didn't want the girl for himself – she was sure he didn't – he felt protective, she knew. This was his downfall. What Susan did was not his business but they were living in the same house.

Twenty-Two

Zeb suffered. He had not known that he would feel like this. He wanted Dan to be in earnest but to him Dan was like some puffed-up cockerel. Having captured his bird, he was pleased with himself. He didn't say anything to anybody that Zeb knew of but maybe he had boasted at the hostel. The lads at the quarry soon noticed that he was out walking with Susan regularly that summer on Sunday afternoons.

Zeb was close enough to hear one lad say, 'Nice piece of skirt. Nice under it too, I'll warrant.'

Dan laughed. Zeb turned away and said nothing.

'Been under it yet, have you then?' the lad said and Dan shook his head.

'They don't mean anything,' he said to Zeb later.

'No, not to you, but they're being disrespectful about a young woman.'

'That's nothing.'

'I would say it was everything.'

'Yes, but the men know what you're like.'

'What does that mean?'

'You have a quick temper.'

'You haven't even seen it.'

'I've heard about it often enough.'

'In that case perhaps you should be careful.'

Dan laughed again but there was something brittle about it. The Sunday walks went on and then he began buying Susan small presents. He wanted to take her to a dance at the Bonny Moor Hen.

'You can't take her into a pub,' Zeb protested. They were talking on the front street when Zeb had followed him out of the house after hearing his plan.

Dan glared at him.

'I'm getting tired of you telling me what I can and cannot do. She has agreed to it and I'm not asking you or Miss Lee for permission. It's a dozen yards away.'

'That isn't the point.'

'You're treating her like your property,' Dan said and looked hard at him. 'If you want her for yourself then say so.'

'She's not much more than a child.'

'Oh yes? That's not how it felt when I kissed her.'

'Just take care with her.'

'I am taking care.'

'You will look after her?'

Dan promised but he took her to the dance. Susan was very excited about it and Miss Lee, considering it was all she could do, bought her a new dress from Miss Wanless who owned the dress shop and made a lot of the clothes herself.

Because the dance was only yards away, Alice and Zeb could hear it. The music was loud, though not in a bad way; there was a band playing country music with a fiddle and drums, and they heard the couples going in and the talk and the laughter and Alice wished that she could ever have gone to such a dance.

She had spent years listening to things like this going on at the pub but she had never been inside, never had a decent dress nor learned how to dance. When would she cease to feel this horrible smarting envy of people whom she thought were having a better time than she was?

It probably wasn't true, she kept telling herself, but she was only happy when the merriment ended in such places, when the music was stilled and the sound of people's conversation and footsteps had died on the pavement as they wended their way home.

'Did you want to go?' Zeb asked of her, long before it got going.

Alice was startled. Had the ache been clear on her face? She had not realised that she was so transparent.

'The women there are young enough to be my children. How would that look?'

He hesitated and then Alice said, 'I would have liked to go when I was younger.'

'Weren't you asked?'

'I was illegitimate so nobody would ask me. And my parents were in ill health from when I was very young so I had to look after them and learn my trade. You could still go.'

Zeb smiled.

'Who would dance with a murderer?' he said.

Twenty-Three

Susan regretted having gone to the pub. It started as a dance but became a romp when the men had drunk too much. Dan drank too and although he stayed by her side, she was not happy and wanted to go home. She watched him change from a kind and loving man to somebody she didn't understand and hadn't seen before. He didn't bother with her, he didn't ask her to dance or talk to her; he just kept shouting across to other men and they shouted back and they came over and carried on conversation which excluded her, all about work. She was forgotten.

She could just go and leave him, she knew, but that didn't seem right. So she stayed and watched and was appalled by the drunken men falling down the steps that led to the stage where the band was playing. The landlady became very vexed, telling them to go home. The fiddlers gave up, the piano player went too and the men were left singing drunken songs.

She had thought about what it would be like when she went to her first dance. Miss Frost had told her all about when she was young and how she had worn pretty dresses in dark red velvet and matching ribbons in her hair.

Her father would take her to stay with the gypsies and she would dance around the fire and they would drink Spanish wine and eat food cooked over big fires and people would sing and everybody would dance. She had had a lover then, a man who had ridden a black horse, and he had wanted to carry her off with him but her father had forbidden it.

'At the time,' she said, 'I thought it would break my heart but in the end I was glad. He was the kind of man who took a girl for as long as he wanted and then threw her away. I never wanted any man to tell me what to do or to be able to treat me badly. My sister married and I never envied her.'

'Was her husband harsh to her?'

'No, it was worse than that: he was boring,' Miss Frost said and she laughed at the recollection. 'Husbands must always be boring. How could they be otherwise? Some men are the kind that one should yearn for but never marry. And don't get me started on childbirth, it is horrific.'

Susan managed to get herself outside when she couldn't stand any more. Dan followed her and she could smell the beer on his breath.

'I can see myself home,' she said.

'I'm sorry,' he said, lurching forward, 'I didn't know it would be like that.' He went with her to Alice's front walk.

'Goodnight,' she said and ran the few yards to the shop and down the lane and in by the back door. There Zeb was, standing up in the firelight at the sudden noise.

'Are you all right?' he said.

'Of course I'm all right,' she said, impatiently, closing the door and taking off her outdoor things. 'It just wasn't as I thought it would be. I think I will go to bed now.' She choked on a sob, went upstairs and clashed the bedroom door.

He heard Miss Lee say, 'Susan?'

'It was awful,' Susan said and burst into tears.

Zeb sat down, so grateful to have her safely back under Alice

Lee's roof and apparently unhurt that he was shaking. He should have been able to trust Dan but Dan had not come back with her. Maybe he just left her outside in front of the pub. The truth was that Zeb trusted no one to bring any woman safely home. He could not help the way that he felt, though he knew that he should. Just because he had met so many bad men in prison didn't mean there weren't good ones out there. He tried to understand that it was nothing to do with him. On this note, he took himself to bed and tried to comfort himself in the knowledge that Susan was fine and Dan meant no harm and everything would be all right. Somehow he got himself to sleep on that lie.

The following day was Sunday and Alice went off to chapel, taking Susan with her because Susan was still upset and needed something to do. They had not been long gone when Dan banged on the back door. When Zeb opened it, he stood there, cap in hand, looking sheepishly at Zeb.

'I did see her to the front door but I didn't like to come further because I could tell I upset her. Can I see her and tell her how sorry I am?'

'She's not here.'

'Chapel? Look, Zeb, I'm really sorry. I drank too much. I should have taken her out of there sooner and I didn't. I'd forgotten how young she was. Is she all right?'

'No,' Zeb said, not inclined to spare him. 'She came here all in a state and cried her eyes out, what do you think? I told you not to take her there, that sort of thing isn't for her, and if you cared anything for her you wouldn't have done it.'

'I wanted to take her somewhere and there's not much choice. You can only have so many walks on Sunday afternoons. I want to spend a time with her. I want to work for her and have her for mine. I want to marry her.'

'And how would you treat her then?'

Dan's eyes hardened.

'I think you're mixing me up with Alec White. I'm not him; I'm decent. I mean well and I love her. I want to set up house with her and have children. What's wrong with that? And who are you to say that I can't see her, that I can't tell her what I feel? I know I let her down and I'm sorry but it won't happen again. I'll come back later when she's here,' and Dan turned and left.

Alice and Susan came home and though Zeb said nothing Alice kept looking at him. She sent Susan out the back to get some herbs for the salad to go with the Sunday dinner and turned to him.

'He was here, wasn't he?'

'He's coming back later.'

Alice frowned.

'He's going to ask her to marry him,' Zeb said.

Alice stared and groaned and then she sighed a deep sigh.

'I don't think he understands how young she is or how to treat her. You would never have taken her there and I think a lot of other young men would have known. He seems to lack the basics. But she's the only one who can decide what she's going to do and if we somehow put him off, he will come round and talk to her anyway. I would hate to think that she married him for all the wrong reasons because she knew that you and I were against it.'

It was like being a parent, Zeb thought, and winced. Alice was right, they could not interfere. Susan came back into the kitchen and helped Alice with the dinner.

'He came round, didn't he?' she said to Zeb.

Zeb nodded.

Susan's eyes sparkled with temper.

'I don't want to see him ever again.'

It wasn't very convincing. She didn't eat her dinner and after it she went upstairs and spent a long time looking into the mirror and putting ribbons into her hair. She went downstairs and back up at least twice before the knock on the door made her cheeks flush and her eyes sparkle in quite a different way.

It was pouring with rain so Dan could hardly ask her to go for a walk. When he came inside Alice and Zeb went into the shop and left them alone.

'I feel like this is my fault,' Alice said, 'for inviting him here.'

'You didn't know. And it's me who works with him.'

'I think she's too young to marry, though lots of girls her age do.'

They waited for perhaps half an hour though it felt like longer and when they went back inside, the two lovers were close together by the fire. When Susan looked up, Zeb knew that Dan had asked her to marry him. She glowed like a happy little beacon.

He and Alice pretended to be pleased and they all sat down and had cake and tea and Dan was in better spirits than Zeb had seen him before. He said he knew of a really good house that they could rent, with a pretty garden, just across the street.

Susan looked shyly at Alice.

'You will come with me to see the rector, Miss Lee, to sort things out after Danny and I go there?'

Alice said she would be glad to.

They agreed to be married in August when they could be fairly sure of the weather. Alice said she could ask Miss Wanless to fashion Susan a lovely dress and she would make all manner of dainties. They could probably have the church hall, or if not they could manage something here if the weather was fine.

'The wedding should be very small,' Susan said. 'I have no friends but you two and I don't think Danny cares, do you?' She turned to her betrothed and he nodded. 'Here would be lovely.'

They therefore set the day for the second Saturday in August and the rector, Mr Sowerby, was happy for them to have a reception at the vicarage. He was another good customer of Alice's. He loved chocolate, that and whisky were his vices, he told her.

The rectory was big and overlooked the river and it was very often used for receptions since it was large and ornate and the rector was so accommodating. If it was a fine day people could eat, drink and make merry in the gardens.

By the time Susan and Dan came back and told Alice that the rector was happy to marry them, she was full of plans for the reception. She was thinking of all the wonderful cakes and sweets she would make, and now that they had the rectory and the beautiful parish church, Alice was as enthusiastic as the lovers. Only Zeb was quiet.

Susan and Alice went to take a look at the house across the road that Dan had spoken of.

'I'll be able to come and help you in the shop just as usual,' Susan said.

'I think you'll have sufficient to do here,' Alice said, looking around at the big bay windows that had a view of the river and a long narrow garden filled with flowers in full bloom. They were rather like Susan's hopes, Alice thought. The girl was so much more beautiful now than she had been before becoming betrothed to Dan and she had been a bonny lass then.

The house had two big bedrooms, a proper dining room, a

sitting room that looked out over the garden and a big kitchen
at the back that led into the yard.

Alice couldn't have been happier for the pair, though Zeb
was doing a lot of hovering over the small fire, which the fine
weather made almost unnecessary except for cooking and hot
water. She kept the shop door open and fought with the flies
that got in.

One Sunday not long before the wedding, when Dan and Susan
were over at the house putting up curtains and Zeb was sitting
over the fire, she said to him, 'Why don't you go for a walk?'

He looked up as though he had only half-heard her.

'I think I'd better move out, you know, if Susan gets married.'

Alice stared at him.

'Whatever for?' she said.

She watched his face colour.

'Well, didn't you think about how it will look, you and me
living here together?'

Alice was astonished. She had not even considered the prospect of living here alone with the murderer. Besides, she thought
of Zeb as little more than a child, which she saw now was ridiculous. She wanted to protest that she was old enough to be
his mother, but she realised she wasn't. For the first time, she
thought of him as a man. Would anybody else think like that?
Perhaps they would.

'I didn't think about it,' she said, not being able to come up
with something better.

He looked at her and smiled.

'You'd feel safe here with me, without Susan?'

That made her laugh.

'If you had been the wrong sort of lad, I don't think Susan
would have made much difference.'

'And I'm not the wrong sort of lad?'

'Of course not.'

Zeb was on his feet but looking down at them.

'I think that's the nicest thing anybody ever said to me, Miss Lee. I don't want to leave,' he said, sounding desperate. 'I don't think anybody else would have me, and I don't want to go to the hostel where Mrs Smithers makes awful meals and I'd have to share a mucky bed with other men.'

Alice shook her head and said what she thought would soothe him.

'It probably won't be much different,' she said. 'Susan will be here most of the time just like she is now.'

Zeb hesitated as if he didn't know what to say.

'Why don't we just wait and see,' Alice said which was always her answer when things had not happened. You had to wait for the problem to arrive. 'Things sort themselves out. Susan will be happy and you and Dan might get on better once you get used to them being married. I think you'll manage when you don't work so closely together.'

It was true, they hardly saw one another now that Zeb could manage the blasting by himself and Mr Almond relied on Dan at the office. Dan was going up in the world, so the men said. They didn't say much to Zeb but neither did they spit or call him names anymore. Their safety depended on him; they could not afford to distract him from what he was doing. They kept their ideas to themselves and he ate by himself and worked alone.

Twenty-Four

Alice liked the new deacon. She thought he had a lot about him. As she and Susan walked away from the manse after they had met him, she asked Susan, 'What did you think of Mr Westbrooke?'

Susan looked at her and wrinkled her nose.

'He's a churchman, isn't he?'

'You mean like a cleric?'

'Is that what you call it? Not the sort of lad a dales lass would want, is he? Sitting there with his nose in books all the time.'

'I thought you quite liked chapel now.'

'I do sometimes, but the lads that go, well, you wouldn't want anything to do with them, would you? A bit of the dull sort.'

Alice considered this and she knew that at Susan's age she probably wouldn't have wanted the church boys, either.

'Especially not somebody like Mr Westbrooke who's so shaffling,' Susan said.

It meant little and skinny. Alice hadn't heard the term in a while. She could see what Susan meant, he wasn't a big bonny lad like Dan Wearmouth. On the other hand he was kind, caring and had the sweetest face and the gentlest eyes that Alice thought she had ever seen. And there was strength in him somehow.

He was learned, that was the word for it, and knowledgeable and he was intelligent enough to look after people. She thought those were much more important qualities for a man to have, but then she was not young and wanting to be in a lover's arms. At near forty you had got well past thinking about such things and longing for somebody's kisses. She could look objectively at all men now. She had her shop and her customers and she thought that in time maybe even Zeb would marry some nice lass, if people could forget what he had done when he was young and foolish. Although she would regret both of them leaving, she would be glad if they were happy. You could never tell what time did for these things.

After Susan married, Alice would miss her. While she had quite enjoyed living alone, all the things that had happened to her since Miss Frost had died had changed her and she did not look forward to the prospect of being alone again. She was surprised at that. She kept thinking that Susan and Zeb were a burden to her but burdens once lifted could leave a great gaping hole in your life. That was when you knew that you had loved them.

It was the following weekend that Ella Martin, the minister's wife, having made sure her guests had tea and scones and the children had cake and milk, came over to Susan while Alice was talking to other people.

'Miss Wilson, I wonder if I could ask a favour.'

Susan was amazed. She couldn't think of anything she might do that would help Mrs Martin.

'I need some help with the Sunday school. I do my best but the girls have been so troublesome lately and I don't like to think of Mr Westbrooke having to cope alone. He isn't local and the children aren't used to him, and I just haven't found the time to help him with the two classes.'

She stopped when she saw that Susan was panicking.

'I don't know anything about such things. I haven't had any formal education,' Susan said.

'No, but you lived with Miss Frost all your life and I know that she gave you a very good schooling in many things. You're closer in age to the children than anybody else and they like you.'

'Do they?' Susan was astonished.

'They know you from the sweet shop and they associate you with good things. Why wouldn't they? Please will you help, just once this week and then if you hate it I won't ask you again. I know it's an imposition. Will you mind if Mr Westbrooke came to see you, or could you come to the manse some time soon? I would be so grateful. He hasn't been here long and I think he's finding it hard.'

Susan wondered why he was finding it hard. He didn't have to go out and work in the fields, the mines or the quarries like many a lad. He had a good thing going here. Surely he hadn't had the nerve to complain about the Sunday school. He wasn't the minister so he didn't have to work at much and Susan felt sure that Mrs Martin and Jane looked after everybody in their house very well. Maybe it was his family that he missed. Maybe his father was a preacher and he had sisters and brothers to keep.

Susan only agreed to help because she could see that Mrs Martin was overburdened, but she worried. She told Miss Lee about it on the way home.

'Oh, but Susan, you'd be so good at it!' she exclaimed. 'You are wonderful with the children when they come into the shop. I think half of them come in just to see you.'

Susan hadn't considered this but when she saw herself in the shop, remembering the children's names and sharing their laughter, and how they always lingered, she began to understand what Miss Lee meant. She had thought it was because they wanted free sweets but they never got any. She talked to them about their families and their lives and what school was like. She hadn't understood before then that she was interested in them.

She went up to the chapel the following evening and found Mr Westbrooke in the chapel. He turned when he heard her and smiled.

'Thank you so much, Miss Wilson, for offering to help. The girls haven't been very well and Mrs Martin has a lot to do.'

Susan hadn't known the children had been ill, which made her feel worse.

'But I don't know anything about teaching,' she said.

'Neither do I,' he admitted, which made her feel better because everybody was aware of how clever he was. 'It isn't ordinary teaching, I feel, it's just to help them enjoy Sunday instead of it being as hard as all the other days.'

Susan thought it was a lovely idea and he was good and kind to think of it like that. She did enjoy Sundays but that had always been down to Miss Frost and now Miss Lee in different ways. She loved Sundays but a lot of that was caught up in dinner and the afternoons and walking with Danny. It was the best time of the week.

'Is it the younger children you find difficult?' Susan said.

'I find the older lads hard to keep there,' he replied, to her dismay. 'And I understand it. Why wouldn't they want to be outside in the fresh air? It seems dull to them but their parents make them come to chapel and I'm completely at a loss. They think I don't know much about their way of life and they're right, of course.'

Susan was astonished by his frankness.

'I wouldn't know what to do either,' she said, horrified at the whole idea.

'You aren't that much older than them,' he said.

That, Susan thought, was not fair though it was true. Those lads were at that awkward stage. She didn't know how to tell him that she didn't want to do it, that she was scared, that she wouldn't be able to sleep or eat until the following Sunday. But she must have said what she should have said, because shortly after that he thanked her profusely. Then she ran off down the cobbled lane so fast that she almost skidded and came to grief. She ran inside the shop, panting.

'He thinks I can teach the older children, Miss Lee, and I really can't. Whatever gave him that idea?'

Alice soothed her and when they sat down over the fire that evening she suggested, 'Children will do anything for sweets. Why don't you give them a sweet when they come in and another sweet when Sunday school is over?'

'I don't know what to say. I've never talked in front of anybody before.'

'Just be honest. You could tell them about how you were found and how Miss Frost took you in and how the good shepherd looks after his flock. You could talk about what the dale is like and how the Bible is relevant here. You could tell them all sorts of stories that will matter to their lives. What about how the sower went forth and sowed some seeds on stony ground?

You can relate it to their lives. They understand that. Some of them have to walk a long way and they have to sit and listen and then they have to walk back, unless they're lucky enough for their father to have a horse and cart. If you can be kind to them and give them a bit of chocolate, they'll like Sundays a whole lot more.'

'Won't it seem like bribery?'

'Everything has to be worth doing. They need to see a result.' Susan smiled.

'I knew that somehow you would tell me that,' she said.

The following Sunday, Susan, terrified and quaking, was left with a dozen big lads, some of them much taller than she was, and half a dozen lasses who weren't interested. She kept the sweets for the end. She stood before them and told them about how her parents had abandoned her and how Miss Frost had taken her in, like the good shepherd who wouldn't leave one lamb to be lost.

They were mesmerised. She was pleased that she held their attention. Nobody's eyes moved around in boredom, no boy shifted his feet in big boots, no girl fidgeted on the hard benches. When Susan had finished speaking to them, she asked if they had any questions and one big lad got up at the back.

'You had no parents then, Miss?'

'I didn't know them.'

'So you were born from sin.'

'I don't know anything about them. I don't think that makes me sinful. I was found here on the chapel steps and I'm very grateful for it, too. I don't mean to keep you long; you have been so good in listening to me. I have sweets here for you all because Sunday should be the best day. You must line up and no pushing. You will all get the same. I said no pushing, Willie Johnson.' He blushed in confusion and got back in line.

Susan wasn't sure whether the sweets were what carried her day but she was so pleased that later she told Alice about it, who said that if the young learned that Bible classes and sweets went together it wasn't a bad idea.

The following Sunday, other children – those who didn't go to chapel – must have heard that sweets were being given away because the room was crowded. Susan told them stories and encouraged them to join in and they talked about how hard ordinary school was and she let them discuss it between themselves without interruption.

They talked about how they were expected to do so much at their farms. Some of them – and not just the boys – had to milk several cows in the morning and then again in the evening, every day. A lot of the lads couldn't go to school: their fathers couldn't cope with the animals and the land without them because they were lead miners or quarrymen. A lot of the girls had to look after their smaller sisters and brothers and put up with their moods and their crying. They also had to scrub floors and wash clothes and see to food because their mothers had too much to do and grew tired.

Susan listened and sympathised and told them all how wonderful they were being. She began to read to them, not just texts from the Bible – which also bored her sometimes – but other stories that Miss Frost had read to her. Fairy stories had a lesson to teach. She wasn't sure whether she should be doing it considering it was chapel, but then nobody else had offered to help Mr Westbrooke. If they complained she would tell them that if they thought they could do better to go ahead and do it. But nobody said anything.

Mr Westbrooke told her that he was amazed that she had encouraged so many children to come to chapel.

'I give them a sweet at the beginning and at the end.'

'What an excellent idea,' he said.

Susan was surprised.

'Do you think so?' she asked.

'It's just a little something and some of them walk miles to get here. They work hard all week so why shouldn't they think of this place with sweetness? I think it's wonderful,' he said.

Four weeks after she had begun her teaching, one hand shot up before the Sunday school began.

'Will you tell us again about how Miss Frost took you in when you were like Moses in the bulrushes?' Willie Johnson asked. And so she did. They sat there silent and listened and she could not help being proud of how she had filled that room to capacity. Even Mr Martin told her how good she was. He asked her whether she might get up in front of the adults and preach. Susan was astonished and said no but she had liked being asked.

'You have a gift,' Mr Martin said. 'You should be a teacher.'

'I don't think I'd want to do that every day,' Susan excused herself.

'Neither would I,' Mr Westbrooke said. When they had tea, he followed her out into the neglected garden where most of the flowers had given up the fight and it was nothing but grass nine inches tall and the odd rosebush, shrinking with black spots on its leaves. Miss Frost would have had a fit, Susan thought.

'It all depended on you,' she told him.

'No, it didn't. If you couldn't have coped you would have run out the first time.'

'Did you expect me to?'

He gazed at her for a few seconds.

'No. No, I didn't. I thought you'd be really good at it, as you could be at anything you chose to tackle. I think that you have a great many talents.'

Nobody had ever said that kind of thing to her before, except Miss Lee, of course, who was always kind and encouraging. And because it was only Mr Westbooke she dared to say, 'Are we talking about the virgins with the lamps and hiding your light under a bushel?'

'You would have had them listening to you in no time,' he said.

Twenty-Five

Charles Westbooke had left home long ago. He dreamt about Westmorland. He had loved it so much. Stanhope was just close enough and yet far away that nightly he dreamed himself back in that big, shabby old house where his father was the local squire and everybody looked up to him.

Charles was happy now but he had tried hard to quench his feelings for his home. Here he could be who he was and his father would not come after him. At least he hoped not. He didn't want to be his father. He never could be his father; he never could go back.

At first he couldn't understand why the ministers' houses were so small but he was used to these houses now. He had been shocked when he first went to train for the ministry at how narrow and mean everything was and he had no good food or fire or bed to himself, just a cot in a room full of other men.

He missed his brother, Henry. He hoped that his father would not take out on his brother that he had left. He was almost certain that wouldn't happen because his brother loved the estate and everything on it; he belonged to it.

He had told Henry that he must write if things were very bad but he wasn't sure that his brother would. But then, Henry didn't see the things he saw. Henry loved the land and the people and the animals. He loved the hunting and the fishing and the shooting. Everything about him was what his father wanted. The only problem was that Henry was not the first son.

Henry was the kindest man who had ever been born, Charles felt sure. Charles had tried to hide from him the way that their parents quarrelled and how his father would hit his mother until she hid away under a table or beside a wall. She never cried. That was what upset Charles most. Aware of her children, she did not cry.

Charles tried not to think of how bad things had been. He knew that his father, having wanted to love his firstborn better, had found what he wanted in his younger son. Henry was everything that Charles should have been. His father hated that Charles was scholarly, that he was clever and loved books.

He wanted him to be able to shoot and fish and ride a horse better than anyone but Charles was slightly built and not above medium height. He could not handle a gun well or mount a horse with ease, or catch even a small fish. And the more your father raged at you, he discovered, the less you could please him. Henry pleased him and Charles would have been happy for Henry to have had everything.

Now he was homesick for something that he had not liked and could never go back to. He had no good memories to rely on. He had no childhood to yearn for. He remembered how at a very young age Henry had pushed Charles behind him and shouted, 'Leave him alone!' at their father. It was the first time that he had not endured his father's fists and his father's boots and the whip and the blood and the hatred which his father had for him. He was the firstborn and he was not good enough. His father did not beat Henry.

His father blamed his mother for having birthed such a paltry creature as he was. Charles was sick all his young life. He suspected it was because his father had beaten his mother when she was pregnant with him and he had not grown and developed as he should have. As he got older and tried to protect his mother and his brother, he knew that he had only to wait until Henry could face his father and was as big as him. Then he had left.

He missed his brother; Henry had been the world to him. But he couldn't stay there once his mother had died, after his father knocked her down the stairs. They said you couldn't die of a broken heart but their mother had, along with her broken body. Once she was gone and Henry could manage, Charles got out of there and pursued his dream to be a Methodist minister, even though his family had been Church of England.

Henry, as clever as he was, had encouraged him to go.

'I'll handle him,' he said, referring to their father. Though neither of them said it, they both knew that Henry was the boy his father loved. Henry had never been beaten to the floor. Henry had not had to stand over his mother so that his father would not kill her and was not there to stop his father from throwing her down the stairs to her death. Charles had gone to him before he left.

'Are you sure you want to stay here with him? You can come with me. I'll look after you.'

Henry smiled and shook his head.

'And who will look after this place?'

Charles couldn't understand why anybody should care but Henry did. Charles thought – without envy, because he loved Henry so much – that Henry was exactly as he should have been: so handsome, tall and lean and disarming with his beautiful smile and his bright blue eyes. Henry was brilliant at all the things that Charles couldn't do. He was an excellent fisherman and a dead shot. He rode to hounds and took every jump, every gate and every stream. He loved the horses, he loved the house, he was charming to everyone who came to his parents' famous dinners before their mother had died. His father idolised him.

Even after his father beat his mother to death, somehow Henry could stand it. But then it had been Charles who found her dying. The doctor said she had fallen down the stairs and nobody dared say any more.

Charles hadn't lied to his brother; he just hadn't said very much. Henry loved their home so much that he could bear it; he could stay. Charles couldn't. He thought that if he had to spend any more time there he would kill his father or at least try to. Henry urged him to go and when he did he found Methodism and it had yet to disappoint him.

Here in the dale he could lie with the windows open at night and not be afraid that his father was beating his mother and that he must go down and confront a man who despised him, who would beat him too if he got in the way. He had wanted a way out and here it was, a religion that cared for people who had nothing.

Charles loved the idea of Wesley coming here on his horse and preaching outside. He loved that Wesley had cared for education and that the Methodist men had sought to gain political power. Although that might seem ungodly, they had wanted to improve conditions where people were badly treated. The religion suited him, as though it had been made especially for people like him who needed a new place to be.

His faith had saved him, not just from bitterness, but from complete annihilation. It had saved him from thinking he was nothing and had failed before he began. He was lucky to be in this place where people worked hard but knew rest; where the minister, Mr Martin, talked to him about everything that they were concerned for.

He loved that he had nothing but a room of his own. He was responsible for everybody but he could choose what he wanted and he was grateful to this church for having given him options. Mrs Martin and Jane looked after his every need and he was so grateful to them. He could talk for hours on end to Mr Martin about the ministry and what it meant. His three little girls were wonderful and it made Charles wish for a wife and a child, but for now he was happy just to have found a new home.

He was happy until the day that he met Susan Wilson. He knew straight away that he loved her. He hadn't ever thought that you fell in love. He had dismissed the idea. He thought of his parents and how awful their marriage had been. Love had nothing to do with real life. And then he saw Susan Wilson and changed his mind.

She was not the sort of woman he had thought he would care for. What was it about her? She was not educated. She had a thick local accent but the dales accent was sweet and had a lilt to it. Here he was still in the borders; it was a home from home.

Susan was slight and did not put herself forward and yet he remembered the moment when she stepped into the chapel on the first day that he was there. He was not prepared for it but then his ancestors had not married for love but for gain and for land and where had it got them? But he – he fell so far in love that he could have fallen off a cliff from it. He was dismayed. Susan Wilson was betrothed to another man.

He pretended to himself that it hadn't happened, that he didn't care about her. It would wear off after a few days. When it persisted, he told himself that surely it wouldn't last much longer than a month. But then it did; it went on and on.

He was angry that he had fallen in love. What a stupid thing to do.

He mentioned to Mr Martin that he thought Miss Wilson might be the right person to help with the Sunday school and Mr Martin had said that he didn't think she had the time.

'Why not?' Charles said.

'She's walking out – I think that is the term here – with the young man who is in management with Mr Almond at the quarry.'

Charles had known this but he had never thought that a heart could really slump until his did. Somewhere down towards his stomach it took up so much space that he couldn't breathe.

'But I will ask her,' Mr Martin had said, oblivious.

Part of Charles Westbrooke was relieved that Susan was about to be married. It took the emphasis off the whole thing. He could try to retrieve his heart. He could go back to thinking about his work and glorying that he had left Westmorland and everything was behind him. But then Susan would come to the chapel with Miss Lee on Sundays and undo all his progress. He grew to dread it and to wish he could move on but he also knew that he could not keep escaping from every problem that presented itself. Somewhere, at some time, he had to stop running.

He stayed. He was glad in a way. He didn't want to run any more. But he had to endure the sight of Susan Wilson with her young man, and Daniel Wearmouth was like Henry, his brother. He was tall and slender and handsome and laughing and clever such as so many men were not, and he certainly was not. Charles tried not to envy Daniel Wearmouth but it was a hard-won battle.

He made himself envisage at night what it would be like for

him when they were married. He would get through it somehow. He knew that to the Almonds, Daniel Wearmouth was like the North Star: so bright, so clever, so above all other men. And Susan Wilson had captured his heart.

Charles tried to be glad that she was happy. He tried not to wish that he was Daniel Wearmouth or even his brother, tall and capable and able to jump ditches and fences and go on with the hunt until the day was done and he was happy and exhausted and muddy. He imagined what it would be like to be them, coming home in the twilight to a house alight with candles, to bathe and change into evening dress and go down to a sumptuous meal and talk over the day with like-minded people who loved the hunt as they did.

Charles had always hated hunting small animals. He had never forgotten the day that a vixen was pulled from the earth after a three-hour dig when her mate had gone to ground and the hounds had savaged her to death and ripped open her belly and throat and the huntsmen had stamped on the three cubs inside her.

Twenty-Six

Dan felt quite different after he took over the office. Mr Almond said Dan could manage most things so Mr Almond would work from home. Mr Almond had spent time teaching him how to do almost everything in the quarry. It had always been Dan's ambition to learn and he thought that but for his father he could have achieved it long ago. He was grateful that Mr Almond had no son and needed him now. Recently, however, Mr Almond had taken the odd day off and while it was strange without him, Dan found that after a few initial panics he could manage. Mr Paterson was so reliable that it helped.

Dan liked that Mr Almond let him run the office himself but he took comfort in knowing that he could refer to the boss about anything and he was always there if there was trouble. He thought that maybe Mr Almond was getting tired of running things by himself. He had one child – a daughter, Arabella – who must be almost thirty and had never married for some reason. Dan had caught nothing but glances of her, but she was said to be very beautiful. Since she never came into the village, nobody there knew her well.

Some of the other men of his age and older resented Dan, he knew, but since he was the obvious choice he didn't think it mattered. They would get used to it and the men who didn't want any promotion were happy about it. Eventually they chose to forget that his father had killed his mother since Dan caught on so fast to the work and they were contented when he could put things right. Dan became quick and confident and was pleased at his ability.

The trouble was that the men came to him with their complaints and he found that he was not the person to deal with their petty squabbles. He decided to get Zeb to do it, at least for a try.

Summoned to the office for this reason, Zeb stared.

'Me?'

'Why not? They're all scared of you.'

Zeb went on staring.

'Just try,' Dan said.

In a way Zeb was flattered that he was sent for. He spent time in the office helping with other things and even Mr Almond spoke to him and told him he was doing a good job and the clerk, Mr Paterson, nodded now and then. Things were getting better all round, but he was worried that Dan thought he could manage the men better than Dan could.

The lad that they gave Zeb to help him with the explosives was Tommy Hudson, who was not the brightest. Zeb didn't like to leave him alone in case he blew off his foot – or worse still, somebody else's – and he had had to reprimand him twice that week for carelessness.

'Me Dad says I shouldn't have to work with the likes of you,' Tommy complained.

Zeb looked into his very young face.

'You're right,' he said, 'you shouldn't. You're useless at it. You'll blow somebody up if you stay here. Off you go.'

Tommy stared.

'But – '

'Go back to your dad. Lucky him, eh?'

Zeb found himself in the office more and more and he grew to like that Dan would discuss everything with him, just as though Zeb knew what he was talking about. He didn't, but it was good to be asked. He was learning to be involved and when Mr Almond came up, which he did for a part of every day now, and found them both poring over figures, he looked differently at Zeb and told them both that they were doing a good job. Zeb had never been told such a thing in his life and couldn't help telling Alice all about it. She nodded her head.

'Whoever would have thought it?' she said at least twice so that he knew he was boasting.

The disputes between the men were usually about where they were working; some places were a lot better than others. Other times they just didn't get on. Fathers and sons often worked together, it had always been the way, but Zeb could see that this didn't necessarily make for good work because the fathers were too keen on telling their sons what to do and the sons didn't want to listen.

So the old traditions were changed under Dan's orders at Zeb's suggestion. Sometimes now they were split up and the men worked with other men's sons. It made for better talk and teamwork and easier days.

Often Dan and Zeb would sit in the office when the work was finished and drink tea and talk. Zeb had not known that men could work like this and be happy. Dan was about to get married and his whole face glowed at his future prospects.

Twenty-Seven

Not long after Dan's engagement, Mr Almond called him to his office.

'Why don't you come to the house and meet the family?'

Dan was speechless. He hadn't expected anything like that.

'Come to Sunday dinner,' Mr Almond said.

There had been no mention of Susan and Dan didn't want to ask about her in case they thought he was being impolite and implying that they should have extended the invitation. But because he went to the sweet shop for dinner every Sunday after Susan and Miss Lee came back from chapel, he was obliged to tell them about his other engagement. And that wasn't easy.

'I must go.'

'They haven't asked me?' Susan said, ready to be offended.

'We aren't married yet. I'm sure they would have done. But I have to go, Mr Almond has asked me as a special favour.'

Zeb and Alice agreed but Susan was silent. When she saw him to the door that evening he whispered to her in the darkness.

'It's only one time, you know, and it's important that I get on.'

'I know,' she said and kissed him in repentance, but after he had gone she lingered over the fire long after the others would have gone to bed. In the end Alice went upstairs and Susan was left sitting over the dying fire with Zeb.

'I wanted to be asked.'

'I'm sure you will be.'

'What if he changes?'

'What do you mean?'

'What if he becomes like the Almonds and wants more?'

'I don't see why he should: after all, he has everything.'

She jumped up and kissed his cheek for that and then ran upstairs. Zeb sat over the fire, brooding for a long time.

The following Sunday Dan put on a new suit and walked the fifteen minutes to Ash House, Mr Almond's home. Mr Almond had had the house built a dozen years ago, when the quarry became so prosperous that he decided to move from the small terraced house where he and his wife and daughter had lived in Stanhope.

Mrs Almond wasn't happy about it. She was afraid that folk would think she was getting beyond herself.

'But we're going up in the world,' her husband said. 'I've lived among the workmen all my life and we've worked hard for what we've got. I see no reason not to spend some of it before we are too old to enjoy it,' and so the house had been built, halfway up Crawleyside bank.

Mrs Almond hated the place, though of course she couldn't tell him. He had done so well and was working so hard. They had only the one child – and more to the point, they had no son – and not once had he reproached her or said that he needed one, which of course he did.

All her young married life she had prayed for a son. Was God laughing at her need and her husband's need for somebody to carry on the work? Daughters couldn't do it. She loved Arabella very much but a son would have made such a difference. She couldn't tell her husband that she wanted to go back to the little terraced house, two up, two down, where they had lived when first married and so happy. But she was no longer like everybody else and there was nothing she could do to better it, so she went halfway up Crawleyside bank. She told him over and over how beautiful the house was, how much she liked it and how she admired all he had done.

It was true but sometimes she looked at him and saw the deep grooves in his cheeks and wondered whether it had been worth it. They couldn't retire because there was no son to take care of the quarry and it didn't matter how much money they had if nobody was there for them. She had come to the conclusion that Arabella would never marry and they would never be free of the burden that the quarry had become.

Arabella remembered the tiny cottage and her mother going out to work. She would go with her and be neglected because her mother was cleaning other people's houses. She would cry and cry.

Mrs Almond could remember when the folk of Crawleyside didn't mix with the people from the village and nobody wanted to live up there among them. Now she had to and worst of all she had to pretend that she was happy about it.

Her face ached for how enthusiastic she had to be to please her husband. He was a kind man, a good man, and had looked after her all these years. She had looked after him in the early years, going out to work, doing anything she could manage to keep the quarry going. This was his present to her and she tried not to hate it. It was huge, made of stone and set back in an acre of ground. They had a cook, several housemaids and two gardeners.

Quite often Mr and Mrs Almond had taken Arabella into

Newcastle or Hexham to social events, to try to find their daughter a husband. There had been plenty of offers for Arabella's hand when she had been eighteen and nineteen, from good businessmen who knew that Arabella, being her father's only child, would inherit everything, but Arabella had remained unimpressed and turned them all down.

'Oh Mama, can't we go home?' she would say and although Mrs Almond despaired, she liked that her child was not impressed by their money or connections. Mrs Almond was pleased that her daughter, though beautiful, was modest. All Arabella wanted to do was organise the gardens, read by the fire and talk to her parents. She seemed not to care that she had no friends. Mrs Almond could not help hankering after the old days, when the girls married the boys across the street and brought up their children nearby.

After he took on Mr Wearmouth full time at the office in the quarry, her husband was at home more and she was glad of it. He still did work in what he called the study, but it meant that she could consult him and chat to him about household matters. She came to be glad of Mr Wearmouth.

Because of what Daniel's father had done, Mrs Almond had not been happy when her husband wanted to promote him, but she had grown used to it. And to be fair, Mr Almond had taken years to decide and had brought the young man on carefully. He was not the person to make mistakes.

As for that other man he had employed, the murderer, well, she had plenty she might have said on that score. But it was not her business to tell her husband what to do at the quarry so she kept quiet. And he came home sometimes and told her that he thought Zebediah Bailey had always been a good quarryman and he was clever too, so she came to be glad of that.

Zeb Bailey spent a lot of time around the office because he and Mr Wearmouth worked well together. Mr Wearmouth knew that he could pass on the lesser, non-office jobs to Mr Bailey, and Mr Almond was by now desperate to be free of some aspects of his business.

He had become tired and longed to go home in the middle of the afternoons and Mrs Almond became grateful that the two young men and Mr Paterson could run the office fairly well without her husband's presence. She and Mr Almond had never been free, never had a holiday, never been able to go away. She dreamed of Europe and hoped one day her wish to go might come true.

Twenty-Eight

Dan found a great many people at the house on the Sunday afternoon that he had been asked to dinner. Mr Almond introduced his wife and she was vaguely polite, as though having him there had not been her idea but since he was she might as well get on with it. The meal was all white cloths and silver cutlery and huge plates. The food was very good, though rather tepid by the time everyone had been served.

Miss Almond, Arabella, was tall and slender, dark-haired and dark-eyed and pale-skinned and altogether lovely. She dressed well; her skirts swished around her and her bare neck was creamy and slender. She smiled at him from time to time though he had the idea that she didn't know who he was. However, when the meal was over, she came to him, extending a pale, slender hand.

'How are you enjoying being manager at the quarry, Mr Wearmouth?'

He was astonished that she spoke to him when all the businessmen and their wives of the area were in attendance, including the people who owned the big house, the squire and his family, the Oswalds and the Quaker family, the Wests, who owned the iron works. There were also people whom he didn't recognise but they seemed so very important. He couldn't imagine why she singled him out and he couldn't think of what to say. He did not think of himself as a manager and smiled in slight embarrassment.

'I'm just helping.'

'My father is full of praise for you.'

'That's very nice,' was all Dan could come up with.

'I know that you have had your difficulties, but I know even so that your family has lived in this area for a great many years.'

At last Dan had something to make him proud.

'I believe we have lived in this region upward of a thousand years.'

'That is a heritage to be commended.'

'I don't know whether it's true. Perhaps my parents told me that to please me.'

'I think it's wonderful to have a lineage such as that,' she said and Dan was prouder than ever. He felt like a prosperous man for the first time, as though he belonged among these people. His family had been better than theirs by origin; they were late-comers, intruders here in Weardale. They did not go back so very far, not a thousand years. Few people could say so but his father had always told him how long they had lived here. Dan was very pleased with that now.

'There is to be a dance next week,' Miss Almond continued, 'for my parents' wedding anniversary. Everybody who is anyone in the dale has been invited.' She rolled her eyes at this and then smiled at him. 'You must come.'

Dan was amazed, felt completely out of place. Also he was sure that her mother would not want him there. He was a workman as far as she was concerned.

'I'm not certain I can.'

'Oh please do, my father speaks well of you and wants you around. He has no son, you see, and would always keep a clever young man nearby if he could. You could be that person if you chose.'

Dan had coffee with her in a huge room that looked out at the view over the village and the surrounding hills and thought about what it would be like to live in a magnificent house such as this. He couldn't think why she was being nice to him when there were lots of other people to talk to, but nobody took any notice. The men were standing about together talking, and the women were sitting down together talking.

There were several other young men, sons of businessmen, he thought, well-dressed and southern-voiced but they had congregated together in the hall and ignored him. There were also several young women, none of whom threw him so much as a glance. They must know by his dress and how he spoke that he was a workman. He hated to feel that he was below his company. Eventually he took his leave, expressing his appreciation to his hosts for their hospitality.

He walked back to the village, thinking of how much the visit had meant to him. He had enjoyed being there among people who could be his equal. And Miss Almond was so elegant and had such good manners, and wore dresses that he thought must have been made for her in the city by a wonderful dressmaker.

She was beautiful, refined, educated. He had been cowed by this but she didn't seem to notice and had gone on talking to him about books. He did get the impression that she liked him, though he convinced himself that this was just his pride.

Mrs Almond put cream on her hands and turned to her husband as they got ready for bed.

'You do realise that that young man, Mr Wearmouth, has been invited to the dance next week by our daughter?'

'Has he?' Her husband looked astonished. 'She's never invited anybody to anything before. Well, he's a nice lad and intelligent. I'm very grateful to him and you should be, too, because if it hadn't been for him I couldn't have had any time off. When I make him manager and Zeb Bailey undermanager, if he keeps going on like he is, we will be able to have what we deserve: some time to ourselves after working so hard for years.'

His wife was still frowning. He leaned over and kissed her.

'I shouldn't worry too much,' he said. 'He's getting married to that little girl who used to be Miss Frost's companion.'

'I wish we could find somebody for Arabella to marry,' his wife said for at least the hundredth time.

'You have tried, my dear, very hard if I may say so.'

'But it's such a let-down. If she doesn't marry soon she never will. She doesn't seem to like any of the young men we've introduced her to the times we've taken her to Hexham and Newcastle. We know a good many people beyond the dale, like the owners of the iron works and the other quarry managers and various businessmen and their sons. She doesn't have any friends, she doesn't seem to like anybody. What on earth are we to do with the quarry if she doesn't marry?'

Mr Almond was too tired to hear any more. He had been listening to this for the past ten years. He blew out the candle and turned over away from his wife, into the bliss of dark solitude.

Twenty-Nine

That week Alice had asked Miss Wanless to the shop to discuss the wedding and in particular the bride's dress. There was also much talk about the wedding itself and Zeb was tired of listening to it so he suggested that he and Dan go to the Bonny Moor Hen for a drink.

Dan hesitated.

'The workmen go there.'

'All right then, the Grey Bull.'

The Grey Bull was a farmer's pub on the edge of the village and only five minutes' walk away. They hadn't been in much because it was more a place for the farmers who had quite a bit of land and didn't need mining and quarrying to help their living along. The shopkeepers and businessmen also gathered there. Zeb felt very out of it though he thought that Dan looked very much at home.

Dan didn't realise that he was going on and on about the Almond family until he noticed Zeb looking at him carefully over the top of a pint glass.

'So you liked them?' Zeb said finally.

Dan didn't miss the sarcasm in Zeb's voice though it was very slight.

'Well, I – ' Dan hadn't known until then that he had been

impressed not only with them but also with himself. In a strange way, he was pleased that he could aspire to such company when he had been nobody in the village until Mr Almond took him up. 'I'm just not used to people like that. It's all new.'

'Have they asked you back?'

That was when Dan knew he could not tell Zeb about the dance. Newly engaged men did not usually go to dances without their betrothed. He felt as if he shouldn't go. He didn't have a good enough suit for starters, and besides he couldn't tell Susan that he intended to go by himself. He decided that he wouldn't go and that he would therefore not need to mention it to anyone.

'I think it was just a visit so that I might understand things better,' he said evasively.

'Miss Arabella is said to be beautiful, though I haven't seen her close up,' Zeb said.

'She's as old as we are,' Dan said and pulled a face and that was when Zeb relaxed, he could tell.

Mr Almond mentioned the anniversary the following week. It was upon Dan's tongue to say that it was very kind but he couldn't possibly come without Susan, but somehow he didn't say it. He knew instinctively that people like them would not want Susan there.

She was pretty and he loved her but he felt that if he took her to such a place, he would be ashamed of her and she would know it. She would not want to stay and then he would have ruined his chance to be invited back. He could not let himself be held back by her.

He felt awful as soon as he thought such a thing. He knew

he should be ashamed of himself. Instead, he found himself smiling and saying that he was pleased to have been asked to such an important occasion.

He didn't want to talk to Zeb after work on Monday evening as they usually did when everybody else had gone home. He didn't want to meet Zeb's gaze. Zeb had had such a hard time that he knew a lot of things that other people didn't understand and Dan was aware of it. He made an excuse.

'Susan said you were coming to the sweet shop. Something to do with the rector,' Zeb said.

'I was, but I'm sick of talking about it,' Dan said and Zeb agreed.

'I don't see why there has to be all this fuss,' he added.

Susan was happy. She had been happy with Miss Frost but this went beyond anything she had hoped for. Not only had Miss Lee taken her in and helped her so much but because of Miss Lee and Zeb, she had met the man she had wanted, longed for. He was not rich as she had told Miss Lee laughingly that he should be, but he was young and good-looking and he had been promoted and they would have a lovely house and everything she had ever wanted.

She thought she would burst. She went about singing all day. She and Miss Lee spent every available moment over at the new house, which needed curtains and furniture. Though they were determined not to spend much money, she did have her own money that Miss Frost had left her.

She told Dan this and he said she should spend it how she wanted to. He didn't know anything about houses anyway, but he had some put by too, and she could have that for the wedding and the house as well. She hugged him and told him he was the kindest lad in the world.

'You didn't come to talk to the rector again, though,' she said. 'Susan – '

'I forgive you. It was only details. You are happy, aren't you?' she ventured, looking into his face. He found himself not wanting to meet her gaze. 'You've been so quiet.'

'I have a lot to do at work right now.'

'I know you do and I won't bother you. I understand that you aren't interested in wedding planning and houses and such, but when we are married I will make the best wife ever. I will do everything for you; I love you so very much. No woman ever loved a man more than I love you.'

Alice enjoyed all aspects of the coming wedding. Having never been married herself she was ready to have a good time. And since the rector had offered them the use of the rectory for the reception, they revised their plans for asking few people.

Susan wanted to invite everybody from the chapel and Alice wanted everybody who came to the sweet shop who had been kind to Susan. They thought they would have a great big table spread with lots of good things, and that way people could come and go as they wanted to after the ceremony.

Alice was so pleased when it looked as if all the village would be there. Every time somebody came into the shop they asked about the wedding and said how wonderful it was. Even if they hadn't been asked to the wedding breakfast, they thought they might attend the church service. Alice found herself saying that they might come to it all, Susan had said she was so happy she wanted the whole village at her wedding.

Miss Wanless had promised Susan the most beautiful dress in the world. Not white, that was too showy and people would think she had gone too far. She made her a dress of pale blue silk with little puff sleeves. Susan looked into the mirror and couldn't believe how it set off her eyes. She had never thought she could look so pretty. Miss Wanless, who was a devout Christian, told Susan that blue signified purity, piety and faithfulness.

The rector's wife was very helpful and the ladies of both churches, even though they were often in enmity, thought that to accommodate so many people they would use long trestle tables and wooden benches. If it was a fine day they could put the tables and benches out into the main street so that it would be a celebration for the whole village.

So many women offered to help. They volunteered to make various dishes for the wedding or to decorate the church and the rectory. Other women were pleased that it would be August and there would be lots of flowers for them to gather both from the countryside and from their gardens. The church would be decorated in blue and white. Alice couldn't believe the response. She thought it was because Susan was not their daughter and there was no rivalry. Everybody wanted to help.

One of the farmers, Mr Moore, had offered his gig and grey pony to take the bride the short distance to the church. He would drive her up and down the main street first so that people could turn out and see her and wish her well. There had never been anything like it in the village.

Dan was told that he should have a new suit made. The tailor, Mr Mortimer, was happy with this but rather taken aback when the groom went to be measured and asked Mr Mortimer if he also had any evening dress among his secondhand suits.

Mr Mortimer did indeed but he was surprised to find that Mr

Wearmouth had need of it. He told his wife about it when they sat down to their tea that evening, though he acknowledged that it was none of his business why people wanted the clothes they did. His wife said that she thought Mr Wearmouth was going up in the world.

Dan was thoroughly at odds with himself. One minute he thought that Mr Almond would be offended if he did not go to the anniversary celebration, the next he thought that he could not go at all because Susan would find out. People would talk, somebody always did.

The thing was, he had never been to a grand party and this was going to be very grand indeed. Mr Almond, not usually given to talking about such things, said that his wife was making sure it was going to be the best party in the dale for years. Mr Almond even boasted about the feast. There would be champagne on ice, whole salmon on silver platters and rare beef on lettuce. A quartet had been hired to play in the drawing room and there would be exotic fruit from greenhouses at a special place in Newcastle.

'I have a lot to do, Mr Almond,' Dan stuttered. 'I shouldn't really be away from the quarry.'

Mr Almond looked on him almost fondly.

'Just come for an hour or two. Why shouldn't you enjoy yourself for once?'

And with that, Dan persuaded himself that an hour or two was not a real evening out, just a glimpse of a society to which he would never belong. He could not resist. He saw himself in the glass when he was dressed and was amazed: he looked almost like a gentleman.

He slid out of the back door and was grateful for the dry weather; it would not make a mess of his new patent leather shoes that he had got secondhand. He set off up the back streets as far as he could until he reached the corner that took him up the hill towards Ash House.

He could see carriages turning into the drive and there was music coming from inside as people got down and went in. The house was glittering with candelabras and there was laughter and chatter. He was entranced.

All the doors to the various rooms were open and Mr and Mrs Almond were greeting their guests just inside the hallway, which was big and opened out on either side. Mrs Almond treated him as though he was important, and said how very pleased they were that he could come and share with them their ruby wedding anniversary.

He went off into the nearest reception room. It was packed and waiters were moving around with big trays of bowl-type glasses on long stems. In them was white, sparkling wine of some kind. It had to be champagne.

He took the glass that he was offered and then was worried because he didn't know anybody. And why would he? At that moment he saw Miss Arabella Almond, waving her white, feathered fan at him and smiling.

She came across and put her hand through his arm and offered to introduce him to other people. She told them he was her father's manager and people congratulated him. The stuff in his glass was wonderful and unlike anything he had ever tasted. After a second glass, he felt quite at home and then he danced with Arabella.

He had forgotten how beautiful she was. She wore a dress so expensive that it shimmered silver and white and her blue eyes were like velvet and her bare arms looked soft and round. She danced lightly and told him he danced well, too. That was good because he hadn't danced in twelve years and only then at village hops.

The food was the kind of thing he had never seen before. There was an ice swan in the centre of the table and there was ice cream. People helped themselves to chicken and salmon, and tomatoes that had been grown in hot houses where the heating was always on, some impressed man told him. There were pine-apples, which he had never seen or tasted before, and grapes.

It made him dizzy. He wanted to go on dancing with Miss Almond for the rest of his life. She was so light in his arms.

He stayed all evening. It was fine so people took food and drink into the gardens. He found a plate of desserts for Arabella and more champagne. He had lost track of how many glasses he had drunk by now but it was very light in comparison with beer, which was what he usually drank. It made him feel happy and he hadn't been happy in so very long, except for when he was with Susan. He wouldn't think of that now; he had a whole lifetime in which to think of her.

Thirty

It was very late indeed when the darkness hid Dan's return. He crept back into the boarding house to find that his bed was inhabited by two other people. He could not wait to get out of there, to the lovely little house when he and Susan were married.

On the Monday he didn't see Zeb much; they were very busy. At the end of the day Zeb called in at the office and said that Susan was expecting him that evening.

'I wasn't going to call in tonight.'

'I think you should.'

'Why?'

Zeb didn't look at him.

'Susan heard you went to a party up at the house.'

Oh hell, he hadn't counted on that. The servants, no doubt, and then he felt mean and stupid.

'I went because I thought it might further me.'

'I know but I don't think she sees it that way.'

'Did you tell her?'

'I didn't know about it,' Zeb said. 'And anyroad, why would I? If Mr Almond wants you there, you're lucky, and I'm doing all right as well. I have good wages. I just don't think women see it like that.'

Dan was thankful for the understanding.

*

He duly turned up at the house and resented explaining himself to Susan.

'I'm doing it for us,' he said.

He hated this. It was hot and they were all sitting outside, Susan and Miss Lee on chairs and he and Zeb on the garden wall and he could have done without this and without everybody there to hear it.

'So why didn't you tell me?' she said, blue eyes alight.

'Because I knew you wouldn't understand and I was right, wasn't I?'

'It was their ruby wedding. Why wasn't I asked?'

'I didn't go as a normal guest. I just went as the new man running the quarry. Surely you can see the difference. We're lucky that he has recognised my ability and wants me around. I have to do as I'm told until I'm sure of my place. He could get rid of me tomorrow if he wanted. He asked me to go as his undermanager, just to be there.'

'And is that what you'll do in the future? I'll sit at home while you go out and socialise with the Almond family and their friends?'

'Sometimes you might have to, yes.'

'Am I not good enough?'

'You are deliberately misunderstanding me. I have to safe-guard my position at the quarry. I could lose it. Then what?'

She said nothing.

'And I think that it is very bad for you to distrust me, to think that I am not doing all this for us. And we are about to be married! If you don't want to marry me, Susan, just say so now and I'll cancel everything.'

He had forgotten that Zeb and Miss Lee were present. He

was so upset that Susan would question him when he was doing everything he could to better himself for their future and their marriage. But now he could hear how loud his voice was, how unforgiving. He was not proud of it but he was blameless, he knew he was.

She started and her eyes filled with tears.

'Of course I want to marry you,' she said.

'So try to be a bit more generous.'

She burst into tears and ran inside. Oh God, he thought. He got himself out of there as soon as he could and stood in the street, appreciating the quiet.

'You all right?' Zeb spoke behind him. Dan turned.

'She should know how much I care about her.'

'She had no parents and nobody to care until Miss Frost and then you. She's bound to wonder if you are about to turn into fresh air. Everybody who loved her so far has died.'

'I am doing my best,' Dan said.

'Women seem to think differently.'

'How would you bloody know?'

Zeb laughed and said he didn't and they got to talking about work as they made their way slowly down the street toward the Grey Bull. And then it seemed silly not to go in there and sink a couple of pints before bed.

Thirty-One

It was full summer when John Bailey came home to the dale. Home. He had long since stopped regarding it as such. He had left it – no, his essentially honest self corrected, he ran – after his wife died in childbirth. He didn't want to come back; it was only that he no longer knew how to stay away. Nightly his dreams showed him his dead wife and son. His grieving was so great that he didn't know what to do.

He had thought that he could run away from the life he had made a mess of, but it wasn't true. God wouldn't let him do it, especially when he had blamed God for what had happened to him. How stupid, how naïve, but grief got you that way. Somebody had to be blamed. Why shouldn't it be God?

He had abandoned everything when he left, but he hadn't had much. He didn't own his house, and what little remained after that, he had given away. He left Stanhope with nothing but a few clothes, what money he possessed and his Bible. His life had been over.

Unfortunately, it wasn't that easy. God expected people to get on with things. John was hungry, cold, needed somewhere to shelter, and had no coat. Whatever had he been thinking when he gave that away? He had been a fool to think that he could manage through the winter. It was laughable, really. He had thought of himself like Cuthbert, giving everything up and living on nothing, in spite of the weather and the problems, but he wasn't.

He had walked. He hadn't even had a horse like Wesley. He kept thinking of how Wesley worked and managed everything, but Wesley had faith and people who believed in him and a family who loved him, his mother and brother. He, John Bailey, had nobody.

His wife had been dead for what felt to him like a very long time and yet it wasn't. He hadn't understood that time changes based on how you feel and when you feel bad it slows down so that every second hurts. Each breath was hard and the days became months and the weeks years, and even to get from one morning to the next felt almost impossible.

How stupid he had been. What did he think he would live on now? He had been paid so little as minister that he had been able to save nothing and then he had had to pay out for his wife's funeral.

He had not known that he was little liked in Stanhope and that his wife was not liked at all. Did Zebediah's sin cause them both to be shunned? He thought it must be so for they had done nothing wrong.

She had lost child after child and each time he told himself that the next would live. She believed it, too, and it didn't matter how many times she conceived, they knew that eventually they would have another child. Perhaps another boy, who would make up for the son that had cost them so dearly and shamed them so that they found it hard to stay in Weardale. It was as if the community blamed them for what he did. How could that be? Was his son not a living being with a will, such a will right from a young age?

He thought that perhaps his son carried the devil in him. He was nothing like them; he was like some orphaned child brought in that they knew nothing about. Zeb had broken their hearts. And John and his dear wife had thought that they could mend their hearts with another child.

It had never occurred to him that she would die trying. The local doctor, a man of about his own age whom he had never liked, told him after the third miscarriage that his wife should not carry another child.

John Bailey stared at him. Did this man of supposed science not recognise a man of God?

'We take what God gives us,' he said.

'That may be, but if your wife conceives again and loses another child you will risk losing her as well.'

'Thank you, Dr McKenna.'

At the time he just wished that Dr McKenna would not try to interfere. He saw men who used their wives for breeding and as soon as the first died, they married a second and even sometimes a third. But he knew he and his wife were not like that. She wanted another child as badly as he did. They had so much to make up for the Lord and yet He treated them badly. If He had looked kindly on them, they could have started again and wiped out the memory of the son who had disgraced them and made them feel as though they were not worthy to be a Methodist minister and his wife. That was why after Mrs Bailey died, John had gone away. He could not help people here in the dale when he could not help himself.

All there was to do was to get away and hide somewhere and try not to think about her burial and her grave. He left. He walked. He was used to walking. He had walked by the river when he was thinking about his work. As he walked, he thought what it had been like when Zebediah was a small child and how happy they had been then and what plans they had made for him.

Between them they would raise a brilliant child. Zeb was so beautiful even when small; he had thick, black hair and grey eyes almost silver and a ready smile. He would be the best of both of them and make them proud. He was their wonderful boy. He would make sure that his child had everything to help him and they would teach him all the things they knew.

After his wife died he had walked away. He was pleased at his decision, he was sure that it was the only thing to do. For the first few days while he could afford to pay for his food and lodging, it was fine. But as he walked on, for some reason he had decided to go up the dale rather than down. This was his first mistake: the places where he could have stayed dwindled to nothing.

These working farms were just a few acres and their men were miners and quarrymen and had little. They knew nothing of folk moving around and would give him no place. They were suspicious of strangers and the further up the dale he trod the more suspicious they were and he could see why. They had so little and distrusted everybody but those they knew well, which was mostly family. They did what was called 'keeping yourself to yourself'.

He had not experienced the kind of loneliness that he felt then, wandering and alone. It was not a vague threat in his mind; it was a permanent thing. He missed her voice and how she would turn over in bed, he missed her being there for him in the evenings. Her conversation, her soft skin, the smell of the lavender water she used when she washed, and that irredeemable sense of somebody else being in the room that you could not replace.

He walked to Hexham over several days, tiring easily because he was not used to the activity, and there he saw a man who was also in the ministry who hailed him with joy. And then he saw his face.

'My dear friend, whatever is wrong?' and that was when John Bailey told him that his wife had died. His friend already knew of what Zebediah had done and had sent letters saying how sorry he was and how he hoped there was something he could help with.

He helped now and took Mr Bailey into his home. There his wife fed him and they gave him a bed and were kind to him. It was hard for him to see their children grown and their grandchildren. They were so respectable and so good that he could not understand why he had nothing but one son who was bad.

He hated his self-pity but it was difficult not to feel like that when he was among these people. They had been just like he was and now he had nothing and they had everything. He didn't wish them ill; he just wished that he could have had even a tenth of the joy they had every day of their lives.

There was a lot of work to do and he helped. He took no money for it though his friend attempted to insist. John tried also not to get in the way of their family. In the end he knew that he must not stay for too long, so when he had been there a month he moved on.

He went to Newcastle and there he looked up another friend in the ministry but didn't stay with him. It seemed unfair to foist himself on people who would have him. He called in, and his friend, who realised he had nothing to do and nowhere to go, found him work in the seaman's hostel down by the quayside.

He made enough by ministering to the men to live and have

his meals but he had no life of any kind. He had thought he would be content just to do this, but only a few weeks later, everything began to jar and night after night he dreamt of how his life in the dale had been. He wanted to go back.

He argued with himself that his wife was what had made his life good and there was nothing left. All he had in the dale was the memory of how things had been. You should never go back, he knew that. But he had nothing here.

Mr Martin had taken over his ministry. What would he do, penniless and poor? He began to wish that he had not been so eager to relinquish his job to another man and give up all that he had left. From where he was now, it looked like a great deal.

Each week it was harder to stay but he was beginning to understand why people remained in one place: it was because they might starve if they gave up what employment they had. He had been lucky and had not appreciated it. He would have tried so much harder now.

He was caught; he couldn't move. He wasn't making any money and then, just as he was beginning to think nothing would ever happen to help, his friend's wife, Isobel Wharton, came to him. Her husband was ill and she wanted to know if he could possibly come and help out.

He was sorry that his friend was ill and did everything he could to help. He was grateful for the change in employment but hoped it didn't show. It wasn't good to do well from another's man's misfortune, but Bill Wharton looked pleased to see him.

'I fell on my head,' he said cheerfully. He had been unconscious for several days after falling off his horse. The fall had affected him so that he was not to do anything, the doctors said, for at least a month. It took much longer than that to bring him back to full strength. John Bailey took care of his work in that time so that the people in his care should not be missing anything.

Mrs Wharton good-naturedly accused him of doing too much and laughed, saying that the people would not want her husband back. Though it made John smile, he knew that there could be a little truth in it. But he liked being among the people again and being useful.

Bill tried to pay him at the end of three months but he would take nothing. He helped his friend back into the ministry and was glad to do so. Being unselfish made him feel good like nothing had before. So when Bill was able to work again and no longer had need of his services, John said that all he would like was his train fare back to Weardale and a little more in case he got stuck.

Leaving was hard. He wished he could keep on going and avoid returning. He knew he'd be confronted with what he had most cared for. He could not come home without thinking that his dear Mary was waiting for him.

His pace slowed the nearer he got to the village and then he was glad he had come back. He would be able to go and see Mary's grave and put some flowers on it. And Mr Martin had always said that if there was anything he could do to help, he would do it. Mr Bailey was certain that this was something one said without necessarily meaning it, but he had to take it literally; it gave him hope of being reasonably well-received.

He did not want to be recognised but it was difficult because it was the afternoon and a lot of people were about. At least it was during the week and people were at work so it wasn't as bad as it could have been. He managed to walk up the main street with his hat pulled well down over his eyes and avoid looking at people or being hailed by those who knew him. But then, he had become scruffy and unkempt and when he had lived among them he had been neat and tidy and organised. So perhaps they would not recognise him as the man he was now; he had changed so very much.

Things had not altered in the dale, he thought, but it was not so very long since he had left and things here were slow to change. He saw the sweet shop open and Miss Lee was smiling and serving a woman and two children. He went past the public house and up the narrow cobbled street to where the chapel and the manse lay. It felt very strange, as it had not when he left.

The afternoon sunshine was beginning to cast long shadows there. He went to the front door and banged confidently on it, anticipating how pleased Mr Martin would be to see him. A small maid opened the door. He was astonished. There had never been a maid to open the front door when he lived there. He and his wife had believed in doing the work they had to do themselves. He asked whether Mr Martin was at home and when he had ascertained that he was, gave her his name and waited.

Mr Martin came to the door, smiling.

'Why, Mr Bailey,' Mr Martin said.

'I did not think you would mind – you said if I were to come back at any time . . .'

'Of course, of course, come in.'

Mr Martin looked surprised to see him, as Mr Bailey supposed he would. He stepped into the hall and it smelled like home.

'Would you – would you like some tea?'

Mr Bailey said that would be very nice and Mr Martin disappeared for a few moments and then came back, taking Mr Bailey into the study where he had spent so many happy days with his books. The big glass doors were open to the garden. The room was not changed. Mr Martin obviously used it as he had, reading and studying, writing and thinking about the various problems people had and how they would come to him for help and what he would say to them on Sundays. However had he given this up? Grief had done it. It had lost him his home, his place and his calling.

Mr Martin came back and urged him to sit down and so they sat by the open windows. Mr Martin's children were playing in the garden, three little girls. Mr Bailey felt the sting of envy once again.

'They grow up so fast,' he said.

'How have you been?' Mr Martin asked him and that was when Mr Bailey told him of his difficulties and how he regretted leaving. He made much of having helped their Newcastle friend and all the other work that he had achieved.

'I was hoping that I might come back in some capacity and help you here.'

Mr Martin looked flustered.

'I have a new deacon,' he said, 'Mr Westbrooke, a very fine gentleman from Westmorland.'

'Oh,' Mr Bailey said. He had not expected anything of the kind. It made him feel cold and unwanted.

'He is staying with us. In fact, he will probably be here in a few moments so that you can meet him. He is in the chapel at present, taking a Bible class.'

Mr Bailey was not impressed with this, though he should have been because he approved of education. But to think that another man was doing one of the things his wife had been in charge of was almost too much to bear.

'It has been hard for you since Mrs Bailey died,' Mr Martin said.

'I did not understand how much it had affected me. I think that's why I left but I was wrong to do so. I have wanted to come back here so very much.'

'I can see why.'

The tea arrived and there was chocolate cake.

'Courtesy of Miss Lee,' Mr Martin said. 'She is always giving us presents. She makes the best chocolate cake in the whole world.'

'I'm sure,' Mr Bailey said stiffly. It would have choked him to have eaten a piece, even though the smell of the chocolate was wonderful. He remembered Miss Lee. He had never liked her. Unmarried women were strange, he thought. They had no true function.

'Have you somewhere to stay?'

That took him by surprise; he had assumed he could stay here.

'I have only just arrived.'

'Well then, you must spend the night with us.'

As though he would be moving on in the morning. But he thanked Mr Martin.

When they had drunk their tea, Mr Martin made an excuse and escaped to the sitting room where his wife was busy with the accounts.

'Mr Bailey is here.'

'I didn't hear his voice,' she said, looking up and smiling.

'No, his father.'

The horror on her face nearly satisfied him.

'Oh no,' she said. 'What is he doing here?'

'He has nowhere to go. He wants to come back.'

'But he can't.'

'I have had to ask him to spend the night.'

'Dear Lord,' his wife said, forgetting who she was. 'Of course you must, but does he know about Zeb?'

Mr Bailey the younger was on first name terms with them, at least when they talked about him. It was a sure sign that he was liked. Also they were pleased because they had helped him to come back and pick up his life again.

'He can't, can he? Do I tell him?'

'Shouldn't you warn Zeb?'

'I don't know that either. I'm panicking.'

'Oh my goodness me,' his wife said. 'I'll go down to the sweet shop and alert them. You keep him busy, give him chocolate cake.'

'I tried, he wouldn't have it,' and at that moment they heard the sound of Mr Westbrooke's always-happy voice, talking sweetly to their only maid, Jane, in the kitchen. They could hear her voice uplifted. Everybody liked Mr Westbrooke, though he had been there only a matter of weeks.

'Oh heavens,' his wife said, and she whisked herself out of the front door while nobody was in the hall, calling back to the kitchen, 'Jane, watch the children. I won't be long.' She scurried down the path and into the street as Jane shouted back and said she would.

Zeb would not be home before six so at least she had some time and the shop was still open. Alice had a queue of customers so Ella waited until everyone was gone.

'May I talk to you for a moment?' she asked.

Alice frowned but nodded and she called Susan in from the back. They closed the middle door and then Ella said, 'Mr Bailey is back.'

For a few moments there was incomprehension in Alice's face and when Ella's meaning dawned, she stood there, dumbstruck.

'He thought he could just come back here and pick up where he left off.' Ella said. 'James will think of something but I had to warn you. He so obviously doesn't know that his son is here. What are we to do?'

'They must both be told,' Alice said. 'We can't have them meeting without knowing the other is here. '

'There is no place for him here but what are we to do with him? He might have had the delicacy to stay away.'

'His wife is buried here,' Alice said and though this was obvious to both of them, somehow it needed to be said.

'James says he looks awful.'

'I'll tell Zeb when he comes home.'

'I'll not say anything until after the girls have gone to bed. Even then, I don't know what we can say,' Ella said and then she shot out of the back door and ran up the lane as though somebody was chasing her.

John Bailey was certain that he would hate Mr Westbrooke on sight and so it proved. Mr Westbrooke was the kind of man that he wished his son had been. While Mr Westbrooke was young, slight, and plain, he was also intelligent and kind such as Zebediah had never been.

He was smiling as he came into the room and was introduced. Mr Bailey was taken aback. It was not the smile that startled him, it was the fact that he was elegantly dressed and so well-bred; he had perfect manners and a refined accent. This man was from Westmorland? He didn't sound it.

He wore what looked to John Bailey like very expensive clothes such as Methodist ministers should never have worn but at least they were appropriately sombre. The cloth looked so soft, and it fit so well. They had obviously been made for him with care. John Bailey knew about these things, for his great-uncle on his mother's side had been a tailor.

Mr Westbrooke shook his hand on being introduced.

'I understand that you are looking after the Bible class,' Mr Bailey said. 'My wife used to do that.'

'She must have been very good; it has been organised so beautifully,' Mr Westbrooke said.

Mr Bailey hated him even more for his graciousness. Mr Westbrooke ate a huge piece of chocolate cake. Mr Bailey felt sure that if he went on eating cake like that very soon he wouldn't fit his slender form into his neat clothes. But he was young and no doubt energetic and he got down two cups of tea and asked all the proper questions of Mr Bailey. He even remembered that the man's wife had been buried not that long since and offered him sympathy.

'Are you married?' Mr Bailey said.

'I would like to marry. A minister needs a wife to do all the difficult things and take care of everything.' Mr Westbrooke smiled at his own attempted joke. Mr Bailey didn't.

'I'm sure,' he said, though he didn't mean it. 'My wife was a wonderful woman. Mr Martin is so lucky in his wife and children. I wasn't lucky with mine. I had only one child and he broke our hearts.'

'How was that?' Mr Westbrooke knew Zeb but managed to look so sympathetic that John Bailey went on.

'He was nothing like us. He was like some orphaned child. He shamed us with his drinking and fighting. He ran away from home so young and we could never hold up our heads here, even though I was the minister. It killed his mother and I had to leave. Why have I come back here, where we were so unhappy and people despised our only child? I had made my parents proud. I had no idea that some sons are not made like that. He murdered another man and from that day we couldn't hold up our heads, though we did our best here. For years we tried to forget him, we wanted another child to make things right, but nothing happened and then my wife died. I wanted to get away . . . yet here I am.'

There was a short silence and then he realised that he had given way to all his feelings when he should not have done so.

'Sometimes it's right to follow your instincts,' Mr Westbrooke said.

John Bailey blinked. He couldn't believe how much he had said; he had never confided so much to anyone. This man was dangerous. He inspired confidences. Though he was going to be a minister, he was not one yet and he should have discouraged such an outpouring, instead of allowing it and making him feel ashamed. The blood had run into John Bailey's face and he resented Mr Westbrooke. He made an excuse and left the room. He found himself longing for his wife so much that his throat constricted and he began to wish he had stayed away.

Surely he could have managed things better than this. Coming back here opened every wound, reminded him of his failures and his son's failures. It was easy to hate his son when he was away from here but now he remembered Zebediah as a small child and how beautiful he had been with his black hair and grey eyes. He was so clever. He remembered how he would read to Zeb at night, telling him old Bible stories that the child loved. He remembered Zeb falling asleep to his favourite story of Daniel and the lion. John Bailey's eyes filled with tears so that he could not see whatever was in front of him.

Thirty-Two

Alice couldn't settle. It was another hour and a half before Zeb would come home. She went back into the sweet shop and happily Susan had half a dozen people waiting in line. It was always like that. If there was only one of you the place was full, if two of you were there, it was empty. And so it proved: within five minutes they were standing looking at one another.

Susan was quiet these days and Alice herself was worried about what Dan was doing. Even so, Susan knew something had happened and when she looked curiously at her, Alice told her. At least it would distract her from her own troubles.

'Do we have to tell Zeb?' Susan said.

'What if he sees his father in the street and we haven't told him? They haven't spoken since Zeb was fourteen.'

They lingered, though there was little business at this hour. The quarrymen's wives had children to watch and houses to clean and a meal to make and were not doing their shopping now. Alice didn't like to acknowledge that she could shut the shop during this time. Besides, she could justify staying open: sometimes a quarryman would call in, hovering in the doorway, asking for a few black bullets for his ma or fudge for his children if it was payday. And the old women and the old men tended to shop at this time, as well. Having been alone all day, they needed the company of Alice's sweet shop. Everybody was a special customer. She talked to them all and that was one of the reasons they called in so often, buying small quantities so that it would not be too long before they could come back.

Children also came now. Later they would play outside their houses in the back streets but now their attention was all on sweets. They would offer a farthing and Alice prided herself on the number of enticing sweets she had at that price. And off they would go, white bag clutched in fingers with some prize inside, to be consumed out of sight of the houses, in the company of other children.

Thirty-Three

Pat McFadden had broken his leg. Zeb was first to reach him after the daily explosion had finished raining stones and the dust had settled. Pat was lying, wincing with pain. It had rained hard that day and they had been glad of it but it had created a mess in the quarry so it was not surprising somebody had slipped and lost his balance.

'Go for Dr McKenna,' Zeb yelled at the quarryman who first reached him. They had become used to following his directions because if they didn't obey him, explosions could go wrong. Although this had nothing directly to do with that, the man nodded and ran. He would have had to be mean not to, Pat was one of the nicest men in the area, not just in the quarry. Everybody liked him.

'Can you move it?' Zeb enquired, squatting down next to him.

'Of course I can't move it, idiot,' Pat said. He spoke to everybody like that, it was one of the reasons he was so well-liked. He treated them all like they were his brothers. 'It's bloody knackered, isn't it?'

'It could just be sprained.'

'Aye, Zeb, likely. Get me the hell up anyroad, I'm lying in the wet muck here.'

'It'll hurt.'

'It bloody hurts anyway, give us a hand.'

So Zeb did and Pat gritted his teeth but said nothing more. The other men helped to get Pat back to the office where Dan was silent. Dr McKenna came and after the doctor had taken Pat away, Zeb hovered, even though Mr Paterson, the clerk, was looking under his spectacles at the two of them. Dan hated accidents; he took them personally and they put him in a bad mood. Zeb realised later that he should have let the matter alone and waited a day or two, but he was daft enough not to.

'Well?' Zeb said.

'Well what?'

'He won't be able to work, will he?'

'That's not my fault. He should've got out of the way quicker than that.'

'He fell.'

'Everybody else managed it, even you and you had a lot further to run.'

'He has a wife and three bairns and his parents to look after. What are they supposed to do? You heard what the doctor said. It could be weeks.'

'He'll have a job when he comes back. The quarry isn't to blame for men falling over. Otherwise everybody would be after me for every small thing that happened. Can you stop arguing with me and get out? I have work to do.'

Zeb lingered.

'Like now?' Dan said.

Zeb went, shutting his lips firmly. There was no point in saying any more. Dan wouldn't budge, he could see.

He got on with his work and they moved the stone and broke it up so that it could be loaded and carried away to the iron works.

*

Zeb was late. And wasn't that typical? the two women said to one another. He was half an hour behind his usual time. Alice wanted to accuse him of having called in at the pub except that when he did get home he looked so dirty and tired that she couldn't.

He went upstairs with a big jug of hot water and washed and changed and then they had something to eat. Conversation was stilted. She and Susan were worried and he was obviously very tired. She didn't like to ask him whether he had had a bad day. He clearly had, she could see by the way that he didn't look much at her.

Susan cleared and washed up and said she was going out for a walk, just for a little while, and left. Zeb looked suspiciously at Alice.

'What's the matter?' he asked.

Alice hesitated.

'Tell me.'

Alice looked straight at him.

'Your father has come back,' she said. 'Mrs Martin came from the manse a little while since. He has turned up at their door.'

Zeb stared at her for what felt like a long time.

'Does he know I'm here?' he asked finally.

'Nobody will tell him until you say so. He's staying overnight at the manse.'

'But he has no place here. What will he do, where will he go? You won't have him here, will you? I'm not sharing a bedroom with my father.' Alice was appalled at his insensitivity but she understood it. He felt threatened just when he was trying to get his life back together again.

'No, no, nothing like that,' she said, soothingly.

'Why would he come back now?'

'He left when he was grieving for your mother.'

'And he isn't now?' Zeb's face was full of panic.

'Perhaps he has realised that he was wrong to go.'

'He won't think that when he knows I'm here,' Zeb said, getting up in agitation. 'Why can't anybody ever have any peace?'

'I think that's what graves are for,' Alice said. She meant to make him smile but he didn't.

'Whatever would I say to him? I haven't spoken to him since I was fourteen and then we shouted at one another.'

'You don't have to speak to him. He was there before you went away. You didn't speak to him then.'

'That was different.'

'You don't have to do anything you don't want to do, except go to work of course. Was it a bad day?'

'I thought so until I got back here.'

'What happened?

'Pat McFadden broke his leg. Dr McKenna thinks it's a bad break, he spent ages examining it. Pat has such a lot of people relying on him and the damned quarry won't pay him, even though it was really their fault. It's been a rough day; I could have done without my father.'

Alice thought how much she would give to have either of her parents about her now, but they had not been judgemental like his parents. Even though she was not their natural child they had always loved her very much and never hidden from her that she was not theirs. In so many ways she had been.

What must it be like when you had only one son and he overturned every hope that you had? If he murdered another young man and went to gaol? She tried to imagine the shame in such a place as this, where people always talked about one another because they had so little else in their lives but want and hardship and work.

'What do you think you should do?' she said.

'I think I should go and see him but it will have to wait until Sunday. I have a lot to do.'

That was all their conversation but that night he walked the floor and she listened to him. She couldn't conceive what it must be like to have your father come back into your life when you were trying to pull about you the shreds of what you had left.

It was three days until Sunday. They must get through it as best they could. She tried to put it from her mind but it kept popping back up again like overheated fudge.

Thirty-Four

Zeb tried telling himself that it was nothing to do with him how the McFadden family got on. He knew very well that Pat's wife, Shirley, disliked him. He didn't remember her well, they were older than he was, but she remembered what had happened. She had obviously come down on the side of those who thought he should have been hanged or at the least transported, so Zeb tried to keep away. She would cross the street if she saw him.

After work, after talking to Alice and having something to eat, he couldn't disabuse his mind of the fact that his father had come back. He was in some kind of shock over it. Going to Pat's house was the easier option; he couldn't just sit there and do nothing.

Pat lived halfway up Crawleyside. It was one of the terraced houses that had been built sideways on because of the wind and rain. It had been Pat's parents' house when they came to Stanhope. They had been at Tow Law at the iron works and before that they lived in Northern Ireland, escaping to what they thought was a better life. When Pat married he and his wife stayed there. Many people lived that way. Some prospered and moved on, others found their own house. But Pat's dad hadn't been well in a long time and now his mother was poorly too.

Pat was the only wage earner they had with three children to feed as well.

Shirley opened the door. She looked blankly at him.

'What have you come for?' she snapped, sharp face glaring up at him.

'I thought I might help.'

'Oh, aye?'

'I don't have to come in – '

'You're right, you don't. I blame you for this.' She blamed him for everything else, so why not? 'You could have helped him away from the explosion.'

'He wasn't near me when he tripped.'

'That's not what Dan Wearmouth says, is it, or the quarry would have paid when he couldn't work? He didn't even come to see us. Getting far too big and mighty he is, he's forgotten what his father did and where he came from.'

'All I want is to give you this.' He took from his pocket a small brown envelope, thrust it at her and walked away. Several moments later she yelled at him, and then again, but he picked up the pace down the hill and he knew that she wouldn't run after him or throw the money back. She had Pat's parents, three bairns and her husband to look after. She couldn't run anywhere or refuse help of any kind.

It was half the money he had saved.

Thirty-Five

Alice gradually became aware that people in the village were talking about how Dan had wormed his way into the Almond family and was acting like a gentleman. She had tried to ignore the talk after he had gone for the second time and wore a good suit and was apparently putting on airs.

She didn't talk to Susan about it either. It would have done no good, though it seemed to her that she and Dan were spending a lot of time apart. Susan said only that Dan was very busy at work and Mr Almond was so impressed with him that he was talking about paying him a lot more money since he was now a manager. And wasn't that wonderful?

Therefore Alice was rather surprised on the day that Susan burst into tears while they were in the shop. Luckily there was nobody else around but maybe that was why it happened. Alice put up the closed sign – it was that dead time in the middle of the afternoon and everybody would know she wouldn't be closed for long, she never was.

Susan would not be calmed. She sat and cried over the back-room fire and talked about how beautiful Arabella Almond was. Alice had the opinion that a woman such as Arabella Almond would never look at a village lad, but he was now so well-turned-out that perhaps she might. Though it seemed unlikely since the woman was thirty and had turned down half the area's eligible men by all accounts.

Susan sat there with swollen eyes and then she gazed into the fire.

'I think I should offer to release him, Miss Lee.'

So that was it. Alice was sure Susan had been worrying about this for a long time.

'What?'

'I don't think he cares for me as he thought he did. If I married him, I would be holding him back and then where would we be? If he didn't want to come home to me but had to – maybe because I was having his child – that would be awful. And the more he resented me, the less he would love me and then what would happen? What if he went and left me after we were wed?'

Alice knew that this was Susan's greatest fear. All the people she had cared for had left her and she doubted the man she had entrusted her heart to. Susan let Alice lead her upstairs where she cried herself to sleep. Alice trudged back downstairs feeling weary. Zeb was sitting over the fire.

'How is she?' he asked.

'Worried. She thinks he's going to go and leave her but also that he's blaming her for feeling like that. Is it fair to go to parties with such people and not take her with him?'

'It's common, I feel sure,' Zeb said.

'You think he means to better them by such means?'

'He has become Mr Almond's right-hand man and he's clever.'

Alice smiled.

'You're right,' she said, 'but I don't think it makes him a nicer person.'

Thirty-Six

Sir Harry Westbrooke, Charles' father, had never been in this area before. He had heard of Durham Cathedral but the Durham dale was narrow with little stone villages and he could not see anything beautiful in it. He couldn't understand why his son had left Westmorland for this place, but then he had never understood his elder son. He found the man unlike him and unlike anyone in his family had ever been.

The Westbrookes were proud people, squires who had a country seat near Penrith, five miles from the village of Shap. They had lived there for at least four centuries and each son had carried on where his father left off and so it had been down the ages until now.

Sir Harry could not understand why things had gone wrong. He had been delighted with the birth of his two sons and they had been the treasures of his life. That is, until several years ago when his elder son had decided he wanted to become a minister – and worse still, a Methodist minister.

Sir Harry had decided it was a joke and it was just that his son had an odd sense of humour. In vain he had talked about their proud lineage, house, land and responsibilities, which the first son always took, but Charles wouldn't listen and he had left.

Sir Harry had expected him back. It must be cold out there

beyond the money and prestige of their lives. But his son had not returned. Now he felt obliged to follow his son to this little valley. He had had news of him all this time from friends who had estates in Durham and Charles wrote to his brother, Henry, but the lad had not been seen or heard from for a good long time. Apparently he had gone to Nottingham for his ministerial training and had lately returned to this barren place.

Sir Harry's heart was so heavy that he didn't know how he could keep upright as he completed the final leg of his journey and got off the train. There was a pony and trap to meet him. He was staying with the Oswalds, the squires of Weardale, another old family who owned a good many farms here.

It was late afternoon when he arrived and since the main meal here – as for so many people in the country – was at five, he made haste and came downstairs to be greeted by his host and hostess. He spent a pleasant evening. The Oswalds had only one son but he was dutiful. He had married and produced a son within a year and they were obviously proud of him.

His wife was bonny in the way that border lasses were, dark-haired and cream-skinned like morning mist, and she was fat with her second. She didn't say much and he approved of that. Women were for looks and breeding, not for offering opinions. The young man's good fortune just furthered Sir Harry's sense of personal injustice; neither of his sons had yet married.

His younger son, named after himself, was a good son and loved the estate and everything in it, but – though his father had given him plenty of hints – he was still single. That didn't really matter, though: it was the elder son, named after his own father, who had to produce an heir.

If he didn't, then of course Henry's son would inherit, but since neither of them had married he was worried. He had no idea who would come next if neither of his sons had a boy. He had few cousins and no brothers. They were not a fecund family. He had been so pleased to have two sons but look at what had happened. Since his wife had died several years ago, Sir Harry sat over his dinner in the early evenings and his fire in the late evenings and drank his brandy and wondered why God was so cruel to him.

The following day after he had reached Weardale, he set out to walk the half-mile into the village of Stanhope. He could not believe his son was living in such an ordinary place when he came from the most beautiful area in the world. He found the parish church and the market square and then was directed up the steep cobbled hill toward the chapel. Beyond it was a fairly big house, though nothing compared to a rectory, where no doubt the minister lived.

A pretty young woman with three little girls was just coming out of the front door. She smiled and nodded when he doffed his hat.

'May I help you, sir?'

'I've come to see Charles Westbrooke.'

'Oh, yes, he is inside. I'm Mrs Martin, the minister's wife.'

'I am Mr Westbrooke's father.'

She went back and opened the door and called for the maid. She told her to show Mr Westbrooke inside to the study, where her husband and Charles were talking over chapel business.

The maid led him through a dark hall, opened a door and announced him. When he went in, he found the two men dressed almost exactly alike in clerical black garb. His son had not had time to compose himself and stared at him. What Sir Harry felt first of all was disappointment. He had forgotten how small, how seemingly delicate, his elder son was. He had always been a disappointment. He was not exactly ugly but he lacked grace. Sir Harry remembered how badly his son sat on a horse. He had no decent seat at all and had refused to go hunting. He couldn't fish – he had never caught anything – and he couldn't hit a barn door if it had been offered to him to shoot at.

It also made Sir Harry glad of his younger son. Henry was somebody to be proud of. This man was not worthy to be called his son. His limbs looked like they didn't belong to him, and Sir Harry remembered he was clumsy in his gait.

Charles didn't even smile. Sir Harry didn't smile either.

'Good morning.' He took them both in with one glance. Mr Martin looked puzzled but it was the look on his son's face that worried him. There was nothing open about it. Mr Martin came forward and shook his hand. Charles didn't move.

'I have come a very long way to speak to my son, Mr Martin. I would like to see him privately.'

'Yes, of course, sir. I'll ask Jane to make some tea.'

'Not on my account,' Sir Harry said. Tea was for women in the afternoons. He never drank such muck.

It was a small dark room and nothing like the lovely old rooms in his own house, Sir Harry thought. There the ceilings were low with age but wide with huge fireplaces and oak-panelled walls. Nobody spoke after Mr Martin left them.

'Have you no greeting for me? So much for your piety.'

'How is Henry?'

'He is doing a lot of good work on the estate.'

'That must be a source of pleasure for you.'

'Had he been my elder son I would have nothing to complain about.'

'Father, we've been through all this a dozen times. I won't come back. I've said to you that Henry can have the place.'

'You know very well that the estate has to come down to the first son.'

'The law is there to suit the men who make it. I always thought it was a stupid idea.'

'That is how it works.'

'Well, it isn't going to do it through me.'

'May I at least sit down?'

'Do.'

Sir Harry took a chair. It was lumpy and uncomfortable, like a great many things in the Methodist church, he thought. He could not imagine what on earth his son was getting out of this. He was ashamed that he had had to come to such a place to seek out a son who was as pale and milky as an unwanted daughter.

Charles was thinner, shorter, plainer and less interesting in every possible way than his father had remembered. He had not hoped for a great deal, but he had forgotten that his son had become a cleric, and not even a cleric in the Church. Instead he joined one of those stupid ideologies that didn't believe in a man drinking and was largely made up of common men. He was ashamed to be here. His son, he thought now, was ugly with stupidity.

Charles waited.

'I have come here because my doctor tells me I have not long to live,' Sir Harry said.

Charles uttered an exclamation of disgust.

'You've told me this before.'

'My health hasn't been good since your mother died and I had no one to see to my needs.'

Charles managed the nearest thing to a snort that any Methodist minister could manage.

'I would not have come all the way here if I did not need

your help,' his father said. 'We have never pretended to like one another. I too have always wished that Henry had been the first child because there is nothing I can do about the way that the estate is left. I want you to give up this religious nonsense and come home so that you can learn everything there is to learn before I die. It's my one hope and it is your duty as my son.'

Charles laughed. That was the awful thing about it.

'My duty? I am not your son. I am my mother's son, the woman you treated so badly that she died. I won't do it. I don't care about land and houses and things like that.'

'It isn't about land and houses; it's about tenants, farmers, the people we have in our care – '

'Our care?' Charles said scornfully. 'They should have been given their own places long since, having worked for so many years. Everything would have been better. Instead they're stuck down there, so far below us apparently.'

'It's easy to talk like that when you are young but things like that cannot be done. The estate is worth twenty thousand a year.'

'I know.'

'Then come back and assure me that it is in safe hands before I die. The doctor says that my heart isn't good. It took everything I had to come here and plead with you. It's a very long way.'

'That was never what I wanted.'

'This is not about what you want; this is about your duty as my son and as a son of our family. You must come back. Please.'

'How many times did our mother plead with you when you beat her?'

Sir Harry had heard this nonsense before.

'She was disobedient. I was always master in my own house.'

'Then go and be master there now. I will never come back,' and Charles walked out.

Thirty-Seven

'You made quite a hit with my wife and daughter on Saturday evening,' Mr Almond said to Dan on Monday afternoon.

'That's very kind of you, sir,' Dan said.

'You must come and see us again. You have good ideas. You save me many hours and you are looking after the workmen so well. Between you and Bailey, I believe you can run the place. I want to have more time at home – you know I'm trying to – and I trust you and Zeb to get it right. He should have more responsibility for the men, I think. He's good with them.'

The following day when two men began fighting below in the quarry, Zeb told them to go and cool off and he would see them later. That evening Zeb went to the boarding house where the two lived. It was hard there, he knew. A lot of men had nothing beyond their work and went home to bad food and dirty beds. They never seemed to change their clothes and they had no women to care for them and no child to urge them on. Others sent money home to their families and caused no trouble but they were usually older. These two were young and had thick accents. They possibly even came from the same Scottish village.

He talked to them. He told them that they were good together and that their conflict had been nothing but a solvable problem;

the quarry benefited from their work. Neither of them looked up as he spoke.

They had come into the dale because they were desperate and had nothing to eat. They were from Berwick and beyond into Scotland, and there was nothing in that place to keep them, he knew. He explained to them that if they stuck together they would prosper.

He didn't know whether these men had families they were sending money home to, he only knew that they needed to go on working. He would talk them into it so that they would not regret the argument and could go back the next day and carry on as though nothing had happened.

He took them to the Bonny Moor Hen and bought them a meal and a couple of pints and he could see that they hadn't had a decent meal in months. As soon as they were properly fed and had some beer inside them, they forgot their disagreement. He remembered their names and knew he must tell Dan they needed more money and somewhere better to live. Both these men needed more money because at the moment they were sending it back to whatever hillside they had come from. They needed a little more so that they need not live like savages.

The following day he tried to talk to Dan about a better place for the men to be housed.

'I live there,' Dan said.

'Then you know how bad it is. We have to find something better.'

'This is a quarry, not an orphanage.'

'You would get more and better work out of them if you could provide decent accommodation. You have to admit there could be so much more with so very little effort.'

'How would that be?'

'We find a decent-sized house, we find a woman who can cook to run it, and another woman or two to keep it clean and organised and do washing for them. Men work better on a full stomach. You know that. Wouldn't you like to move?'

'Badly. All right, see what you can do,' Dan said.

Thirty-Eight

Mr Bailey felt like an intruder in his own house. It was the strangest feeling he had ever encountered and he hated every second of it. He had no place to go and no money and he wished now that he had taken more for the work that he had done while he was away. Whatever was he to do?

Mr and Mrs Martin were not the kind of people that he would ever have wanted to stay with. They treated their children with such levity that he was appalled. The little girls were there most of the evening, instead of being sent upstairs to bed, and there was no maid to take them since Jane went home. They were there for a long time, until eventually supper was served at almost nine o' clock. His stomach had long since given in and he could barely eat, he was so hungry.

The meal was good and Mrs Martin presided and was kind and pleasant to both Mr Bailey and Mr Westbrooke. But the conversation was of other people and books and nothing to do with the ministry and he was not used to such talk. It was all so light and airy, like a spring wind over new grass.

When they went to bed he was taken into the small bedroom that had been his son's. He knew he could not complain. Mr Westbrooke had the big bedroom that was across the hall from the bedroom where Mr and Mrs Martin slept. The house seemed bigger than it had done and more precious than ever. He didn't sleep; he longed for his wife and his home and his ministry. He had thrown away the small amount he had left after his wife had died.

He could not stand it. Little had he realised that his best option would have been to remain where he was. He could have married again. He was shocked when he thought of it, but now he began to think that he could have had half a dozen children with another woman if he had done things differently. Why had he not?

He lay awake, listening to the clock in the parish church tower and thinking of all the widows – and more especially, of all the maiden ladies – here in Stanhope. In particular he thought of Miss Lee. Now that would be a good idea. She had her own business; she was well-off. She was not much to look at – skinny and rather opinionated – but he could change that. Maiden ladies in Stanhope were many and she could not afford to be choosy. And with her, he could eat as much chocolate cake as he desired. That made him smile and after that he slept.

Consequently he went down to breakfast in a completely different mood. The little girls were there so it was difficult to make conversation, but when they had gone away with Mrs Martin, the men were still sitting. He took the opportunity to suggest to Mr Martin that he might find some kind of work within the district.

'I can't say that there is any,' said Mr Martin.

'Then I don't know what I am to do.'

'I'm afraid I can't help you there.'

'I have no money. Are you going to turn me out?'

'I can't afford to keep you here,' Mr Martin said apologetically.

'Perhaps you could ask people if they need help.'

'Shop-keeping, perhaps? Or something like that?'

'I am a minister of the church. I could not possibly do anything like that. And besides, they know me here.'

'I don't know what to suggest then.'

'What about other places?'

'Weardale is a very small area, as you know. A lot of people have to come to Stanhope to worship.'

'I could preach.'

'Mr Bailey, we have no opening for you here. We have lots of people who will preach, we don't have to pay anyone to do it.'

'They cannot be experts, as I am.'

'It doesn't require expertise, just care and a little speech. People appreciate that we all have the same problems, don't you think?'

Mr Bailey didn't think. These people knew nothing of the Bible or the teachings of Wesley. It was his job to interpret the ministry to them. Mr Martin obviously did not care about such things.

Breakfast was over and Mr Martin and Mr Westbrooke went up to the chapel. Mr Bailey didn't want to leave the house but he knew he was no longer welcome there. He couldn't think what to do now. He walked up the lane toward the quarry. It was a fine day and he had nothing else to do. He left his small bundle of belongings inside, by the front door of the manse. He would claim them on coming back.

People weren't meant to go near the quarry and he had no plan to go that far. It was dangerous work and strangers were unwelcome. But as he drew near, he saw the quarrymen working and observed a young man entering the office. His heart clutched. The man moved like his son.

It couldn't be his son; he was safely locked away in Durham gaol or maybe had even died. Yet there was something about the way that the tall, slender young man stood that was just the same way that Zebediah had been. That kind of thing was unmistakable.

. Mr Bailey forgot that nobody was allowed in and he walked up toward the office. And then, since the man had gone inside, he followed. The young man was leaning over a desk. He looked nothing like a man who had been in gaol for all those years. He had not suffered. He was tanned from working outside and he was smiling down at the man behind the desk and they were talking. But Mr Bailey knew that he was not deceived and he was appalled. His son looked so very young. After all those years in gaol how could he look like that?

'Zebediah,' he said and that was when the man sitting down stared. The man leaning over the desk straightened and turned around. And there Mr Bailey's son was, his grey eyes clear, his hair so black beneath his hat that it shone. Mr Bailey could see that Zebediah had known he was there.

'Father,' Zeb said.

'What are you doing here?'

'Working. What are you doing?'

'Trying to find my way back. I shouldn't have left. After your mother died I didn't know what to do, but now I want to be here. Are you staying where you used to live with the other men?'

'You'll have to forgive me; I'm at work here,' Zeb said and he turned around and began talking again.

'Someone took you in then? The minister didn't tell me. Why did he keep such information from me?'

Zeb turned to him.

'Maybe he thought it had nothing to do with you.'

'You are my son.'

'Not according to you,' Zeb said and he walked out of the office.

The other man got on with the paperwork he was dealing with and the clerk at the far end of the office hadn't even looked up. Mr Bailey followed his son outside.

'You must help me.'

Zeb ignored him and in the end Mr Bailey left the quarry. He went back to the manse and up the path further to the chapel. He found Mr Martin and Mr Westbrooke there and he broke straight into their conversation.

'You ought to have told me that my son was here.'

Mr Martin glanced at him.

'I didn't think I should.'

'But he's working at the quarry, the place I never wanted him to go to. Has he learned nothing from what he did? He'll end up back in gaol, having killed somebody else and they'll hang him. He knew that I was here. You told him, didn't you?'

'Mr Bailey, you will have to excuse us,' Mr Martin said and they went into the little back room that Mr Bailey had known so well and closed the door.

Mr Bailey wandered out of the chapel. He sat outside and remembered how things had been when he was first married, how happy he had felt when Zebediah was a small child. The devil's child seemed to be prospering. He couldn't understand it. He had nothing and yet his son had work and a place to live.

He went off to the boarding house where the men lived but the woman who ran it wouldn't let him past the front door.

'Nobody gets in here until I've seen his money,' she declared.

'My son will pay for me when he gets back from the quarry.' The place stank and the woman reeked; she had long, greasy hair and black teeth. Her face was white and her dress stiff and smudged with various foodstuffs from never being washed.

'Send him in then when he comes down and we'll talk about it,' she said.

After that he sat under the trees; the afternoon had turned hot. Some of the men would not come that way, no doubt, but those who lodged there would so he waited. But even when the last of the stragglers was gone, his son was not there.

He was just about to give up when he saw the two young men from the office. They didn't seem to notice him and they walked up the main street and into a vennel that led to the back of the sweet shop. Mr Bailey was amazed. Did the old maid who ran the sweet shop take in lodgers or was his son living in sin with a middle-aged spinster? Here in Stanhope? He could not believe such things.

He went to the front but the shop was locked so he walked down the yard after them. He banged hard at the back door and when a pretty young woman came to the door, he gestured.

'My son is here. May I come in?' He pushed past her and into the room. He observed what he thought were two couples. 'Is this a house of sin?'

'What on earth are you doing here?' Zebediah said.

'I have nowhere to go and no money.'

'You can't stay here,' his son said.

Mr Bailey looked past him to the old maid. She was the one to appeal to, she owned the place.

'Miss Lee,' he managed after a slight pause, 'won't you let me stay here, just for the night? I will go in the morning. You are taking in lodgers.'

'I'm not,' she said and that was when he remembered how much he had disliked her and other women like her, spinsters.

'Mr Martin has refused to let me stay with him. Not so long

ago that chapel and the house was mine. If this is not a house of sin, I would like to stay.'

'What on earth makes you think something so silly?' she said. 'You may stay but don't say things like that to me.'

Mr Bailey had never heard a woman talk in this manner and was aghast. He stopped thinking about her as a possible wife for a respectable clergyman. He said nothing, though, since his remaining relied on her goodwill. He remembered that he had left his Bible and other books at Mr Martin's but he was afraid to go out in case he should not be allowed in again. He stood in the middle of the floor until she asked him to sit down.

Coming here had been a good idea, he thought, when she gave him sponge cake with raspberry jam and several cups of tea. He hadn't eaten since breakfast and was very hungry. He did not miss the look that Zebediah flung at her when she said she would take him in but she ignored him. He was obviously not her husband then. Mr Bailey should have known: she was a middle-aged woman and men never married women older than them. And she was far from handsome; she was scraggy and plain-faced and rather frightening, he acknowledged.

The young woman and the young man went off together after that but they were not long away. Maybe they were the kind of people who would sneak around corners together. Miss Lee made dinner and Zebediah went out, slamming the back door, though he came back within minutes. Mr Bailey did not realise that he had fallen asleep until he heard her voice calling him to dinner.

It was one of the best dinners he had ever eaten: local trout, he was sure, with new potatoes and peas and a kind of butter sauce that he had never tasted before. After it was a summer pudding, thick with raspberries and dense with cream. Mr Bailey thought he might have died and gone to heaven. She gave him tea and then he fell asleep again.

Susan and Dan went out and Zeb looked sheepishly at Alice.

'I'm sorry to bring this on you,' he said. 'I knew things were too good to last. Why couldn't he stay away?'

'He has nothing.'

'In the morning I will move out and take him to the hostel with me.'

'Indeed you will not. We will manage.'

'With him here?'

'He is still your father.'

Mr Bailey didn't know how long he had slept but he was awakened by Miss Lee telling him that he must take off his clothes, all of them, and wash. She would bring him a nightshirt. When he protested she spoke firmly.

'I don't allow dirty people into my house. You are sleeping down here and nobody will interrupt you, but you must wash first.' She indicated the tin bath and the nightshirt and handed him a big towel. Then she went upstairs and left him.

When she came back down he was dry and in the nightshirt.

'Do you need to go down the yard?' she asked him.

He was mortified but shook his head.

'I will leave you a candle and pot and you can sleep on the couch. I have made it up for you with pillows, sheets and blankets.'

He was so tired that he did not even wish her goodnight; he just went straight to bed. The couch, as she called it, was a lot more comfortable than many places he had been since his wife had died.

He was astonished at the lack of noise. He had no idea who was upstairs. Presumably they were not sleeping together as couples, or were they married? He no longer knew. In the morning he would go to the manse for his belongings. No, perhaps he wouldn't, because if he left here she might not allow him back inside. He slept without dreaming and he thought it had something to do with the smell of chocolate.

Thirty-Nine

Susan and Dan were looking around their new house. She had done quite a lot of work since he had been there and he knew that she was eager to please. But in some ways it worried him, as though his future was all mapped out for him.

'The new house seems to be costing a lot more money than it should,' he ventured.

'But you told me to go ahead and do what I wanted.'

'I didn't realise we needed all these pots and pans.'

'I didn't buy them. Miss Lee gave them to me. She said she had too many.'

'I was speaking generally; you know what I mean. And why are so many people coming to the wedding?'

'I thought we had agreed.'

'What about Mr and Mrs Almond? As my employer, surely he should be asked?'

'I didn't think they would come.'

'If they don't get asked then they can't, can they?' Dan said.

'Then you must ask them.' She looked into his face. 'Danny, I want to say something to you. No, please, it's important. Just listen.'

'All right, I'm listening.'

'If you don't want to marry me, it's all right, you know.'

Dan stared at her.

'What?' he said.

'I can feel you drawing back from me – '

'I'm not.'

'We haven't seen one another in days. We used to meet almost every day. I think you're avoiding me.'

'I want to make it right for us. I want to be a real manager. I want to go as far as I can. Mr Almond is learning to trust me beyond anything I ever hoped. I thought you understood that I went to his home because it's moving me on to another level in all sorts of ways. In the end, you'll see; it'll be good for us. One day we'll have a lot more than this.' He swept a hand around the kitchen as he spoke.

'I don't want more than this. I just want you. And if you being a manager takes you away from me all the time, then I think we'd best stay as we are.'

'Susan, I'm working really hard and it's for our future. Mr Almond trusts me and I can't give it up. I want to get somewhere and be somebody and have a lovely house and nice things and I'm beginning to like my work now that I'm really moving forward. I want you to come with me and when the time is right you'll mix with people like the Almonds; we'll be like them.'

He could hear himself being impatient but he was finding everything so dull other than work. Susan talked of nothing but the wedding and he was dreading it. August was never a beautiful month weather-wise; it was cold and rainy, but all he thought was that it was drawing him closer to that little house and a woman who never shut up about trivial things.

Susan didn't look happy; she just shook her head.

'All I want is to be with you.'

'We will be and I'll give you the whole world.'

One late afternoon more than two weeks before the wedding Dan, had left the quarry and was making his way down Crawleyside bank toward the village when he saw the Almonds' carriage.

It was a long way round to go that way but he wanted a walk. Nothing was drawing him into the village. He went up to the top of the hill and walked toward Crawleyside before going back down the hill. He was feeling a lot better about everything. Perhaps he was getting used to the way that he was living now and thinking more positively about marriage.

He thought of how Susan would look after him and make him lovely meals. He would be able to sit out in the garden that autumn if the weather was fine and drink beer and look down on the river. It would be so pleasant. Then his thoughts turned: when the winter came, the little house would be – oh, it would be so dull. There would be dark days and nothing to do once he came back from work. And maybe by next summer, there'd be a child and what if Susan was like so many dales women and bred a child a year until he was exhausted and she was worn out and they had nothing left? It terrified him.

He heard the noise of the carriage and then it stopped. Miss Almond's voice called his name. He moved back to the carriage and she opened the door and invited him in.

'I'm on my way home. Do come with me. Mama will be pleased to see you. We've been so dull since the wedding anniversary party. She would love to get away but my father says he is much too busy.'

He didn't see that there would be any harm in having tea at Ash House. He could not quench the pleasure when he went into the wide gates by carriage and was put down at the front door, though he felt as if he was doing something wrong.

Mrs Almond greeted him like a lost cousin with a smile and an outstretched hand.

'Mr Wearmouth,' she said. 'What a nice surprise.'

They had tea out of china so delicate that he could see his fingers through his cup and there were scones so light that they did not require any chewing. There were tiny, diamond-shaped sandwiches, and cake such as he had never seen before, in three colours, surrounded by marzipan. The teacloth had delicate embroidery in its corners; pansies they were, black and yellow, and there were napkins to match.

Mr Almond came out of the study and greeted him as though they were old friends.

'I see,' he said, 'leaving the quarry early, eh?'

'No, sir, everything is done.'

Mr Almond smiled on him.

'If I had known you were going to be this good, I would have given you the chance years ago. But I could never delegate. I don't understand how these things work since I've always managed everything by myself.'

'It has been very hard,' his wife said. 'I've begged him to find someone young enough with sufficient ability to look after the place.'

'It's very complicated,' Mr Almond protested good-naturedly.

'Surely we could have a few days away; anywhere would do.'

'Mr Wearmouth is not very experienced yet. I don't want the place to fall to pieces while I'm not there,' Mr Almond said but he was still smiling.

Dan wished he didn't have to leave. After they had tea, Arabella suggested that she show him around the garden, where so many beautiful flowers were holding up their heads. He liked it; it was big and had huge glasshouses and a pond where silver fish glided through the water. The sun was hot and there was a summer-house. He and Miss Almond sat there in the shade.

She heaved a sigh.

'The summer is so lovely.'

'Do you wish you could go somewhere else to appreciate it?'

'Not really.'

He was surprised.

'Couldn't you?'

She looked wryly at him.

'Away from here I'm nobody but a quarryman's daughter.'

'I don't understand.'

'My father was a workman when he set out; I'm nobody in society. And I don't have many female friends – they care about nothing but what they look like and the getting of husbands. I don't fit in with them because of my bookish tendencies. I love reading history and I like being here in the dale. It's my place.'

'But you must have had many offers of marriage, you're so clever and so beautiful.'

'Businessmen like these men don't want clever wives. They want women who sit back and tell them how wonderful they are. I would have to pretend all the time. They're all so dull; they're young men who depend on their fathers for everything and they drink too much and never read and they dare to think they are doing me a favour because I'm nobody. I couldn't marry like that.

'Then there are the others who want my money and that is even worse. They pretend that they care for me – at least some of them do – but you can tell that they too think they are doing me a favour. Such arrogance. Now I have nothing but to dwindle into being an old maid, sitting on my sofa with cats and a box of chocolates, reading. Not so very bad but it did not occur to me that it would be so. There are worse things. What about you? You are getting married, I understand.'

Dan looked down at his fingers.

'They tell me she's very pretty,' Miss Almond said.

'I don't think I care for her any more.' There, it was said. He felt better for it. He didn't want Susan's silly little presence, the small, stifling house and her ordinary dales ways. She was not beautifully-spoken like Miss Almond; she didn't read books or have fine, white hands. She wasn't even amusing or lighthearted or clever or funny.

'My life has changed so much since your father made me his manager. I don't think like I did.'

'You have had your head turned by our glamour,' she said and laughed.

'I'm afraid it's true.'

'But it isn't like that. All you have seen are the good parts. My mother frets and my father is always at work. We lead a very dull life.'

'It can't be any worse than mine.'

'I don't think you're dull,' and then she looked at him and made him smile. 'I like having you around me.'

'I don't read much,' he admitted.

'I think you are very like my father and I like that about you. You work hard and you care about the quarry. My father's always been like that and my mother has always been there to support him and I think that's wonderful. I shall miss you very much when you get married. But you will bring your wife to see us, and if you care for her, I'm sure we will too. Why haven't you invited us to the wedding?'

'I thought you would think it was beneath you.'

'That's not fair,' she said. 'We aren't like that. Tell me about the girl you love. She must be very special.'

Dan couldn't speak; he couldn't say anything. He was panicking. He didn't want to marry Susan; he didn't want to leave here. He wanted to stay with Arabella Almond and her parents in the small paradise that her father had provided for them. He wanted to be with her for the rest of his life.

'I don't – I don't want to marry her.'

She laughed.

'Oh, Mr Wearmouth, that's just cowardice. If you didn't care for her you wouldn't have asked her.'

'I've been alone for so long after my mother died and my father went to gaol. I got tired of being alone. I've had nobody all these years so when I met her and she seemed to like me, I clutched at the whole idea of having somebody. But as the weeks have gone on, I've found it harder and harder to spend time with her.'

'I know about your parents and I'm very sorry. It must have been so awful for you all these years and living at that boarding house.'

He smiled.

'It was dreadful,' he said. 'Miss Almond. You do like me?'

'Of course I do. I think you're the most interesting man I've known since my father. You brighten my days. I just wish we had met like this earlier, before you found someone you really care for.'

'I don't care for her since I met you.'

There was silence and even the birds in the garden didn't make a sound.

'You don't mean it. It isn't fair to her.'

'Yes, I do. I love being here with you. Who wouldn't? But it isn't just the house and how rich you are and everything that comes with it. I wouldn't ask you to marry me from ambition – '

'Marry you?' she stared.

'Oh, I'm sorry. I didn't mean to say that. Why would you want somebody like me?'

She continued looking at him.

'I have never thought positively of marriage. I have always preferred to be alone and to do as I please. But now I think that being with you would please me. I do like you very much.'

'You do?' It was his turn to stare with disbelief.

She laughed.

'Actually, I do. I didn't think of it like that but I knew you were about to get married so it would have been silly to. But I do like you being here and being around me. But you can't leave her for me. That would be awful.'

'Marrying her when I didn't want to – wouldn't that be awful as well? And we would both be trapped in a marriage that wasn't right for us. Do you think you might be persuaded to marry me?'

She hesitated.

'Are you thinking that your father and mother would be horrified?' he said.

'I don't think they would be pleased. Why don't you talk to my father?'

'I would never dare.'

'You must. You have to have courage to get the things that you want most.'

'You do want me then, Arabella?'

He didn't know what happened after that – just that he was kissing her and the garden was full of sunshine and if he had been in love before now, he didn't remember it. He could smell roses and hear the birds singing but best of all – unlike Susan who would allow nothing but a slight meeting of lips – she let him take her into his arms and kiss her as he had wanted to kiss a woman for so long.

Susan was not a woman; she was just a silly girl, with dreams filling her head. Arabella put her arms up to his neck and drew closer so that he could feel the softness of her breasts. When the kiss was over, he was still holding her close. He looked into her eyes.

'I hardly dare to ask, Miss Almond, but will you marry me?'

Forty

Zeb went off to work as usual. His father was still lying asleep on the couch in the back room and after he had gone, Alice felt slightly easier with only one of them in the house. After they had had breakfast and opened the shop, her unwelcome guest came into the shop while she was busy.

'Miss Lee, I wondered if I might bother you for some breakfast.'

'I'm very busy now.' Alice was aware of the women in the shop. They would know who he was even though he didn't acknowledge them. Alice asked Susan to go through and make some tea and Mr Bailey followed her, asking at least three times when the kettle would boil.

'We let the fire go down because it's too warm. I have to rebuild it now for your kettle,' Susan said.

'Then what do you do for tea during the day?'

'We drink cold water.'

'That won't do for me,' he said. He watched her cut the loaf and put out butter and jam.

'I thought I smelled bacon earlier.'

'Much earlier,' she said. 'You'll have to make do with this; it's halfway through the morning and we have a lot to do.'

'You are very impertinent for a maid.'

'I am not a servant,' she said. She made the tea and went out and left him to his bread and jam.

Since Miss Frost had died, they could not make ice cream or even chocolate when the weather was warm because it wouldn't keep. If the weather went on being hot, many of the other sweets also didn't set and everything was more difficult. That day it rained but it was still warm. They hated rainy days. People went out for necessities, not sweets, at such times. But today there was a good trade.

Mr Bailey came into the shop at about one, complaining that he had nothing to eat and Susan again made him a sandwich. He looked at it in disgust.

'That's not a dinner,' he said.

'We don't eat much during the day. Dinner is tonight.'

She and Alice had no time to eat; they made sweets as soon as the shop was closed. By the time Zeb came back from work, Alice was hastily putting together fried eggs and chips.

He went over to his father.

'What are you still doing here?'

'I have nowhere to go,' his father said.

'I'll give you some money in the morning and then you must go.'

'Where to, the poor house?'

'I don't care. I don't want you still here when I come back from work.'

They sat down to eat at the table in silence and Mr Bailey looked at his dinner.

'This isn't a proper dinner. There's no meat.'

'We don't eat meat every day,' Alice said. 'It gets very dear. This is all there is. If you don't like it you can leave it.'

'Isn't there anything else?'

'There isn't,' she said.

That evening, when Susan had gone off to bed and Mr Bailey had fallen asleep on the sofa, Alice turned to Zeb.

'He is going to have to sleep with you.'

Zeb looked hard at her.

'I don't want him here.'

'None of us wants him but we can't put him out, can we?'

'I'll give him what money I have.'

'Don't you think he'll just come back when he has none left? What would be the point in that?'

When Zeb came home the following day, he stared. His father ignored him; he was deep into a book, though he had earlier told Alice that her books were ungodly.

'Please yourself,' she had said, and went off back to work.

That night Zeb had to put up with his father in his bed again. It was harder than sharing a bed with Eli in gaol. His father did not talk to him, did not listen to him, and was more intrusive than anybody had been in years. Zeb had gloried in having such a space to himself. Now he felt as if all his privacy was gone.

He lay awake, listening to his father snoring loudly. He took up a huge amount of space and turned over and over as though he was having bad dreams. He even cried out at one point. Zeb was just about to dig him in the ribs when he quietened and went back to snoring.

In the end Zeb took a pillow and a quilt and slept downstairs on the sofa where Alice found him in the morning.

'That bad, was it?' she said.

'Couldn't you hear him?'

'I should think the neighbours could hear him,' she said but with a slight smile to take the sting away.

'I will leave and take him with me, it's only fair.'

'No, you won't,' Alice said. 'How can you do that? There's only the hostel and it's filthy. The new house where the men sleep is full so you can't go there. And the pub is dear and folk there will not want you and your father foisted on them.'

'Well, thank you for that,' he retorted, but he was secretly pleased that he didn't have to leave. The idea of living with his father not at the sweet shop was unbearable.

He tried to think of a use for his father and couldn't. All his father had done was be a Methodist minister. Zeb didn't think he was bad at it; it was just that now he had no place to go and nothing to do.

Forty-One

Dan left Ash House without seeing Mr Almond. He had gone inside, full of hope, but the maid told him that Mr and Mrs Almond had gone to dress for dinner as they had friends coming. He would not be able to see Mr Almond that evening. So he went back down into the village and tried to keep his spirits high but when it got late he couldn't sleep.

He lay there amidst the dirty sheets and the fetid air and the men and thought that Arabella Almond was nothing but a dream and in the morning he would wake up to find himself still betrothed to Susan with no alternative in sight.

There was no problem about waking up since he didn't sleep. He lay there until it was time to go to work. He didn't eat breakfast, though there was nothing new about that. Miss Lee would send him a hearty lunch as she always did. Guilt weighed him down as he trod slowly up toward the quarry.

Soon after he got there, Zeb appeared in the doorway with the bottle of cold tea and his bait.

'No chocolate cake,' he said. 'It's too hot.'

Dan nodded and got on, at least he tried to, but when Mr Almond came in it was so difficult to concentrate. He knew that he must ask sometime, somehow, so there was no point in letting the day go by. The trouble was that there was only one room in the office and he wanted to speak to Mr Almond by himself. He had to wait until Mr Almond determined to go into the quarry to see what was happening, as he did every day. Dan followed him out.

'I would like to speak to you, sir.'

Mr Almond, surprised at the tone – and of course he would be – stopped.

'Is everything all right?' he said.

'Would you give me five minutes with nobody else there?'

'Certainly, if you need it.'

Mr Almond trod on, up beyond the quarry so that no one could hear them. The bell heather was bright. A few birds soared in the sky and it was very warm.

'What is it?' Mr Almond said, smiling on him.

'You understand that I am about to be married?'

'I will put your wage up and we are still hoping to gain an invitation.'

Dan couldn't speak. He felt so wretched, both at treating Susan in such a way and at having the gall to ask this man for his daughter's hand when he was nothing more than a glorified quarryman.

'The thing is,' Dan said and then stopped. He wanted to say, 'it doesn't matter, sir, and I would like you to come to my wedding,' but then he had a vision of Arabella Almond and he couldn't do it.

'I want to marry your daughter, sir,' he said.

There was so much time between his words and when Mr Almond opened his mouth again that Dan wanted to fall into the silence and be extinguished. Mr Almond began to speak more than once and then stood still for a long time. He turned around and looked up the valley and then back down towards the quarry.

'You've spoken to her.'

'I wanted to ask you first but I think she is in favour of me.'

'It must be the first time she's ever been in favour of any man,' Mr Almond said roundly. 'I'm astonished.'

He said nothing more. Dan got to the point when he couldn't stand the waiting; Mr Almond was gazing up at the sky.

'Do you have some particular objection, sir?'

'I have a great many objections,' Mr Almond said, looking so straight at him that Dan wished himself away. 'Unlike most other men, I didn't want my daughter to marry someone like me. Saving the fact that you aren't my son, you are the only man I know who could possibly take on the quarry after me, so there's that, at least. I know that's very blunt but it's true. I wanted a son. I wanted half a dozen sons so that they would fight over my job and marry and have children and what do I get? One daughter who won't marry above us. It grieves me and it grieves her mother even more. We dreamed of a grand marriage. But how could we break into another level of society? We belong nowhere: we aren't down with the workmen or up with the rich and educated folk. They're nice to us because I've made money but we wanted to move on, to move up, and Arabella has stopped us from doing that. It's a huge disappointment. But I also love how she doesn't care for any of that, so what can I do?'

Dan was taken aback at the frankness of Mr Almond's speech but he wasn't surprised. He too was a nobody in such ways.

'Perhaps I should have come to you first but I didn't intend any of this. I didn't know that she cared for me. If you and her mother are against it, then I will go to some other quarry and find work.'

Mr Almond looked kindly at him.

'You're a good lad,' he said.

'No, I'm not. I've let down the girl who trusted me. It was a mistake.'

'I think that a great many men feel the same way. But you can get used to your mistakes when the first flush of marriage is over and you have someone to go home to every night.'

'I don't want to go home to Susan Wilson,' Dan said. 'Do you feel that I am too low to ask for your daughter?'

'Certainly not, you're a great deal higher than I was when I asked her mother. But are you sure? Having let one woman down, you might do the same a second time.'

'I know I deserve that but I haven't seen anyone like your daughter.'

'Or her wealth or her position or her intelligence.'

'I won't deny that played a part, but I truly love her. If you think I'm not worthy of her, I won't come near again.'

'I can't do that if you are what she wants. She has turned down half a dozen proposals, though it was a very long time ago. You would not be taking my daughter in the first flush of youth. She is almost as old as you.'

'I think that may be an advantage. We seem to think the same way. No, I shouldn't say that. Would you at least consider it?'

'I will. What her mother will say, goodness only knows,' Mr Almond said. 'But if you ever let her down, then God help you.'

It was early evening when Mr Almond arrived home to find his daughter in a hammock beneath the trees, reading. His wife was drinking tea under another set of trees nearer the house. She gave him tea, though he refused cake since he thought he was getting fat from so much sitting down in his job. Then he told her what Daniel Wearmouth had said. He expected his wife to be upset, he expected her to refuse the whole idea – in which case it would have been difficult – but she sighed over her teacup and sat back.

'I was afraid of this.'

'Why afraid?'

'She likes him. She did from the first. She talked about him so much and when he came to the anniversary she stood about waiting for him. For the last ten years I have tried to find her a husband. She would have none of them. And for the last five years, I have despaired that we should ever have a holiday from this place and that she would live with us for always. I have nothing against old maids, but for Arabella to be so intelligent and so beautiful and for nobody to want her that she wanted in turn . . . Could she have been made to go into old age alone?'

'Does that mean you don't mind?'

'Of course I mind. I wanted her to marry a squire or a businessman or at least a decent clergyman. The bishop of Durham, perhaps,' she laughed, trying for a little levity. 'But she is always more clever than they are or more beautiful than they think they deserve. I never thought beauty would be an encumbrance. Does she really like this man?'

'He says she does.'

'You want me to talk to her.'

'That would help,' he said.

When it was late, Mrs Almond went to her daughter's bedroom and knocked lightly on the door. She liked to hear the 'come in' from Arabella before she entered the room.

It was a lovely room. There were no lights on because Arabella had the windows open and the night was as fine as the day had been. It was perfect weather, though they both knew Mr Almond would consider it 'too damned hot' for lead mining and quarrying.

Arabella's maid had just left her; her mother had timed it. There Arabella sat with her hair plaited almost as though she were a child. She turned and smiled at her mother as she had smiled at her every night of their lives. Mrs Almond's one daughter was all the world to her.

'You come from my father,' Arabella said.

'You could have told me.'

'Mr Wearmouth was so worried and afraid that you and Father would hate it and forbid him to come near me.'

'We were surprised.'

'But not pleased.'

Mrs Almond sank down on the bed.

'I couldn't say it was what we wanted for you, but when does a mother think any man is good enough for her daughter?'

'I had so many chances. You did everything you could for me. Your mistake was introducing me to books and my own will.'

'Every woman should have books and her own will,' her mother said. Arabella cast herself into her mother's arms and thanked her for being so lovely.

'You do want him then?' her mother asked.

'I have never wanted anything more in my life. I'm sorry to make you so disappointed in me.'

'We aren't disappointed,' her mother lied bravely. 'I'm glad you have found someone that you care for so very much.'

After she left Arabella, Mrs Almond went to bed. She and her husband shared a room, which showed how un-aristocratic they were. Mrs Almond loved to turn over in the night and smell her husband's sweat-salt back and feel his warm skin under her fingers. She would blush in the daytime, remembering how sweet the taste of his skin was under her mouth. Sometimes he would turn to her and gently draw her into his embrace and call her his dear Nell. She was never happier than when she was in his arms.

Tonight, however, she sensed that her husband was restless because of his knowledge of the affair between their daughter and Dan Wearmouth. She sank down on the big bed beside him, pleased that he had left the windows wide open. What little breeze there was came from up the top of the land where the bell heather was bright purple and the wind moaned softly.

'He has a woman in the village he is supposed to marry,' she said. 'If he doesn't marry her, how will people feel?'

'I'm not sure that matters beside Arabella's happiness.'

'But is it the right thing?'

'She has spent ten years deciding what was wrong for her, why shouldn't we trust her now?'

It was two days later, on the Saturday, when Dan found the courage to tell Susan of his decision. He couldn't rest so after working that morning as he usually did he had gone for a walk. He knew that he must tell Susan what he had done but he didn't want to go to the sweet shop. He couldn't imagine what Zeb would say or do. He was putting it off, telling himself that there was no hurry, that nobody knew, and anyway if he left it, it would look better. He would tell her tonight, though; he couldn't lie awake worrying any longer.

Perhaps she was over the road in their new house and alone.

And so, ignoring the sweet shop where he thought everything was locked up, he went across the street.

He went round the back as they all did and up the garden. The back door was open. He went in and called Susan's name and she came quickly down the stairs. Her face lit when she saw who it was. He felt even worse for that.

'Oh,' she said, 'I didn't expect you. I assumed you were working late and then going straight to the pub to eat. You've been doing that a lot lately.'

'Are you on your own?'

'Miss Lee is making sweets because the day is cooler now and I think Zeb has probably gone to the pub. I was just finishing the curtains in the upstairs bedroom. They look so beautiful. Would you like to see them?'

'Not just now.'

'Oh, well, why don't we go over the road if you've had nothing to eat? Miss Lee will be ready to stop working by now and there's plenty of supper.'

'I – I already had something to eat.'

Susan looked at him. She studied his face as though she knew he was concealing something there. He didn't want to look at her.

'Susan, I can't marry you.' He said it in a rush because he didn't know any other way to say it. He was dreading it but it had to be said, so quick was best, surely.

That was all he said. Five small words to cause Susan's world to crash around her. She stared at him. He glanced quickly at her and then away, not able to meet her eyes.

'You can't marry me?' Her voice was faint. He hoped she wasn't going to pass out; that would cause even more problems. He would have to call for help and explain himself to Miss Lee.

'I've proposed to Arabella Almond and she has said yes.'

Susan still said nothing.

He walked around as though he was a visitor, pausing before various pieces of furniture, seeing none of it. He turned around and tried to look her in the eyes but he couldn't.

'I'm sorry, I really am, but you wouldn't want me to marry you, knowing that I no longer cared for you. It wouldn't work. It would just be a lie and would be no good. I thought I loved you but this is different. I have changed so much. I'm not the same person who wanted to marry you.'

Susan stood there like she was stuffed.

'I thought I'd better tell you straight away,' he said lying, to his own discomfort.

'But I asked you just the other day and you said it was all right and we should go ahead. The arrangements are made and Miss Wanless has made me the prettiest dress – '

'I'm sure you'll find plenty of places to wear it.'

He couldn't believe that he had said such a crass thing. She flinched.

'I'm sorry,' he said. He didn't look at her and then he left.

Forty-Two

It was late when Alice finished making sweets. What had become of Susan? She was usually back at the shop well before now. They had decided to have supper at nine but it was after that and there was no light in the windows across the street.

It was raining and that made the darkness fall earlier than it should have at this time of year. Being almost the end of summer, everything looked tired in the garden. She was already imagining cooler days when the sweets set so much more easily.

Alice washed and put everything away and when she was tired of waiting, she left the back door open and ventured across the empty road. It was much too soon for the men to come out of the pubs but the noise sounded as though they were having a very good time.

She went to the front door and banged on it. The day was so wet that she didn't want to go through the garden, but there was no reply. She wondered whether Dan had come by and taken Susan out but since it was raining there was nowhere to go. And they had decided on supper at home, so surely she would have brought him across the road.

It had rained so much during the past few days that the hem of her dress was soaked as she went to the back. The wet on her skirt was almost as far as her knees from brushing against the grass and shrubs at the sides of the garden path. She reached the back door, aware of the cloth sticking to her legs.

She opened it. It was never locked unless there was no one at home. Darkness held the house at bay because of the rain, which had found a sideways wind from the fells and was throwing itself at the windows. It was more like October than summer.

Alice called Susan's name but there was no reply. A small fear caught at Alice's heart. When she made her way into the kitchen, down the step from the pantry, she saw a small figure hunched over a fire that was laid but not lit. It was gloomy and the whole house was dark. Rain pounded on the roof and ran down the windows. The sound it made on the glass was usually friendly but not tonight. It threw itself sideways like an assault.

'Susan?'

Susan looked up.

'Miss Lee.'

The look on Susan's face caused Alice's heart to do horrible banging things inside her chest. Something horrible had happened, she could tell.

'What's wrong?' It occurred to Alice – and she was so ashamed she blushed at the idea – that perhaps Susan had let Dan nearer than she should have done and was having a baby. They were getting married very soon. Alice could make light of it and tell Susan that she was being much too serious. They would get through it.

'Are you coming back for supper?' she tried.

Susan spoke her name again and then she put both hands over her face.

Alice went to her, pulling up a chair beside her.

'Whatever has happened? Tell me.'

Susan didn't for a few moments but Alice waited, knowing that Susan was collecting both voice and strength.

'Dan doesn't want to marry me any more.' Susan's voice wobbled and then ceased.

Alice stared at her.

'That can't be right.'

'He came here and told me.'

Alice groped for explanation.

'He's been to the pub and has cold feet,' she offered.

Susan shook her head as though she could shake off Dan somehow.

'He's asked Miss Almond to marry him and she has said yes.'

Alice's throat constricted so badly that she couldn't speak or swallow to clear it. It couldn't be true, she thought. Arabella Almond had turned down every eligible man for miles over the past ten years, she was noted for it. She would never accept a lad like Dan, who was nobody.

'He told me he's changed because he's the manager now and the Almonds like him.' Susan's voice gave up at that point and she broke into huge sobs, her breathing all over the place and her words incoherent. Her body shook with distress.

'He can't just drop you like that,' Alice said, horrified.

Susan cried so much that Alice thought she would be sick. At last Alice managed to get her across the street and into the kitchen. Unfortunately Zeb chose just that moment to come in.

'What's the matter?' he said, eyes all at once piercing.

'Nothing,' Alice said hurriedly but he could see Susan's face. 'Susan isn't feeling well and she needs to go to bed.'

'He's left me,' Susan wept. 'He's marrying Miss Almond.' And she ran away up the stairs so quickly that the bedroom door had clicked shut before Alice had taken a breath.

Alice had to make a decision and did it immediately. Susan would come to no harm upstairs but she couldn't rely on Zeb not to kill Dan. She flew to the back door and stood against it. She looked into his eyes and it took some doing. They were alight like black fire. She held his gaze.

'Come out of the way,' he said.

'I will not,' Alice said. 'I did not go to all the trouble of bringing you home for you to kill another man and let them hang you.'

'Come out of the way.'

'If you touch me, you will leave here, take your father with you and never come back. And I will never speak to you again.'

'I'm not going to kill him.'

'No, you aren't because you are staying here. This is nothing to do with you. This is not the same thing as happened to you the first time, you know it isn't.'

She was aware of Mr Bailey standing behind Zeb, his face contorted. She had not seen until then that he was crying.

'Don't you trust me?'

'I don't trust any man,' Alice said, 'and you let your temper get the better of you once. I won't let you do it again. Susan is not yours and even if you want her to be, you cannot kill a man for changing his mind. That is what he has done. Yes, people will be saying that he jilted her, but at least he changed his mind before he got married. At least he was honest.'

Zeb stood for some time.

'I don't love her like that,' he said and Alice relaxed.

'I didn't think you did. Now she will need you to help her as a friend. And you have a good job at the quarry that you have worked long and hard for so you will not make an enemy of Daniel Wearmouth. You will stay here. Promise me you will or I will guard this door all night.'

He stood there with his head down for such a long time that Alice quaked but in the end he looked straight at her and smiled.

'All right,' he said.

'You won't go out.'

'No.'

'You won't hurt him now or ever?'

'I won't hurt him.'

'Right,' Alice let go of her breath, 'then I shall go and see how Susan fares.'

Zeb did not know how long it was before he noticed that his father was in tears. He was amazed.

'Father – '

'I'm sorry, I just thought you were going to – '

'I'm sorry too. I'm sorry to have put you through such grief all these years.'

'I wasn't a good father. I wanted a son in my image. How stupid is that? You were never like me. What would be the point in life going on if we were just like our fathers? I've never forgotten how clever my own father was.'

Zeb didn't remember his grandfather.

'Did he make you feel unworthy?'

'He was too kind for that, and too clever to make anybody feel that they were less than he was, less than anybody was. I thought I would be as good as him but I wasn't. He spoke so many languages. He knew Greek and Latin and he had been to France. He was so much more intelligent than anybody else that he spent a lot of time apologising for it. At least I didn't have to do that.'

That was when his father looked at Zeb and they laughed.

*

Susan awoke and knew that something had gone wrong and then she recalled what it was. She was too tired to cry any more, her eyes ached. She wanted tea; she was thirsty. She made her way downstairs after she had put on Miss Lee's white robe and she found Zeb sitting at the fire.

'I've just made some tea,' he said and poured her a cup, strong with milk and no sugar, just as she liked it. She sat down across from him and over the kitchen fire.

'He fell in love with Arabella Almond. She is very beautiful.'

'How could he change his mind, just like that?' Zeb said.

'I don't know but he did. Everybody will talk and I will have to give up the house. I can't afford to keep it on. I've spent every penny I had on it. I had saved for years and I also spent the money that Miss Frost left me. Now I've nothing.'

He offered to make toast over the fire but she finished her tea and shook her head and went back upstairs.

Zeb did what was expected on Sunday mornings. He had become used to cooking while Miss Lee and Susan went to chapel. Miss Lee would leave the Yorkshire pudding mix to go into the oven and the vegetables already peeled to go on to the stove. At the right time he put everything on and the joint into the oven, just as Susan usually did.

Miss Lee went off with his father, putting her hand through his arm in the sweet way that she did.

He was making the gravy and worrying about whether it would work without lumps since he never did it, when they came back.

'Did Susan get up?' Alice said.

'Not since I gave her tea and then she went back to bed.'

They ate.

Alice watched him carefully. She had the feeling that he was going to find Dan that afternoon despite what he had said and she couldn't let him.

'I'm going for a walk,' he announced as soon as they had finished.

'Why don't you take your father with you?' Alice suggested. 'It'll do him good to get out.' She smiled serenely so that Zeb had no choice but to take his father with him.

Susan didn't come back downstairs. At teatime Alice took tea and cake and spoke to her but Susan didn't move and when Alice went back much later it had not been touched.

Alice still lived in hope. She imagined Dan rethinking his new relationship and coming back, begging for a second chance. And although Susan would be offended, she would take him and be grateful. Alice was not given to cursing but she wanted to do a lot of it as Susan lay silent by her side, saying nothing, barely moving and rarely sleeping. She understood why Zeb wanted to kill Dan.

She also thought of herself left here with Zeb and his father if Susan did marry. It was enough to turn a decent woman's stomach. Yet Zeb had offered to leave with his father and she had turned him down. That week when he was paid he gave her all of it and she did not refuse.

The following day was Monday and Alice made sure that she was up before Zeb. She made up the food for him to take and spoke softly to him.

'You will be careful? I don't care how you feel about this, it's Susan's problem. She will need both of us so if you do anything to endanger that, you are in serious trouble.'

'I promise I won't.'

He sauntered out with his lunch tin and Dan's. She had kept that right, how generous of her.

When Zeb sat down to eat, it made him remember how good Alice was. Inside the tin were sugar mice that she had made when the rain dropped the temperature and he was glad of it. She had also packed a huge piece of Victoria sponge cake, and wrapped separately were beef sandwiches, his favourite, thick with a smudge of horseradish. Alice baked most days and her favourite was a white bread made with milk instead of water. It was exquisite. It made him smile just to sit there and eat.

Another man of his age, Abraham West, came over to him when they stopped.

'Is it right about Miss Wilson and him?' Dan had become 'him' since he had been promoted.

'What?' Zeb said.

'That he's marrying the boss's daughter and has let Miss Wilson down?'

'Why don't you ask him?'

'Miss Wilson is lovely,' Abe said. 'I could get a few of the lads and – '

'No.'

'You scared?'

Zeb looked at him.

'Don't be daft, man,' he said. 'There isn't a law against changing your mind.'

'Well, there should be,' Abe said. 'She's a lovely lass. Half the lads in the dale would have loved to wed her and she chose him. And now what's happened?'

Zeb said nothing.

'Is she all right?' Abe said.

'How would you feel?'

Abe stuttered.

'I'm not a lass,' he said.

This was the truth, Zeb had to acknowledge. He half-expected Dan to have the bloody nerve to ask him up over some problem that day but it didn't happen. He had dropped off the lunch Miss Lee had made for Dan and tried not to hope that it would choke him.

Forty-Three

Mr Bailey went to the subscription library that was run by the Vernon sisters. They were gentlewomen, he knew, who had run out of money, but their father had collected books and they had a huge library in their house. They had many of John Wesley's books, which Mr Bailey knew well, as well as science, poetry, encyclopaedias, history and geography. But he realised that the main reason women went was because there were modern novels. Among these were Jane Austen's books that Mr Bailey had developed a weakness for.

They also ran the local newspaper, the *Stanhope Gazette*, and Mr Vernon, their brother, was a printer and he published the newspaper. Because their house was the kind of place where older people liked to gather, the Vernon sisters had begun putting up little tables in the library and the newspaper office. The house that their father had left them was big and here the fires were always burning when the weather was cold, and people could sit about and talk of books.

Miss Harriet had begun a book club for various ladies in the village to read and talk and it became a place for women to gather. Men had the pubs, or if they were non-drinkers, the chapel and its meetings, but gradually they came here as well. Mr Bailey discovered that he could sit there with a cup of coffee and talk for half the day. He could borrow books and socialise with other men his age and older. There was even a smoking room because Mr Vernon loved his pipe. In fine weather they would sit in the garden and in bad weather they had the back room.

The library even held the odd poetry reading and Miss Harriet would read fairy stories to the children on Saturday afternoons. It was a new place for him to become involved and before long he had offered to read to the children. He joined the book club as well, which encouraged other men to do the same.

Miss Lee provided cakes for Mr Bailey to take with him and he became very pleased about that, and grateful because he hadn't even asked her to. The other people were always so enthusiastic about her baking. On some days she provided sweets and to his chagrin, Mr Bailey had come to be glad of cold days because then she made chocolate. She would send it with him and it was exquisite. She also gave him so much cake that he was weighed down with it.

Zeb had, in an embarrassed fashion, started giving his father money each week. Mr Bailey tried to give it back to him but Zeb wouldn't take it, so Mr Bailey spent his money at the library on the newspapers and books, borrowing them for Miss Lee to read. He had grown to think of her as a daughter. And he could not forget the night she had stopped Zebediah from attacking Daniel Wearmouth.

Zeb was astonished that his father had taken to going so often to the subscription library. He was very pleased when he found out that not only was his father reading stories to the children on Saturdays but also making them up. And according to Alice, who heard all the gossip, they were well-received. Alice provided sweets for the children, which undoubtedly helped.

His father was happy, Zeb thought in amazement one warm day. He was sitting outside and even smiled now and then. The day was bright with a few high, white clouds in the blue sky. His father had stopped complaining and started enjoying himself. How strange and how lovely to feel that Miss Lee could work miracles. But then he had known that from the day she rescued him. There must be angels lower than she was and he adored her.

It was a difficult thing to admit, that he could never envisage a day without her in it, looking suspiciously at him to see whether he was going to knock somebody to the ground. She thought her sweets and cakes and dinners could mend things and they had.

Susan was still not coming downstairs. One day when Zeb was having tea and cake with Miss Lee, he asked her about it.

'Do you think we should have the doctor?'

'I'm not sure yet. I think perhaps we should wait a little while. I need to go and see the rector.'

'He probably knows. The lads at the quarry do.'

'Already?' Alice said.

Alice knew when the rector's wife opened the door that the news had travelled. She said nothing but gently led her into the study where the rector had been seated behind his desk. He came forward, hands out to clasp hers. His hands were warm and his gaze was kind.

'I know why you're here,' he said. 'I'm so very sorry. How is Miss Wilson?'

'As you can imagine.'

'I will sort things out. I think almost everybody understands.'

'How could he do it?'

The rector sighed.

'Men have their heads turned by opportunity and the chance of prosperity.'

'If he could have stayed where he was, everything would have worked out.'

'Mr Almond needed a manager and it has long been understood that Mr Wearmouth has a good grasp of quarry management. It was only a matter of time.'

'I'm so worried about her.'

'I would come if I thought it would help, but I don't want to get in the way. Have you talked to Mr Martin?' This was generous of him, Alice thought.

'Not yet.'

Alice trod up to the chapel after checking that Susan was breathing. She had eaten nothing and was drinking only water but she would do for now. Her temperature was normal, Alice thought, feeling her brow so often that she was glad Susan didn't care sufficiently to notice.

Mr Martin came forward, pale of cheek.

'Oh, Miss Lee,' he said, 'I'm so very sorry. I would have come to you but I wasn't sure of my welcome. Clergymen can be so intrusive in such times but I will come gladly if you think I can be of any help.'

Alice thanked him but didn't say that he should come to the house. They were both right, at the moment. She went home and Susan was in bed. Alice thought again of the doctor but did nothing. Even Mr Bailey seemed concerned.

'Is she going to be all right?' he said.

'I'm sure she will be in time.'

'I could read to her – '

'When she is well enough to come downstairs that would be lovely,' Alice said.

Forty-Four

Mr Almond called his daughter into the study.

'So you want to marry him?' he said as she sat down.

Arabella hesitated and said nothing and he thought, yes, she has fallen in love but she doesn't want to displease you.

'You mustn't marry unless you please,' he managed, 'and if you don't want to, say so. You can stay here with us always.'

'I want him,' she said, with a resigned sigh.

'But still, a quarryman?'

'You were a quarryman and Mama married you. He is terribly attractive and you have said yourself that he has a great deal to offer at the quarry. If he is that good, you and Mother could take some time away and do all those things you've always wanted to. You won't refuse?'

'Would you like a house for yourselves?'

'I don't really care for such things.'

'Does he?'

'He loves it here,' she said with a smile.

When Mr Almond told his wife that he wanted a small wedding, she sighed.

'I think you're right. Why make a fuss? They'll be married in

Stanhope and that will be embarrassing enough. Let's do it in a very discreet way so that it doesn't bother anyone too much.'

'Arabella says they will be happy living here but do you think I should buy them a house? Both of them say they don't care.'

'It would be nice for us not to lose her,' his wife said.

'He's running the quarry and no doubt will eventually manage without us, so we can go abroad for a few weeks if you so choose, my dear.'

'Really?' His wife's face brightened. 'I would like that.'

Dan couldn't sleep. The quarrymen looked sideways at him as though for twopence they would pitch him into the bottom for what he had done. He blamed himself. He wished he had approached Susan differently; he wished he had never set eyes on Arabella Almond. But then he went to the house and the same wonderful feeling of well-being, so new, enveloped him like a dream.

'Papa says he can afford a house for us but I wondered very much if you would mind living here,' she said.

He was amazed.

'Why would I mind? It's a lovely house.'

'Really? I thought that perhaps you would like to be just you and me.'

'If you want that – '

'I don't want to leave my parents but for you I would,' she said and because they were alone in the summerhouse, he took her into his arms. It was even better than before.

'Besides,' she said later, 'my father is convinced you could probably manage without him for a few weeks and he is going to take my mother to Italy the minute we are married. It's years since they went anywhere.'

Mrs Almond therefore shone on him like a sunbeam. Although they talked about the wedding, it was the trip to Italy she most cared about. She had never been to Florence or Venice or Rome and now her husband was taking time off and they were going to stay in beautiful hotels.

Arabella and Dan would go away after the wedding but only for a few days. Her parents would be going after that and they agreed it would be wonderful to have the house to themselves and the late autumn in which to enjoy it.

Dan liked that there were gardeners at the house. He liked the servants, even though he couldn't meet their eyes. They had been friends or were known to him. There was a cook, a parlourmaid, a kitchenmaid, and Arabella's own maid. She had nothing to do but follow the gardeners around asking for flowers for the house and then she would read and sit outside. Sometimes she chose to pot a few plants and when the weather was inclement she sat and watched from the conservatory.

Sometimes they had tea outside and after a couple of weeks Arabella turned to Dan.

'My mother thinks you should move in here now. After all, you can't be comfortable at the hostel.'

Dan was grateful and so pleased. He was given an enormous bedroom, not near hers, and he was aware of the distinction. He must behave properly. He had a huge, feather bed and his clothes were always laundered. In the evenings when he came home, he and Arabella would sit in the shade and drink champagne, cool from an ice bucket. He would change for dinner and the dinner was always good. They dined with white cloths and silver cutlery and her father insisted on giving him the very best wine. Mr Almond liked claret and then port and there were vegetables from the garden and it was the best time of the year for such things. Trout were taken from the Wear and there was plenty of lamb.

Her parents were so kind. Dan couldn't think how he had ever got to this wonderful place where he was so well thought of. He went to work each day and did everything he could for the quarry because it had given him all he ever wanted.

Dan and Arabella were married at the end of October. He had stopped having nightmares that Zeb would come for him, though he had no reason to suspect he would. Zeb was polite and helpful and Dan was relieved.

After the wedding Dan and Arabella went to Hexham and there he had his bride to himself. The evening was warm and the windows were open to the square that made up the marketplace just beside the abbey. Arabella came out from her dressing room wearing a thin, light garment, which showed the contours of her body.

He had to remind himself that they were married, that he could lust over her as much as he wanted and that he could have her. He couldn't believe that he could ever have such a woman. She stood outside on the balcony. It was quiet and there was no one about. She turned to him.

'You haven't undressed.'

'I'm not sure what to do.'

'Neither am I, but if you come over here, I can help.' She undressed him and he slid off the flimsy robe she wore and they went to bed naked. He loved how immodest she was, how she laughed and gave herself so readily. They drank chilled champagne – he might never grow used to it – and she was as insatiable as he was for touch and feel and kisses.

Forty-Five

Susan sat in the back garden watching Zeb work on the day of Dan and Arabella's wedding. He didn't often do it – there wasn't much to do – but she thought he enjoyed it. She liked just sitting there. His father would sit with her and read or offer an occasional comment or doze.

She had stopped eating and sleeping. The doctor had shaken his head. Alice had had to fight with Susan to allow the doctor to come but he had been so kind, sitting on the bed and speaking softly to her. Alice sat in a chair nearby, trying to smile.

Alice followed the doctor downstairs.

'What can I do?' she begged.

'Young people usually recover from such things. Try not to worry too much.'

Alice offered to pay him and he shook his head.

'What, after all the wonderful sweets we have had from you?'

'I will send you more.'

'Miss Lee, you are paid up for a very long time ahead. I will come back in a few days but if you are worried at all send for me,' he said and off he went.

Alice begged Susan to eat but when she did, she was sick almost straight away. She could keep down nothing but plain water. The shadows under her eyes were nearly black and her gaze was dull. She did not come to the table for her meals; she stayed upstairs. It was all she could do to get out of bed when she had to use the pot beneath it.

Alice tried to coax her down the stairs and for the first three weeks she made no progress. Susan was very thin; her bones stuck out everywhere. Then came the day when the house across the road was rented by someone else. Susan was supposed to go and get her things but it seemed pointless to ask her. And Alice didn't want to leave her.

'What shall we do?' she asked Zeb. 'We don't have room for more furniture here.'

'Why don't I go and talk to the couple and see if they want any of the stuff? Maybe I could get back some of Susan's money.'

Alice knew that he was right so she let him go. He did very well and got all of Susan's money back. Alice told Susan but Susan didn't react so she took the money to the bank opposite the rectory on the main street and deposited it in Susan's depleted account.

The house across the street was let to a young couple with one child and the wife was openly pregnant with another. How it must have hurt Susan, Alice thought. It even hurt Alice, and she had had nothing to hope for other than her friend's happiness.

She didn't tell Susan of the wedding day but somehow Susan knew. She came down and sat in the garden and they all sat with her. They needed to somehow. It was a glorious October day.

Susan sat there, tiny and shrivelled, holding a blanket around her. Even though the sun was bright, she could not keep warm. She drank the tea that Alice brought her but she did not eat the cake. Alice had made every sort of cake she could think of to tempt Susan's appetite as well as chocolate since the evenings were cool. She made it just for Susan but Susan couldn't eat and stared endlessly at the wall.

By five o' clock Susan was weary and went to bed. Dan was married. Zeb and Alice and Mr Bailey had sat in the garden with her and they didn't eat the cake either; they just drank tea.

'They say you don't die of a broken heart but I think she might,' Alice said. 'I've never seen anybody take on so. I don't know what more to do. It must be so hard to have the person you loved do so well without you. What is that about? There's no justice.'

Forty-Six

'I want to stay in bed with you for the rest of my life,' Dan told his bride.

'May we have something to eat?'

'Anything you wish for.'

The food came to the bedroom and there they stayed. After all he had been through with his father and mother, he finally felt as though his life was turning around. The windows were open and there was now a cooling breeze.

Arabella was everything he had ever wanted a woman to be. She was passionate, she adored him, she was kind and funny and beautiful. Her lips were sweet and her body was soft and yielding and she wanted him as much as he wanted her.

He could not have had a bride who was more matched to him than this gorgeous woman who was his. He had been right to marry her, despite what he felt for Susan Wilson. He would always feel guilty about that but it was the better path that he trod.

Five days later they went reluctantly back to Weardale. Arabella's parents were going away in less than a week so he must go to the quarry and get back to work.

On the first day he stayed there until the usual hour and went back to the house. It was full of trunks for her parents' journey. He could barely wait and neither could she and soon they were waving them away from the door. They went almost mischievously back into the house, which was theirs for weeks and weeks.

Forty-Seven

It was the first of December when Susan finally made her way downstairs and collapsed into a heap on the back-room floor. Zeb ran toward her but he wasn't fast enough. He picked her up and put her on to the sofa and there Alice revived her with cold water. When she opened her eyes, she said, 'Will you make me some toast, please? I'm hungry.'

Alice didn't think she had ever heard a more beautiful sentence. She made herself go carefully. She toasted bread over the fire and put just a scraping of butter on it. Susan ate two slices, had a cup of tea, and then Zeb carried her back upstairs to bed.

Alice kept leaving the shop when there was no custom and creeping upstairs but Susan was sleeping. Often Mr Bailey was there – watching over her, he said – but he often nodded off and would wake when Alice came into the room. But still she was glad of him there. At midday Alice made potato, leek and carrot soup and took it upstairs and Susan ate it all. Alice was triumphant. That evening Susan ate some dinner.

The following day she was exhausted and ate nothing, but the day after that she tried again. And then she began to get better. It was a slow process but Alice thanked God every night that Susan was recovering. The doctor called in and declared that there would soon be roses in Susan's cheeks. All that winter Susan slept but she ate three meals almost every day.

Mr Bailey had taken to reading novels aloud to her. Zeb was amazed at his father. He had never read a novel in his life before he came here. But Susan liked the sound of the older man's voice and would lie there with her eyes shut and an almost-smile on her face. He did funny voices for her and it brought a choke into Zeb's throat because it was exactly what his father had done when he was very small, entertaining him.

Zeb didn't understand where it had gone wrong in his upbringing. Now it was too late but Susan was benefiting from it. Zeb had never thought about it before, but his father had a wonderful voice, so good for preaching, so lilting for reading such as he was doing now, and he didn't tire. If there were amusing parts in the book he made her laugh. To keep the serious bits light, he had only to read in a strange voice and she still laughed. It was the best thing for her, Alice said.

Alice thought they might enjoy Christmas after all. Zeb was making good money and so was the shop. The weather was soft and Alice was happy at work. She went back to see to Susan every so often, probably more than she needed to, and Susan was now up and dressed and sitting over the fire with a book. She was nodding in the afternoons but Alice could see an improvement every few days.

Zeb had begun playing cards with Susan again. Alice didn't care for such things herself but she liked to sit and watch them. She liked it even better when they played draughts and chess. Susan seemed to have the right kind of mind and could beat him every time.

Mr Bailey said nothing nor tried to take part, but that was

another memory for Zeb because his father had taught him these games. Zeb had the feeling his father had let him win at them when he was very small.

One day the week before Christmas, when Alice was feeling particularly light-hearted, old Mrs Asquith, who lived on the edge of the village and had been alone for so long that she loved chatting whenever she had the opportunity, came into the sweet shop for chocolate for Christmas.

'Did you hear the news from the big house?' she asked.

The big house was Ash House. Alice didn't want to talk about anything to do with the family but Mrs Asquith was unstoppable. She was also somewhat deaf so it didn't matter what you said, she got on with what she had to say.

'Daniel Wearmouth's bride is with child.'

Alice could only hope that Susan did not hear but Mrs Asquith, like a lot of deaf people, shouted. Alice got rid of her as quickly as she could. There were two customers after her in the queue, it being almost Christmas and busy, so it was several minutes before she could go into the back. She knew by then that the damage was done.

Susan wasn't crying; she was just sitting, whey-faced over the fire, Mr Bailey beside her but sensibly saying nothing. When Alice came in, he went down the yard, or pretended that he had to – she didn't know which but was grateful either way.

'It could be a mistake,' Alice said. 'It does seem awfully early to me for her to be sure of anything.'

'Miss Frost used to say that some women just feel different, even after a month.'

'I'm so sorry if it's true,' Alice said.

'Why wouldn't she be having a baby?'

It was far too soon, Alice thought again, trying to convince herself. Perhaps the news was wrong and had been put about by gossips.

She heard the shop bell tinkle just then and they both rose to answer it.

It was only when Susan went early to bed that Alice could talk to Zeb, softly because the ceiling was wooden.

'It's common knowledge,' he said.

Alice didn't think she could go into the intricacy of these things with a man, however close they were, so she said nothing. She was just grateful that Mr Bailey had a nice habit of going to sleep early in the evenings. Or maybe he just pretended to – she felt he did that a lot, and she was beginning to love his tact – even though he might hear everything. She didn't care, she was happy as long as he said nothing and he was very good at this. Perhaps hardship had taught him that he should do better, as it had taught them all.

Forty-Eight

Dan was so excited. He couldn't believe that his wife was having his child. The baby would be born in August. Mrs Almond told him that summer could be difficult for pregnant women, carrying a baby in the heat

Arabella was not excited and he couldn't blame her. First of all she was sick, not just in the mornings but all day and sometimes all night, and she was weary. She spent a lot of time in bed so in a way he lost his wife and he regretted it. Though what else he could have done, he had no idea.

Eating dinner without her was hard though her parents did their best. Coming back to the quiet house was hard too. He could not complain but he found it difficult that she was so ill. He summoned the doctor – not the local doctor, he couldn't face that – a doctor from Hexham that his father and mother-in-law told him was good. He was glad they were now at home because he was so worried. When they came back, it took some of the responsibility from his shoulders, but it did not make him feel better. The doctor said nothing was wrong that he could tell.

Dan now slept across the hall from his wife because she was hot and restless and did not want him there. No, that was not fair; she would want him had she been well. But she could not bear anybody near her while she felt so sick.

After the sickness, she began to feel better and he rejoiced. Her parents seemed ten years younger and Mrs Almond said that if he thought Arabella was up to it, they would have a party. He said that he hoped she would be.

Arabella was all for the idea of parties and they slept in the same room again and ate the same food. He was very careful with her in bed, though.

'For goodness' sake, I do want you, you know,' she said impatiently one night.

'I'm worried about the baby.'

'You don't need to be; he'll be fine. You are always so careful and caring. I do love you so very much.'

Dan laughed.

'I don't think I ever lived until I found you,' he said and then he made love to her very carefully. He heard the sounds in her throat, slight, but there to tell him how welcome he was.

'Arabella, you are everything that I have ever wanted,' he said and she told him that she had never been happier.

Dan could go to the quarry now with her father and show him how much things had come on and Mr Almond admired his work. He was the better for having taken his wife to Italy and pleased that the quarry was making money without him. Dan was so grateful that Mr Almond was generous enough to give him the credit for what he had done while they were away. From then on, Dan thought that Mr Almond kept back a little so that Dan would take the lead in everything they did. His confidence grew and the quarry did better and better.

Dan went back to his loving wife and his parents-in-law every evening. His wife was still slender and kind and they were so obviously pleased with how he was running the quarry. He couldn't believe it. He hadn't known he had any talents in business; he just worked hard.

Sometimes, when his wife slept, he would get up and push back the curtains and gaze at how beautiful she was. He could not believe how his luck had changed. She was his and he lived this wonderful life where his every need was met. He had managed to keep the quarry going better than he would ever have thought he could.

He got down on his knees and thanked God for having given him such blessings. He was grateful that he was here and he had his wife. It would be good when they had a child.

Arabella slept long and deeply. Often he slept in the bedroom across the hall when he could bear to because it was not fair that he might disturb her. He went to work and was happy there. He was glad that the weather was so mild because a great many quarrymen went back to lead mining if the weather was too harsh, although lead mining was not doing as well as it had. So he was pleased that the men stayed. He insisted on paying them more, though Mr Almond was unsure. But Dan thought that the more they were paid, the better they would work. Why would any man work more for not being paid?

Also he and Zeb had opened another house for the men because they wanted all of them in decent clean accommodation. Although the quarry had mostly subsidized it so far, Mr Almond baulked at paying for all of it so a great many of the men stayed in the hostel instead. The food was bad and the beds were dirty but it was much cheaper and most sent their wages back home to Northumberland and the Scottish border. Zeb complained bitterly to Dan about it, but Dan didn't like to say any more. He had won better wages for the men and now they must wait.

Forty-Nine

Arabella began to get fat, so she said.

'Oh, look at me,' she begged, gazing hopelessly at herself in the big, wide mirror in their room.

He couldn't see the difference.

'You've never looked so beautiful.'

'You are a bloody liar.'

He liked the way that his wife was given to cursing in such a polite tone; it sounded humorous. He did like how she looked but he could tell that she didn't believe him and the change came so rapidly. She went from being her usual slender self to being clumsy, as she called it, in a matter of days. Also it affected her in other ways. Her moods were low. If it rained, she sat over the fire. If it was fine, she complained that she was too hot and as Mrs Almond had forecast the fine weather started early and went on getting hotter and hotter.

It occurred to Dan that if they had been ordinary people and she had had to work she might have been a little better off. But she didn't have to do anything she didn't want to do. She wished he would come home sooner and then she wanted him to have days off. That spring he worked every day and began coming home to a discontented, red-faced harpy whom he did not recognise. His mother-in-law was very kind.

'It's only for a short time, be good to her. She is in great discomfort.'

'You went through this.'

'We had no money then and I had no leisure to lament my condition,' she said. 'I was terrified that we would starve. I had to go out cleaning because we were so badly off. I don't talk of it now, Mr Almond gets upset, but I remember because otherwise I would take things for granted as Arabella is able to.'

It didn't help that the weather was searing. The farmers rejoiced because the lambs were born into sunshine and were soon dry and skipping about the fields. Then the farmers complained about the lack of rain for the growing crops.

Dan loved Arabella's parents as he had never loved his own. He was ashamed of it. His parents had done their best but he thought he would be eternally grateful that Arabella's parents had let him marry her. They had accepted him freely into their family and he was happier now than he had ever been.

Arabella noticed his good mood even though by early summer she was 'as big as a house end', she complained. She was so grateful when there were thunderstorms. She would sit with the doors of the orangery open and tell him how grateful she was.

'I can't wait for this child to be born and I will never let you near me again,' she said.

'Yes, you will.'

'Dan, you won't be disappointed if it isn't a boy?'

She looked so anxious that he laughed.

'Why would I care?'

'That is what marks you out as a workman,' she said, 'and I am so thankful for it.'

He kissed her.

'I don't care whether it's a boy or a girl so long as you are both well,' he said. He didn't say to her that he couldn't sleep for worrying about work and his wife and the whole place so that he was continually exhausted. But every day he still went down among the men so that at least they knew he was there and not hiding in the office away from them.

That was how he thought of it. Hiding in there. He wouldn't hide. Yes, he had let Susan Wilson down, but wasn't it better than marrying her when he loved another woman? He wished he could have gone to see her, to be reassured that she had recovered. He could tell just by the set of Zeb's face that she was ill, even after his marriage. And why wouldn't she be? All her hopes were gone.

He tried not to go into the village but when he had to, he avoided looking at the house across the road from the sweet shop where they had thought to be so happy. He caught a glimpse of a man and his wife and two children coming out of the house and he remembered the last time he had been there and how cruel he had been to her. How horrible and stupid and hurtful. He heard nothing of her and had nobody to ask. He looked at the sweet shop and just hoped that Miss Lee was looking after her. There was no way in which he could put this right. He would live with his guilt always.

Arabella found everything so difficult right from the beginning that he hoped the baby would be born soon. She was huge and her ankles had swollen to an enormous size and her eyes displayed her tiredness, with great bags beneath them. After the sickness left her and her body began to change shape, she was pale and listless and became more and more tired. He begged her to call the doctor but she insisted there was nothing wrong with her. He appealed to Mrs Almond.

'I'm not happy about it but she won't have the doctor here.'

'Is it usual for women to be this size?'

'Everybody is different.'

Dan was so worried that they called the doctor in and he said that she must rest completely now. During the last few weeks before the baby was due to be born, Arabella must not get out of bed unless she needed to. Dan prayed that the baby would be born soon. Arabella was suffering so much and the weather was so hot.

Two days later, halfway through the afternoon, a boy came with a written message from his mother-in-law. All it said was, 'Come home.'

He went there with as much speed as his panic would allow. When he bounded into the house and reached the upstairs, Arabella was lying on the bed slick and crimson with sweat and fatigue. She smiled at him.

'I knew it would be all right, if you were here,' and then she closed her eyes.

He went on looking down at her, knowing that she would open her eyes and his world would be normal and everything would be all right, but she didn't. He hadn't noticed before then that the doctor stood there, ashen-faced and narrow-eyed with disappointment and despair. Dan had known Dr McKenna all his life.

'I'm so sorry, Dan,' he said. 'It was the childbed fever. I'm afraid it's very common.'

'But it can't have happened so quickly. It can't have.'

The doctor said nothing but only shook his head.

It was only then that Dan saw the nurse and the baby in her

arms. He stared. The child had survived and his wife had died? He turned away from the nurse and he could see Dr McKenna motion her out of the room. Then he went out himself and left Dan to the howling and despair and rage of his grief.

Dan sat there with his wife's body and never wanted to move. He couldn't believe she could have been taken from him with such speed.

He wanted to go back in time, to when they were talking about baby names. He wanted to go back even further to their wedding night, and before that to the night he had kissed her, when he had asked her to marry him. He had known then that Susan Wilson had been a first love but Arabella had been the love that took his heart.

He gazed down at her. The problem was that she was not there and he could see it instantly. The soul, if that was what you called it, had already gone.

Mrs Almond had more sense than to try to comfort him, neither could she find comfort for herself or her husband. Why was it that when they were poor, she had been able to give her husband a daughter, but when Dan and Arabella had tried for a child, she died and it was all over? She could not believe that her only child had died giving birth. It was too cruel.

Dan felt that if he could just sleep, he could go back and none of this would be true. But the trouble was that the nightmare went on and on and he was in it and could not escape. There would be no waking up from this.

It seemed to him that the child screamed from the moment that Arabella died and he could not bear it. He told the nurse to take it away and when she did nothing but stare at him with the baby in her arms, he shouted at her to get out of the room with it. At that moment Mrs Almond came in.

'What on earth is going on?' she said.

'I want that thing out of my house,' Dan said hoarsely. 'She's dead because of it.'

Mrs Almond looked at him.

'You're overwrought,' she said.

Dan glared at her.

'I want it out. Do you understand me?'

'Dan – '

'Get out with it.'

Mrs Almond took the baby and went from the room without another word. She was very worried now. She was grieving that her child had died and so suddenly and now there was this extra responsibility. She knew that if she did not find somebody to feed the little boy he wouldn't survive for long.

Pat and Shirley's third child, born on the same day as Arabella's, was stillborn. It was also a boy. Pat knew why it had happened: his wife had far too much to do dealing with ill parents and he was off his feet for so long when he broke his ankle. The two small children ran her ragged. He was not surprised when the baby didn't make it.

Shirley wept.

'I so much wanted to give you a son,' she said.

He understood that. They had two lovely, little girls and dearly would have liked a boy even though they knew that the whole thing was stupid.

'Never mind, Shirley,' he said, sitting down on the bed and taking her into his arms. Dr McKenna had said that Shirley would be all right and as far as Pat was concerned, that was the most important thing of all.

Dr McKenna had come straight from the big house and by the looks of things it hadn't gone well there. His face was pale and sweaty and his eyes were dull. He was so obviously relieved that Shirley lived even though the boy had died. Pat followed him on to the landing.

'I'm so sorry, Patrick,' the doctor said, and Pat managed a smile.

'You did your best and at least she's still here.'

That was when Dr McKenna hesitated.

'Mrs Wearmouth?' Pat ventured.

The doctor shook his head. Pat was stunned. It had never occurred to him that Dan Wearmouth could have problems like the rest of the world now that he was so high and mighty.

'And the baby?'

'It's a boy. It won't last long without its mother,' Dr McKenna said. He left and Pat hoped he was going home for some rest.

Pat went back into the bedroom. His wife was sitting up and looking extremely alert considering what she had just been through.

'What was it that Dr McKenna said?'

'Nothing.'

'Yes, he did. What was it?'

So Pat, wishing his wife had less sharp hearing, told her.

'Go and offer to take the baby,' she said.

Pat didn't look at her.

'Did you hear me, Patrick?'

She only called him Patrick when she was very angry and since now she was upset as well, she was not easy to deal with. Pat didn't answer.

'Don't be like that,' she said.

'He wouldn't help us when we were having a bad time.'

'And so you'd have his baby suffer? Where will they find somebody to take it?'

Pat got off the bed. He walked out of the room but as he closed the door, he heard Shirley getting out of bed. He went back inside.

'The doctor said you are to stay there.'

She glared at him.

'Then go down and offer as I told you to. Right now, I mean it, Pat. Don't you come back here without the bairn.'

'That is not our problem,' Pat said and his wife stared.

'My God and you brought up a good Catholic. Everybody's problem is ours and this child will not die while we can keep it alive.'

'We're not doing it!' Pat yelled and he slammed outside, following the doctor who was just getting on to his horse.

Fifty

Dr McKenna came to the sweet shop. He had never done so before as directly as this and Alice thought he looked more tired than she had ever seen him. Luckily the place was empty and she and Susan were both there.

'May I see you for a moment, Miss Lee?' he asked, very softly, and he went up the vennel, bag in hand. She went into the back and let him in.

'Are you ill, sir?' she asked kindly.

'No, no, Miss Lee, there's nothing wrong with me but I need help and I don't know who else to talk to.'

Alice was astonished. Dr McKenna's lovely wife, Iris, had died almost a year ago. It was something he needed to consult a woman about, then. She was flattered and rather pleased that he came to her but she didn't think he looked well. He worked too hard; he did too much. His children were grown up and married and they had children too, but still he went on. Though there was no other doctor, so perhaps he felt as if he had no choice.

'Sit down.'

'I am breaking confidences here but I feel I must do so. Mrs Wearmouth's child has survived but she has died – '

'Oh no, oh, how awful.'

'Yes, but there is more. Mrs McFadden has lost her child. She will be well soon and the Almonds will need someone to look after the Wearmouth child.' He hesitated.

'Surely she would help,' Alice said.

'It's her husband, I fear. He doesn't want her to. Will you go to the quarry and talk to him?'

'Me?'

'Somebody has to. He wouldn't listen; he strode away like all the devils in hell were after him. I know of no one else at this time able to help in this way. Will you try?'

'To talk to a man about such things?'

'Please?'

Alice agreed and told the doctor to go home and rest and he smiled and nodded and went off. His horse was waiting patiently outside but he was so tired that he didn't even climb back on to it. He took hold of the reins and walked home.

Alice knew Pat vaguely, as she knew most of the quarrymen. She had never had cause to go to the quarry before and she didn't relish this but she knew that somebody must do something. And she was not involved as the others were: she had never borne or lost a child. Did that make it better or worse?

She set off and then changed her mind and changed her mind again. But within a few minutes she steadied her resolve and went to Ash House. She was led inside. There Mrs Almond sat with a howling baby in her arms.

'Oh, Miss Lee,' she said, 'see what we have come to. I don't know what to do. Daniel seems to have lost his mind over my daughter's death and Mr Almond has become ill and the doctor has sent him to bed. Daniel is trying to make me get rid of the baby.'

'I heard from the doctor.'

Alice never remembered how tiny babies were. She felt sure that mothers didn't feel like that when they were giving birth but now as Mrs Almond put the child into her arms, she felt his warmth and saw his tiny fists and his screwed-up face and knew how badly he needed his mother.

'Would you let me try to find him help?'

Mrs Almond looked old for the first time that Alice could remember.

'I don't see what you can do,' she said.

Alice could hear Dan's voice loud from a room nearby and though she would have liked to remonstrate with him, she knew how dearly he had loved Arabella and what he had given up for her. It was not the time.

'The doctor says that Mrs McFadden has lost her baby and that Mr McFadden won't let her take this one, but he must.'

'He doesn't get on with Daniel; I know he doesn't. Daniel is always saying so. I worry that if this baby leaves the house, he may never come back because Dan won't have it. He's behaving like the master here and my husband is too ill to do anything.'

'Mr McFadden resents Daniel for the way that he reacted when they needed help but Zeb Bailey helped them. I think he will listen to me now. Let me try. I know you're worried about what will happen but this child needs sustenance now so we can think about the rest later. Don't you think so?'

Mrs Almond gave her the baby and the carriage and Alice went off in style to the quarry. When she got as near as she could, she got down and carried the baby to the office.

There Zeb stared at her but he said nothing.

'I need you to call Mr McFadden in here,' she said as she explained.

'He won't do it.'

'I need you to call him in here,' she said again, not looking at him.

'You aren't supposed to know about that.'

'Get him in here,' she repeated, and this time she held his gaze. He threw Mr Paterson a glance and went off.

Mr Paterson merely shook his head and invited her to take a shabby chair.

It could not have been a long time but as the child went on crying for nourishment and its mother, she became more and more anxious. Zeb came in with Pat McFadden. Alice knew Pat as the most popular and well-tempered man in the village but she quailed before him now. She had forgotten how big he was, how sharp-eyed, and how when he didn't choose to be good-natured he could be hard to deal with. Only she hadn't had to deal with him before.

He was angry. He had not only lost his child but now he was being asked to take in the son of a man he did not like or respect. His role in his home was being questioned and he was proud, as all men were of such things. Alice couldn't think of anything to say. The baby screamed harder and his tiny fists clenched and unclenched.

She sat there as Pat stood before her, looking very tall and sturdy. His mouth was set in a hard line and his eyes were almost burning with temper.

'I know what you think you are doing here,' Pat told her, 'but you mistake your man, Miss Lee.'

Alice didn't care.

'The child will die without help,' she said, as the baby was obliged to take a breath between his screams.

'I'm not having it in my house, not after what Dan did to us. So don't come here with your clever ideas – '

Zeb stepped forward as though to say something but Alice held him with her gaze.

Pat fell silent and his head went down. Alice realised he was grieving for his own son and he wanted nothing to do with this one. She knew now that she had to win this, that she had to talk Pat into it, that the child's whole life depended on her powers of persuasion. Pat was a proud man.

'Please, Mr McFadden, help him. He's only a few hours old. He won't live without you. Does it matter whose son he is? Please help him.'

Pat choked.

'I've got no son,' he said.

'You have a wife and two beautiful daughters. Does your wife not care to do this? If she has refused, then – '

'She didn't refuse. I refused. I'm the man in my house, unlike a lot of other places where women won't be told,' and he glared at her. Normally she would have given him what for, but this was different. She needed to succeed here whatever it took. So she said nothing.

'When we were in a bad way, he wouldn't help us,' Pat said.

'But you did have help,' she said and she looked pointedly at Zeb and then back at Pat.

Pat threw Zeb the kind of look that would have felled him had he been that way given. Zeb ignored him.

'Zeb helped you,' Alice said when neither of them spoke. 'He kept you when nobody else would, you and your family and your parents, and now you can pay him back with this, even if neither of you thinks it a good idea.'

'The one has nothing to do with the other,' Pat said.

Zeb looked down at his feet but after a few seconds he spoke. 'Go on, Pat.' That was all, as though he was half-ashamed to be there, and didn't want to have to beg another man to take yet another man's child. Especially when neither of them wanted to be involved.

Pat started to say something and then he looked sideways at the wall, as though there was a lovely painting hanging there.

'Do you think my Shirley would feed a bairn like that and then give it up to a man we despise?'

'It's not for him,' Alice said. 'Men's quarrels aren't worth a baby's life.'

'There'll be another way around it, there'll be some lass – '

'Is that what Mrs McFadden said?' Alice persevered.

Pat turned aside, but it wasn't that he didn't care, it was just that he didn't want anyone to see the emotion on his face.

'Our bairn died and we have to take in his?'

'Your Shirley would take it, wouldn't she? Are you going to go home and face her and tell her that you refused this baby, that you refused to let her help a small child when her own had died? Are you going to go back there and do that? What kind of man will she think you are then?'

Nobody spoke.

'What kind of a man will you be in your house if you do such a thing? Is that what the master in your house looks like?'

Nobody said anything and the baby screamed and screamed until Alice wanted to scream too. How stupid men were, they cared about things that didn't matter.

Pat sighed and then he glanced just slightly at the baby. He took a deep breath.

'All right then, I'll talk to Shirley. But if that bastard offers me money, I will kill him.'

So Pat got into the carriage in all his quarry muck with Alice and the baby and they went on up to Pat's house. There the carriage stopped. Pat gestured for her to go forward with the baby but Alice urged him to get out and then she put the child into his arms. And so Pat carried the baby to Shirley. She must have seen him because she ran out of the house.

That was not the first time Alice wished she had a child. She felt as though he had been snatched from her. Her breasts ached. How stupid. Her arms ached for the warmth and feel of the baby. Her whole body yearned toward the way that Pat gave the tiny being into his wife's arms. It was not the first time she had felt shut out, but the hurt went all the way through her body.

'Dan lost his wife,' Susan said, eyes glazed, running through into the back room when she heard Alice come in.

Alice scanned through her memory and hoped that even when things were at their worst she had not wished that woman dead. She hadn't. She was grateful and then acknowledged that her power was hardly such that the good Lord would care for her stupidity.

When Zeb came home, rather late, Susan had gone into the front. He hesitated in the doorway.

'Miss Lee, I'm sorry I – '

'No, don't be sorry,' she said, taking his hands. She was only glad that his father was upstairs and Susan had retreated to the shop and was fussing over the shelves for something to do. 'You can't help being a man,' she said and pulled a face at him. Then she became aware that she still had hold of his hands and she let go.

'Mrs McFadden took the child straight into her arms and you were partly to thank for that. You kept them all those weeks when Mr McFadden was so poorly. Go and get changed. The supper's ready.'

Zeb put down his bait tin and went off upstairs to wash and change as he always did. When he came down, she gave him a big glass of sloe gin since it was all she had from Christmas that was strong enough to help.

He looked at it.

'It's pink,' he objected.

'Just down it,' she said and after he had, they ate and went to bed early because they were worn out.

Susan was not asleep.

'Why did she have to die?' she said.

Alice talked to her, mostly comforting nonsense about how the garden was looking and how the blackbirds were throwing the flowers out of the pots. She talked about how the fish loved the pond and the small birds were sitting on stones and drinking out of the water, continuing until Susan fell asleep. Alice could hear Zeb's footsteps in the room across the landing because he could not sleep. Alice was only grateful to fall off the cliff into unconsciousness to the rhythm of his feet. Mr Bailey's snoring had become such a comfort.

It was two weeks after that when Alice was setting off for church that Susan asked if would she mind if she came too. Alice was so astonished and pleased that she said no, of course not. They went out, arm-in-arm and in good humour, turning the corner just beyond the shop and plodding up the steep cobbles until they turned left. There just in front of them was the chapel.

It had come to represent stability for Alice and a whole lot of other things. It was imperfect, as they all were, but Mr Martin and his wife were kind and their children were always there and Alice was reassured by the way that the services went on.

She understood now about chant, about prayers, about how you needed familiar words and music and rhythm to sustain your daily life. She loved it more than ever when things had been so hard for Susan and for Zeb. She was so grateful that her religion had seen her to here. She hoped it would always be there, comforting, warm, and understanding. And she could go back to her house and her sweet shop and be thankful for all those things she had that so many people did not.

Fifty-One

When Dan awoke, he was lying on the floor in the dining room. Pale light made its way through the nearest window and he could hardly move, he felt so awful. Then he remembered that Arabella was dead and he groaned. No noise came from anywhere and he remembered the child. What had been done with the child?

He sat up. He felt sick, his head was heavy and as he got slowly to his feet, he gazed at the debris around him. Somebody had smashed the place up; there was broken crockery everywhere and shattered glasses. There was the awful smell of old brandy and the white cloth that had covered the table was half off it. The chairs were broken and even the chandelier had been abused; there were pieces of it on the table.

As he stood there the door opened tentatively and one of the maids put her head around it.

'Get out!' he yelled and the door closed promptly.

There was a bottle of brandy untouched on the sideboard. He took it and he lay back down on the floor and opened it and put it to his lips.

Mr Almond didn't come back to the quarry after his daughter died, and neither did Dan, but Zeb stayed away from the office.

It was not his job to go in there without their say-so. He was worried, though. Mr Paterson was in the office by himself and nobody was looking to see whether things were going well.

One day two of the men weren't getting on and Zeb went up to the office to ask if something could be done. They were causing disruption and disruption led to loss of work and loss of work cost money.

As he opened the office door, Mr Paterson shot towards it and blocked the entrance. He wasn't usually like this; he was too old to move that fast. Zeb stared at him.

'Is there something wrong, Mr Bailey?' Mr Paterson said. He was always polite and almost warm toward Zeb, something Zeb had not worked out. He could feel himself frowning at the man.

'The Nattrass lads are causing trouble,' Zeb said.

Mr Paterson hesitated and then he came out of the office and closed the door behind him.

'It'll have to wait,' he said, looking anywhere but at Zeb.

Zeb looked hard at him. He knew something was the matter and it wouldn't get him anywhere if he didn't sort this out.

'Why don't you deal with it?' Mr Paterson suggested.

'I don't have authority here.'

Mr Paterson hesitated and then he looked back, as though the door had opened behind him.

'Come in,' he said wearily, as though he had carried the burden alone for too long, and he opened the door wide.

Zeb stared. Dan was face down on the desk. Zeb didn't even know he was there. Arabella had been dead for two weeks and he had seen nothing of either Dan or Mr Almond.

'What's the matter with him?'

'He's drunk.'

'What?'

'He gets drunk every day now. Sometimes he stays all night and when he doesn't, he comes in early with a bottle and is asleep by eight. Mr Almond is poorly and I can't do everything myself. I know folk think badly of him but we have a quarry to run, or two hundred men will be out of work. Now can you settle it yourself? I don't like to ask but he thinks well of you and I've got nobody else. I can't run this place on my own.'

'The men know who I am.'

'You're the explosions man. That's the hardest job in the quarry outside of this office and you've got plenty of ability. I've seen you in here often. I know you got fed up of Mr Wearmouth, but he's having a really bad time here. He thinks the boss is dying. You don't tell anybody that, do you hear?'

'All right, I'll try,' Zeb said.

'And you need to come and be in the office.'

'I don't know what I'm doing in the office without Daniel.'

'Well, somebody has to be here,' Mr Paterson said.

The two men who had quarrelled were brothers. They had always worked together but this time they had fallen out. Zeb guessed it was about a woman.

Their father, who had died several years since, had a small farm between Stanhope and Eastgate, down by the river about half a mile away from Stanhope. It was already getting dark by the time Zeb set off, on a nasty night that was cloudy and spitting rain. The last thing he wanted was to have to go there and tackle two lads on Dan's behalf, but he had said he would do it so he did.

The road curved once it left Stanhope and went into a big bend, with a house here and there. On the right the road turned up past Greenfoot toward Rookhope, a steep climb. There the wind blew sideways into him and he could barely stand up.

There was very little light but the farm was sideways across the edge of the field so that he could see it before he reached it. The track down from the road was muddy and he almost fell into it. The place seemed a hell of a lot further than the half-mile Mr Paterson had told him it would be and he cursed Dan as he banged on the door. For a long while nothing happened. He hammered twice more before the bolts were shot back and the key was turned. There stood a young woman with a child hiding against her skirts.

He had expected one or other of the lads to open the door. He told her who he was and then the younger lad, Kenny, came to the door.

'What do you want?' he said, glaring.

'Mr Wearmouth sent me.'

'What does he want?'

'He wants to know why you haven't been at work. He won't keep your jobs for you if you aren't coming back.'

The other lad, Albert, appeared behind him.

'Let him in. It's the only way we'll get any place.'

Inside, the one-storey-high building was as low-ceilinged as it could be, to stop the wind getting anywhere near it. The builder had been clever, cutting it off from the worst of the weather as it crouched here, up from the river and low in the valley.

A big fire burned in the kitchen and there was the smell of just-eaten dinner but nobody offered him as much as a cup of tea. Neither did they ask him to sit down.

Zeb let the silence fall and grow cold before one of them, the elder one, said, 'What did he send you for?'

Zeb was losing patience.

'You thought he'd come himself?' he said, glaring back.

The girl with the child had disappeared into a far room but he could hear it wailing.

He subsided into a chair by the fire and was glad of it.

'What was it between you?' he said.

They looked at one another again.

'It was nothing,' Albert said.

'Can you afford to stop working? How are you going to pay for things?'

'That's not your business,' Kenny said and Albert put a hand on his arm to shut him up.

'If it's nothing to do with work, then why not come back and let your problem sort itself out here?' Zeb suggested.

'It won't sort itself out,' Kenny said.

'Why not?'

Both brothers glared at him now.

'Do you think if we could have sorted it here, we would have brought it to work?' Albert said.

'If you don't make money at the quarry, what will you do?'

The child was crying harder than ever and they both gazed at the closed door that presumably led into the sitting room or maybe into a bedroom.

'You could work with other people. Mr Wearmouth has said that he will alter things if it suits you better.'

They both looked impressed with this and well they might, Zeb thought, since Dan had said nothing of the sort and never would have, even sober.

Kenny nodded at the door.

'It's her,' he said.

'What?'

'The lass, she's what we're fighting about.'

'That's not true,' his brother said, ready for combat.

'Yes, it is.'

'Just a minute,' Zeb said. 'Is she your wife or your wife?' He nodded at them separately.

'Neither,' the elder said. 'She was our brother's wife. He was older than us. He died and she was left here. The trouble is that we both care for her and neither of us can marry her. It just gets so awful between the three of us. She's such a lovely lass and she has nowhere to go.'

Zeb could only imagine the frustration. They needed to get out and find themselves wives. But living in that place with the two of them and the lass with a half-grown child, how would it ever work out?

'She likes me,' Kenny said.

Albert was too canny to say anything but he looked down and was silent.

'Do you own this place?' Zeb asked.

Albert shook his head. Zeb had thought they would not. Most of the farms up and down the valley belonged to the Oswald family who lived at the hall on the opposite side of the river from Eastgate.

'You don't have to stay here.'

They had not thought that far, he could see. Their family had probably lived here for hundreds of years; it would never occur to them to move. People got tied up to land and that was fine as long as it worked, but it was doing them a disservice now. If they could think beyond it they might prosper.

'If you come back and work it doesn't have to be like it was. You will make a lot of money; you're good workers. Mr Wearmouth said you were his best. Maybe you could afford a cottage for your brother's wife in Stanhope. There she could have the company of other women, and you could move closer into the village and go to the pub and meet the local lasses. You never know what might happen.'

Their countenances cleared. It had seemed to them that because this had been their parents' farm they could not move. It was one of the saddest things, people thinking they had to stay tied to the land because their ancestors had lived there. If it was not working they should move forward. All these lads had needed was a suggestion that they might move on. Sometimes somebody else had to give you permission to go.

As Zeb walked back, he was pleased at what he had done, until he got to the sweet shop and realised that he had not asked them if and when they would come back to work.

He went into work the following morning and Dan, looking remarkably sober though pale-faced, routed him out very early before most of the men had arrived. He called Zeb up to the office.

'Mr Paterson told me you went to see the Nattrass lads. So what happened?' and at that moment, just as though miracles did occur, Zeb could see the brothers making their way up the almost flat land in front.

'You did it?' Dan said.

'I told them you'd pay them more money.'

'You didn't.'

'Oh aye, I did,' Zeb said and he ducked out of the office.

Fifty-Two

One cold day, about noon, Zeb was set to blow a big wall. He had told the men to stand as far back as they could get because he didn't want anybody hurt. After they had retreated, he found Dan, drunk and staggering, coming to him.

'Are you going to blow this some time today or are you bloody not?'

'In a few minutes I am. Just hang on.'

'We need this as of a week since. For God's sake, let it go.'

'Not yet,' Zeb said.

'It's well-covered. You've told everybody to clear. Why isn't it ready?' and Dan reached forward and lit it. It blew before Zeb got chance to pull him out of the way to safety.

Dan should have known better. Maybe he did know but he didn't care. Zeb could tell he was frustrated with so many problems, and now that Mr Almond wasn't there because of his illness, maybe it was too much for him. Especially since his wife had died. Or maybe he just wanted to take some kind of risk, the way that some people wanted to venture beyond what was safe in their lives just to see whether they could get back. When you felt you had nothing to lose and you didn't care, that was how you behaved.

Zeb was vaguely aware that there was the most awful

God-Almighty bang and he knew then what he had known all along – that no matter how long he delayed a fuse, it was always going to cause a problem for the man or men who had lingered to light it. It was such a big fall and such a long way that every time he blew the hillside, he was not sure he would have time to get out of the way. It was always a slight risk but never like this. He calculated that here he only had so many seconds; he might not make it.

Maybe Dan was worried about Zeb lighting this particular fuse; it was more dangerous than the usual. Maybe that was why he came and pushed at him. Maybe Dan didn't want to lose his explosives man or a friend. At that moment Zeb knew that he hadn't wanted to take the responsibility by himself. Maybe he had willed Dan to come down there and blow it for him. Though his sensible self argued that if Dan had not stumbled and overreached, then the accident would never have happened. All this went through his mind as the hillside blew itself to hell and rained stones.

The men were well out of the way; Zeb had made sure of it. But all he got time to say was, 'You stupid bastard,' before the whole quarry-side caved in and he was blown sideways. He just had time to throw himself on top of Dan – who was drunk and stumbling and not clear of the fall – right before he lost consciousness.

When he came to he could taste and smell blood; it was running into his mouth. He ached and smarted but it couldn't be that bad because he was conscious. Although it hurt, it could not be that a big stone that had hit him. He was fortunate that the shower he felt was little stones that stung and pinged off his body and the earth.

He had known when he started this job that there was a chance that he would lose his life like this. But if the quarry was to survive, they needed to get stone out of there as quickly as possible, so somebody had to be the explosives man and take a risk. It was only when he lay there, amazed that he was still alive, not yet worried about Dan beneath him, that he saw how different he was now from the man who had left Durham prison. He wanted to live.

He came round and moved and then he saw Dan. He remembered that he had pulled Dan down with him, away from the heart of the explosion, and realised that if he hadn't, Dan would be dead. He was lying there unconscious. Zeb stared. A big rock had hit him on the side of the head, despite Zeb trying to protect him. It was right beside him, looking huge, and the wound on his head gushed bright, red blood.

Zeb sat there, staring, as the dust and noise cleared.

'Get Dr McKenna, somebody, quick,' he yelled and as one lad dashed away the others gathered around.

'What the hell was he doing?' Davy Hunt said. 'We could all have been bloody killed.'

'Shut up,' was all Zeb said, 'and get started on the bloody stone. This isn't a tea party. Move it!'

Somebody grumbled. Zeb got slowly to his feet. As he did so, they all melted away.

Dan wasn't moving. Zeb had seen dead men in gaol. All he could think was to feel for a pulse and he couldn't feel anything. What if Dan had done this on purpose because he couldn't stand his life without Arabella?

'Don't you die on me, you stupid bloody bastard,' Zeb told

him, but softly in case anybody should hear. If Dan gave up now they were all finished, he thought.

When the dust and noise cleared, Dan opened his eyes.

'I didn't mean to do it,' he said.

Fifty-Three

Zeb went to Ash House because Dan kept insisting he follow the doctor.

The place was enormous. Zeb couldn't imagine why on earth anybody needed such a huge house. He thought of the men crammed into the hostel despite the two new houses and it occurred to him that Mr Almond could have spent his money in better ways. Surely men who were well-fed and looked after worked better?

The doctor went with the housekeeper to see that Dan was well settled in his bedroom. Zeb wanted to leave. He hadn't wanted to come at all; it was just Dan insisting so much that Dr McKenna had said that he thought Zeb should go along if that was what it took to keep the patient quiet.

Zeb was turning to go when he heard Mrs Almond's voice ringing through the hall as she came to the bottom of the stairs.

'What are you doing still here?' like he was muck that had come in on somebody's shoes.

'Nothing, Mrs Almond, I just wanted to make sure he was all right.'

'What happened?' Mrs Almond asked and Zeb thought how much she had aged since her child had died. She was bent and skinny and her face had dropped almost to her shoulders.

'There was an accident,' Zeb said.

Zeb didn't want to tell her that her son-in-law had been drunk and stupid so he stood there with his hat in his hand and said nothing.

'Mr Wearmouth got hurt when I blew the wall.'

'Did he now?'

She had the coldest, most piercing eyes that he had ever seen.

'Was anybody else hurt?'

Zeb shook his head.

'You were,' Mrs Almond said.

Zeb was surprised.

'No, Mrs Almond.'

'There's blood on your head and on your hands.'

'I fell. Dr McKenna says it's nothing.'

'You were blown off your feet.'

'Yes, I was.'

'Why was Daniel there? Aren't you capable of doing that by yourself?'

'He wanted to help.'

'I see,' she said. 'Well, you'd better get back to work then, hadn't you?' and she turned and walked away through the hall and up the big stairs.

Fifty-Four

To say that Charles Westbrooke was pleased when Dan decided to marry Arabella Almond and not Susan would be to do him a wrong. He wasn't pleased with any of it. His feelings had started when Susan began teaching Sunday school though he had pretended to himself for quite a long time that she was nothing to him. Having sworn never to marry, never to put himself into the awful position of being squire and following his father, he was most unhappy to find that he admired Susan. He told himself that it was a stupid passing idea and that he merely admired what she was doing.

It did occur to him that she would make a very good wife for a minister but he had meant this generally because of her character. Besides which he could see that Susan – and presumably all the girls around there – admired and loved Dan, and Charles understood why. He was a very superior kind of quarryman: clever, handsome, tall and slender. He reminded Charles of his own brother, Henry, and he felt sad and then guilty because he wanted to be like that and not this slight, scholarly figure. He appreciated that he was kind and that the old ladies liked him, but it wasn't the same.

Nobody in the village knew the kind of background he came from: the country brutality – both to children and animals – the hunting and shooting, the general slaughter, the way that men got drunk in the evenings and regaled one another with hunting stories. The way that women were treated like property and bought for breeding. Had he always hated it or had his drunken, brutal father left him like that?

He cared nothing for the prosperity, the carelessness, the pride that came from owning thousands of acres, farms and horses, or for the rich countrymen who never read a book, or spoke to a child except to scold and beat. He had been afraid of his father for as long as he could remember. He would not become that man. He would stay in the church and love his God and not go near a woman.

This made him laugh after he stopped being able to put Susan from his mind. His love for her was not something high and mighty; he wanted her in his arms and in his bed. There was even a pathetic part of him that proudly wanted to show her the place that had been in his family for four hundred years. He was ashamed of himself.

He had thought that he was safe as long as Susan was engaged to marry Daniel Wearmouth but when he heard that Daniel had let her down to marry Arabella Almond he was hurt for Susan and dismayed for himself. He knew it was selfish but he had already talked himself into letting her go. He knew they would be married and he would even be polite about it, though he wasn't sure he could attend the ceremony. It wasn't usual for ministers of the church to go to one another's parishioners' weddings but here in Stanhope things were different. He was so glad to be part of this community. Yes, there were endless petty jealousies, but Susan was well-liked and everybody went to Miss Lee's shop, so they all wanted to attend her wedding.

Mr and Mrs Martin were going and the little girls were getting new dresses. In fact so many women in Stanhope were having new dresses that Miss Wanless was hard pushed to see to everybody's needs. Mrs Martin said she had taken on her niece to help her.

There was nothing better than a summer wedding and he was generous enough to wish Susan well but when Daniel Wearmouth jilted her, he wanted to go and beat him into the ground, which was exactly what his father would have done. He was very upset for her and when she became ill, he had to stop himself from doing more than enquiring about her.

He worried that she might die and then that she might live sorrowfully for the rest of her life. Mrs Martin, Ella, refused to believe this.

'Susan is very young. She will learn to love again, I'm sure. She is so pretty and pleasing, who wouldn't want to marry her. The pavements will be thick with lads ready to walk out with her.'

Susan, however, did not do this. After she got better, the only place she began to go again was the chapel and there nobody fussed. They smiled to see her and Charles was pleased, not only because she was there, but because he had had to try to take on the bigger boys and girls of the Sunday school. Mrs Martin had said Susan had no intention of facing them but attendance had gone down and very often the boys were so sullen that he felt he was wasting his time.

Willie Johnson spoke for all of them as he asked, 'When is Miss Wilson coming back?'

Even when Charles got sweets for them, they did not stay. He did not blame them. There was nothing like the countenance of such a bonny person as Susan. She was their sweet shop girl; they loved her like they loved chocolate, not seeing the difference.

After she came back to the chapel services, Charles did not dare to ask if she would help. He did not even talk to her; he merely smiled. When their paths crossed, he said how pleased he was to see her. She looked awful. She was pale and thin and her eyes were dimmed and she barely looked up. She was not ready to face the scholars. Later he was told that the children had gone into the shop, headed by Willie Johnson, and asked her if she was going to teach at the Sunday school.

Charles just wished he had been there to see it.

Willie Johnson was the biggest of the lads, which wasn't to say that he was necessarily the brightest. He either got pushed into the shop or entered first anyway, and with him were a number of older boys and girls. Susan was alone in the shop.

They had been hovering outside, she didn't know why, and when Miss Lee had been in the shop they hadn't come in. But now that the shop was empty and it was late afternoon, she could see they had timed it. In they came.

Nobody said anything. Susan stared at them. She was surprised they had money for sweets. Most of these children were from poor families; that was why she had wanted to give them sweets at chapel.

Willie was then pushed up to the counter and Susan smiled on him. She hadn't seen him in ages and her heart ached for the last time she had seen them and how happy she had been.

'Willie, how are you and how are you all?'

'We want you to come back,' Willie said in a rush, not looking at her, cheeks crimson.

'What?'

'To teach in the chapel. Mr Westbrooke is rubbish at it.'

Susan wanted to tell him not to say that but she was beginning to understand what it had cost these children to come to her.

'Even though he gives us sweets,' said Clara Hobson, 'he doesn't tell us stories the same way you do. Will you come back?'

'Will you please?' Patience Hobson said.

Susan wanted to cry. She didn't say anything.

'We know that man was horrible to you but we don't care about him. We want you to come back,' Eliza Egglestone said.

Miss Lee, unaware of all this, came into the shop and the children rushed out like they were being chased. Miss Lee stared.

'What was that about?' she said and Susan ran into the back and started to cry.

The following day, therefore, Mr Westbrooke had a visitor. When Susan told him what her mission was, he laughed and looked relieved.

'I can't tell you how pleased I am that you will do it. Willie Johnson has told me how bad I am.'

Susan started to laugh too and was pleased to do it.

'He said you were rubbish,' she said.

'I am,' Mr Westbrooke said and they laughed together.

Over the next few weeks Susan took on more and more work at the chapel and Alice was so glad of it. Susan put on weight and, as Dr McKenna had said, she began to blossom. Alice was so pleased that Daniel Wearmouth could not extinguish that light. Nobody had the right to do that to another person.

Susan was so closely involved that Ella had told Alice she didn't know what she would do without her. She was good with the little girls, she helped at the various classes, and she talked to

Mr Westbrooke for hours about what more they could do with the Sunday school and the Bible classes. Ella said they discussed Willie Johnson and one or two other souls with hilarity and respect. They were a good team.

Fifty-Five

Dan stopped drinking during the day after he caused the accident. Zeb actually took a flask off him the first day they were in the office together after Dan came back, calling him a bloody stupid bastard. Mr Paterson coughed but Zeb glared at him.

'Don't you come on like that, Bill, I can remember you cursing when I worked at the quarry when I was fourteen before you aspired to the office.'

Mr Paterson had the sense to say nothing and get on with his work in the corner.

'I wasn't going to drink it,' Dan said. 'I just need to have it.'

'No, you don't. You need to get over your bloody self,' Zeb said.

'My wife is dead.'

'Well that stuff won't bring her back,' Zeb said.

It wasn't long after this that Dan went through the village and saw Susan. He got a shock. She was so beautiful. He hadn't seen her since he had married Arabella, or at least if he had, he hadn't noticed her. It made him stop in his tracks. She didn't see him; she was talking animatedly to some short, skinny bloke in clerical garb. The thing that insulted him most was that she looked happy. She was laughing.

He tried to put it from his mind and couldn't. He kept on thinking of what she had been like and what she was like now. She had been a girl, now she was a woman. He tried not to mind her being happy and laughing because that wasn't right but he did mind.

The following day he spoke to Zeb.

'Is that the minister, the little skinny bloke who wears black?'

Zeb frowned.

'No, that's the deacon, Mr Westbrooke. Mr Martin's as tall as you, surely you remember him. He's getting fat from all the sitting down he does. Why?'

'I just saw him and wondered.'

Zeb now did the outside work at the quarry. Dan kept the office and occasionally Zeb came back in to help. The men seemed to like it better that way.

Less than a week later Dan asked Zeb how Susan was. He immediately wished he hadn't.

'What do you mean?' Zeb stared at him very hard indeed.

'I'm just asking after her.'

'Well, don't,' Zeb said.

'Is she going to marry that bloke?'

'What bloke?'

'That clergyman.'

'Don't be soft,' Zeb said.

That evening Zeb went home thinking about Susan. He went into the shop when Alice finished making the sweets. Susan, like most of the time, was up at the chapel.

'Do you think Susan's going to marry Mr Westbrooke?'

Alice looked astonished.

'Marry him?'

'Yes.'

'I have no idea. What brought this on?'

He didn't want to tell her that Dan had asked.

'Just seeing them together.'

'He'd make a lovely husband,' Alice said, considering it now.

'He would?' Zeb couldn't understand this. The man was short, plain, and did nothing but read books. He could never have done any outside work. What use would that be? And anyway, he couldn't be making any money; clerical blokes never did, like his father.

Alice stood there, considering; she moved from one foot to the other like an indecisive sparrow.

'He's kind and gentle and well-spoken. He's really good with the little children at the Sunday school and with the three girls. He's educated and he'll do well in the church and –' Alice was looking hard at him now. 'Why?'

'Nothing to do with me,' he said hastily.

'Then who?'

Zeb didn't answer. Alice stood there patiently and he knew she wouldn't let it go.

'Dan.'

Alice stared.

'He asked about her?'

'I thought that now things were different. Mr Almond is so poorly that Dan runs everything now. He stands to get the quarry so she might take him on.'

'Do you really think he would have the gall to ask her when his wife's just died?'

'He did care about her.'

'But after what he did?' Alice ran out of words. Then she said, 'You may be right. She cared very much for him and she hasn't shown any sign of liking any other lad. And nice as Charles Westbrooke is, I don't think any lass as young as Susan would look twice at him.'

'Mr Westbrooke will never make a lot of money. Dan will,' was all Zeb said.

Charles Westbrooke badly wanted to ask Susan to marry him and he was more scared than he had been of anything in his life. He was afraid that she wouldn't have him and then he thought he would never marry. He hadn't loved anybody before her and he didn't think of any woman in the same way.

Every moment he spent with her was bliss. He liked her laughter, the fleeting expressions on her face, the way that she moved and how she looked at him. He was terrified that at any moment Daniel Wearmouth would come down from that big house where he lived and the quarry where he ruled and ask her to marry him and that she would say yes.

Charles could not stop this from happening. He had seen Daniel Wearmouth in the village, passing by on a fine, grey horse, and had not failed to observe that the man looked hard at the lovely young woman Charles was talking to. It haunted him day and night even though Susan was with him every evening. Charles worried that Miss Lee must think she was making the sweets and running the shop alone, but he knew she was not like that – she would not begrudge Susan anything that brought her pleasure. And besides, Miss Lee was very fond of Mr and Mrs Martin and the children and himself and they loved her. And Miss Lee loved the chapel and everything it stood for.

She was now notorious as the woman who had come to the quarry with Dan Wearmouth's babe in her arms and taken on Pat McFadden, and there weren't many people who would do that. Pat was good-tempered but also scary and you never knew which way he would go. And yet Miss Lee had done it and she had triumphed.

She was a legend at the quarry and the men adored her. She was the chocolate woman, the sweets girl. Had there ever been danger, they would have stood around her in a circle and let no harm come to her.

Fifty-Six

Charles Westbrooke's father had gone back to Westmorland with a heart as heavy as it had ever been when Charles refused to go home. Sir Harry was so angry with his elder son. The doctor had said his heart would not hold out much longer but he could not relay this to Charles in any manner that might make him come home. He knew that now. Charles didn't care about anybody or anything related to his family or his home. His father tried not to hate him.

Henry was there when he got to the station.

'I told you to send somebody,' his father said, trying not to be pleased.

'I did. Me.'

He took his father's suitcase and led him out to the pony and trap. It was just like him, so modest, his father thought, and his heart squeezed a little with joy. Henry didn't care about appearances or he would have ordered the carriage. It was difficult not to love him and God knew that Sir Harry had tried. He was angry that this boy was his second son; he wanted to love his firstborn better. But there was nothing to endear Charles to his father. What he could do for Henry was limited.

He was so glad when they came in sight of the house. There all his frustrations ceased, as they had done for as long as he could remember. He loved this long, low house with its narrow, mullioned windows. Some parts were almost a thousand years old. His family had lived here for so very long that nobody knew where they had lived before. He would have done anything to protect his land.

He was sorry his wife had given him but two children. Other men had six or seven. It was not as though he could not afford to have them, educate them, give them everything. He had been an only child and had determined to do better. He had chosen the wrong woman. He chose his livestock better than that, he reproached himself. He could have had half a dozen fine sons but for the stupid, puking woman who was so afraid of child-birth and of him. She hated him in their marriage bed. She had done right from the beginning.

He had chosen her, an earl's daughter, from among the bevy of beauties in London. She was the most admired that season and she was but eighteen. He had been determined to have her, stupidly he now thought, because every man had wanted her. And he had won.

They were married and he took her back to Westmorland. She cried when she left her mother. She cried all the way to the north. She complained about how cold it was, and she hated the darkness and the snow, the very things he loved best.

She screamed on their wedding night, begged him not to take her but he was triumphant; he had won and he was lusty. He had had no other woman in a very long time, thinking that he should be faithful to her. He felt triumph when the blood ran down her thighs; it was part of the conqueror's due. But within days of their marriage he found himself going to the girls in Penrith. After that when she tried to deny him, he was so angry that he beat and then had her.

A wife who did not like your advances was only engaging for so long. She did not want him near her once she was impregnated and he did not want to be there. He wanted her with child and that was all; he was glad to be done with her.

There were plenty of lasses who would have him and they did not cost him nearly what she had. He became impatient and because she did not want him, he did not want her. There were no more children after the two boys and three miscarriages. He hated her for all of it. After the third time she miscarried, he lost patience and pulled her out of bed by the hair and knocked her across the room. He wasn't proud of himself but he couldn't stand any more of her incompetence. It was all she had to do and she couldn't even manage that.

As the two boys grew he was horrified how like her Charles was. Charles had been named for his grandfather and Sir Harry was ready to admire the child but the first time that Charles was put on a horse he screamed in terror. His father was obliged to thrash him in the stableyard before the servants. He could not endure the humiliation of his child's fear. Worst of all, Charles was stubborn and refused to cry. It made Sir Harry dislike him even more.

Now, coming upon his home, he felt the tears spring to his eyes. Why had Henry not been his first son? Why was he this unlucky? Henry kept him engaged in conversation about the horses and dogs that his father loved so much, and about the cats that would sleep on his father's lap in the evening. Sir Harry pretended to send them outside to sleep in the stables but he never did and they kittened in the cupboards and under the beds and he loved their mewling offspring.

Dogs fawned and horses had small brains, but cats were disdainful and he could not help loving them. Every morning he would go outside in the stableyard where he poured a big vat of milk for them. They kept down the rats and the mice and earned their place in his house and at his table. They were almost sacred beings to him. Sometimes they brought in presents for him, a small vole at his feet or a half-dead mouse that would run around the room and make him smile. One time the big ginger tom dragged a dead hare in and laid it by the sitting room fire. It had made him laugh so hard that he choked over his brandy.

The best time of year for him was the autumn when the nights here in the north became long and cold and the wind screamed around this house where his ancestors knew him. Summer was always a disappointment, in spite of the way that it was better for the crops and the lambs and a lot of the creatures that depended on him, including the tenant farmers. He was generous with them, kept their rents very low so that they could bring up their families in peace and prosperity.

They each had a big garden to back and front, to grow what they chose, and they could keep pigs and hens. He would loan them money and let them pay him back when they could, if ever, because their enthusiasm improved the land and the place which had been given him. He was known to be a good master and he thought they loved him for it.

He let them shoot over his land as long as they told somebody so that there were no accidents, and they could fish in the river as often as they wanted to. When they came to the shoots as beaters in the autumn he always made sure they had big meals and that they took home pheasants, partridges, or whatever had been shot. Since they helped and were part of it, they got the spoils too. He had no poachers on his land. Nobody needed to poach.

His tenants and their families were well-looked-after. He had provided the schooling in the area and enabled their children to have time to go. No child was obliged to work on his land until he was fourteen and the girls were not just given sewing and cookery lessons. Every girl was taught to read and write and add up, just like the boys, and he provided books and chalk and boards and anything else that his teachers needed. An educated child had far more to offer the world. They did not have to go to the parish church if they didn't care to. Other landowners might look askance at this but he knew better. People who had to obey rules were less inclined to. They worshipped where they chose. He thought he was God's equal, so it didn't matter.

When his tenants married he put on wedding breakfasts, and at least twice a year, at harvest and at Christmas, there were big spreads. The children got presents and sweets and there was dancing and singing. These were his people, they were his care of duty and he loved them like a father.

As he grew nearer to home now the rain began to fall. He was glad that when they stopped beside the house and Henry helped him down from the trap that he had not far to go to be indoors. The rain was hard and cold but so welcome. He had felt parched in Weardale where his elder son was disgracing the family name. He never wanted to see Charles again.

That evening they sat over the fire. It was one of his favourite things, to sit there with his son. He was glad that one of his sons loved him and was devoted to the estate and all the people there.

Henry would match him when they drank claret and after a good dinner there was port by the fire, or more often brandy since Harry knew that Henry preferred it. Henry had a good head such as he had at that age. Henry could drink all night and hunt all day.

His father admired him for it and wished to be young again. That was just another thing he had against Charles. The lad had never been able to take his drink. He was too small, too thin, he had no muscle on his bone to absorb it. He was better off as a Methodist, born for it, goddamn him.

'Charles isn't coming home,' Sir Harry managed finally as they drank their second lot of brandy. 'He wouldn't listen though I tried to tell him I wasn't well.'

'Shall I go and see him?'

'There is no point. He won't come back. I begged him.'

Henry wouldn't meet his gaze. Sir Harry knew why. Henry loved his brother and it was commendable in some ways. Charles had been a poor son but Sir Harry was still pleased that Henry regarded his elder brother with respect. That was how it was meant to be. Family mattered beyond anything and the going on of it, the passing of the estate down from father to son, was the most enduring thing of all.

'He as much as told me that he would never marry. I don't think he's a real man at all. He cares too much for religion and as far as I can judge, has never looked at a woman in the whole of his life,' Sir Harry said, disgusted.

Henry said nothing to this and the log fire sparkled and crackled.

'So you must marry and soon,' he said. 'We must have an heir and it's clear that Charles won't provide it.'

Henry gazed at him but said nothing.

'I will invite people here and then we will have a grand ball in Penrith. You are the catch of the county. We will find you a wife.'

Henry still said nothing but they had drunk quite a lot of brandy and soon after that they went to bed. Sir Harry stood in front of his bedroom fire with the rest of the brandy in his glass and he thought, yes, this could be rescued by his younger son. The line would go on in the way that he wanted it to.

*

Perhaps it was the memory of Daniel Wearmouth, so tall and elegant on his horse, that spurred Charles on to think seriously about asking Susan to marry him. He wanted to marry her but he had no experience of women beyond his mother, the servants and the local families.

When his parents had entertained he had tried to keep out of the way, but then none of the women had admired him. He was so physically imperfect that they slighted him. He would have liked not to have cared. Women did not respect him, they respected his money and his rank, but he was not fooled and went nowhere near them.

The trouble was that he did care now very much and the more he thought about asking Susan Wilson to marry him the more afraid he was.

He tried not to look into the mirror. When he had to, he looked himself straight in the eyes and the rest of the time he tried to forget his body. But the trouble was that his body had now decided to trouble him; he could not stop thinking about what it would be like when he took Susan Wilson into his arms and asked her to be his bride.

Fifty-Seven

Dan had not intended to go into the sweet shop but then again perhaps he had because he waited until he saw Miss Lee go into the back before he walked inside. It smelled as it always had, of chocolate and daydreams. Susan was not looking up, fussing with some of the sweets, but when she did and saw who it was, her face carefully rearranged itself until she was professional. She smiled.

'Mr Wearmouth,' she said, 'how lovely to see you.'

'Miss Wilson,' was all Daniel managed. He had almost forgotten her name and wasn't sure he could remember his own.

'I thought I would – I thought I might buy some peppermints.'

'Peppermints?' Susan repeated the word as though she had never heard of the sweet.

'Yes, for – for Mrs Almond.'

'Oh, right. Only she usually likes chocolate.'

'She has a cough,' Dan said, lying frantically, 'and says that only peppermint will help.'

'Miss Lee swears by peppermint oil but I'm sure the sweets will help.'

Susan weighed them out, screwing up her eyes at the scales and then putting the peppermints, a quarter as she told him, into a little white bag and twisting the top to keep the sweets safe. She told him how much it was and somehow Dan found the money to give her and then he hurried from the shop, sweat dripping into his eyes.

Alice came back into the shop at that point.

'What did he want?' she said.

'Peppermint creams, apparently.'

'How odd.'

'For Mrs Almond. He says she has a cough.'

'Cream won't help,' Alice said. 'Are you all right?'

Susan looked at her, eyes large and frank.

'I don't think I love him any more. There are a great many better men in the world, Miss Lee, don't you think?'

'I suppose so, but he is tall and handsome and rich.'

'I'm not sure I care for such things now,' Susan said. She said nothing for a few moments but when nobody came into the shop Susan turned to Alice once again.

'Do you think that Mr Westbrooke likes me?'

Alice was surprised and yet not; Susan spent most of her free time at the chapel. And yet Mr Westbrooke was as different from Dan as any man could be.

'I haven't seen you together enough to say. Do you like him?'

Susan nodded gravely.

'Not as I liked Dan, it's nothing to do with that. He's so clever and kind and he looks after people and he's just so nice to me. He doesn't go on and on about himself like most men do and Dan always did. I couldn't help how I felt about Dan. This is different.'

Dan went back to Ash House where his father-in-law had almost stopped coming downstairs, he was so ill. Dr McKenna was there most days and Mrs Almond had said to him that he must run the quarry without her husband. Dan could have told her that he had been running it with Zeb's help without her husband most of the time for months but he didn't.

Mrs Almond didn't have dinner with him so Dan was left alone. It was this time of day that he thought most about Arabella and how much he missed her. But now his mind strayed back to what a fool he had made of himself in the sweet shop and how beautiful Susan had become. He did not regret Arabella; he just knew that he couldn't love anybody like that again. But Susan would make a good wife and she would appreciate how important he was now.

He knew he had behaved like an idiot but he didn't think she had noticed or cared. She was probably just glad he had gone in. He should call by and ask her to go for a walk with him, or better still he might take her to the house. He thought Mrs Almond would not object – how could she – but he would talk to her first.

That evening when she was about to go upstairs to see to her husband, he stopped her in the hall.

'Mrs Almond, I wondered whether you would mind very much if I thought about marrying again. I know it isn't long but I miss Arabella so much. I'm sorry if it looks awful but I have nobody.'

'I understand,' she said stiffly.

'I wouldn't necessarily have to bring her here. I know how much Arabella meant to you. I could take a little house in the village and not bother you and I would work very hard.'

'You have someone in mind?' she asked coolly.

'Yes, the girl I was going to marry, Susan Wilson. I haven't done anything about it. I didn't want to upset you and Mr Almond when he is so unwell.'

'Perhaps we can talk about it another time,' she said.

'Yes, I know, I just didn't want you to hear talk and be upset.'

'I shall be on my guard,' she said and went off back upstairs.

When she ventured into her husband's bedroom he was awake.

'Did I hear you and Dan talking?'

'He wants to marry Susan Wilson.'

'Much good may it do him,' Mr Almond said. He looked keenly at her. 'I don't want him to have anything, you know.'

Mrs Almond shook her head and looked down.

'Let's not pretend I'm going to get better,' he said.

'I want to. I don't want to be left on my own with nobody but Dan for company.'

'He'll be moving out, regardless,' her husband said. 'It's all arranged.'

She stared at him.

'You can't blame Daniel for what happened to Arabella.'

'I don't want him owning my quarry, and he's the kind of man who would try to take everything. After I die I want him out, him and Zeb Bailey. They are clever young men but there are other men I can find to take over. I have already put the wheels in motion. There is an experienced quarryman called Bernard Lennox who operates out of Durham.'

'You haven't mentioned him.'

'He knows what is happening and he will help you. I've long since been in touch with him.'

'I didn't know you'd arranged anything.'

'Did you think I was going to go and leave you to the wolves?' he said and that was when she burst into tears.

When she went to bed that night, Mrs Almond was comforted. Her husband had made provision as she should have known he would, and in the end Arabella's child would inherit everything.

Fifty-Eight

The ball in Penrith had been a great success, Sir Harry could see. He was pleased with himself. He had gone to a lot of trouble that season to make sure that his son saw as many eligible young women as it was possible for him to see. He should have his choice. His pedigree was flawless and the money was huge. Nobody would turn down Henry Westbrooke.

People came to stay and there were many dinners and he did his very best to entertain. That autumn they were never alone. He wasn't sure whether Henry appreciated it. He was difficult to fathom. He was not withdrawn like his elder brother had been – he was always courteous and able to speak on any given topic – but he didn't always seem present. Though he did dance with every young woman; he was such a good dancer.

After the ball in Penrith they were asked to many similar occasions. Sir Harry kept telling himself that it was important for the estate and that what he was doing now would bear wonderful fruit. They stood it together and he went to bed at night and was pleased. His elder son may be pathetic and would never have a child, but Henry would do all those things that were expected of him.

Lady Catherine Boldon was the most beautiful girl in the area. Sir Harry worried about her beauty, thinking she would be like his wife, until he met her and saw that she was not. She was confident and worldly. She was dark-eyed and pale-skinned and made him wish he was still young and could put his hands about her slender waist. She had breasts so milky-coloured and round that it left him dry-mouthed. Best of all she was rich and Henry liked her.

Her parents smiled on him and came over and said that their children made a pretty pair. Sir Harry was so proud. He took her father aside and said that his first son was a waste of time and would not marry. He had taken to religion. He implied that his son had become a priest – which he didn't think was far from the truth – and while there was shock on the other man's face, it ensured that Henry would have a great opportunity here. He could tell that this girl liked his son very much. Their first son would be Sir Harry's natural heir.

It was very late indeed when they got home from that ball, almost morning, but he could not go to bed without telling Henry how pleased he was with him and with this girl. She was obviously waiting for him to make an offer for her. He could not understand why Henry seemed unaware of this.

'You danced with her twice.'

'Three times,' Henry said.

Sir Harry could not help but see his hesitancy.

'Does that mean nothing to you?' he said.

'We like one another. I've known her so long, she's like a sister to me.'

'She's what?' his father said.

Henry, face closed now, seemed to understand that this would not do. He was about to amend what he had said but his father got there first. Henry already knew how generous his father was to him always.

'Is there some other woman you would rather have?' his father said. 'If there is and she has face and fortune, let me hear it.'

'No, sir, there's nobody.'

'Then let us leave it that you will offer for her?'

'Yes, sir,' Henry said.

'Is there something you aren't telling me?'

Henry didn't reply. His father hesitated.

'I don't want to push you into this. If you loved a kitchenmaid, she shall be the next lady here.' He smiled but his son did not respond.

'No, sir, there is no one else and of course I shall offer for her.'

Sir Harry didn't know what else to say but he could not help feeling disappointment. He wanted his son to marry but he also wanted him to be happy.

Lady Catherine was pleased to see Henry, he could tell. She came forward straight away and smiled on him. She was so beautiful and he asked her to marry him. He didn't remember the words or the day or the time, or even which room in her home they were in; he just felt sick all the way through it. She looked so pleased, as though relieved, and as though she loved him.

'Oh, Henry,' she said, 'I have been holding off other men. I'm sorry to be conceited but I wanted you and I have waited for you to ask me for so long.' She kissed him, though only briefly because it was more than she should have done.

He tried not to think of marriage, of how he would have to go to bed with her. She was very beautiful and he tried to persuade himself that it would be just what he wanted, but he knew after the kiss that it would not be.

He wanted his brother to come back, to come home so that he

should not have to do this, to face taking on the elder brother's role. He didn't want to do it; he didn't want to be there. He began to imagine what it would be like when he was dead. It seemed so cosy. No more worries, no more trying to please his father when he could remember his mother screaming under blows and how Charles had always tried to defend her. He knew how many beatings Charles had endured trying to defend his mother and his little brother. He hated how their father called Charles weak when Charles would have died to protect them.

No wonder Charles had left. Henry knew that he would do almost anything so that his brother did not have to come home and bear how his father hated him, despised him, got drunk and called him names. He would humiliate himself because he could no longer let Charles be hurt. Henry could bear being at home; his father loved him. He could stand it, for Charles' and for his mother's sake. His father adored him.

Henry wanted to call Charles selfish for having gone away, but he could have left, too. Charles had offered to take his younger brother with him but Henry didn't want to leave this land. He cleaved to it, but it had become obvious to him that he did not want to cleave to a woman. He did not want to leave an heir sufficiently so that he could lie with his wife.

This wonderful country was his. He had wanted it his whole life but now he couldn't see straight any more. If he could have stayed here and not married and not had to father a son everything would have been all right. He had not realised until now that he had waited and waited for Charles to marry. But then perhaps Charles felt like he did, and though he might admire and like women, he didn't want one.

Catherine was the kind of girl who cared what a man looked like and how he sat a horse. She loved hunting.

There was nothing wrong with that, it was one thing they had in common, but he could not imagine what it would be like when they were married and he had to bring her home. He could not think of being tied to her for the rest of his life. It shouldn't have mattered. He had few friends so he ought to have been glad of the companionship but somehow he was not.

She was pleasing to him. She did everything she could. She was kind to the servants; she was affectionate to his father. It was obvious to him by now that she had been honest: she loved him – perhaps had always loved him – and now she didn't have to hide her feelings. She would be his wife.

They went about a lot together and he was glad not to have to go to places he didn't wish to go to. She said that she didn't care for company, either, and wouldn't it be wonderful when they were married and could stay at home over the fire together.

'We'll have to live with my father,' he said, grimacing, and Catherine laughed.

'I can handle him,' she said, 'you need have no fear, my love.' And she was so good that he thought he might manage this.

His life with Catherine would be full of good things. She always approved of everything he said and everything he did. She loved to go riding with him and she admired him in the hunting field. She loved his horses and she liked nothing better than to come home at the end of the day and then, bathed and dressed, to come down to dinner and discuss the hunting.

He loved this too and as the time drew nearer for them to marry, he began to be glad that he had chosen her – or as she laughingly said, she had chosen him. His father and her parents were so glad of it. Her fortune was equal to his; she was the match for him. His father, Henry dared say, had never been happier.

That winter she and her parents stayed at Westbrooke Hall and there was dancing and feasts. He loved the music and the way she was always by his side. She drank wine and in privacy, sometimes brandy.

She and her parents and many friends came to celebrate her birthday. That night, when everybody had gone to bed, Henry and Catherine took brandy to his bedchamber and sat over the fire, giggling.

There was always a decanter in the room. She should not have been there but that was part of the fun. And since they had become engaged, people did not seem to expect as much propriety. They would soon be married. They were allowed out together but there were always a great many people about, either at the hunt or at the various dinners and dances, so they spent little time alone. Now they had sneaked away and they sat before his fire in the bedchamber that had been his for years.

It was huge and the great, roaring, log fire was always lit except in summer. It was his favourite room. She had never been in it before.

'Oh Henry,' she said, gazing around her, 'will this be ours?'

He had not thought of it.

'I didn't mean to say that,' she said, and he could see her blushes, even in the firelight. 'Of course we will have a room each as people do, but it's just that I like this room. It speaks to me of you. I am glad you allowed me here even if it is just for a few minutes. Though I ought to go very soon.'

They sat over the fire and talked about the hunting and their favourite horses and they drank more brandy and giggled and then she kissed him or he kissed her. He could never remember afterwards. He had never been touched before by anyone and her mouth was sweet and her body solid and well-rounded from hunting and dancing. Her face glowed apricot by firelight.

He liked how his hands found the fastenings on her clothes and how she was equally adept at helping him undress until they were naked and rolling around on the bed. He was unable to stop himself and she didn't help him to stop. Her giggling was like music. He thought he would never forget it.

He liked being close against her in the cold night. Even with the fire, the room was old and big and wide and full of whistling draughts. Even not knowing what to do, his body still guided him towards her. And even though he was appalled at what was happening, his body drove him forward and into her and she cried out at the invasion. It was pain but also something much more exciting. She was whimpering with desire and the more he drove into her, the more she whimpered, until it was a long note, all together. It spurred him on so that he put himself further and further into her body and when the climax came he was astonished, pleased, grateful, happy, joyful and satisfied with himself. Like a tom cat, he thought afterward. When he was spent, he came out of her body and turned slightly away, shocked and not knowing what to think. She called him her love and told him how wonderful he was and how wonderful she felt.

'Oh Henry,' she said, 'I will make you the best wife that a man ever had, I promise you.'

The bed was sticky and messy and so was the lower half of his body and he wanted to get out and wash. When she slept, which she seemed to almost straight away, he got up and went across the room and found the water that had been left for him. It was cool rather than cold and there was a flannel and a big towel. He washed almost brutally to get rid of the feel and taste of her. All he felt now was disgust that he had let himself do such a thing, and resentment against her that she had not gone to her own room when she should have. He towelled off his body and sat by the dying fire. From time to time he watched her but she was sleeping so deeply that she was aware of nothing.

So this was it. This was the big secret of men and women getting together. You let your body get out of control and do things you never thought possible – and in his case, never imagined real – and that was all it was. He couldn't sleep. He couldn't get back into the messy bed somehow. It made him feel nothing but revulsion.

She was not a neat sleeper. She turned over and over, like somebody who has always slept alone. He too had always slept alone and she was taking up a great deal of room in his bed that had always been for him only. He felt as though the room and the bed now held secrets about him and she was a part of the bed and the secrets and the room.

He wished she would wake up and go to her own room and he could be left in peace to think about what had happened but she went on sleeping. He went on watching her until the morning came and she awoke. He got out of the room at that point because she held out her arms to him and he didn't want to be there. He had already dressed; he made an excuse and walked away.

After breakfast she managed to take him aside.

'You are all right, aren't you?'

'Of course. Why wouldn't I be? I have you. I was just surprised. Having you to love will take some getting used to.'

He was lying to her now but she didn't seem to know it. She smiled and kissed him and her eyes were full of love.

He felt as if he could not breathe while she was still there. After she and her family had gone later that day, his father clapped him on the back and said to him, 'Good thing you're marrying her soon. She's ripe for the plucking.' And he went off, sniggering.

Henry needed to get away. His father understood, teased him a little about cards and wenches, but all he wanted was room and quiet. He had endured a solid fortnight of regret and hatred for himself and for Catherine and he could stand no more. The inn that he frequented at Shap was an obvious place but it was only five miles away from the estate so Henry went there. He liked being away, even just for a night, and the inn was good. They gave him brandy and water, meat and cheese, and a fire if the weather was bad. He sat over it and looked back at what he had and was pleased that he had endured it.

He listened to the men playing dominoes and darts. He liked the sound of their voices, the old men who had nothing better to do. They did not bother him; they knew he was a Westbrooke of Westbrooke Hall and respected his privacy. He liked it that way. Then one evening, two young men were staying and they asked him if they could sit by the fire with him. He was so pleased with their company that he allowed it.

They made him laugh. They talked of various hunting stories the year before and of how they had gone home for Christmas and of their houses in London and their clubs. He was dazzled by them. After a great deal of brandy, he parted company with them, thanked them for the evening and staggered upstairs.

It was not long before they followed him. They came into his room and gently stripped him and touched him. When they offered to stop, he begged them to go on and so they pleasured him over and over. He heard himself whimper and keen so that they would go on with their hands and their mouths. He knew that he had what he wanted, and for the first time in his life, his body was satisfied.

The three of them slept naked but when he awoke in the late morning with the sunshine streaming past his curtains, he was disappointed. They were not there. Hastily he put on clothes and went downstairs, thinking they might be eating breakfast.

Here he tried to appear casual but upon enquiry he found that the gentlemen had gone. He was afraid then that they might tell people what they had done and what he had done and what he was. He couldn't eat or drink. He slunk back to Westbrooke Hall and there he remained for many days, afraid that somebody should find out.

It was a month before he realised that it had been nothing to them, that they too had enjoyed it and that he owed nobody anything. It was nowhere near as big as he had thought; to them it didn't matter, to him it mattered more than anything ever had before. That was when he broke down.

He saw that he could never love a woman. He had not understood it before now. He longed for their touch, he wanted another man, anybody who would take him and pleasure him and be there in the light for him such as they had not been. But there was no one.

He lay among his twisted sheets and wanted to cry aloud in his disgust at himself and his horror of what he had done. He could never be Westbrooke of Westbrooke Hall; he did not deserve it. He couldn't marry and be the squire here. It would be dishonest and wrong and he felt nothing but disgust for the woman he was meant to marry.

After that he thought he should write to his brother and tell him what had happened but he was too ashamed to do it.

Charles would try to understand but as far as he knew, Charles had no idea what it was to crave what you should not want; to be so guilty, so against God that you did dreadful things in order to satisfy your body.

He told himself that Charles was just as unnatural as he was because Charles didn't seem to want a woman, either. Maybe Charles was like he was; maybe their parents had brought this upon them. He could ask Charles nothing.

When Henry went hunting he was more reckless than he had ever been. He enjoyed the feeling of being able to control how dangerous he made things. Nothing mattered now. He had gone beyond the point where he could be redeemed. He liked jumping the fences that were too big, time after time. He could never be what his father wanted. He could not face the person that he had become.

Day after day he risked all and came back feeling triumphant. Each day he cheated death until he had no fear left to him. He would regale his father with hunting stories such as he had never done before. His father loved to hear them, looked so proud of him. His father thought there was a future with Catherine and Henry and they would carry on the line, just as his father had wanted him to do. Night after night they sat about the table eating and drinking before moving over to the fire, drinking brandy until his father nodded off to sleep.

Henry then sat there on his own wishing things were different but he could not put from his mind the ecstasy of the young men's bodies, how he had screamed with want and begged and cried and then moaned in pleasure. How they had laughed and then lay down to sleep all together like puppies. It was the happiest night that he had ever known and yet it had ruined him. He could not forget that they had left him. They had not thought it anything important. And so he had gone home and tried to quiet his body and get it ready for marriage. At first it seemed there might be a way round it but he also could not forget how Catherine's body had nauseated him. Was he to be condemned to a lifetime of her?

Henry hated himself more each day until he could hardly bear the light. He stopped sleeping and so the nights too became endless and black. The day that he missed clearing the ditch he knew he should not have attempted it. He couldn't remember the last sleep he had had; even brandy didn't get him there any more. When he did sleep, his nightmares woke him in terror, though it was less terror than not being able to sleep at all.

Somehow missing the ditch as he hunted was such a small thing compared to all the other things in his life that were beyond his ability and his love. He felt sorry for the horse because even as he pushed it forward, he knew it was too much. He felt the horse pause, sensing it couldn't manage the jump. But because of the way that Henry had – perhaps deliberately – set the course, it went anyway.

It occurred to him that he and the horse would end up dead together and that wouldn't be so bad, would it? But it would be his fault. He felt guilt but that wouldn't last, he knew. He would not have to lie there blaming himself for long, in this semi-conscious state where he felt nothing. Maybe in paradise – if horses were allowed there – his beautiful steed would forgive him. As for the rest, he didn't care. It was so much easier not to fight on any more.

The water was cold and the cries shrill. The horse screamed. Oh God, would he never be forgiven for having taken it with him? He was too selfish, he didn't deserve such an animal. He didn't deserve to exist. He had so much wanted to be the man who could love Catherine. He had wanted to be the son that his father had been so proud of. But it was not going to happen and in his despair he saw it and knew that this was the end. Charles was so far away. He had got free and now Henry too would be free.

He would not have to fail in front of his father. He would not have to live up to anything any more. He would not have to relive hiding under the table or behind the furniture while Charles held him close and his mother screamed and screamed. Only at Charles' shoulder could he subdue the cries that would have brought their father's wrath down on them. Sometimes when his mother had been beaten to the floor and lay there quite still, his father would drag his brother from him and knock Charles down again and again until he too did not get up. Henry tried to make himself invisible during those times. Now he really would be and what a relief it was.

Henry had been only just conscious when the doctor reached him. It was as well they knew one another. Henry even managed to smile.

'Ah, Dr Philips,' he said. 'Is my horse all right?'

'He scrambled up the side,' the doctor said, lying despite the fact that Henry had heard the horse's screams.

'Useless beggar,' Henry said.

'It was doubtless all your fault,' the doctor told him gently.

'It was,' Henry said.

*

'My son is dead?' Sir Harry didn't understand.

'I'm afraid so. He broke his neck. The horse had to be destroyed, of course, but it was nobody's fault. It was too far a jump and the ground was so wet with the weather we've had lately that the horse lost its footing.'

'My son died in a ditch?'

The doctor coughed.

'I don't think he knew much about it.'

'Are you sure?'

'Certain,' the doctor lied.

Fifty-Nine

Charles had been glad to receive a letter from his father telling him that Henry was to marry. His father made much of the fact that the young woman was beautiful and rich and Charles dared say that she was. He remembered her, though he thought she had been nothing beyond a spoiled and wilful child.

He had the awful feeling that his father might have talked his brother into this. Since Charles had shown no signs of marriage, Henry must produce the heir. Carrying on the bloodline was the most important thing; it had long since been drummed into them. He had always hated the idea.

It was early afternoon now and he was coming back from visiting some of the poorest people in the village. He saw old women mostly, who had nothing and whose husbands had died. Some women had young children and their husbands had left them. All of them had little.

It was always women who bore the brunt of it, he thought. He was making his way back up the lane from the main street when he heard a cry behind him. As he turned, he saw a young man coming towards him and there was something about his gait that Charles remembered.

It was one of his father's trusted men, Joseph Galway. But as the man drew nearer, Charles realised that it was not Mr Galway, his father's lawyer, it was his son, Jack. He was also a lawyer. Charles and Jack were the same age and had played together as children.

Charles stared. If his father had sent Jack there, then something was very much the matter. He let Jack walk all the way toward him, and although it was not far up the lane, it felt like an hour before they were near enough to greet one another.

'Jack,' he said softly. The other man bowed and his face was very pale.

'Sir.'

Nobody said anything else but Charles motioned in the direction of the manse. He took Jack in and invited him to sit down in the study since Mr Martin was not about. He asked Jane for food and drink and then he turned and tried to smile at his old friend.

'Is it my father?'

'No, sir.'

'You don't have to call me "sir". We're not at Westbrooke Hall, you know, Jack.'

Jack said nothing but lost his breath and caught at it again. To Charles' dismay, he sobbed for a moment before collecting himself. It was as though he had been on the road a long time and had contained himself too far.

Charles said nothing more. Jane came in with a huge beef sandwich and some ginger beer. She always found what people needed. Charles nodded his thanks but he doubted his friend could eat.

He went to the sideboard and got out big glasses and poured brandy into both. He thrust one glass at Jack and bade him to take it. Jack swallowed the brandy and coughed, the tears running down his face. He had an excuse when he choked.

'It's your – it's your brother,' he managed.

'Is he ill?'

Jack shook his head.

'He had an accident.'

'What kind of an accident?'

'Hunting.'

'He's badly hurt?'

'No, sir. He's dead.' Jack's voice gave up this time completely and he sobbed openly. The tears ran down his face like rain down a window, straight down on to his neck and inside his shirt collar where it must have pooled, tight and cold.

Charles could not imagine his brother dead, or even hurt. Henry loved hunting but he was not stupid about it. He didn't hunt his horses to exhaustion; he didn't take chances. If he was hunting all day, he had three horses at his calling and he loved them all dearly.

'What happened?'

'It was a ditch.'

'He came off in a ditch?' Charles was astonished. His brother was an accomplished rider, he knew more about horses than any man Charles had ever met.

'Aye.'

'Which horse was it?'

Jack sniffled.

'Shap's Lad.'

Charles almost smiled at that. His brother's favourite horse; he had never had a problem with it.

'They had to shoot him, his legs were broken. But we told Henry the horse had scrambled out.'

'Which ditch was it?'

'Over at Gray's well.'

'The deep one?'

'No, the other.'

'How in hell did he have a problem with that?'

'I don't know, sir.'

'Stop calling me "sir"!'

Jack turned reproachful eyes on him.

'I'm sorry,' Charles said. 'You've had to bottle up your feelings until now, knowing you had to tell me. I'm sorry, Jack. I just don't know what to say.'

They stayed silent for a little while. Charles heard the master come into the house and he left the room.

'Would you mind if I kept to the study for a little while longer, sir?' he asked Mr Martin. 'I have had grave news from home.'

'Not at all. Do you want to share it with me?'

'May I tell you later?'

'Yes, of course.' Mr Martin put a hand on his shoulder. Charles was so touched that he almost broke down. 'My father has sent a man. May he stay? He could share my room.'

'Jane will make up the bed in the blue room,' Mr Martin said. 'He shall have a fire and a good dinner. Whatever you need, you shall have for him.'

Charles nodded his thanks and went back into the study. Jack had not touched his sandwich.

'Jane will be upset if you don't eat it,' Charles said. 'She prides herself on her doorsteps.'

Jack smiled wanly.

'I will in a minute.'

'So, my brother was unhappy.'

Jack, startled, stared at him, didn't speak. Charles pursued it.

'Did he not want to marry Miss Catherine Boldon?'

'Did I say that?'

'Men make mistakes when they are miserable, isn't that so?'

Jack didn't answer.

'You aren't going to lie to me and tell me that he wanted to marry her?'

'How am I supposed to know?'

'You're a lawyer.'

'She is a lovely lady.'

'She's nothing of the kind. She's a lot more than that: she's a spoiled bitch. But she's beautiful and wealthy, isn't that right?'

'What do you want me to say?'

For a few moments Jack looked as old as his father.

'I want you to tell me the truth,' Charles insisted.

'I don't know the truth.'

'Was there another woman?'

'No. Though I don't think your father would have minded what woman Henry married as long as she cared about him and he did about her. Lady Catherine adored your brother, everybody agreed. Nothing was her fault.'

Jack was starting to recover his composure and lose his temper. Charles was glad of that.

'Then why was my brother so unhappy?'

'I said I didn't know.'

'But you do.'

'Your father sent me here but I shouldn't have to put up with this. Why should I know about your brother? He was never my friend.'

'He didn't seem to have any friends. Not real ones,' Charles said.

Jack said nothing.

'Eat your sandwich,' Charles offered and he sat there while Jack attempted to eat. Charles took a mouthful of brandy. He hadn't had brandy in years but it felt good in his mouth.

They sat before the fire as the logs fell apart. Charles was glad that rain assaulted the windows. His brother, whom he had loved so much and saved so often from his father's fists and his father's whip and his father's words, had died. He should not have been surprised. Henry – while big and handsome and socially superb, as well as a keen shot, a good rider and a skilled fisherman – was not the man his father wanted him to be. Neither of them was. No man could have been. His father thought that his sons should be gods because he imagined himself so high.

Jack gave up over the sandwich and the beer. He didn't even finish his brandy. Charles gave him five more minutes.

'So, why did my brother end up dying in a ditch?'

'I said I didn't know.'

'You're a bloody liar.'

'It happens.' Jack glared at him.

'What, when you're fit and young and know the place so well? And Shap's Lad is the best you've got? It just happens?'

Jack got to his feet.

'What do you want me to say?'

'I want you to tell me why my brother was unhappy.'

Jack faltered.

'I don't know. And you have no right to shout at me like this and expect me to tell you things that can't be told.'

Charles tried to calm himself.

'I didn't mean to shout at you. I am a minister of the Methodist church.'

'You're nothing of the sort. You're a Westbrooke through and through and you're bullying me now, just like your father would have done. You don't have any scruples. You're as big a bastard as your bloody father.'

'So tell me.'

'All right, then,' Jack said, glaring into his face. 'Your brother didn't like women. He was unnatural. He went to bed with a couple of men at the pub in Shap, even though – even though he was getting married. Maybe you're like that too, maybe that's why you ran away.'

Jack was so easy to read, Charles thought, shocked but steady. Jack wanted him to hit him; he couldn't take any more provocation. Both of them were on their feet. They stood there for what felt to him like such a long time.

'He went to bed with two men?' he finally asked.

Jack broke his gaze and nodded and broke down again. His tears chased the others down his pale, thin cheeks.

'Aye,' he said. 'Everybody knew. You can't keep owt secret. The disgrace of it all and when he was marrying.'

'And my father?'

'He wants you to come home.'

Sixty

Alice was surprised when Dr McKenna came to the sweet shop for the third time in a week. The doctor had never had a sweet tooth. Since his lovely wife, Iris, had been dead for some months and he would buy her chocolate almost every week, Alice suspected that the doctor had a sweetheart. She wouldn't say so to anybody of course, but she was pleased for him. She thought that a man such as he was a catch in the dale. And given his position of authority, he needed a capable wife. She had no doubt that the doctor had been courting.

He had a lovely house in its own grounds at the far side of the village just before the road went down to Frosterley. There he had a housekeeper, Mrs Farrell, whose husband, Fred, was a quarryman. Mrs Farrell made the meals and went to the markets and had a couple of maids to do the washing and cleaning; another man did the outside work and looked after the garden. A young lad did the heavy work, like seeing to the doctor's horse, polishing the trap, and bringing in the coal. The doctor was well-looked-after. Alice could only wonder at who the lucky woman was that invited the doctor's attention.

There was no gossip for her to go by. She heard nothing. The following Wednesday he came back in again and she greeted him cheerily just as she always did. The doctor stood in the doorway awkwardly. She thought his horse and trap must be waiting but she couldn't see anything on the road.

She said that she hoped she found him well. He replied, with a smile, that she was the only person who ever asked after his own health. Alice said she couldn't believe it. He glanced behind her as though he thought somebody might come in. She could have told him they wouldn't. Wednesday was always a slow day since all the shops shut at noon. Now it was half past eleven and Susan had gone up to the chapel to deal with something.

'Are you all right, Dr McKenna?' she asked.

'Miss Lee, I wanted to ask you something, but I didn't want anyone to overhear.'

He was going to confide in her. Most people did.

'Hold on, I was about to close for the afternoon,' she said. She did so and then she asked him through into the back room, which was always as clean and tidy as she and Susan could make it.

The stove burned bravely in there. Earlier she had made mushroom soup and it gave off a lovely smell. She always dried mushrooms; she loved picking them from the fields behind the house. For the soup all she needed was an onion, nutmeg, some water, salt and pepper, and a little cream and butter. With freshly made bread, it was a treat.

'Would you like some soup?' she offered.

'That's very kind of you,' the doctor said, 'but I think I should not.'

No doubt Mrs Farrell prepared much better meals for him. She waited. She asked him to sit down but he didn't. She wondered if he wasn't feeling well but he would hardly have come to her if he was ill.

'How can I help you?' she prompted him. The doctor flushed and didn't look at her.

'Miss Lee, you know that my wife has died, more than a year since. My daughter wants me to retire and go and live with her in Frosterley but I don't want to give up my profession.'

Alice was startled at the idea that he might even contemplate retiring. What if there was no doctor to replace him? Besides, he couldn't be more than mid-fifties.

'I'm not about to,' he said hastily and with a bit of a smile. 'I'm not that decrepit; it's just that she fusses and she has two small boys. But I'm not ready to fade into the background. Miss Lee, I have a very high regard for you and I would like to ask you to be my wife.'

Alice felt as though she had fallen down a hole in the floor and lay there, dazed.

'Me?' she finally managed.

'Well, yes. I think that you would make an excellent doctor's wife. That sounds awful, I know, but you are so good with people and considerate of their feelings. And to be fair to you, I like you very well. I really do. I can offer you a beautiful house and you would have to do no work there. And if you didn't like the house – it is, after all, the house that I took Iris to when we were first married – we could move somewhere else within the dale. I would be glad to do so. I would do everything in my power to make you happy if you would marry me. I don't need an answer now. I am amazed to have got this far. But if you would consider it, over a period of a week, perhaps, I could call on you or you could come to me then. Whatever your decision, I would accept it, of course, but remember this: I – I have thought about you day and night for so very long and I couldn't wait any longer.'

He left very swiftly, Alice thought.

Sixty-One

Charles knew that he must not linger but he could not leave without seeing Susan Wilson and so he ran down the cobbled lane toward the sweet shop. He paused to collect himself before he opened the sweet shop door, hearing the little bell tinkle. Miss Lee came out smiling and then looked surprised, because as a friend he always came to the back door.

'Mr Westbrooke,' she said.

Charles, who had hoped to see Susan, was dismayed but didn't like to show it.

'Oh,' he said. 'Is Miss Wilson not about?'

'She went to see one of her scholars at the top of Greenfoot, I believe.'

Susan, he thought with joy, was given to doing such things, even in bad weather. It was a long hard climb but she would go there to help out at any farm, any house, any village. It was one of the reasons that he loved her. But that she had chosen today made everything so very hard for him. He looked down.

'I must go back to Westmorland, I have grave family business there.'

Miss Lee looked at him and he thought that many a man had seen the sympathetic gaze and told her all his troubles.

'My brother has died,' he said. He hadn't meant to say anything but somehow the words came out.

Alice stared and then she came forward and took his hands.

'I am so sorry, Mr Westbrooke, how very dreadful for you. Is there anything I can do to help?'

Even though he said there wasn't, she brought him necessities for the journey, such as chocolate mice, cinder toffee and even Turkish delight. She said she hadn't known how to make it until recently and he must take it because it would be essential on his journey. He remembered himself sufficiently to thank her.

'You will tell Miss Wilson that I have gone and that I will come back?'

She said that she would and he went forth with his stack of goodies and the smell of chocolate in his nose.

Sixty-Two

Dan found his nerve and made his way to the sweet shop. He didn't want to be there but he didn't think he could manage alone any longer. He had to be there, he had to find some way of appealing to Susan.

He didn't hesitate. He went straight into the shop, making sure that it was the right time of day just before they closed. He had watched Miss Lee go into the back so that Susan was by herself. It was after half past five and he knew they would close at six and it was likely that nobody would call. Susan would clear up and clean and close the shop ready for the next day while Miss Lee went into the back and began the evening meal. She would see how Mr Bailey fared and then Zeb would come back from the quarry. But not yet, Dan had made sure that Zeb had work to do before he stole away. If Zeb found out what he was doing, Dan didn't know what would happen. So he made his way across the road in what small light was left and he opened the door. Susan was behind the counter. As she looked up and her eyes registered dismay, he closed the door behind him.

'Miss Wilson,' Dan said, hastily, in case he should lose his nerve again, 'I wondered whether I might come to see you. Not here but somewhere we can be alone.'

She stared at him.

'Why?' she said.

Dan took a deep breath.

'I would like to talk to you.'

'You can talk to me here.'

Her gaze was glittery, her eyes were bright, and her mouth was tight and small, an expression he had never liked. But it was no good to think of that now. Dan urged himself to speak and since it was the only chance she was going to give him, he did.

'I know that I did you a grave injury when I married Arabella, and I'm sure this must sound overbearing and insensitive, but I want to marry again. I remember how much we had together and I am sorry for what I did. I wish to spend time with you so that we could both see if it's something we could contemplate in the future.'

Dan was rather pleased with this speech. It was much more eloquent than he had thought he might manage.

She stared. He waited for her to say something. He thought she was going to slam into the back and he wouldn't dare to follow her. When she didn't say anything, he went on but his voice wasn't quite steady. He was ashamed of that. He was ashamed to be here, of his weakness. But he couldn't bear the nights alone; he couldn't bear that Arabella had died for the sake of some bloody, puking, puling child. The child had smelled; it smelled of death to him. The only good thing was that it was gone now. He didn't care where it had gone to, he hadn't even asked. It was just something else he didn't have to deal with, something that wouldn't remind him of how his wife had died. He had loved her so very much. Now he needed saving, he needed Susan to save him.

Susan didn't move and she didn't stop looking at him so he was encouraged to go on. He had rehearsed what he would say next, but it felt as though it was falling from his mouth like rotten teeth.

'I have a great deal to give you. I will inherit the quarry. I can build you a big house and take you on holiday to Paris and to Rome. I can afford to buy you fine dresses and you could have servants and jewellery. Anything, anything at all but that you will marry me. I always loved you. I'm sorry that I did you so wrong. Let us spend time together and I will prove to you that when you are my wife you will not regret it. Please, Susan, marry me; I'm so alone and I need you.'

Susan still didn't say anything. Dan went on looking into her face and hoped that he might still win the day.

'Everybody's alone, Daniel,' she said softly and after so long that he had begun to think she would say nothing at all.

'I know but we don't have to be. I could get it right this time; I know I could. Please, will you just consider it? I will try so very hard to make you happy.'

Susan stood like a statue.

'I know what I did to you – '

'Do you? I sat in the garden and listened to the church bells on your wedding day. I know that you took your bride to a lovely place after you were married. And that you lived in a beautiful house and that you were very happy and you had servants and – '

'I could give you all that.'

'And I don't believe you cared about me at all.'

Dan didn't know what to say.

'I was ambitious and she was – clever. She knew all about books and – '

'I don't know anything about books,' Susan said.

'No, well, neither do I.'

'And what about the child? Did you think another wife would take on her child?'

'No, no, the child is looked after.'

'Do you see him?'

Dan said nothing.

'So, you don't see the child that your wife died giving you and you didn't want me. But now that you are alone, you don't like it. I'm so sorry about that but I don't love you or want you any more. I'm sure that you could finds dozens of women who would marry you for your money but I'm not one of them. Now I think you had better go, because when Zeb comes home he will be very angry if he finds you here.'

'Zeb understands how I feel.'

'So you told him? And did he think it was a good idea?'

'No,' Dan said softly.

'What?'

'I said "no"!'

'Well then, I think you should go now, don't you?'

Sixty-Three

Charles did not expect Catherine's father and was surprised when the gentleman came calling, shortly after Henry was buried.

Sir Archibald had been at the funeral and Charles could vaguely remember how polite he had been to people. So many had turned up and most of them felt obliged, he knew. There were the servants who gathered outside the house, and many villagers and all the gentry from round about, so the church was packed. But he did remember seeing Sir Archibald and Catherine's white face and slender form, as much as he could tell amid the black. She stumbled and had to be supported by her parents, as though she had really cared.

So when Sir Archibald turned up at the house, Charles was surprised. He had not expected him but shook him warmly by the hand and apologised for his father's absence.

'No matter,' Sir Archibald said. 'I know that he has not been well these twelve months and more. We had thought you might come back sooner.'

It could not be seen as anything more than a reproach, gentle as it was.

Sir Archibald coughed and looked down. Charles had offered him tea or coffee. Now he rather wished he had offered him something stronger. Perhaps it was not too late. He had forgotten such niceties. He longed for Stanhope and the people and the chapel and the Martin family and most of all Susan. He wished he could run away. He could never run away now. It was strange how he thought of Stanhope as his home whereas this was really his home. And now it always would be. He tried not to think about Susan; she was far beyond his reach.

'My daughter, as you can imagine, is distraught,' Sir Archibald said.

'I'm sorry.'

'She loved your brother.'

Charles found this difficult to imagine but then he had not seen Catherine in a long time. Certainly at the church she had been a shock, tiny and bent over, leaning on her father's arm, not like the petulant, half-grown child he had remembered.

'The thing is – ' Sir Archibald didn't go on to say what the thing was. Charles waited. 'The thing is – ' Charles took a deep breath because he had the feeling that the thing was not going to be good news, '– that she must marry.'

It was assumed, Charles thought. She wouldn't get very far if she didn't marry. He waited and then he waited and then he waited a bit more. Sir Archibald stood there like a statue.

Charles went to the decanters on the sideboard that were brought in newly-filled from the kitchen every day. He hadn't known how much he was going to need things like this until recently.

'Brandy, sir?'

The man shook his head.

'Whisky, then?'

'You're very kind.'

Charles had somehow forgotten how near the border he was. He poured generous amounts of something that made his nose prickle into two glasses. He had never drunk much at all and could barely remember the taste of whisky, but he had the feeling he would need it soon, in spite of the Methodist leanings that were pulling at his conscience. He carried the glasses across. Sir Archibald took his but his hand shook so much that the whisky rolled about in the glass like gold tears. He took an enormous swig, choked, and then water filled his eyes. He didn't look at Charles.

'Would you like to sit down, sir?' Charles offered.

Sir Archibald shook his head.

'I didn't want to come here.'

'I understand how very upset you and your family must be.'

'My daughter is having a child.'

Charles stared and Sir Archibald's cheeks suffused with crimson. He had been right, he thought now; he did need a drink. He tipped the golden liquid down his throat like he was dying of thirst until the glass was empty and even then it wasn't enough. It occurred to him that he needed this. He was not strong, he was not a real Methodist, and he could not manage now. He was pathetic, just like other men who couldn't get by without the bottle.

'I think because they were betrothed that Henry thought –' Sir Archibald stopped again.

Charles' mind brought to his lips words that he had not used in a long time and had to prevent himself from uttering now.

'The wedding was all planned,' Sir Archibald said.

Charles had spent some time considering whether to come back for the wedding and now he wanted to laugh. Such a small decision and he had been unable to make it. And now Catherine Boldon was carrying the heir to the Westbrooke estate. Wouldn't it have been wonderful had Henry been alive? But of course it wouldn't, because Charles now knew that his brother did not want a woman. It would not be fair, he thought, to accuse Catherine Boldon of seducing his brother but right now he wanted to kill her.

Perhaps she had wondered about Henry's fidelity, perhaps she had been making sure of him. Perhaps she had just loved and wanted him. Why should she not? He was tall, handsome. Everyone he met loved him, except the two men who had seduced him. But that was not fair to them, either. His brother, discovering what he wanted, had allowed himself not only to sleep with the woman he was to marry but to bed two others. Perhaps the one had been caused by the other. Charles was near to resenting him; it was just as well he had loved Henry so much.

If Charles had married Susan and they had a son, then Henry and Catherine's child would not have inherited the estate. His child would have come first. If he had married Susan before coming back, then everything would have been all right. Why did he not ask her? Why had he not the courage to go to her? His dreams were shattered now.

Sir Archibald continued.

'I thought you should know. I understand the child is not the heir to the estate because they were not married. We plan to send her away to have her child and perhaps – especially if it is a girl – never to come back. But I did not want you to think that we were trying to achieve something behind your back. I have no idea as to your plans, but if you are hoping to marry, then this won't affect you. While we are ashamed at what she did, we cannot deny that there is to be a child. I won't take up any more of your time. I am sorry you have had to come home to such circumstances,' and Sir Archibald took his leave. Charles thought how very old and tired he looked as he got into the carriage and was driven away.

Sixty-Four

Two days after the doctor's visit to Alice, she received another visit in the afternoon. She had been somewhat distracted since the doctor had proposed and could not think about anything else. It was unusual for her not to know her own mind almost immediately, but this was different. Nobody had ever proposed to her before, nobody had even asked her to dance. Nobody had kissed her or held her or even suggested to her that they liked her, so it was unsurprising that her mind was a mess.

She went back and forth between the idea of being married to the doctor and the idea of turning him down and going on as she had, except of course, everything would be different. This was likely her first and last opportunity to marry, and not just anybody, but one of the cleverest, warmest men in the dale. She might even have a child. That made her lie awake at night, imagining holding her own child in her arms, living in the doctor's house, helping him with his practice and sitting over the fireside with him in the evenings, cradling his child in her arms.

She hoped the others didn't notice what she was going through. She felt that she could tell nobody because she couldn't stand anyone's advice if they dared give it; she could not tolerate anyone's opinion. She felt that she might be able to leave the sweet shop: she had been there for so long that she might tire of standing behind the counter, of making sweets in the evening, of having very little time to herself. But she thought that if she moved, everything must change.

Susan would probably keep on the shop but would Zeb and his father stay there or would they want to move? Would Susan want to be alone? Maybe Mr Westbrooke would come back and ask Susan to marry him. It was one of Alice's favourite daydreams, that Susan would be happy after all she had been through. But now Mr Westbrooke had gone and Susan was quiet. In fact, around the shop and its little house not a lot of conversation was going on.

It was mid-afternoon when the woman came to the house. Luckily Alice was alone. Susan had gone visiting some family whose child came to Sunday school, Zeb was at work and Mr Bailey was along visiting the Vernon sisters and no doubt reading the newspapers.

She had closed the shop for half an hour. She was so tired with worrying all night that she just wanted to go and sit down. She had subsided into the back room by the fire and the next thing she heard was banging on the outside door. She had dropped off to sleep, something she rarely did.

As quickly as she could, she got up and made her way to it. Outside stood a woman of about thirty with two small boys. She did not smile.

'Miss Lee, I am Edith Scott and I would like to have a few words with you if you don't mind.'

'Of course not,' Alice said. She knew exactly who the woman was. She was the doctor's only child and it could not be good that she was here.

Alice ushered her unwelcome visitor into the house. The little boys hid against their mother's skirts and when Alice asked her to sit down, she was obliged to take the smaller one on to her knee while the other slid down beside her chair.

Alice offered her tea but she shook her head.

'I'm sure you have some idea of what I am doing here and who I am. I understand that my father has offered you marriage.'

Alice could hardly do more than nod her head.

'The thing is, Miss Lee, that I am hoping that my father will retire and sell the house and come and live at Frosterley with us. This was, I thought, the general plan after my mother died. It didn't occur to me that he might marry again. We have very little money. My husband is ill and cannot work and all we have is what my father spares us. If he should marry again, I have the feeling that we could not carry on.'

'Surely he would always help you.'

Mrs Scott looked confused.

'He doesn't like my husband. He didn't want us to be married; I went against his wishes. But he is older now and I thought that if he came to live with us, we could buy a much bigger house. He is very fond of his grandchildren and I think that would be the basis on which he would come to us. He has worked very hard and gets so tired.'

Alice had heard that Mrs Scott's husband was a known idler and had married her because she was the doctor's only child and doubtless would inherit everything. Perhaps he had encouraged her to come here because he was afraid that this planned future would come to nothing.

Mrs Scott, colour high in her cheeks, said, 'If my father married again, he might have other children. You must see how my circumstances are, Miss Lee. I must appeal to you to think of my children and me and consider very carefully what you might do. My father is an old man and you are very much younger than he is. Have you thought also that he may not be able to give you a child? Because I would think – quite aside from the fact that he is so important in the area and has such a lot of money – that surely you would want a child if you were to marry.'

Alice thought she heard footsteps down by the side of the house in the vennel but she couldn't be sure. She held her breath for a few moments. It would be sadly inconvenient if any of her lodgers arrived back now but nobody opened the back door so she let go of her breath and returned to the conversation.

'Have you agreed to marry him?' Mrs Scott said.

'No, not yet.'

'Then let me beseech you to act carefully because the cost to me could be very dear.'

'I don't think your father is as old as you assume him to be.'

'He's sixty and more.'

The back door opened at that point but nobody came in so Alice could only think that it was the wind in the yard. She got up and shut it carefully.

'I will think about what you have said, of course,' she said, 'but you are not thinking about your father's happiness nor mine. Other people do have a right to such things, you know. You have a husband and children; I have none of these things. I have worked hard from a very young age because my parents were ill. To be able to have a husband and a child and a fireside is very enticing. I'm sure you must understand that.'

'Then you force me to be blunt. You are accepted here for what you do but perhaps not for the person that you are.'

'I don't understand you.'

'My father is a well-respected man here, one of the most important, and you are the illegitimate child of people quite unknown. You would be doing him a grave disservice if you married him. I think he has had his head turned by nothing more than too much chocolate. If he considered more carefully, he would not choose to marry someone like you who has neither family nor good looks.'

Alice couldn't think of a thing to say and Mrs Scott had obviously come to the end of her carefully-prepared speech. She got up and made for the door, her two little boys trailing behind her. Alice didn't even get up to usher her out; she was too stunned. She sat in her fireside chair and began to cry. She couldn't remember the last time she had done so, which was of very little comfort now.

And then she was angry. She wanted to run down to the doctor's house and tell him that she would marry him; that they were entitled to go ahead and try for some happiness. But she didn't, she went on sitting there trying to get her passions under control before anybody came home.

Sixty-Five

When Sir Archibald had gone, Charles entertained the most un-Christian desires. Perhaps Catherine would fall over and miscarry. Or if she was still the disagreeable girl that he remembered, she would carry on hunting and lose her baby riding too hard. Had she thought of that?

He went for a walk, thinking that his head might clear. Instead he just exhausted himself, walking around, talking to people and seeing how much work there was to be done. The only good thing about it was that everywhere he went people smiled on him. He thought it was not because of him or of Henry, it was because his father was such a good squire. Now he must try to be the same.

He went back to the house. His father was calling him from upstairs. He climbed the stairs one at a time, slowing his steps, the better to delay the encounter. His father was in bed. His poor health was no pretence; he could not get out of bed without help. Charles had always thought he would be pleased when this happened, instead of which he wanted to cry like a small child.

'Wherever have you been?' his father said.

'Just walking around.'

'Around the fields you hate.'

'I don't hate them.'

'You hate me.'

'I wouldn't pay you the compliment of thinking that I care one way or the other.'

His father laughed.

'You love it here, after all. I knew you would come back. I knew the church couldn't hold you. You must marry her.'

'What?'

'Catherine. You must wed her now.'

Charles stared, thinking his father knew about the baby until Sir Harry said, 'She cannot be let down. She must marry the heir and since Henry is not here to do it, you must take her.'

Charles was inclined to argue but he didn't. His father looked surprised and perhaps dismayed that he was denied the argument that he was so clearly up for. The churchman in Charles tried to drag him back but he was beyond it. He had known when his brother died that the church was over for him. He wouldn't give his father the satisfaction of hearing him say that he would be pleased when he died, but it was the truth.

He merely smiled at his father and asked if he wanted anything and when his father refused, he went downstairs and sat by the fire. He thought over his life and blamed himself for what had happened to his mother and his brother. He did not spare himself.

When Mrs Diamond, the housekeeper, brought in the brandy he didn't refuse it. At first it was not to offend her, but shortly afterwards he poured a good amount into one of his father's exquisite crystal glasses. He leaned over the fire that she had built up while she was there and watched the flames through his glass, wishing he had not turned into the man that brandy was allowing him to be.

He could not escape this place nor his lineage. He had tried so hard. Henry had killed himself because he had been left to cope and it was too much. Charles wished that he had not run away. He was ensnared now. He would never escape it again; the land held him. It was his prison and this place his dungeon.

He wished that he had been able to tell Susan who he was but he had not thought at the time that he could not reach beyond this part of him. How young and stupid he had been. He was glad that he had not offered her marriage. If he had when he wanted to, they would have been married and he could not have helped Catherine. Even now he could not go back to Susan and offer her marriage.

A woman like Susan would never strive for such a thing. She would marry him because she had chosen him and for no other reason. If she did not choose him – he couldn't ask her now. What woman would marry a man knowing she must provide an heir? It was disgusting. It was beyond any honest thing that humanity had taught. It was the bottom of life to treat anyone in such a way. He could not go back. He must stay here and watch his father die.

In the days that followed his father was so pleased that he seemed much better, the doctor reported. He even came downstairs and made merry and drank, though the doctor had told him not to. Each evening he treated Charles to the fact that if he drank too much Charles would be free of him that much the sooner. Charles sat there and endured it. His father did not go to bed early. It became the object of his day to ensure that his father went to bed before he was exhausted but it never happened.

During the day he saw the tenants and the people who worked on the estate. He settled disputes, he looked at figures, and he was grateful that he had men to help him. His father had been a very good manager. Charles was surprised at that; he had thought he would not have been. But this place had meant everything to his father. Charles' religion made him wish to do better; he accepted that God had had a plan for him, it was just not what he had wanted.

Money was so important. He saw that the estate was complicated, how much everything cost. His father bred racehorses. It cost a fortune but Charles could do little about it because he was not yet the master here. Around the horses, he remembered his brother and the horse that had been shot. As he walked the land, he was there in Henry's footsteps and it was hard.

His brother had done so much good work here even though he was not the master. His father had trusted his brother, who made sure that the tenants' houses were sound and they were paid good wages. It was a fine place to live because of what his brother had achieved and his father, from love, had let him. In his more honest moments, Charles acknowledged that his father was also a good master (if good masters could be said to exist, which he did not really believe). He felt so out of place, so out of time. He wanted to go back to Weardale and forget it and yet he could not.

Within a week he rode over to Sir Archibald's estate. There he remembered that Catherine was an only child and the estate was worth as much as the one that he would inherit when his father died.

Her mother greeted him with relief and her father shook his hand and offered him whisky, which Charles declined. He told them that he would like to speak to Catherine and they almost shuddered with gratitude.

They left him alone in the library. Why the library, he couldn't imagine. The smell of the place reminded him of Mr Martin's study and he longed to be there. He had the feeling that he would never see it again.

Usually a woman entered a room with a rustle of skirts but there was little sound when Catherine came in. He was shocked when he saw her. He thought she was going to faint; her whole body shook. She was still swathed in black, as she had been at the funeral, and she didn't even look up, as though it had taken everything she had to get there.

She was the thinnest thing that he had ever seen. Her hair was so sparse that it fell to her neck in wisps, her cheeks were sunken, and her eyes, what he could see of them, were almost black with fatigue and grief and perhaps guilt and regret. If she had ever been as beautiful and impertinent as he remembered her, there was nothing of it left.

'Charles,' she ventured, in a small voice that he could barely hear though it held a vestige of spirit, 'you shouldn't have come. My father had no right to go to you. This is a mess of my own making.'

It was the last thing he had expected her to say. Charles didn't know how to answer her.

'I will go away,' she said, with a hint of acid humour, 'and you will never hear from me again. I have told my father so.'

Charles found his voice and said something almost humorous, to his surprise.

'That was brave of you,' he said.

She attempted a smile and to look at him. She then looked away toward the door, as though somebody had walked into the room, and his eyes followed her gaze. Did she think his brother's ghost had somehow manifested itself in her misery? Or was it that they both wished it?

'Why don't you sit down?' he offered.

She shook her head.

'You sit down,' she said.

'You know I cannot, until the lady does.'

'I'm no lady. I'm a slut. My parents tell me so every day. Please, Charles, leave me alone. It would be the kindest thing that you could do.'

'I'm not here to be kind. You have the Westbrooke heir inside you.' He hated even saying the words. What stupid person had thought such things mattered? How awful.

'Dear God, what am I, a sow? With my luck I would breed only girls, if that. I have wished and wished that it would die. Please go away. I never liked you and you never liked me.'

Charles caught her before she fell. He wasn't quite sure how he managed the distance to her – it was a bloody big library and the space between them was huge – but she was in his arms before he knew it. He cursed under his breath and carried her out of the room. She weighed so little. In the hall he shouted and a maid came and directed him to her room. It was obvious when he reached the door that she was being punished in some hard ways for what she had done. The room was black, the curtains were closed, and there was no fire. In the shadows he laid her down and snapped at the maid to open the curtains to what little light there was. He could hear the rain beating itself hard against the windows.

'They won't even let her have a fire, sir,' the girl said. 'Will you help?'

'Are you her maid?'

'Mary Blamire, yes, sir. Please talk to them.'

'Don't worry, Miss Blamire, this is going to be sorted out.'

Mary nodded but her eyes were full of tears.

*

A short time later he was in the library with her father, glaring at him. Feeling slightly better, he spoke in clipped tones.

'You will treat her properly. She is going to be my wife and therefore you will look after her. I will be back tomorrow and every day afterwards and I expect to see her condition improve. My God, was she not allowed a mistake?'

'It's not just a mistake: it's a sin and cost us all dearly,' her father was not cowed. 'The whole county is laughing at us behind our backs. Your brother killed himself because of it.'

Charles was amazed and then wanted to laugh.

'You think my brother killed himself because his bride was expecting a child? Have you lost your mind? Was that not just an indication of their ability to breed, and isn't that really what you wanted? Isn't that what this bloody stupid way of life is all about?'

Sir Archibald looked shocked.

'They should be joined by God.'

'As soon as Catherine is able, we will be married,' and Charles swept out of the room. He had always wondered how people swept from rooms and yet he accomplished it with ease. He felt taller and more angry than ever before.

By the time he got home, the anger had died and he felt wretched. His father bellowed down the stairs for him and greeted him with a sly smile when he came upstairs to his father's bedroom. It was strange to Charles. He had not smiled since his brother's funeral. He was drunk, of course, in spite of what the doctor had said; he was always drunk.

He must have shouted at the maids and frightened them because the decanter by his bed was three-quarters empty. Charles wanted to ask Mrs Diamond not to give his father brandy but it was unfair to her to carry the responsibility.

'She's in pup, isn't she?'

Charles didn't reply. He wasn't sure how his father had worked this out. He hoped in spite of everything that his father had not heard the stories about Henry in the pub in Shap. But he had obviously understood something of what was going on and now he was pleased.

His father laughed so much that he began to cough and went so scarlet in the face that Charles watched carefully in case he collapsed.

'I am so glad that he left us his child before he died,' his father gasped, 'and the jest is that you will have to marry her because she is carrying the Westbrooke heir. That is very funny. Henry was a real man, not like you.'

The worst thing of all was that Charles had never been at home without his brother. He missed him as though his heart was torn out. He wanted to hear Henry's voice and to see him striding through the hall and he wished that his brother had confided in him. Men had been sleeping with men all throughout history, since Grecian times at least, and probably always. What did it matter? Now his brother had died from shame and grief and even so, he had managed to impregnate the woman he was to marry.

Now Henry was dead and so many people were suffering because of it. Charles sat there and thought of Susan Wilson. He had to hope that she disliked him so much that she would put him from her mind. As for Catherine, if he had not come back here he thought she would have died. She might even now; having a child in such a condition would do neither of them any good. He had to make sure she was looked after and had some kind of life.

Not only did men who preferred women think that men who preferred men were strange but they also thought that women who couldn't or didn't marry were not up to scratch either. It made Charles want to weep that people who called themselves Christians behaved in such dismal and appalling ways, censuring people as they did.

All Charles had wanted was a decent life with the woman he loved amongst kind people and it was all gone. It was obviously far too much to try for. It had cost he and his brother everything.

Sixty-Six

Zeb was most surprised to find his father waiting for him in the lane. It was raining hard and he was irritated anyway; at the quarry Dan had become short-tempered and was drinking again, Mr Paterson was threatening to leave, and according to Dan it was only a matter of time before Mr Almond died and left him everything. When he was drunk, he bragged worse than ever. Zeb wanted to hit him but he had far too much to do. So to see his father standing there, blocking his path at the bottom of Church Lane when he was imagining a warm fire and his supper, was no help.

'Is something wrong?' he ventured.

'Very wrong,' his father said.

'We'd better go back to the shop and you can tell me about it.'

'We can't go back there.'

Zeb stared through the grey evening and the darker rain.

'Father, I'm soaked. We have nowhere to go.'

'The pub across the market place will do.'

Zeb stared at him. This was desperation. His father hadn't stepped inside a pub at all that he could remember.

The pub across the market place was the one the workmen went to so he couldn't really go in there. In the end they walked all the way down to the Grey Bull. Since it was early evening there were not too many farmers about or business people.

Zeb told him to sit down and said he would go to the bar.

'What for?' his father said.

'Beer.'

'I don't drink beer.'

'Selling beer is their business. We can hardly sit here without,' Zeb pointed out and he went off to the bar.

It was warm by the fire and when he brought the beer back, his father gazed at it disdainfully. He took a sip, though, and said that it wasn't too bad. Zeb also swallowed some. He was glad of it a moment later.

'What's the matter?' he asked.

'Miss Lee is thinking of getting married,' his father replied.

Zeb choked anyway.

'She's what?'

'The doctor has asked her to marry him.'

Zeb stared at his father for the second time in half an hour.

'It must be gossip.'

'I heard her talking about it,' Mr Bailey said. He explained how he had come home and found the back door slightly ajar and overheard the doctor's daughter trying to dissuade Miss Lee from marrying her father.

'And we all know the best thing to do is to tell a strong woman not to do something and what does she do?' His father took a big swallow of beer and then sighed.

'She must be twenty years younger than him.'

'Does that matter?'

'I don't know.'

'It's not as if she's awash with offers.'

'What do you mean?'

His father looked impatiently at him.

'She's plain and clever. Why on earth he wants to marry her, I have no idea. He could have any woman, beautiful and charming and young. He doesn't have to settle for an old maid.'

'Maybe he cares about her,' Zeb defended.

His father grunted and pushed the beer away.

'She's a lovely woman but I can't see anybody ever marrying her.'

Zeb wanted to say that Miss Lee had the loveliest silver-grey eyes that he had ever seen but he couldn't. He thought she was beautiful, but then he had never forgotten her standing in the street outside Durham gaol. She had been all grey and silver and white, like the early mornings in July in the dale when pale clouds touched the darkness of the hills. She smelled of chocolate and he had often wondered whether she would taste of it. It was probably how the doctor felt.

Zeb wondered that every man in the dale didn't want to marry her. He certainly did but he knew that he couldn't ask her. A murderer couldn't ask for anything. If she wanted to marry the doctor, she must go ahead and do it, and he must make sure that he and his father did not stand in her way. He wanted to cry into his beer, to howl all the way home and fling himself into bed.

'What are we going to do?' his father asked now.

'There's nothing we can do except wait for her to make up her mind. Do you know how long she has?'

'I don't.'

His father didn't recognise the irony.

'You didn't overhear that bit,' Zeb said and his father smiled at him in acknowledgement.

'You don't need to worry,' Zeb went on. 'I make good money and I've got some saved. We'll be all right.'

'But I like being there. I like Miss Lee. She's probably the only woman who would ever have taken me in.'

'Or me, or Susan probably.'

'What will Susan do? Do you think she knows?'

'I shouldn't imagine so. I think Miss Lee will decide before she tells us. We'd better go home. She doesn't know you were there?'

'We'll soon find out,' his father said and they set off as the rain poured down.

Sixty-Seven

'Do you think Mr Westbrooke is coming back, Miss Lee?' Susan said.

'I'm sure of it,' Alice said and yet when Susan had gone to bed and Mr Bailey was snoring upstairs she said to Zeb, 'I think she loves him.'

Zeb looked at her and shook his head.

'He did say that he would come back,' Alice said, 'but it's been weeks and she is beginning to think that she'll never find a man to take her.'

'Shall I go to Westmorland and talk to him?'

'Would you?'

'Why not?'

'That would be wonderful. Do you mind?'

'Of course not,' he said and smiled at her. 'I'll go and ask Mr Martin for directions.'

'You're going away?' Dan looked closely at him across the desk.

Zeb didn't want to tell him why.

'Just for a couple of days. I've never taken a day off.'

'I can't manage without you.'

'I'll be back on Monday.' This wasn't necessarily true but Zeb wasn't going to tell him that.

'Is it something special?'

'Just family stuff,' Zeb said.

Dan might have remarked that Zeb didn't have any family but he didn't so that was good.

Zeb was astonished at how beautiful his journey to Westmorland was. The further up Weardale he got, the more extreme the scenery and the higher the hills. The houses were brave there and stood against the wind and rain but he was lucky. The weather was kind and he appreciated it.

When he got to the very top before the plunge over into Cumberland he looked at the view. It was the best he thought he had ever seen. The lakes, the mountains and valleys, the whole area, was just so beautiful that he could barely breathe; he was two thousand feet above sea level, on top of the world.

After that it was the road to Penrith. Although he was worried about Charles' circumstances, when he got to Shap and there found a horse and trap and driver to take him to the Westbrooke house, he had to make himself more clear.

'The Hall?' the driver asked.

'Is it?' Zeb said. 'Mr Charles Westbrooke is the man I'm wanting to find.'

'Yes, sir. That's it.'

The next five miles beyond Shap went off into the hills and he had not seen more wild country. There were lovely cream and brown sheep grazing the land and ponies free everywhere and when he came closer to the house, further down from the tops, he saw cattle such as he had not seen before. They were black with a white belt around their bodies, short and round and fat.

Everything was so well-kept. He had not understood that Charles' father owned anything more than a house yet here he was being driven through the gates of a big place. There was a long drive to the estate with rough fields on either side. He beheld a huge – and by the look of it, a very old – house, built low but well and extending a long way on either side.

When the carriage stopped, a young woman in a black dress came to the door and greeted him. Zeb smiled and introduced himself. She told him that she was the housekeeper, Mrs Diamond, and she led him into the enormous, dark building. When he got inside, he liked it straight away. There was a big fire in the hall and in front of it sat two black Labradors, who yawned and stretched and got up and waved their tails at him. They settled down once again as though they knew he was a friend. Their glossy black coats shone in the firelight.

He was led into a huge room with fires at either end and there Charles sat in an armchair. He got up, hand extended and greeted Zeb with great enthusiasm.

'Zeb, how are you? I'm so pleased to see you. Thank you for coming here. You are so good.'

He was different, Zeb thought, nothing like the minister he had been, but well-bred and confident. Zeb tried to be easy.

'Not really,' he said, 'Miss Lee made me come. I hope you don't mind. I didn't have a proper address for you and the minister said to find a farm which bore your name not far from Shap.'

'That's as much as he knew. I didn't want people to know the way that my family has lived. You will stay here?' Charles said, looking eagerly at him.

'Well, I thought I might find an inn – '

'It's Saturday tomorrow. Surely you can spare me the weekend?'

Zeb hesitated.

'This is yours?' he said, finally. 'I mean your – your father is master here.'

'It's our home, yes.'

'It's a very fine place.'

'It's been in our family for hundreds of years.' Charles stopped there and offered Zeb food and wine. 'Forgive my father's absence,' Charles said, 'he isn't well.'

'Is he a lord?' Zeb didn't usually ask questions like that; he knew it was rude but he couldn't help it.

'Only a baronet.'

'Only?'

Charles grinned and then sobered.

'I didn't mean to hurt anybody by not returning to Stanhope. I thought I could have a life away from here. I wanted to be somebody else. I thought I had succeeded but it doesn't seem to have worked that way.'

They sat down in a small but elegant dining room where the furniture was solid and dark. Charles asked about Miss Lee and then about Susan and his eyes betrayed him, Zeb thought. This man loved Susan Wilson.

They talked of trivialities: the weather and how well the quarry was doing and how Zeb thought the sheep and cattle were. When they had finished eating, Zeb sat back in his chair.

'We hoped you were coming back.'

Charles didn't reply and Zeb thought how different he was from the man they had known. He looked tired, burdened, older.

'I thought my brother would take this place over,' Charles said, finally meeting his eyes, 'and that I wouldn't have to come back.

He loved it so much and I wanted to go on being a Methodist minister and – and leading the life I cared for so very much. It's all gone now. My brother died in a hunting accident and the girl my brother was going to marry is having his child.'

Zeb was astonished. Charles' brother was stupid enough to get a girl pregnant and then get killed hunting? What sort of an idiot did that?

'And I must marry her,' Charles said. 'The estate has to have an heir. It has been so for hundreds of years.'

Zeb thought he had never heard anything quite so stupid.

'But you love Susan?'

Charles looked so far down that Zeb thought the floor beneath the table would scorch.

'This is the second time she has been let down,' Zeb said.

'She loves me?' Charles looked up quickly.

'You doubted it?'

'I didn't ask her, you see. I felt that I couldn't. Daniel Wearmouth – '

'Oh, to hell with Daniel Wearmouth,' Zeb said. 'She cares about you very much, asks about you every day. That's why I'm here.'

'Oh Lord,' Charles said almost comically and Zeb could see why. Without the humour he would break down. 'But I cannot marry her.'

'I'm supposed to go back and tell her that?'

'Tell her anything that will make her feel better. That I was not a good sort of man, that I cheated or lied or came from a dreadful background. Most of it's true. Look at me, I'm so stupid.'

'I don't know much,' Zeb said, 'but I think you should marry where you love.'

'She is my whole life,' Charles said and his voice broke. 'I blame my brother for doing this to me and how unfair is that?'

Zeb didn't think it was unfair. He thought Charles was mad to stay there when he had made a life for himself, but then a place like this held huge responsibilities and Charles could not get past those. Zeb felt sorry for him and even sorrier for himself, having to go back and face Susan.

Later when they went to bed a manservant came to Zeb and offered to unpack his meagre bag.

'I have little,' Zeb said and smiled on the young man and thanked him for his trouble.

'I understand you're from Weardale, sir?' the man asked, his whole face hungry.

'I am.'

'I'm from Alston.'

'I know it well. It is a lovely place.'

'It is indeed.'

'You miss it?'

'Yes, but since Mr Charles came home things have been better. We were very sad.'

Zeb didn't want to go back. He didn't want Susan to feel as if she had been jilted again. Though he knew there had been no vocal understanding that she loved Charles Westbrooke. Whatever would he say? And he also knew that Dan had proposed to Susan. If she married him it would be a huge mistake but she might think it was her only option, especially if Miss Lee was leaving the shop. Zeb couldn't envisage his life without the shop, without Alice.

He lay awake all that night in his beautiful chamber with the fire and the view over the fells where the moon shone clear in the sky. He had no doubt that Charles was awake too.

Sixty-Eight

When Zeb got back to Stanhope, Alice and Susan were waiting for him. They sat down to supper almost immediately so he had no escape.

'How is Mr Westbrooke?' was Susan's eager greeting.

'Having a bad time. His brother died in an accident – '

'Miss Lee told me.'

'And his father is old and ill.'

'What about his mother?'

'She has been dead for a very long time, I gather.'

'Do you think he will come back to see us?'

'I'm sure he will,' Zeb said and then he knew that it wasn't right. He couldn't say that to her, it wasn't true and that was disrespectful towards her. 'But not for a long time.'

Susan looked suspiciously at him.

'His father is a farmer?'

'His father is titled. They have a big estate with lots of tenants who rely on the baronet. His brother has died and Charles feels obliged to marry the woman his brother was to marry.'

Susan stared, which was hardly surprising. Zeb made himself meet her gaze.

'Why?'

'Because she – because she is carrying his brother's child.'

Susan went on staring but her face got pinker and pinker and her eyes became like glass.

'What?'

'She is carrying the heir.'

Susan's face wrinkled as though she would cry and then her eyes narrowed.

'Charles could marry – somebody else.'

'He couldn't let the family be disgraced.'

'You mean it, don't you?'

'Susan – '

'So are you telling me that his brother and this woman lay together when they weren't married and he got her pregnant and then he died and because of this Mr Westbrooke will not come back?'

Zeb said nothing.

'Is that right?' Susan's gaze was like a knife.

'He feels he has to marry her. His family has lived there a very long time and hundreds of people rely on them.'

'Well, when I lie in my bed I shall remember that his brother and his brother's woman sinned so that I could not marry the man I wanted. What a comfort that will be,' and she got up and left the table.

Alice looked after her and half got up and then sat down again.

'This is the second time.'

She didn't need to say it, they both knew. They went on sitting there. His father as usual had gone to sleep after eating.

'The trouble is,' Zeb said, 'that I could see how much he loves Susan.'

'He shouldn't have pretended to be someone else.'

'I think he was trying to get away from the life he didn't want there. And maybe he would have if his brother had married.'

'But isn't it always the firstborn son who inherits? So the moment Charles and his wife had a child, the younger son's child wouldn't matter, unless one was a girl and one a boy.'

'I think that's why he deceived us as he did. He so much wanted to get away. The place is huge. If it's any comfort, I think he is very unhappy.'

Sixty-Nine

Dan hated going back to Ash House. He felt as though he was living all alone. He was trying not to drink during the day but it was so very hard. In his mind, especially when he drank, he confused Arabella and Susan, and not being able to have the one he very much wanted the other. He thought about her body so much that his life felt tainted.

Mrs Almond ignored him. The doctor was there every day and she took all her meals upstairs. Dan was eating less and less and drinking more and more, blotting out not just the house and the quarry but the fact that Susan wouldn't marry him. He wanted her now as much as he had wanted Arabella and the fact that she wouldn't have him made it so bad that he could hardly bear it.

Getting back on that particular night he was surprised to find Mrs Almond downstairs.

'Is Mr Almond feeling better?'

'My husband is dying.'

'I'm so sorry, especially after Arabella.'

'It would have been a different thing altogether if we could have had the child here,' she said.

'You must pardon what I did. I know it was horrible to blame the little boy.'

'Perhaps you should go and see him,' she suggested.

He could have told her that it was the last thing on earth that he wanted to do but he was aware that his position here was delicate and he should be nice to this woman, so he agreed. He was just glad that every day he didn't have to look on the face of a child that might resemble Arabella even in the slightest way; he couldn't have borne it. She would still be here if she had not had that child. Some days he tried to pretend she wasn't dead. He thought of how she would be here waiting for him in the garden, laughing, and they would drink champagne and later she would come to him in bed, naked and wanton as she always was.

Mrs Almond went back upstairs before dinner. He didn't change his clothes for the meals anymore, there didn't seem to be any point. He had not even begun eating though he had begun drinking. Shortly after that, as he was sitting over the drawing room fire wondering whether he might manage some dinner, one of the maids – he never remembered their names – came through and said that he had visitor, a woman.

She didn't even bother to say 'lady' though she wouldn't recognise one if she saw one. Anyway, it couldn't be anything important. It must be something to do with disgruntled staff – or worse still, some wife of a quarryman who thought she had a grievance and had been angry enough to bring it here. The visitor wouldn't be anybody who mattered to him.

He got up and the visitor was ushered in and he didn't mistake who it was for a second. He knew Susan from her gait, from the way that her body moved. He remembered spending nights imagining himself with that sweet body in his arms, submissive and sweat-slick for him.

It was raining again. Did it never do anything but rain, he wondered idly. He felt the happiness surge through him because she could not be here for any reason other than that she would marry him. He had longed for this, thought of it, and hoped just a little, but he had never quite believed it.

'Susan.'

'Yes. I had to come. It is a very fine house.' She stumbled and didn't look at him. She was so nervous, he thought.

'Isn't it?' he said.

'I'm sorry to hear that Mr Almond is so ill and I wouldn't have come here without a very good reason. I knew that you wouldn't come back after the way that I treated you and why would you, I was so sure of myself, so awful.' This all came out in a rush and she was looking appealingly at him.

'No, you weren't. I was to blame. I treated you badly first and so much more badly later.' He laughed and then she laughed even though the whole thing was awkward. 'Could it be that you have changed your mind?'

'I – I thought about it more. I thought that you could give me a life I could never have down there in the village. Although it seems dreadful to want a rich life and a big house, I find that I do want them. I do want to be with you, I do want to marry you and if it's because of all that, then I'm sorry.'

Dan hesitated.

'It's a very sudden change of mind.'

'Isn't it?' she said and her eyes glittered.

Dan smiled. Susan smiled just a little. Dan was so nervous. He felt as though he had no right to have her be this kind to him, but he was so desperate to have back the joy of marriage.

Susan let the silence fall for a couple of minutes although to him it felt like a couple of hours.

'Will you have me then, Daniel?' she said and her voice broke on a little sob and Dan thought that she had never stopped caring about him. She loved him too much to turn him down now and he was triumphant.

He had not expected her to capitulate so suddenly and he was so pleased with himself, so proud. He could go back to being the man who had everything. He would have the quarry, and even if Mr and Mrs Almond didn't want Susan in their house, he would buy her a fine house here in Stanhope. He might even build it.

'You really mean it?' he said.

'Let's be married as soon as we can,' she said.

Mrs Almond, halfway down the stairs, held her breath as Daniel followed Susan out. She had not realised that he was serious about this woman. And so soon after Arabella had died having his child. It was disgusting. Did he really think he could bring that common young woman here to be his wife as though nothing had happened?

Mrs Almond choked over her tears. She would make him pay for this. She would never have Susan Wilson here. She had stood enough from Daniel Wearmouth.

She was therefore surprised later that evening when Dan came into her sitting room rather abruptly and, for once, sober. Her husband was upstairs sleeping. Dan said that he was sorry for interrupting whatever she was doing but he had something to tell her.

She pretended she didn't know what it was and nodded her head. He didn't even sit down. He told her very quietly that he had asked Susan Wilson to marry him.

'I know that it's very soon and wouldn't have been what you wanted but I'm very lonely and I'm finding it very hard. I wouldn't expect to bring her here, of course, I am going to rent a cottage in the village.'

He had found breaking this news to Susan harder than he had thought. He had not forgotten that she was pleased at the idea of living at Ash House and when he told her that they would not be doing so, he could see that she took it hard.

'Oh,' was all she said.

'I'm sorry but you can understand how Mr and Mrs Almond may feel. And he is so ill. You don't mind, do you?'

'Of course not,' was all she had said.

'I see. And when is the wedding to be?' Mrs Almond said now.

'In a month. I promise you, Mrs Almond, I will work harder than ever to make things go well at the quarry. I know I haven't been a lot of help since Arabella died, but I will do my best so that Mr Almond doesn't worry about it.'

Mrs Almond said very little and Dan went off to bed very pleased with his day. Things would get better now. The world wasn't coming to an end and he had finally done right by the girl he had fallen in love with in the beginning.

Seventy

Susan wanted to tell Alice that she had accepted a proposal of marriage from Dan but she couldn't. Alice would be horrified. Dan had hurt her so much, and Alice and Zeb had been so kind. Although Zeb had known that Dan wanted to marry her, he wouldn't approve of her saying yes, so she slid back into the house and lied, saying she had been visiting people from the chapel. She did visit a lot of people, she liked the children, but she had never told such a lie before and she was ashamed of herself.

By the following day, however, the lie had grown as big as a house. She told Alice when they were working together and the shop was empty. Alice's reaction startled her.

'I'm so glad you did,' she said and hugged Susan to her.

'I didn't think you wanted me to.'

Alice let her go and looked into her face.

'It's all about having somebody to come home to,' she said simply. Susan thought yes, that was what the best of life was about, two of you to take on the world so that you had a reasonable defence mechanism when life threw awful things at you. And she did want to have children.

'Are you pleased for me?'

'I'm delighted.'

'The wedding will be very small, not like last time and not like his marriage to Arabella. And I would like Zeb and his father there if they will come. Zeb doesn't know the news yet. Would you speak to him, Miss Lee? Because I think he already knows that Dan has asked me.'

'Is it Zeb you want?' Alice asked. She was surprised to feel a little pang of hurt. She hadn't known until then that she cared so very much about the man she had rescued that she didn't want him to marry even Susan.

'No, no, it isn't that, it's just that he's the nearest I've ever had to a brother and I care about him and I don't think he wants me to marry Dan. I don't want us to be estranged because of it.'

It was so difficult to find the right time, Alice thought. His father was always around or Susan was there. Therefore it was late at night when she told him that Susan was to be married.

He stood in the middle of the room and nodded his head.

'I thought she might,' he said. 'I knew he had asked her but I didn't like to say anything because I thought she had given up on him and had feelings for Charles Westbrooke.'

'I doubt Dan's ability to make her happy considering the circumstances but sometimes people come to a certain time in their lives. She is ready for marriage, perhaps. She wants us there and your father.'

'Then I think we should be there for her, don't you?' he said.

Alice had still not replied to the doctor's offer of marriage. He had said that she could take as many days as she needed but she could not make up her mind. Every time she thought about it, a new argument presented itself. She didn't know what it was or she would have sorted it out. She was aware that the atmosphere in the house was changing.

Susan was silent, Zeb's father crept about and Zeb avoided her eyes. She didn't think they knew anything but people's instincts were quite different so perhaps she didn't need to tell them. It was almost a week and she knew that she couldn't keep the doctor hanging on for much longer. It was downright rude.

One afternoon they were all together in the house. She wished that they were not but the weather kept them in. She wished that it would not rain every day. It wasn't good for sales and it wasn't good when they all sat together like this. It was such a small room in the back.

Susan was supposed to be knitting and Alice reading. Zeb was staring into the fire and his father was also pretending to read, though he hadn't turned a page in half an hour. She knew because neither had she. She didn't even wish it was time to go to bed, because when she got there, she lay staring up into the darkness wondering what on earth she would do.

Then she looked up and her eyes met Zeb's gaze across the fire. At that moment, she knew that she couldn't marry the doctor.

It wasn't him directly, she thought; it was because the doctor was older. She didn't want to marry an old man. Even if she should never feel anyone's arms around her, she didn't want to marry a man who had grandchildren, a man who had had a wife before her for so many years. And no doubt he would compare them, even if he didn't mean to.

Even if they moved, he would still be a grandfather. He would still be concerned with his daughter and her sons. And Alice already knew how his daughter felt about her. Alice had even thought that if she married the doctor she could persuade him to help his daughter more, but if they had children, his attentions would be divided. It was all too much to contemplate. She would rather be Alice Lee, sweet shop owner, and alone and proud of it.

'Is there something the matter, Miss Lee?' Zeb asked.

'Nothing at all. Shall I make some tea? Or better still, some hot chocolate?'

At that, they put down their books and needles and said it was a wonderful idea. She heated milk on the fire and she put chocolate into it to melt and when it was thick and ready, she poured it out into big cups. They sat over the fire and sipped at their chocolate while the rain poured down.

The following night the rain and wind was even worse but Alice didn't think she could keep the doctor waiting any longer. When Susan had gone to bed with a headache, Mr Bailey had fallen asleep, and she thought Zeb was upstairs, Alice put on her outdoor things.

'Shall I come with you, Miss Lee?' a soft voice behind her asked.

She turned and there he was.

'I'll be fine alone.'

Zeb hesitated.

'I know where you're going,' he said.

'How do you know that?'

'My father overheard you with the doctor's daughter.'

Alice gave a sigh of exasperation.

'Am I never to have anything to myself?'

'It's late and it's dark and the pubs are open. I won't bother you. Let me just be there. I'll wait outside.'

'All right then, but you will stay back, you won't come inside?'

'I won't do that,' he said, so they set off down the street.

Nobody spoke and Alice was both horrified and comforted to have Zeb by her side when she went to the doctor's house. She had so much wanted to handle this by herself but it was late and dark and he was right, as usual. She turned in at the gates and he hung back, but when she approached the house she was aware of his presence.

Alice suspected that Mrs Scott had been speaking to her father and that he thought she had given him up for that reason. She could see also that he was not surprised when she told him that she couldn't marry him. She didn't think he would consider anything else a good reason. She was, after all, not going to get another offer. No, she would stay in her little home and then Susan would marry and after that Zeb and his father would probably find a house. She would be left as she had been before Miss Frost died, before Susan came to live with her and she took in Zeb and then Mr Bailey.

All of it had been done for them, and yet now she didn't want them to go. It was selfish, she knew, but she had grown fond of them. She thought that eventually Zeb might talk a local girl into marrying him. He was a man now, not a foolish boy. He had a good job and decent prospects. She would be left where she had been all those years ago, when she was lonely and did not think her circumstances would ever change.

This had been, she saw now, the main argument for saying yes to the doctor but she still couldn't do it. She wanted her sweet shop, she wanted her own life. She didn't want to be there in the doctor's house being nice to his awful daughter and her children, as though she was sixty, with nothing but his company to keep her. It wouldn't be enough.

She hoped that it did not show on her face; she hoped that the doctor had no idea she didn't want him. She hoped that she wouldn't regret it. It had been the hardest decision of her life. And then she thought no, that wasn't right, the hardest decision of her life was whether to take in the young man who was standing outside getting soaked because of her. And that had been the right decision; he was a decent man.

The doctor was quiet and kind and when he saw her to the door, the rain was pouring down. He offered to see her along the street and she couldn't see Zeb at all but she refused and thanked him. And then she was back in the rain. She wanted nothing more than to run back inside, into his big, warm house with its perpetual smell of camphor, and she waited there for a few seconds after the door shut.

A tall, dark figure emerged out of the darkness.

'Are you all right, Miss Lee?' Zeb asked.

'Was I a long time? Oh dear, you're drenched.'

'I'm fine. What about you?'

'I don't know. It seemed like a good idea for so many days. He has so much to offer. I just hope I don't regret telling him no.' They set off along the street, aware of the lights shining out of the pubs as they went. Further over, two men were fighting in the street. Zeb had been right to come with her. Drunk, these men might not remember who she was; they might offer her insult. She didn't think they would touch her but the rain was ceasing and she could hear raised voices.

As she and Zeb walked up the far side of the street, somebody threw a missile. Zeb grabbed her and pulled her away and the bottle smashed where she had been standing.

'Idiots,' was all he said as he let her go.

She was pleased then. He had mastered his temper. Not long ago he would have been inclined to cross the road and shout and possibly even knock them down. While she had to admit it made him very useful, she had never been quite certain that he knew when to stop. She put her hand through his arm as they walked. She wished it had been a longer walk; she rarely got him to herself. And as soon as that thought crossed her mind, she knew. She stopped. He stopped too.

Zeb enquired if she was tired.

'No, I'm not tired.'

'Upset, then? It must have been really hard. The doctor is so good and fine and respected.'

'I feel as if he's too old. Does that sound silly?'

'Not to me. He must be at least twenty years older than you. Why would you marry an old man?'

'I suppose it's because men of my age are married and have children.'

'You must have had proposals?'

'Me? No. I never fitted in, I was a – an orphan, as you know, and it was different when I was young than it is now for Susan. I was never considered respectable.'

'Well, you are now and you've done it yourself. And not just that, you're – well, you took us all in, and who else would have done it. Especially me. If I haven't said it, Miss Lee, I am very grateful to you for everything. For me and for my father. We can bear one another now. I never thought that would happen. You've made us all happy. You have a gift for being kind to other people. You and your chocolate orphanage.'

Alice stopped and laughed.

'That's a lovely way of looking at it. Susan is the first bird to fly my nest. You and your father I hope will stay.'

'I don't ever want to leave,' he said and Alice hung on to his arm as they made their way up the street. She didn't ever want him to leave either.

Seventy-One

It was night-time and cold when Catherine Boldon ran away. She had hoped that nobody knew. She had waited until it was dark and the stars were out. She picked up her bag. As she did so, her maid, Mary, appeared in the doorway.

'Mary, what on earth are you doing up so late?'

'Same as you, I think,' Mary said.

'You cannot be. You have a chance. You have Rob and marriage and a future. You don't need to come with me. I have nothing.'

'I don't want to stay here and marry. A baby a year and him when he's nowt to begin with. What's the point? Let's get out of here. I'll help you. I've got money saved.'

Catherine sobbed.

'You can't do that for me.'

'It isn't for you, it's for me,' Mary said. 'Now let's get out before somebody notices.'

She picked up one bag and Catherine picked up the other and Mary shouldered the few possessions she had. They picked their way across Shap Fell by moonlight. Catherine had thought it would be hard but she had not imagined that her maid would go with her. She liked Mary very much but Mary owed her nothing.

Before they reached Shap, Mary was singing and Catherine

knew that she had done the right thing. She needed to get away from here and with their resources they might do so. She had deceived Charles out of necessity, she thought. She had hoarded money, she had sold jewels, and even now she had a thick wad of money on her and a purse full of golden guineas. She had jewellery with her but nowhere in sight. She needed not to be robbed nor to look robbable, she thought, shabbily dressed as she was.

She thought Charles was a gentleman and that he had tried to do the right thing, but she didn't like him and she thought if he was honest, he didn't like her either. He was little and scatty and read too many books. What she had wanted was Henry. Now all she was left with was his wretched child, if it lived. And despite everything, she wanted it to live.

She just hoped it was a girl. If she had a boy and Charles found out about it, she had the feeling he would come and take the child. That was how men behaved over property and titles. She and Mary – and she was glad that Mary had come with her – they would go as far away as they could, hopefully somewhere they could not be found. Not a big place, but big enough that nobody would know or care who she was. She prayed never to come back here.

She had thought quite a bit about how and when she would leave. She would have liked to have left before now. She did feel slightly guilty about leaving Charles on their wedding day but it made her laugh. She only wished that she could see his face when he discovered that his bride had gone. She thought he would be secretly relieved. Or maybe he wouldn't even care. Was he that proud? Or would he just be glad that she had made the decision for him?

She could go north to Carlisle but she was so very well-known there. She would be found; somebody would recognise her. She could go south toward Kendal and perhaps ultimately to Manchester, but Manchester also was a big place and she had been there too many times, going to wonderful dress shops and parties so she didn't feel comfortable. She decided that she would go to Brough and from there into the northeast. She had never been and she knew nothing about it except that there was a fine cathedral in Durham. Nobody knew her there. Perhaps it would be the perfect place to hide.

They came in sight of Shap early and kept to the shadows so that nobody would notice them. When the stagecoach came, Catherine hailed it and they got inside. Soon they were being driven away from what had seemed like the future and was no more.

Mary remembered what a lovely gentleman Charles Westbrooke was. Even when he was in a bad way he had called her Miss Blamire. She had never met a real gentleman before and now as she saw her mistress falling asleep, she wished she had had such an opportunity. She would have given him everything.

Seventy-Two

On the day that he was to be married, Charles got up early. He had not slept but that was nothing new. He had not slept for so many nights that he couldn't remember what it was like. He thought about Susan so much. He didn't want to marry Catherine but he saw her now as neglected and pitiful and his religious self – whatever it might be – could not see her unmarried and dealing with her parents. How stupid they were. How small-minded. But then, so many people were.

Women had to marry. What else could they do? Men married because they wanted to bed a woman, but were they prepared for all those children, were they used to a harpy at breakfast? To most people, marriage meant poverty. So why would anybody want it? Yet women could not get by, it was said, without.

So he got up and tried to eat his breakfast but he had not got far before Mrs Diamond came into the room.

'A man has come from Sir Archibald and he says that you must go to see him.'

Charles didn't ask questions. He went. He did not change into his wedding clothes, he just got on his horse and left. He drove the horse hard and when he got there, he told the stable lad to look after him well. He went to the house and there Sir Archibald came to him. The man looked even older.

'What has happened?' Charles said.

'Come inside.'

Charles did. He could see how agitated the older man was but when he got there Lady Elizabeth appeared and she was crying. They led Charles into the library. He had no good memories of the library and it seemed his memories of it were not to improve.

'She's gone,' Sir Archibald said.

'What?'

'In the night. Catherine has left.'

Charles could not conceive of people being so stupid that they did not know their daughter had left the premises. They had treated her badly and no doubt this contributed to her running away, but he could not fool himself. She didn't want to marry him. He was sorry to know that he felt relief. He didn't want to marry her either. In a way he was grateful to her, but she was weak and he was worried, especially about his brother's child.

'She cannot have gone far.'

Sir Archibald looked patiently at him.

'I have had men out for hours.'

'Then why did you not send for me?'

'You don't know this place any more. My men do but she is not to be found.'

Charles wanted to shout and scream that this was his wedding day. He had not wanted it; he had thought he was doing the right thing and now he was jilted, humiliated and left. There was a side to him that wanted to laugh. Catherine had always had spirit but if they had been married he would have helped her, looked after her. And then he thought of what it must be like being married to a man you didn't love, who didn't love you. Of giving birth to a child whose father had cared so little for you that he let loose his appetites when he was betrothed to you. He thought that she had truly loved his brother and he could forgive her anything for that, but he was worried that she would lose the child. She was so desperately unhappy that she would care for nothing now.

'She went alone?'

Sir Archibald was red in the face.

'No, she took that wretched girl with her.'

Charles remembered the wretched girl and it made him feel better. He thought that Mary Blamire was a very capable woman. Perhaps they would get by. He wished he had had more sense than to think Catherine would marry him. Why should she if she could manage some other way? He blamed himself. She was not the woman to put up with a man who tried to force her into a marriage she didn't want.

He had thought too much of his brother and not enough of the woman who had loved him. He wished he could help Catherine differently now. He wished her well; he wished she would come back. If she did, he would not let her go to her parents, he would give her money and enable her to do whatever she wanted. And maybe in time he could go back to Weardale and offer himself honestly to Susan Wilson.

The idea of being married to the woman he truly loved was too much for him. He tried to talk himself out of it but he couldn't stop himself. He had done what he could here. He had offered marriage to his brother's intended wife who was pregnant with his brother's damned child and it hadn't happened. Why the hell should he stay when he could go back to Weardale and claim Susan Wilson as his bride? She loved him and he loved her and it would be the way that things were meant to be. Just for once it would work out.

There were no reports of Catherine. Her father was sending out messengers to Penrith. Surely she would have gone there, it was the first decent-sized place. But nobody had seen her. His father sent men further afield but even after several days there were no reports. Charles now felt as though he could give up on her. There was no reason why he should deal with this any longer. His father was angry with both Catherine and Charles, saying that he had bungled it. She would have married him had he been like Henry.

Charles wanted badly to tell him that this was all his younger son's fault, and that everything had been ruined because of it, but he couldn't. He knew that his father would not live much longer; there would be nobody but him to live here, to carry things on as he didn't want to and now must. He thought of Susan all day and all night. Would she marry him now after what he had done? Would she have him despite the fact that he was not the man she had fallen in love with? Would she come here to be his wife and to do all the things his wife would have to do? It was no small job on an estate this size. He didn't know but after a week he couldn't wait any longer.

Not ashamed at all, he left and his heart began to sing. Perhaps Catherine's disappearance had been the best thing to happen. Maybe she had thought of him too and not just of herself. If so, then he was grateful for it. If Catherine didn't want him, then he didn't want her. He would go back to Weardale and claim the woman who was his. Susan Wilson would be his wife and he would bring her back here in triumph.

Every hour was savage to him. He wanted to urge the horses forward but you could only go at such a pace. Everything was too slow. He thought of what it would be like when he could go there and honestly offer himself to Susan. He could give her everything. He could show her the house, the land, he could even put up with his father. Charles hoped she could handle the old man, but he would shield her from his father for the short time that his father lived. Henry's death had finished the old man off and although Charles hated him, he understood it must have been a fierce blow to his father's pride.

He and Susan could even live somewhere else. Now that was a good idea. He owned a great many properties. One of them in particular was available and it was such a pretty house with a wide garden that faced south. He and Susan could be happy there. And in spite of his father, they might have children to carry on the estate. Susan would be gracious and kind as she always was and they would sit together every day and be together in bed every night. It made him dizzy to think of it.

He had done his best here and it had not been enough. Catherine could manage for herself now and he would have his heart's desire. He was nearing Weardale now, after several changes of horses and time to rest and eat. He tried not to think of the person he had become and of how disappointed Mr and Mrs Martin might be that he was no longer an acting minister, though he thought they would understand.

He reached Stanhope in the early afternoon and it seemed that there was confusion in the middle of the village. As his carriage stopped, a bride and groom came out of the church and he could see clearly who they were.

There were no guests to greet them. There was nobody to be glad but he did not mistake them. The groom was Daniel Wearmouth and the bride was Susan.

Susan was wearing a pretty blue dress and Charles could see Zeb and his father and Miss Lee. He stopped the carriage well back and hoped that they hadn't seen him. It wasn't likely they would; they were so intent on what they were doing.

He instructed his coachman to go back the way he had come and as confused as the man was, he turned the horses and went back. They wouldn't go far, he thought, the horses were spent and he and his servants were tired.

They got as far as St John's Chapel where there was a good pub in the middle of the village with facilities for travellers. He stepped wearily down and went into the Golden Lion and he could see already that his horses were being attended to. He smiled politely at the young woman who greeted him and answered her like the gracious almost-landowner he was. Soon he would be a baronet. He would have twenty thousand a year and numerous farms and people to look after him and the only thing he wanted was Susan Wilson.

He stayed there listening to the rain falling into the fire of his small private room. It sputtered as it hit the coals and he thought of what it had been like when he was a Methodist minister. Or almost a Methodist minister. He was nothing now except what his father had wanted him to be. He ordered brandy after his dinner. The dinner was not very good but the brandy put from his mind everything that he had ever sought for and that was good. It was over, it was finished. He would be Charles Westbrooke of Westbrooke Hall forever. No, not forever, he was still minister enough to know that life was short. He must go back to his father and his inheritance and live with the fact that Catherine Boldon had so disliked his horrid, meagre form that she had run away.

That was not fair to her or his brother. Why should she care about him when he cared nothing for her? Why would she not love his brother? Henry had been so kind, so endearing. He was a bit like the dogs they kept by the fireside, always willing, always good, always eager for the day. His brother had been destroyed by stupid ways, by narrow men. Why would you not want people to be happy?

His brother had taken his own life, he knew it. Henry didn't want to be in a place where nobody who was any different could be accepted. Right now he felt the same. He felt like drinking too much and throwing himself in the Wear. It was a great shame that he was such a strong swimmer.

It was all gone. Susan was married.

Seventy-Three

Dan had rented a house in the village, nowhere near the place where he had jilted Susan. He would even have moved away had it been practical. Susan didn't seem interested in the idea of a house and he became gradually aware over the coming days that she was not a young girl any more. The person he had fallen in love with was gone. She seemed always at the chapel and though he could not fault her for that, she was distracted. He had thought she would be wildly happy and as the days went by he hesitated, yet he could not jilt her a second time.

The news that Charles Westbrooke was not coming back had seeped through the village so that even Dan knew it. He had dismissed the bookish little man. Susan could never really have cared for him. And even if she had, it could be no lasting matter when somebody as important and manly as Dan was offering her marriage and everything that went with it. She would have been foolish to have turned him down. She had so obviously thought better of her decision. After all, she would not want to end up like Miss Lee, old and sour-faced and plain, working and looking after other people for the rest of her life.

At first he had said to her that he was sorry Mr and Mrs Almond had not offered them a home at Ash House, but she said airily that she didn't care for such things; she wouldn't have wanted to live in such a big place when the workmen lived in tiny houses. She didn't think it was right. Dan thought she had spent too much time around Zeb or perhaps too much time in prayer; she seemed to do a lot of that.

He had thought she would look for a house but it was only when he pointed out that they could not stay at the sweet shop that she became aware of the difficulty. Even then he had to go by himself. It was a strange turning that he could not interest her in something that was particularly women's territory, notably after her enthusiasm in preparing their first home.

The house therefore that he decided to rent for them was near the river.

'What do you think of it?' he asked when she had been right round it and still said nothing. It was a good, big, stone house, much bigger than the sweet shop. He hoped for some positive response from her because he was quite proud of himself. She could never have hoped to live anywhere with such large gardens and big, square rooms. But she saw the huge bedrooms that looked out over the back garden that was laid to vegetables and said nothing. It had greenhouses and leek trenches, gooseberry and currant bushes, and the greenhouse at the back led into the greenhouse at the side of the house that held flowers. The garden at the far side had rose beds and lawns and even fruit trees.

He showed her the spacious kitchen, the lovely reception rooms, and the quiet hall.

All she said was, 'I think it will probably flood.'

He hadn't thought about that.

'And it's very dark, of course, being at the bottom of the hill.'

'We can look at something else.'

'No, no, I'm sure it'll do,' she said and that was all.

After the wedding, there was to be no celebration. Miss Lee had offered a meal at the sweet shop but Susan said no. She wanted everything to be as quiet as possible so they went back to the house down by the river. Susan had been right, he thought. There were already large puddles forming outside the front door from the rain that had begun just after they left the church. And when he ventured into the hall, water was seeping through the front door.

Even that could not quite extinguish the idea of his wedding night. He remembered with such joy the first night that he had spent with Arabella. He had asked Susan if she wanted to go away for a few days. He thought that Zeb could look after the quarry if it was just three or four days. He did not want to go back to Hexham but he thought of Durham. Surely there was a decent hotel there for his new bride. But Susan had said she didn't want to go away and told him that he must not be selfish; Mr Almond was so very ill, he must be there at the quarry. This made him feel better, she was obviously proud of who he was and everything he could do for her.

They sat by the window in the sitting room eating sandwiches that Miss Lee had insisted on, as being the least she could do for them. There was also a cake. Susan ate a small sandwich, had two cups of tea and no cake, and then she took up a book and began to read. Daniel spent his evening watching the rain pour down the windows and seep into the hall and wished that he had not promised to himself that he would stop drinking now that he was married. There wasn't even a bottle of sherry in the house. When he had suggested some for after the ceremony, Susan had frowned and said there was nothing she disliked more than drink.

He hated tea and sandwiches. He wanted to have a good

dinner and some wine and cheese and to sit over the fire making plans for all the lovely things that they would do. Susan made no conversation and when he politely suggested they might go to bed she demurred.

'In a minute, I just want to finish this chapter.'

It was an hour later when they finally went upstairs.

She didn't take any notice of him. She calmly turned her back and took off her clothes and put on some nondescript garment that he had imagined old ladies wore. It was full-length and high-necked and long-sleeved. She also pulled on a nightcap. Dan had never before been afraid of her but he was now. He was intimidated.

She knelt down by the bed and put her hands together and her lips moved in prayer. This went on for such a long time that Dan thought it would never end. Then she got up and climbed into bed.

'Aren't you going to get in?' she said and when he did she lay back and looked at him. He looked back at her and then she leaned over and put out the candle and said, 'Goodnight, Daniel,' just as though they had been married for twenty years.

Dan turned away. There was no way in all the world he could have touched her. He thought he might never be able to.

The following morning she got up and made him breakfast and put some sandwiches together – they were the remains from the day before so not exactly exciting. He duly went off to the quarry. Zeb looked hard at him but said nothing when Dan said nothing. He just sat down and started to work.

Shortly after that, there came a note from Mrs Almond to request his presence at the house.

*

Mrs Almond sat all in black over her fire. She did not get up.

'My husband has died,' she said without preamble.

'I'm so sorry.'

'I trust your wedding went well.'

Daniel flinched.

'The funeral will be in almost a week's time but you need not make arrangements for the quarry to close or anything to change.'

'It must be as you wish, of course,' he said.

'It will be as my husband wished. He thought of all these things, you see.'

'I'm sure,' Daniel said, but even so he felt an excitement. He knew he shouldn't feel like that but he had been married to their only child and was the father of their heir. He was sure that he would now be given full authority at the quarry. He had long wanted it and there was no reason for Mrs Almond to think otherwise. He had always done his best and he was good.

'You will not be expected at his funeral and you will not come back here. I want you to go to the quarry and take what few possessions you may have left there. You're done, Mr Wearmouth.' She spoke firmly and there was a spark of triumph in her eyes.

Dan stared at her.

'That is what my husband wished. You cannot have imagined that he would leave you a penny or a place in the quarry that has been his life. You are to go and you are to take Zebediah Bailey with you. Neither of you will set foot in my quarry again. And don't go anywhere near the child. You had your chance; you didn't care. You have no rights as far as I can see. And if you don't stay away from him, I shall take steps to have you removed

– not just from here, but from everywhere. I take it you know my meaning. You can go now. Close the door after you.'

Telling Susan that he had been sacked was one of the hardest things Daniel had ever done and it wasn't as though he got to tell her in the privacy of their house. He came back to find the place empty and Susan serving on at the sweet shop just as though nothing had happened.

Zeb was there too; he could hear his voice in the back, as no doubt he was telling Miss Lee what had happened.

'Can we go back to our house?' he said.

'Miss Lee's busy. I can't just leave when the shop is open. What's happened, why are you both back here?'

'We've been dismissed.'

Susan stood still. She didn't say anything.

'Mr Almond has died and Mrs Almond says she doesn't want us there any more.'

Still his new wife said nothing and then, at variance with what she had just told him, she went into the back and left the shop to itself.

Miss Lee and Mr Bailey just stared at Zeb.

'But you didn't do anything,' Miss Lee said. 'And I helped with the baby. Why would she be vindictive? It could be just that she's grief-stricken.'

Zeb shook his head.

'I think this goes back a long way. She doesn't want Dan there because of what he has done and she doesn't like me. She never did. So now she can get rid of both of us.'

'I shall go and talk to her.'

'No.'

'But – '

'No. You can't do that.'

'Why not?'

'Because it would be all wrong. Don't you see?'

Alice didn't. She went for her coat and for the first time ever he took her by the arm so that she couldn't.

'Please,' he said.

Alice, having little option but violence, stayed where she was.

'Then what do you propose to do?'

'I don't know yet, I haven't thought about it.'

'Then why won't you let me go?'

'Because it'll look like I can't stand up for myself. How pathetic would that be? If you were my sister or my wife it would be different. Now you do see?'

'No.'

Just then Susan ran into the room and up the stairs, closely followed by Dan who stopped at the foot of the stairs.

'I know you have no money,' Alice let her gaze return to Zeb, 'because you've given it all to other people over time.' She turned. 'Do you have any money?' she said to Dan's side and he stopped looking up into the darkness of the staircase.

'Not much.'

'You didn't save?'

'I spent it on Arabella.'

'Oh wonderful,' Alice said.

'Will you get Susan to come down here? I have paid rent on the house and I'd like my wife in it.'

Alice went upstairs. Susan wasn't crying. She was standing by the window.

'Can you believe it?' she said. 'He promised me Ash House and fine clothes and a carriage and Europe.'

'You didn't marry him for such reasons?'

'What other reasons would I have after what he did to me?' Susan said. 'I stopped loving him a very long time ago. It was Charles Westbrooke that I loved.'

'You're his wife.'

'Not really. I didn't let him touch me. May I stay here?'

'Susan, you can't.'

'Then I'll leave with what little I have. I'm not going back to that house where the river comes in. It creeps under the door.'

'But Susan – '

'Please, Miss Lee, just until I think what else I can do. A ceremony doesn't make a marriage and I don't want him in any bed of mine.'

Alice made her way slowly downstairs and told Daniel.

'I'll go and fetch her,' he said but Zeb moved to the front of the stairs.

'No, you won't,' he said. 'She's not going anywhere until she's ready to.'

'You can't – '

'I can.'

Dan swore vilely and slammed his way out of the back door.

'Miss Lee, my father and I will leave,' Zeb said.

'There's no need.'

'We can't live off you.'

'You've given me plenty of money in the past and you know it. You have nothing because you've given it away but it's benefited us here. You'll find another job.'

'Mrs Almond will probably prevent it. She'll tell other people.'

'The Misses Vernons have a spare room,' Mr Bailey offered

but he looked so miserable that Alice went over and kissed him on both cheeks.

Mr Bailey looked baffled.

'Neither of the Miss Vernons can make cake,' Alice advised him.

'Miss Lee, you can't let us stay,' Zeb protested.

'There you go, telling me what to do again. It's a nasty habit,' she said, 'and I do wish you would get rid of it. I must go and serve on, I heard the bell,' and off she went.

'Will you go over and talk to him?' Miss Lee said later.

Zeb stared at her.

'He doesn't want me there.'

'Yes, he does. You're his best friend.'

'But Miss Lee – '

'No, don't let's blame him for what happened. He made a mess of things but then who doesn't. She says she wants nothing more to do with him.'

'If he hits me, I'll come back.'

'If he hits you, he'll be a very brave man,' Miss Lee said and so Zeb set off down the village, down the bank, wondering why the hell Dan had found a house at the bottom. It was still bloody well raining.

He banged on the door. Dan let him in and there in the hall water was seeping through the rug.

'It's wet,' Zeb ventured.

'I bloody know that,' Dan said.

He went off into the sitting room and Zeb followed him there.

'So,' Zeb guessed, 'you didn't bed your bride.'

'Shut the fuck up. Who did you ever bed?'

'True,' Zeb said.

Dan managed a smidgeon of humour.

'Nobody?'

'I once had a very special bedmate called Eli.'

'A man?'

'He was a rat.'

Dan choked on laughter.

'Aren't most men?'

'Rats are better than men,' Zeb said. 'Less selfish, more sociable. Men never really did it for me, even though I apparently did it for them for a long time.'

Dan looked him in the face.

'I still envy you,' he said.

'Why?'

'Because your father is here.'

'I'm sorry.'

'You were the only person who understood and the only person who ever tried to help him. I'm thinking I might go. I would ask you to come with me but I know you wouldn't leave your father. I wouldn't leave mine if he was anywhere about.'

'You shouldn't go.'

'Susan doesn't want me. She made that perfectly clear last night. I have nothing left here. I think in the morning I will leave. If you change your mind, I think I'll head toward Durham. You could always catch up.'

'You can't just walk off and leave her.'

'Why not? She married me out of revenge for what I did to her.'

'And what did you marry her for?'

'That's not fair. If you wanted to come with me, Miss Lee would look after your dad.'

'I can't do it.'

Dan looked hard at him.

'At least admit it. You don't want to go because of the old maid.'

'Don't call her that.'

'Aren't you ever going to ask her to marry you?'

'She wouldn't have me, and then what? I don't want to have to leave.'

'What if she does want you?'

'She won't.'

'Why did she turn down the doctor?'

'Because he's an old man.'

'Well, you certainly aren't that,' Dan said with a grin.

'She couldn't marry me.'

'I don't think that's true. Now, I'm going to pack up and leave.'

'You should give Susan the right to go with you.'

'I tell you what, Zeb. I'm going to Durham to find some work so I will write to you when I get there. If she has changed her mind when I have a job then she can come after me.'

'You do still have money quite a lot of money, don't you, despite what you told Miss Lee?'

'Quite a bit put by. I've learned the hard way about money, I'm never going to be without it again.'

Zeb delayed going back to the house. He didn't want Susan there; he had been pleased they were married. He wanted Alice to himself but that was gone too. Susan was always her first concern. Why couldn't Susan and Dan have settled for one another after all they had been through, after all that had happened?

When he finally went there, Susan met him at the back door.

'Has he gone?'

'How did you know?'

'I just did.' Her voice broke on a sob. 'Well, he's not going without me, not after all he's done. I won't let him.' She had a bag with her and her coat over her arm. She would just catch him, Zeb thought. And Dan would take her with him and maybe in the end they could work something out.

'I'm too old for all of this,' his father said from the armchair by the fire. 'I'm going to bed.'

'You haven't had anything to eat,' Alice objected.

'Miss Lee, you are the kindest woman in the whole world,' he said.

'All right then, I'll bring up cake and tea in a few minutes.'

'Bless you, my dear,' he said and began taking the stairs. The stairs were steep, Zeb thought, and he really was getting on.

'He's quite fit for his age,' Alice said and smiled at him.

'I'm terrified that he'll die after all those years we were apart.'

'Perhaps you have both come home. Or are you planning to leave with Daniel and Susan? If you think it's the right thing to do for you, then you must go. Your father will be perfectly well off here. He's not difficult any more. You're the difficult one, telling me that I had no rights to intervene on your behalf since I'm not your sister or your – ' She stopped there.

Zeb said nothing.

'You do want some dinner presumably?' she said, back at the fire.

'Miss Lee – '

'Oh dear, when you say "Miss Lee" like that, I know something awful is about to happen. You haven't done something dreadful, have you? I wouldn't put it past you.'

'Nothing,' he said.

'Oh good.'

'Will you miss Susan?'

Alice glanced at him.

'I am praying she doesn't come back,' and that made him smile and so she did too.

'I don't think she will.'

'My heart sank when she ran back in here. In my worst nightmares there she is, sobbing her eyes out over some man again. Dear God. Oh, I'm taking the Lord's name in vain.' She peered into the pot she was stirring. 'This smells awful. I haven't had time to attend to it and it's not done well. I must make some tea for your father. Do you think he will want chocolate cake with coffee icing or coffee cake with chocolate icing?'

'I think he likes the coffee cake best,' Zeb said. 'I can do it and take it up to him.'

'That would be lovely,' she said and so he made the tea and he got the cake and he went up the stairs. His father was there by the big lamp that Miss Lee insisted he have so that he did not spoil his eyes. He was reading and he stopped and smiled.

'Oh, what a good lad you are,' and when Zeb put down the tea and the cake, Mr Bailey beamed at his son and patted his arm.

Zeb went slowly down the stairs but Miss Lee was nowhere to be seen. He found her outside in the tiny shed that lived in the back garden.

'What are you doing out here?' he said.

'I'm looking for some elderberry wine. I'm sure there are a couple of bottles left.'

'Wine?'

'Oh, it's non-alcoholic,' she assured him.

It was nothing of the kind but Zeb wasn't going to say anything. It was wonderful stuff so he wasn't going to stop her.

'There it is,' she said, unearthing it from the depths of the dark shelves. 'You said that you liked it last time.'

'Very much,' Zeb said.

'I think there are probably half a dozen bottles somewhere.'

'Why are we having it now?'

'Because we deserve it,' Alice said and she preceded him into the back room, bottle in hand. 'Open it, will you? We're having badly-burned beef. This will help it down.'

The beef wasn't burned. He couldn't fault it.

'Do you know I think the elderberry tree gives us the best of everything?' Alice said. 'The berry gives us this and the flower gives us champagne. Miss Frost loved the champagne. I still miss her. She wanted to take you in. She was the best-hearted woman I ever met. And then she died. She taught me how to make sweets. She taught me so many good things.'

They sat by the fire with the rest of the bottle and Zeb enjoyed the sound of the rain hammering down. Dan and Susan must be on their way by now. He didn't think they would be wet, Dan wouldn't allow it. He hoped they would be happy.

'Miss Lee – '

'You couldn't start to call me "Alice", could you? I know I'm a lot older than you but it makes me feel ancient. At least just when we're together by the fire with your father.'

'Miss Lee – '

'There you go again,' she said. 'There's nobody here.'

He looked around and she was right.

'I wanted to say something to you.'

'I'm sure it's about work and you don't have to worry. The sweet shop always does well and you will get something else in time. And besides, I still have a great deal of the money that you gave me every month so we can get on well enough for a while. Perhaps you need a break after all the things you've been through.'

'Miss Lee – '

This time she just looked disparagingly at him but she didn't say anything.

Zeb waited a moment in case she should interrupt as she always did.

'You wouldn't want to marry me, would you?' he rushed.

When he heard the echo of his words it sounded so clumsy, but then it was the first time he had proposed. You didn't get a rehearsal of such things.

Alice stared and then looked accusingly at the wine.

'Zeb – '

'No, just consider it for ten seconds. And then if you think I am horrible and not worthy of you, I will leave tomorrow and take my father with me rather than have you put up with us. Miss Lee, ever since the moment I saw you standing across the road from me in Durham I have loved you. You are so beautiful and so kind and I love you as I have never loved anyone in my whole life. I know my record is awful, that in gaol I had dreadful things happen to me so maybe you think I am too dirty for you, too damaged and too stupid – '

He got no further. Alice, throwing wine all over the place to get to him, took him into her arms and called him by his name. That was when he put his arms around her and that was when he tasted a woman's mouth for the first time. It was even sweeter than the first sugar mouse that she had sent him when he had thought his life was over.

She did taste of chocolate and of all the lovely things she had come to represent in his life. She was warm and giving and kind. He had known that but he had not known what it was like to hold her in his arms. She was not middle-aged. She was firm yet soft and she pressed against him so that he wanted to take her upstairs and have her for his own. But it wouldn't have been right, so after the kiss he drew back and let her draw back.

'Will you marry me, Miss Lee?' he asked again.

'Yes, I will, Mr Bailey.'

'Mr Bailey is my dad. You can call me Zeb,' so she did and she stayed there in his arms kissing him. She said only a good deal later, 'I had no idea what that wine contained.'

'I was so worried you were going to marry the doctor. I stood outside and wanted to die.'

Alice laughed.

'You can definitely call me "Alice" now, I think.'

And so he did and after that, after her name was sweet up on his lips, the ex-convict knew that he had lived again. It was much more than he deserved, he felt. Alice Lee and her sweet shop had saved him and he thought that week-to-week and day-to-day she probably saved a great many other people. The children and the older people and the couples and the single women who needed hot chocolate in the evenings, and the farmers who wanted to bring just a little of the sweetness of life to their wives.

Alice remembered the first day that she had seen him through the mist and how lost he was. He wasn't lost any more. And neither was she. And Mr Bailey slept upstairs after his tea and cake. She could hear him snoring through the floorboards. In the morning they would tell him of what they had decided and she would take the short, cobbled bank up to the chapel to talk to Mr Martin.

They would probably be married in the church and she wanted the whole village to be there to celebrate the coming together of such unlikely people. She wanted this man as she had never wanted anything in her life. She would have his children and make dinner for him and turn over in bed to feel his body so sweet and young against hers. She would soothe his nightmares and help him in his troubles and be there for him when he came home in the pale of the evening.

That was the best thing of all, she thought. He would come home to the sweet shop and there she would be waiting for him, always. He would call her name and come inside and kiss her lips. In the mornings he would call up the stairs while she was dealing with his father or perhaps his child and he would tell her he was off to work and she would call back and wish him well and know that he would come home to her.

If you enjoyed *The Guardian Angel*, keep reading for an extract
of Elizabeth Gill's moving novel

Nobody's Child

**'A wonderful book, full of passion, pain,
sweetness, twists and turns'**
Sheila Newberry, author of *The Gingerbread Girl*

One

Christmas was all around. The shops had coloured streamers crisscrossed in their windows and Kath Watson could see chickens, geese and turkeys hanging up in the butcher's. She thought it might be nice to have something good to eat on Christmas Day. The shop had a queue; people here must eat a lot of meat.

She lingered outside the shoe shop. Her family bought their shoes off markets so a shoe shop was a strange place, with its boxes everywhere. She looked through the window and her attention was caught by a pair of black patent leather shoes that she instantly longed for. She was surprised at herself. Clothes were just something to wear to keep you warm and cover you up; she thought pretty clothes were nothing more than a come-on to coarse mucky lads who only wanted to take you behind a hedge.

Her father had wished her married long since and didn't understand why she was so picky. A lot of the gypsy lads had money – those that dealt in scrap metal or horses – but Kath had seen inside other families' wagons and they reeked of filth and disarray. She did not see herself turning out baby after baby, clearing up and putting up with the likes, so she wouldn't have any of them. Her father called her unnatural and asked her what in hell she thought she would do instead.

Her mother had shuddered and said when he was gone, 'I want a better life than this one for my lasses. I don't want them on the road like we are.'

Kath had never ventured this far up the main street of the little pit town, where many people shopped and went out. The street had as many houses on it as shops and children played in the road. She was always afraid that she would be shouted at and since at the moment they could not move on, she didn't want to face their scorn.

Today, however, she made herself take it on. She thought that people stared but that could have been simply because they didn't know her. The shops were mostly repeats of the co-operative department store and every so often there was a little run of terraced houses among them. A picture house called The Palace was at the top of the slight hill that led up past the railway gates where the cattle market was on one side and a foundry on the other.

After the petrol station and some buses, the street evened out and straggled away until it split in two at the top. Yards or passages led into the back streets and she passed several pubs with archways which must have been where the horses and carriages were kept in older times. There were also a number of churches. She didn't know much about churches.

When she reached the top of the street, she crossed over and began to come down the other side until she became aware that somebody was following her. When she stopped and turned around, a middle-aged woman was behind her.

She stared at Kath. 'You're Rose Gurney's lass, aren't you? You look just like her, the mucky slut.'

Kath stared back and replied, 'My name's Watson.'

The woman chuckled but her eyes were full of scorn. 'Is that right and where did you get that from?'

She walked off before Kath had a chance to say anything more. Kath tried not to think about it, but flustered, she hurried home without the shopping she had meant to buy. She had had such plans for Christmas – she was going to bake a cake and stuff a goose. She was so determined that they would have a good holiday this year.

She had not been back long when there was a heavy knocking on the back door. She opened it and beheld a policeman, large and fierce-looking.

'Is your father at home?'

'No.'

'Your mother?'

'My mother is very ill and in bed.'

As she spoke her father appeared behind her. She thought he had gone out and was relieved he was there to handle the problem.

The policeman stared at her father and said, 'You can't stay here. This house is Jonathan Gurney's.'

'He's not here,' Kath's father replied. 'I had to pull the boards from the windows so that we could stay. My wife is ill. When she's better, we'll go.' He slammed shut the door.

Late in the morning Kath went upstairs to check on her mother. She was worried by what she found. Her mother was asleep and her breathing was harsh and uneven. She didn't open her eyes when Kath entered the room. She didn't look like Rose any more. She had turned old, her yellowing skin stretched across her face as though there wasn't enough of it. She was getting worse.

Kath lingered. She wished her mother would open her eyes, that she would say something. Kath didn't like to make any noise, though she hoped her mother would be aware of her presence. It was better for her to sleep.

She swept the ashes from the fireplace then laid sticks and paper and a little coal inside. She put a match to it and watched it light and lick. The growing flame gave her a measure of satisfaction.

The sheets didn't seem to need changing; everything smelled fresh. She was thankful she didn't need to open the window to clear the air – when she drew back the curtains to let a little light in, snow began to fall. She stood there for a few moments, watching it.

She could remember last Christmas. They had gone south as they often did and met up with friends at Thirsk. It was such a pretty town and unlike many places, there were fields they could stay in. Nobody had tried to move them on or got in the way.

The man who owned the land wanted payment, but that was no problem – they had plenty of money and her father was thought by other men to be silver tongued, which helped. Kath's father was a harsh but decent man and kept his family well. He could read and write and talk to the authorities. They stayed several weeks while the weather was bad and left in April when things picked up.

She enjoyed their time there, surrounded by friends and music and dancing. Her pleasure wasn't even diminished by her father's attempts to marry her off. He had insisted that Kath wear beautiful dresses in the camp so that the young lads would court her, which they did. She braved her father's anger when she refused to marry any of them. She had other things to worry about now. Her mother had been ill for four months and was becoming worse each day.

Their father had brought her back here to her hometown only when she broke down and begged. Kath did not think her father told the truth to the policeman about when they would leave – he would never have come back here but to let his wife die where she chose. It was just a question of time.

Christmas morning dawned and was nothing like other Christmases that Kath had known. The house was like a tomb; it had its own atmosphere. She heard voices – sound raging beyond her room. She got out of bed, pulled open the door and in the dimness of the shadowed hall she could see the figures of two men, one half-turned toward her and the other almost completely away.

She heard a sound she didn't know, a man crying. It was her father. The other man was the doctor, whom she recognized from his visit two days before. He was in his shirtsleeves, white shirt stark against the gloom, a jacket over his arm and the black bag he carried in his other hand.

The doctor, ignoring her, went down the stairs. Her father hurled himself into the room and slammed the door. Kath was left in the freezing hall. She wore nothing but a shift and began to shiver, but it was not from cold, it was from dread. She could hear her father sobbing.

Had her mother died? Her father was crying now as he had never cried before. Kath was confused. He had never taken her mother's happiness into consideration.

Like most of the travelling men, he pleased himself and did

whatever he liked. He was the person who dictated how the rest of them went on. It could be nothing but guilt bringing him to tears.

As Kath stood there, Ella, her younger sister, came to the door. Hearing her father crying, she turned back into the room and Kath followed her.

Kath thought that her father would eventually come out and tell them that their mother had died, but he didn't. As the morning wore on, she dressed, went downstairs, saw to the dogs and lit the fire. Ella said she didn't want anything to eat but when Kath made toast over the fire, slick with butter, they downed it with hot, sweet tea.

She could not believe that their father had not invited them to say goodbye to their mother. She felt as though she would never have the strength to move away from the fire again.

When her father staggered down in the early afternoon, she could see that he was drunk. Kath had seen him drunk before but this time felt different. He looked years older. His face was harsh, his hair wild and his eyes unseeing. He blundered to the cupboard where he kept a couple of bottles of whisky, took a bottle and staggered back upstairs.

'I'm scared,' Ella moaned in a tiny voice and she ran from the house and into the wagon that was their usual home.

Ella came back inside when dusk fell and Kath was glad of her company. It was mid-evening when she took Ella upstairs to their bedroom. There was no sound at all from her parents' room. It took a long time for Ella to go to sleep; she turned over and over. She was cried out and exhausted and when she finally slept, Kath listened to her breathing and was thankful for it and for her warmth. Outside a keen frost had set about the town though the snow had stopped falling and the air was clear.

She must have slept at one point because when she awoke in the darkness she knew that something had changed. She didn't know what it was. She thought she heard footsteps on the stairs . . .

You have just read an extract from Elizabeth Gill's
Nobody's Child – a heart-breaking tale about
the power of love and family.

If you enjoyed *The Guardian Angel*, why not try . . .

Snow Angels

Elizabeth Gill

Abby Reed, grieving after the loss of her mother,
finds an unexpected source of comfort exploring the
rugged, snowy countryside with the brooding Gillan
Collingwood, son of a local shipping merchant.
It isn't long before she begins to hope that she and
Gill might someday be more than friends . . .

But then Gill meets his elder brother's new wife Helen,
and falls instantly, deeply in love with her. Abby is shattered
by the news and throws herself into an imprudent love
affair. Her impulse will take her away from the frosty
wilds of her homeland to London's glittering social scene . . .
but can she ever forget the boy she left behind?

**A sparkling winter wonderland of a novel –
the perfect fireside read!**